# EX LIBRIS

# Alastair Campbell

## My Name Is...

HUTCHINSON
LONDON

Published by Hutchinson 2013

2 4 6 8 10 9 7 5 3 1

First published in Great Britain in 2013 by Hutchinson

Random House, 20 Vauxhall Bridge Road,
London SW1V 2SA

www.randomhouse.co.uk

Addresses for companies within The Random House Group Limited can be found at:
www.randomhouse.co.uk/offices.htm

The Random House Group Limited Reg. No. 954009

A CIP catalogue record for this book
is available from the British Library

ISBN 9780091953911

The Random House Group Limited supports the Forest Stewardship Council®
(FSC®), the leading international forest-certification organisation. Our books carrying the
FSC label are printed on FSC®-certified paper. FSC is the only forest-certification scheme
supported by the le⸺                                              Our paper
procurement                                                        nent

Typeset in Perpe⸺                                                  ⸺ingshire
Printe⸺

# Acknowledgements and dedications

The first people to thank are those who responded so kindly to publication of my first novel, *All In The Mind*. It is in no small measure down to them that I was encouraged to write another novel with a mental health theme, this time addiction, and in particular the impact of alcohol abuse on young women. Slowly, attitudes to mental illness are changing, and the cultural space is an important area to make that change accelerate so that one day we can see genuine parity of treatment between physical and mental health – something which now exists in legislation in the NHS Constitution, but which is far from the reality for many people with mental health problems. It was in part as a result of writing *All In The Mind*, and later *The Happy Depressive*, that I became an ambassador for Time to Change, the mental health awareness campaign, and I hope that *My Name Is . . .*, may be of some help to those organisations working so hard to get governments and people around the world to face up to the scale of alcohol abuse and the damage it does to individuals, families, communities and countries. I think there is both an appetite and a need for greater openness about these issues.

The decision to make the subject of this novel a young woman came when I made a documentary for the BBC about alcoholism two years ago, which included an interview with Southampton liver specialist Nick Sheron, who said that whereas once his patients were almost all male, now there was an even split between men and women, so I thank him for unwittingly providing that creative spark.

Random House have been supportive and hugely professional and I would like especially to thank Gail Rebuck, who thoroughly deserves her reputation as something of a giant in publishing, Jocasta Hamilton, my editor, Emma Mitchell, my publicist, Kathy Fry, for her copy-editing skills and Richard Ogle, for the cover. My agent Ed Victor and his team have as ever been a great support. A number of people read several drafts but I would like to thank in particular Charlie Falconer and David Mills, who were enthusiastic from the off, but also had helpful suggestions for change. I am also very grateful to psychiatrist David sturgeon and addiction specialist Rory O'Connor who checked the text from the practitioners' point of view.

As for a dedication, I hope you will allow me several.

To Fiona, for sticking with me through and beyond the descent into alcoholism.

To the French woman who helped lift me from the floor of the buffet of Peterborough railway station, summer 1978, and suggested I got help. It took a while, I never knew her name, but I've never forgotten her.

To the two policemen in Hamilton, Fife, who suggested I accompanied them to the station, March 7, 1986.

To Ernest Bennie, the psychiatrist who helped the penny drop a few days later. And to the memory of Bill W and Dr Bob, founders of Alcoholics Anonymous, who showed that the greatest progress can come from the simplest of ideas, and who can be ranked among that small group of people who have truly changed the world for millions, and continue to do so.

# My Name Is...

# HANNAH

**My name is Hannah. This is their story.**

# KATE

**My name is Kate. I am Hannah's mum.**

I did all that antenatal stuff, but none of it prepared me for what actually happened; the noise I made, the waves of pain, the hour upon hour of willing it to be over, the Scouse midwife telling me 'it's no worse than shitting a melon, love' and me being too weak and angry to say that's the last thing I want to hear right now, thank you very much. And, when finally the baby was out, the realisation that I didn't really know what to do, and I had to ask the nurses as this little creature lay across my chest, eyes closed, scrunched up like a kitten, tiny pink lips puckering out for a first feed from breasts which were larger than I wanted them to be, and uglier too, with veins spidering out from the nipple that her mouth was seeking.

'Do they want milk straight away?' I ask, but now the midwife is all busy busy, clearing up the mess around the baby's head, gently wiping her, and not so gently wiping me, the dopey doctor is writing on a board, and I'm thinking I'll have to work it out for myself, and as the lips move closer, I'm struck for a few moments at the wonder of it all, that she has been growing inside me, I've had no idea who she is or what she looks like, and now she's here, skin, hair, arms, legs, tiny little fingers prodding into my flesh.

A few minutes later, the door swings open. It's Pat. Useless though he was when the waves of pain were at flood levels, I feel bad that he missed the actual moment. We would go on to have another child, Vicki, and he was there for her, but a man only has one firstborn, and he had been hand-patting and there-there-ing for most of the day, and he had even had time for a little kip in the low chair in the corner by the silver-coloured bin, but missed the birth. Of course, he'll tell all his pals at work that he was there, but he missed out really, and all because of a misunderstanding, because he thought I was telling him to 'fuck off out of it' when actually I was telling the baby to 'fuck off out of me' because amid the pain I could think of nothing else to say. I hate swearing. I hardly ever swear, can't remember the last time I used the F-word, yet when I was giving birth it was F this, F that, F the other, and I might even have let out a C-word, so loud they probably heard it in A & E, and maybe he was shocked, and genuinely thought I was telling him to F off out of it, not just pleading with the baby to leave my body and relieve me of the pain. Our life together has been full of little misunderstandings like that. He was what my grandma used to call 'too merry for his own good' when he proposed, and not long after we married, before Hannah arrived even, when he thought I was out but I was actually in the downstairs loo putting on some make-up because I was on the way out for an interview, he was talking to his brother Malcolm in the kitchen, and we had thin walls at that place, really thin, and I heard him say that he had only proposed to me because he was pissed, and it was the worst mistake he'd ever made.

Knowing him, I expect he knew exactly what I meant when I was effing and blinding and asking for more effing pethidine, and could he 'stop patting my hand like I'm a fucking dog', and saying it felt like I had a hod of bricks inside me, but he did that hurt, watery-eyed look – the one he used whenever I caught him cheating on me – and slipped out, doubtless to 'wet the baby's head'. There is always a handy euphemism for drinking. And you'll always find pubs and florists near hospitals and cemeteries. I was at the Whittington, and I could think of at least three pubs instantly, all within staggering distance of the hospital entrance on Magdala Avenue. Right round the corner there was the Whittington Stone with its discount booze for medical students – what sort of example is that to set? – and the New Brunswick wasn't much further in the other direction. I was sure Pat would have gone for the Archway Tavern, though, set in the middle of a busy junction right at the bottom of the hill, because they prided themselves on live music and he'd have got the band to sing a Beatles song to celebrate the pending arrival. I'd spent all my life thinking that having children brought husband and wife closer together. But it never really happened to us, and not just because of the misunderstanding over who or what I was swearing at.

I'm only being honest here, I know we're all meant to say we love our kids, and bringing them into the world was the greatest thing we ever did, and raising them the best time of our lives, and nothing in the world matters more to us than their health and their happiness, and that last bit is true, but I'm not going to pretend I enjoyed the experience. The midwife was right when she said it was like shitting a melon, and when it was out, I was feeling saggy and sore, and a bit scared, because I could tell the doctor and the midwife were already thinking about the next one they had to deliver, and even when Pat came back, I felt alone with this child, and unsure about the future. Maybe I sensed something on that very first day, but nobody ever really tells you how hard it's going to be. Nobody said at those classes that you'll worry you've lost your mind, along with your figure, or that there will be nights when you lie awake torturing yourself about what you can or should be doing for them, and you'll still feel guilty whatever you do. And if nothing matters more to a parent than their child's health and happiness, how are you supposed to feel, and what are you supposed to do, when they're sick and unhappy? For all the advice and the books telling you what position they should and shouldn't sleep in, whether you should pick them up or let them cry, I never found a book telling me what to do when it all goes wrong and you think your world is ending, and your whole life has been a preparation for failure at the thing women are meant to be made for.

So that feeling of wonder in the delivery room didn't last long, before I was frankly just thanking God it was all over, then I'm thinking how weird it is that I keep thinking of God even though I've not been to church since the day we were married, and have not believed in Him for a lot longer (God that is, not Pat. I would never give Pat a capital H, and I'm not sure he deserves a capital P either). Thinking back, about his drinking, his philandering, his lying, and the time he told his brother I was a mistake, I'm amazed I stuck it out as long as I did. I sometimes felt his brother liked me more than he did, and when I was listening to Pat slag me off that time, Malcolm said, 'Come off it, you've done better than most, so stop knocking her,' and Pat must have just nodded, or shrugged, or rolled his eyeballs like he does when he doesn't agree with something but can't be bothered to argue, because there followed a short silence, and then they talked about a horse Malcolm fancied backing in the 3.15 at Sandown Park. When I emerged, and Pat suddenly realised I might have heard what he'd said, his lips parted and his eyes widened in mild panic. It was a look I would get used to as our marriage limped on, and I would find him ending phone calls suddenly and thinking I was born yesterday, but I said nothing, picked up my keys and ran to the door, saying I was late for the interview.

'Good luck,' Malcolm shouted.

'Yeah, good luck,' said Pat. 'You're better than the rest and don't you forget it.' It was his charm I fell for, and even at times like that, he had it, moving effortlessly from little boy caught saying bad things about his wife to loving husband who made her feel he worshipped the air she breathed.

Now he is walking over from the door, past the midwife, staring in wide-eyed wonderment at the creature lying across my breasts. I want to explain that I didn't mean him to get out when I was screaming, I was talking to the child inside me, not to him, but now the child is a real living thing, out in the world, that sounds harsh, and anyway he has that cute little smile on his face and then it spreads and his eyes light up with a joy that I've never seen before, not when we met outside the train station, not when we first kissed, in a lift of all places, not when we first made love, when he was so gentle and kind I thought this man is going to be mine forever, not when we moved in together, not when he asked me to marry him, not when we married and he turned to me after we had done all the ceremonials and whispered, 'You are the most beautiful thing I have seen since Andy Gray's goal for Everton

7

in the 1984 FA Cup Final,' at which point I burst out laughing, and the priest looked cross.

'Wow,' he said. 'Amazing . . . amazing, isn't it?'

'It's a girl,' I said.

'Yeah. So Hannah, yeah?'

'That's what we agreed. Sam for a boy, Hannah for a girl.'

Pat ran his index finger across her cheek, then tapped on her bottom lip. 'Hello, Hannah,' he said. 'Welcome to our world, my little lovely.'

I don't think I had ever seen him so happy. He really did radiate a pure joy and I wanted to forget all the times that hadn't been so great lately, with money tight, and his wanderings probably more frequent than I knew, and I thought this could be the making of him, maybe this – she – would be the thing that brought us back together, like it used to be. That sounds so naive. I try not to feel sorry for myself, but it's hard.

He leaned over and kissed first Hannah, then me, just a gentle peck on my forehead, then he stood up and asked if he could hold her.

'Is it OK if my husband takes the baby?' I asked.

'Course it is,' said the midwife.

I still felt saggy and sore inside, but I was a little less scared, happy that he was happy, and happy I could still feel like that.

He lifted her up to his lips and kissed her little eyelids, and told her she was going to 'light up the world and make it a better place to be'. It reminded me why I fell in love with him in the first place. In fact, I had a vague inkling he may have said the same thing to me the first or second time we made love.

# PAT

**My name is Pat. I am Hannah's dad.**

She was born on the Tuesday night and we had her home by Thursday afternoon. They were a bit worried about her heart rate, and there was even muttering about her going into the Whittington's Special Care Baby Unit, but it settled down quickly enough and we were spared that. I underestimated the impact it was going to have on me, to see her and hold her and whisper sweet nothings while she tried to open her eyes and take in the light. I was annoyed to have missed the moment on one level, but on another I know I wouldn't have coped well seeing all the gubbins and the cord and all the blood and gore. Kate apologised for the misunderstanding a few days later, said she had been shouting at the baby for hurting her, not at me, but it was fine; I'd nipped out for half an hour to the Archway Tavern and there was a band doing Kinks songs, and I told the lead singer about the baby coming and asked them to play 'Tired of Waiting for You' and 'Ev'rybody's Gonna be Happy', which both seemed appropriate. They were a lovely bunch of lads – tribute bands often are – they played the songs, then announced to the pub that I was on my way to see the baby being born. Cue cheers and heightened excitement.

I stayed a couple of hours but Kate was desperate for sleep, and I couldn't wait to spread the news, so I popped into the Herbert Chapman on the way home to tell Ronnie the landlord and a few mates, had a couple of pints, sang a bit, and it was almost midnight by the time I got home to the flat. We were living in one of those brown-stone blocks on the Holloway Road, right opposite the Coronet, that giant pub which always looked more like an amusement arcade to me than a boozer. I much preferred the Herbert Chapman, even if he had been the manager of bloody Arsenal. Once inside the flat, I poured myself a beer, raised a toast to Hannah in the little mirror by the cooker, then phoned a few people . . . my mum, who had wanted to come down from Liverpool, but Kate had said 'let's wait and see'; she was after every detail and was thrilled the midwife had been from Huyton, so wanted to know all about her, like why did she move south and was she married and did she have kids, until my knowledge was exhausted and I steered things back to Hannah. Six pounds eleven ounces, brown eyes, two tiny wisps of black hair on either side of her head, a few strands on top, long fingers that seemed all out of proportion with the rest of her, but Mum said that was quite common and nothing to worry about.

'Who does she look like?'

'Hard to tell really. Maybe my eyes, I think, but they were quite scrunched up most of the time . . . well, shut in fact.'

'Oh, that's quite normal.'

'Features maybe a bit more Katie. Yes, I think so.'

'And Kate's well, yes?'

'She's fine. Oh, Mum, I can't tell you how beautiful she is. I have never, ever felt like I did when I first saw her.'

'Well, she'll change your life, that's for sure, and you'll

have bad times as well as good with her. Heaven knows we did, eh?'

I felt instantly deflated, and then a sharp stab of anger. I know she doesn't always mean to, but Mum has a tendency to inject a little dose of pessimism into any happy scene. It was like when I first got a job with the Post Office in London, which of course is what led me to meet Kate and without that there would have been no marriage and no Hannah and no burst of happiness like I had felt when I lifted her from Kate's chest. So as I try to share that happiness with her, Mum is dragging me back down to earth, which is where I don't want to be right now, I've not had many stratospheric feelings in my twenty-seven years, and I want this one to last because it is telling me that life is going to change for the better. Kate and I have had our ups and downs, but we are going to pull together, and I will become a good husband, stop messing around with other women, stop going out on the piss after work so much, help around the house, and we will both give Hannah all the love and support she needs, and she will have a wonderful life full of hope and opportunity. Instead, I am remembering the row Mum and I had when I said I had got the job, my first proper job with holidays and pension contri-butions, and a line manager called Mr Preston, and I could start on Monday, so I was going to leave the next day and go down to find somewhere to live, and she knew I had been trying and trying and trying, losing count of the rejection letters, and she had been pushing me, but when it came to it, and I got a half-decent job with prospects, suddenly all she could see were the problems – of moving down south, no friends, no family, high cost of living, nowhere to live, and I just wanted her to share my excitement at this sudden success after five months without work, and all I was getting was the downside. And it felt a bit like that now – 'bad times as well as good . . . Heaven knows we did, eh?'

Well, yes, we did, but did she need to remind me right then, when I still had the treacly smell of my beautiful newborn baby on me? It was hardly my fault that our dad legged it. I don't remember much about it, but Malcolm does, and he reckons if he had been Dad he would have thought about going too, because she nagged him and yelled at him when he came in late, and called him a filthy sodden drunk, and once threw a cup of boiling tea at him, before she had even put the milk in it, and if she hadn't been a lousy thrower it would have scarred him, because he was too drunk to duck. We lived a couple of streets back from the Anfield Road in Bootle, not for from Goodison Park, and Malcolm would tell these stories like they were scenes out of an old black-and-white comedy, and we could laugh about them over a pint, but who knows if Mum and Dad splitting up, and Dad being such a drinker, were the reasons my brother went off the rails? Or maybe the reason why I never did as well in exams as the teachers said I would? I was bright, they all said that, and I wasn't scared of work, they said that too. But I fluffed my O levels, left, tried to get an apprenticeship at an aircraft parts factory in Skelmersdale, didn't get it, so started doing labouring jobs mainly while I applied all over the place for better things. To me, the Post Office in London was like Leeds University was to the really bright lads, even if Mum couldn't see it.

Malcolm was ten when Dad left, and I was seven, and by the time I was at senior school, my brother was taking drugs and hanging out with the wrong crowd and coming home high or drunk or more likely both and Mum was at her wits' end not knowing what to do, and desperate to pretend to the neighbours that there wasn't a problem, when everyone knew there was, not least when he was expelled from school. The next-door neighbours, on both sides, knew for sure. The walls were so thin we knew when they changed channels on the telly – it was handy at times, because my mum would forget *Coronation Street* was on but get reminded when she heard the theme tune next door – and for sure they could hear her yelling at Malcolm like she used to yell at Dad, useless layabout, shirker, good-for-nothing, only think about yourself, and her being God-fearing and going to church every Sunday and when things got really bad she started to go every day, and I always knew when things were really, really bad with Malcolm because she was forever popping out to St Monica's, thinking that if she prayed hard enough he might stop smoking weed, stop stealing to pay for his cocaine, stop sitting on walls near off-licences with four cans of lager, where all the neighbourhood could see him bringing shame on her, shame on the house and the family, stop her living in fear of another knock on the door from the cops saying our Malcolm was in trouble again.

Hannah was our first child, Mum's third grandchild, Malcolm and his wife Julie having had two boys already, Alan and Chris. So yes, he gave her lots of problems, the same as Dad did, but if only she could look at him now, not touched drugs for eight years, not been near a court or a jail cell for nine, barely drank, making more money than Kate and me put together, and then some, Julie, a lovely wife who had helped straighten him out, two young boys; if only she could see *that* Malcolm, not the Malcolm who used to keep her awake night after night, she wouldn't have dragged me down the way she did in those early hours of Hannah's life.

I think if Hannah had been her first, she would have insisted on coming down to London, regardless of Kate's objections, but we were living in a two-bedroomed flat, without a spare room now that the second room had gone from being 'the baby's room' to 'Hannah's room', so Mum would have to have slept on the sofa, and even though we never addressed it directly, she knew that Kate didn't really want her down. It wasn't that they got on badly, they just didn't get on well, and I guess we all reached the judgement that with something as important as a new baby, in-law tension was an unnecessary addition. So whenever Mum raised the idea, I just said, 'Let's wait and see,' and we waited long enough for the birth to happen and now, gone midnight, she wasn't even asking any more.

Kate's mum and dad lived about fifteen miles from us, out east, opposite the entrance to Parsloes Park in Dagenham, so they would be able to pop round more easily. I called them, and Kate's mum said she would take care of telling that side of the family in the morning, and visit later, then I called Malcolm and our cousins, one or two of Kate's colleagues at Matheson & Co., a couple of friends, then I put the phone in its socket, and went to fetch another beer from the fridge. It was 1.20 a.m., and I'd told Kate I would take her in some fruit for breakfast, but I was too wired to sleep, too happy, too excited, the excitement now only a little bit contaminated by 'Heaven knows we did, eh?' I think one of the reasons I fell for Kate was that she was more upbeat than my mum, certainly in the early days.

I drank straight from the can, and after two large gulps, I could smile at what Mum said, she didn't mean ill, she'd had a hard time, felt her life was a failure, and so she found it difficult to let happiness in, even when it was gushing at her. I took another swig, closed my eyes and I saw little Hannah lighting up the black back canvas of my mind. 'Fuck me, Patty boy, you made that, you and your little Katie, you made that.' One minute it's just a thing, it's been inside her for months and we're forever asking boy or girl, this name that name, we're buying and borrowing cots and toys and silly pictures of bears and elephants for the walls, but it is still just a thing, and now it is a living, breathing, scowling, crying, heartbreakingly beautiful little human being who will be here God willing long after we've gone, with kids of her own, and a whole life of experiences good and bad that nobody, not even her oh-so-proud dad, can possibly predict. 'How fucking exciting is that?' and this time I am saying it out loud, and I stand up, take another sip from the can, then a bigger sip, then a gulp, then a large swallow, and it's gone, and I raise the can high in salute of my wonderful little princess, then go to the kitchen for another one. Wet the baby's head, that's what they call it. Wet the baby's head. No way could I sleep. I didn't want to lose this feeling. I didn't want ever to stop seeing that perfect little face, stop thinking about my perfect little girl, Hannah Ruth Maynard, made by me and my little Katie. So small, yet so powerful. Couldn't speak, couldn't walk, didn't know her own name, didn't know who the Queen was, or Nelson Mandela, or the Beatles, or Bob Latchford, didn't know that she had a power to move me I had never seen in anyone, not even John Lennon. He was my hero, I guess, part inherited from my mum, but he never made me feel like I felt when I first saw Hannah. Never, not even when he died.

I took our wedding photo from the top of the telly, and sat down on the sofa, flicking open the ringpull as I landed.

What a bad suit that was. I'd bought it in Walton, mid to late eighties I guess, for someone else's wedding as it happens, Ricky Heath, only I never went, because his fiancée called it off with two days to go, so it was 'as new' when I wore it for my own. I should have gone for something dark, more traditional, but I thought light-coloured was trendier, happier. Malcolm was my best man, and made a crack in his speech about how I was always crazy about fast cars as a kid and that must explain why I dressed up like a car dealer on my big day. Kate wore white but we were struggling cash-wise at the time, and so was her dad, who had been laid off from the railways, and it was all a bit cheapo cheapo, only knee-length and not too much fancy stuff around the edges, and looking at it now I wondered if she should have gone for a slightly bigger one, because she looked a bit dumpy as it was too tight round the middle. I saw none of that on the day though, and I honestly did see myself spending my whole life with her, I really did.

I met her coming out of the station at Caledonian Road. My Tube train had been delayed and I was rushing to work because even though there was no clocking in or clocking out, if you were late there was always a bit of a mood developed around you, piss-taking and even a bit of bullying, so when I was on days, I always tried to get there around half seven at the latest. She can't have noticed that I was rushing, because she just stood there and said, 'Excuse me,' blocking my path so I had to slow down. At first I thought she was one of those charity people wanting to have a chat and then skin you for a bit of money, so I carried on, just more slowly, and then she said, 'You wouldn't know where Westbourne Road is, would you?' and I said, 'Yes, it's near where I work, it's only a few minutes.' So I carried on walking and she said, 'Would you mind showing me?' and I said, 'Course, not a problem.'

Amazing, isn't it? . . . If my train had been on time, if I had taken the stairs instead of the lift, if any one of the other travellers milling around me had come out of the lift just as she decided she needed to ask the way and she'd asked one of them not me, we would never have met. Had a single thing changed in either of our lives, we would not have been there at that time, in those circumstances. We would not have met. If we hadn't met, we wouldn't have fallen in love. If we hadn't fallen in love, Hannah would never have been born, and I would never have known the happiest moment of my life, or at least I might have, but it would not have been the one I could now describe as the happiest moment of my life, the moment I set eyes on her. And of course, it is not just the lives of parents that come together like that. Our parents, their parents, their ancestors, every move we make is only possible because of every move they made, because one move different, by any of them, and nothing would have been the same. It was a big thought, and I loved having it, and took a large swig from the beer can to cement it in my mind.

It was spitting with rain when we got out of the station and onto the street, and she tried to get an umbrella out of her bag, but I kept on walking, she gave up on the brolly and we were striding pretty fast along a small parade of shops, and at the end, there was a guy on the pavement, just sitting there, with a blanket drawn over his knees, his bearded head down, a polystyrene cup between his feet, and a sheet of cardboard with 'SMALL CHANGE PLEASE' scrawled over it. I'd seen him before, and always just walked past, often wondered if he wouldn't be better off in Pentonville nick down the road, where at least they'd feed and drug him, but maybe I wanted to impress this young woman, I don't know, but anyway I stopped and fished out a fiver and dropped it into his cup. 'There you go, mate, get yourself a cup of tea and some breakfast now, and promise me you won't spend it on booze.' He looked up, nodded, raised a thumb, took the note from his cup, rammed it into a coat pocket, then let his head sink back to his knees.

'That was nice of you,' she said.

'There but for the grace of . . .' I said. 'I had a brother who was going that way once. Can happen to anyone.'

'Well, yeah,' she said, and I was suddenly struck by her chirpy London accent, 'but in the end he's choosing to be there, ain't he? I mean, if he really wanted to work, he could clean the streets rather than live on them.'

'I dunno about that. You don't know what's gone on in his life, do you? Could be ex-military, ex-jail and can't get work, or kicked out by his parents or a wife and not able to cope. A lot of people can't cope with the practicalities of life, so they try to escape, and that means drink and drugs, and before you know it, they're living on the streets. You see plenty of them round here, a lot more than where I come from.'

'But there are hospitals, doctors, rehab places. There's welfare. Nobody has to starve, not in England, it's not like Africa, is it? I mean, there's got to be something in him that wants to live like that, don't you think?'

'You really think so? I can't imagine anyone wants to live like that.'

'Well, it was nice of you to help him anyway, even if he does spend it all on booze.'

'I guess he will, yeah, you're probably right.'

I'm pretty sure she asked me my name first, so I told her, then she said her name was Kate Anderson, and she was going for a dental appointment at eight, just a check-up. She had lovely teeth, still does.

'Hate dentists,' she said. 'Once had a bad one, his fingers stank of fags and I honestly think he'd been drinking.'

'Bloody hell, a drunk dentist – that's the last thing you want.'

'I know, and I went another time and as I walked in he was sorting out some X-rays and I swear his hands were shaking so I just said "sorry, I don't feel well" and I ran out, never went back. The receptionist barely batted an eyelid, was probably used to it.'

'You should have reported him.'

'Yeah, maybe. Anyway, Sally at work recommended this new chap, so here's hoping.'

'Where do you work?' and as she told me – Matheson's, the hair products place, where she worked in packaging and shipping – I realised I was trying to establish how to get in touch with her again. I wasn't overly conscious of fancying her, maybe it was too early in the day for that, but I must have done, or else why was I trying to find out how to contact her afterwards? She had a nice face, and even though, wrapped up as she was in a thick beige coat, it was hard to get a proper look at the rest of her – apart from the bottom half of her legs, which looked OK, and feet clicking away as she walked along beside me – I felt I was in the presence of an attractive woman. She moved nicely, and there was a lot of warmth to her, and a mix of confidence and shyness which I liked. She tended to look at me when I was talking, but look away when she was. Even though I've always been lucky with the ladies, since my teens in Liverpool, I was a bit shy too back then, and certainly wouldn't have asked her straight out for her number, but I'd got her name, I knew where she worked, and by the time we reached my sorting office, I knew where she lived as well, on her own, in a rented one-bedroom flat. She'd had a cat called Delilah but it died and she wasn't getting a new one, because it would feel like she was being unfaithful to Delilah. It's fabulous what strangers tell each other within minutes of meeting.

I'd been promoted to assistant head of section a few days earlier, which meant I had a small team working direct to me, and although I was still earning just below the national average, which I had heard reported at a union meeting a week earlier, I'd had a pay rise of sorts, which is maybe another reason I chucked a fiver at that down-and-out. Anyway it meant that if I did call her, and if I did get through, and if she did say yes, she would love to meet up for a drink, and maybe go out for dinner, I would be able to take her somewhere half decent. So I did call, and they did put me through and she answered before I had even properly rehearsed what I was going to say, and I ended up just saying 'was the dentist pissed?' and she laughed and said 'no' and then she said 'yes, I'd like that' when I asked if she fancied going out on Friday, and I thought, wow, that was too easy.

I was twenty-three, two years younger than her. She didn't look twenty-five, and when she told me, I said 'no way', and she took it as a big compliment and insisted on rooting through her handbag to find something with her date of birth on it, and she had a National Insurance card in there and, sure enough, she was born in March, the same month as me, but two years earlier, 1966.

'A World Cup baby,' I said. 'So how come you haven't settled down with anyone yet?' and she went all 'hold on a minute, I'm not that old, I could ask you the same thing', and I sort of was settled, but I didn't want to say that, obviously, so I said something like I had been playing the field a bit too much, but it came out badly, and she looked away for a few seconds. I found myself saying 'no, no, sorry, I don't mean like that, I just mean I had a few girlfriends in quick succession but for various reasons nothing quite worked out'.

In fact, I had been with Melanie for eighteen months and we'd been in bed the weekend before at her place, and we'd talked about moving in together finally, only we couldn't decide whether to move into hers or mine, a couple of rented rooms in a house near Arsenal's ground, which for an Everton fan like me was a bit of a pain, but not enough to shift me to Northolt where Melanie lived. I told Kate I had been with a girl called Melanie but we called it off a few weeks ago. 'What about you?'

She'd been engaged when she was twenty-one, to a guy from Barking called Roger who made window frames, but she said once the engagement ring was on, he changed, started behaving as though they had been married forever, expecting her to cook and clean and be at his beck and call, whereas if he fancied a night out with his mates, that was fine and dandy. 'So you dumped him?'

'Yep,' she said. 'Broke his heart, so he said, and so he calls me every now and then, usually Friday nights.'

'Pissed?'

'Imagine so. I never pick up.'

I had no reason to disbelieve her, other than the fact that I hadn't told her the truth about my own situation. But the next day I made it true. I told Mel I was 'really sorry but I've thought long and hard and I just can't commit. I like it when we're together but I also like it when we're apart and that means I'm not ready to move in, not with you, not with anyone.'

Three months later, I moved in with Kate, even though she had gone back on her promise of fidelity to Delilah and got herself a new cat, Primrose, who made me sneeze. Eight months later, we sat down with a council official her dad knew and he helped us get one of the council houses on the Holloway Road, and reckoned that if we pooled our resources, and saved hard, we would soon be able to secure a mortgage to buy it. Nine months after that, we moved to the top floor of Carrington House, two bedrooms, share of a garden five floors down. I carried her over the threshold and we cracked open a bottle of fizzy white wine and we had sex on the new double bed, which was just a mattress because we hadn't even unpacked.

We got married the following spring, 1993. We're not religious but both our mothers are, so we did the church thing, St Cedd's over her parents' way, though even at the time I was I suppose technically in breach of the 'forsaking all others' part of the deal, because I'd had a bit of a fling with a girl at work called Cheryl, and she was the one who said it had to stop, a few days before the wedding, because she said I had to change now I was getting married and she didn't want to ruin things for me. Malcolm's weakness was drugs and drink. Mine was women, and drink, and one leading to the other and then back again. Cheryl wasn't the last, and they never went on for more than a few weeks, and I think I was on Corinne when I realised that Kate knew, or at least heavily suspected, and with reason, that I was not playing the loyal husband role very well. I would just do flat denial, and she never pushed it too hard. The truth is I did have a commitment issue. I fell in love with Kate, for sure, but even as I did so there was a part of me I wanted to hold back, and once we were shacked up, and then married, I think the only part I could guarantee as being me alone, not me as in me and Kate, was the stuff I couldn't tell her about, the guilty secrets, because if I did she would kick me out, and then I really would be on my own. I didn't fancy that. I don't think she did either. It wasn't like my mum with my dad, flying into a rage at the slightest thing. With Kate, it was like she would suppress the rage, not want to know, not want to press too robustly for the truth, in case it hurt her. Lucky me, eh, that's what I would say to myself as I met someone else, and let my instincts lead me. Then silly bastard, that's what I would say to myself as I headed home, and wondered why I couldn't give myself totally to Kate, as I had promised to do. I really did love her, and when I am on my deathbed, and all the women I've had float across my memory, Kate is going to rise to the top of the pile. But whereas she always seemed, so far as I could tell, to be happy just with me, I always had to operate a Kate plus one policy, sometimes Kate plus two and even more.

'It's going to be different now,' I said to the wedding photo. 'You have my unconditional love, Kate, now and forever.' I think I meant it, though perhaps the beer was beginning to talk, as it is prone to do. When I woke up, right there on the sofa, empty can still in hand, I was keen to get showered and changed and head straight to the hospital, to see Hannah. When I arrived, Kate was a lot perkier with her own colour back on her face after the redness and the greyness of last

night. I gave her a little kiss, asked her how she had slept –
badly – then went to the cot at the side of the bed and looked
down on Hannah, asleep on her side, her tiny chest moving
in and out, and recalled something my gran once said, at my
grandad's funeral, when I asked why she didn't seem sad that
he had died, and she banged on about what a drunken waster
he was and said, 'The only truly unconditional love is the love
of a parent for a child. You'll know that yourself one day.'
Now I did. I was asking nothing of Hannah, yet getting so
much, just seeing her breathe.

'Did you bring the fruit?' asked Kate.

'Oh shit, sorry, love, I'll go and get some in a minute. But
let me watch this little thing for a bit.'

# MALCOLM

**My name is Malcolm. I am Hannah's uncle.**

We only lived half an hour north of Pat and Kate's place, near the reservoir at Ponders End, so Julie and I went to the hospital the day after Hannah was born, 12 February 1995. We walked in with our flowers for Kate and a little blue-checked romper suit for the baby, and Pat was like a little kid himself. The only thing that hacked him off was that we hadn't brought our lads, but I thought that might have been a bit much for Kate.

I was there when our Alan was born, at Fazakerley maternity, before we moved south, and yes it was exciting and moving, and I felt a big responsibility falling upon me, and I would have to say it was all very special, having kids, but I didn't go overboard like Pat did when Hannah came along. You'd have thought he was the first man alive to have become a dad. We had to look at the fingers and look at the toes, and isn't she this and isn't she that, and who did we think she looked like, could I see Mum in there? – to be honest I saw more of Dad, but I thought better of saying so. Pat never really talked about Dad. Maybe he thought that with a child of his own he could somehow catch up on what he'd lost, I don't know, but my God he was like a new man. I was happy for him, and I hoped it might make him settle down. I think he told me most things he got up to. I knew there had been a couple of women on the go, one at work, which is always a daft idea, and another an old girlfriend from over the river at Wallasey – he called her 'my ferry fuck' – who looked him up every few weeks when she went down to London.

I don't often do the big brother thing, but I really felt I had to that time. We always met at a gastropub in Park Road, Crouch End, which was halfway between us, and had the added bonus of being called the Maynard Arms, which gave us a running gag about having our own family pub. Once we'd had a couple of relaxers, ordered some food, and done all the football and the news and the bullshit about work, I told him he really had to pack it in with Hilary and Ellen, his 'ferry fuck – and can you stop calling her that?' I said marriage was a big thing and it was time he took it seriously. I said Kate was a fabulous girl and she was as good as he was going to get and he shouldn't be messing her around like this. He said Ellen was nothing, just a shag every now and then, and if need be he could knock her on the head for good. 'Not a problem, Malc.' Hilary was trickier, which was his own bloody fault, because he knew her through work – 'Never shit on your own doorstep,' I said – but I think he did dump her a while after. There was a rhythm to his little wanderings though. It was like he had to have Kate, and I do think he loved her, in his own way, I really do. When you were in their company, you had no doubt they were a couple, and he could be really solicitous of her. But he couldn't resist these little relationships outside the marriage. 'A standing prick knows no conscience,' that's what he used to say, and we'd both laugh, but I always worried for him that one day Kate would flip out and show him the door, just like Mum did to Dad.

'Yeah, but that wasn't because he was out shagging the whole time. He was just a full-on, fat-bellied, fifteen pints a day, "where's my dinner" pisshead, who treated her like shit. I treat Kate well when I'm with her. Just that when I'm not with her, I'm not averse to being with someone else. But the minute they try to get too close in, I level with them – "I will never leave Kate."'

'Well, don't bank on her not leaving you if you play around too long and too often. Our mam put up with him for a fuck of a long time. And then she didn't. I'm just saying . . . don't let history repeat itself.'

Pat always lived in the moment though. That day at the Whittington, with Hannah awake now and Julie and I having had a turn to hold her, he had a camera and he was snapping away – 'Oh look, I'm sure that was a smile, look, Julie, she's smiling at you,' and Kate, who looked shattered, saying, 'Babies don't smile when they're that small,' but he was having none of it, he was sure it was a smile. He said he was going to take a picture of her every day of her life, so that they had a record of how she developed and went from being the most beautiful baby in the world to being the most beautiful young woman in the world. He was going to do little Polaroids and put them on the kitchen wall day by day, and if they ran out of space he would put them up in the entrance, and if need be he would cover every wall in the flat. 'I will record history being made,' he said, 'so the world can see how she changed, day by day by day, slowly, step by step, becoming the eighth wonder of the world.' Then he picked her up again, rubbed his nose against her cheek and said, 'Who's my little eighth wonder then?' He kept up the photography for a few weeks, I reckon, then he went to once a week, then it became less frequent, every few weeks maybe, and eventually he just stopped. I don't even know if he's kept the pictures. I doubt it. He has always had mad passions, but they fizzle out. There were a few years of his life he went to every Everton game, home and away, including Europe, spent a fortune on it. He only sees them when they're in London now, if he can get tickets, and he never seems too bothered if he can't. Too expensive anyway. Then he got into racing, and the bookies was the only place he wanted to be, and he was convinced he had worked out a system for winning. He even had a bloody waistcoat phase, where he collected smart waistcoats, had a cupboard full of them. It was the same with his women, apart from Kate. Meet them, get obsessed with them, dump them. I really hoped Hannah, his own daughter, was more than a passion on the lines of his football team, or his flings.

When Julie and I were walking out of the hospital, I said that Pat reminded me of me when I first got into cocaine, and everything seemed more intense and better and sharper and clearer, and even boring stuff could be fun. I was off everything by then, apart from the odd drink-up every now and then – which I know alarmed Julie and which I always regretted – and Julie didn't much like me talking about my drugs period, which was before her time, but it was the only comparison I could find. I had never known him like it.

But it was never going to last, was it? Kids are hard work. I know that from my own two, and I know it from the kind of kid I was myself, causing no end of grief to my mum especially, because she was the one who stuck with us. She had no choice really. After Dad upped and went, we hardly ever heard from him, just the odd phone call every now and then, and me wanting it to end as soon as it began. I didn't hate him, not like Mum did, but he had gone from our lives and I wished he would stay gone, rather than try to pop in and out on his own terms. Mum made me feel bad even for speaking to him. Christ, she really hated him. I was indifferent really. I don't have that many memories of him when I was growing up, and even though I think I remember him leaving, I can't be sure of what is a real memory and what is the stuff Mum and Pat and I have talked about since. She was always saying we were well shot of him, but she could never stop talking about him either. It was as though he went, as ordered, but he never left us, even when she had rid the place of every item of clothing, every photo, every knickknack he had ever bought, every remnant of him. I wanted Mum to move on, to live with the fact she had kicked him out, and enjoy it, build a new life for herself. But she never did. Maybe he had damaged her too much. Truth is he had been a bastard to her. I know for a fact he hit her at least twice, because once I saw it, even if it was just a drunken lunge and he barely caught the side of her face, and the other time because Mrs Park next door told me she had 'heard a slap one night, then your mum crying, your dad shouting, and do you want me to call anyone?' She was a real nosy cow, but she was probably telling the truth. I said, 'No thanks, we'll manage.'

When Julie and I got engaged Dad phoned up and asked if I wanted him to come to the wedding and I just paused, wondering how to say no without being too hurtful. The words were forming in my mind. I was going to say that it was probably best not to risk upsetting Mum because that would upset us all. It was only a few moments of a pause but long enough for him to know what I was thinking. So he didn't come, didn't send a present or a message, and the next time I saw him I had a boy of my own. I let him come and see the baby, but made him promise not to tell Mum. I hate family secrets, but she would have gone crazy with me, so what was the point of provoking it? I just thought when all was said and done, my son was his grandson and it was only fair to let him see him. He seemed more pleased to be seeing me than seeing Alan. I guess babies were not his thing. If Pat was a nine and a half on a scale of one to ten baby-doolalliness, Dad hovered between two and three.

Julie was worried about Pat too. 'It's like he thinks she's some kind of miracle, going to save his marriage and save his life. You can't expect a baby to do all that. She's only a baby for heaven's sake. It's not Jesus coming on the scene.'

'I wouldn't worry too much,' I said. 'The novelty will wear off soon enough. But he may as well enjoy it while it lasts.'

# CHRISSIE

**My name is Chrissie. I was Hannah's babysitter and part-time childminder.**

Hannah and Vicki were among my first charges when I was still training to be a 'proper' childminder. When Hannah was little, Mr and Mrs Maynard – I could never get used to calling them Pat and Kate, no matter how many times they asked me to – had tried to manage without any help other than family and friends. However, when Vicki came along, once they were both back at work, they realised they had to get some proper help. I'd put a little ad in the window of the newsagent's opposite the cinema on Holloway Road, and Mrs Maynard called me two days later. She wanted to see my references before an interview, and she wanted her husband to be at the interview too, but it turned out he was doing double shifts in the run-up to Christmas, so in the end it was just me and her, with the girls.

Vicki was asleep when I arrived if I remember rightly, and I think Hannah sat next to her mum for a part of the interview, and I do remember her eyeing me up, and she didn't give much away. I smiled every now and then but she had quite a stern face on her. She was very still, not as fidgety as a lot of toddlers are, but I remember she used to tighten her hands together a lot, until the fingers were red. I think that was my first real memory of her, sitting there looking at me a bit suspiciously, with her hands clasped together and her thumbnails almost purple. I suppose it's natural for a child to worry about some stranger wandering in, and your mother sitting there asking her if she can look after you. It's not something I had direct experience of as a child. My father was the sole breadwinner, and my mother a full-time housewife looking after me, my brother and my sisters, in St Albans. So I suppose it is entirely possible Hannah felt a little scared of me, or scared of the situation. After a while she must have got bored, because she went off to the corner and played with some toys. They were never short of things to play with.

Mrs Maynard's main concern was that I knew all the basics of looking after babies. Once Vicki was awake, Mrs Maynard made me change a nappy, even though Vicki hadn't filled it. Hannah didn't appear to have the jealous older sibling thing at all. She seemed fascinated by her little sister, and fond of her too. She was still giving me the beady-eye look, but I think it was as much out of concern for Vicki as it was the suspicion she had for me. Later, we went through to the kitchen where Mrs Maynard had laid out different foods, and asked me to warm some milk, make a hot meal for Hannah, and make a sandwich for myself. It was not at all what I expected. I just thought I would go in, she would say she had read my references and called one of the people, check out the diploma I was working for, and she would decide either she liked me or she didn't. But it was really quite a test, especially considering I was charging bottom rates until I got through my course.

I admitted that I had never looked after anyone as young

as Vicki, and as soon as I said it, I thought I had made a terrible mistake, and regretted it, because suddenly she looked nervous, and nodded. We sat down at the kitchen table and she asked me to hold Vicki. I imagine that if Vicki had burst into tears, that would have been the end of things, but she came to me easily and I held her against my shoulder and then raised her a little so that we were looking into each other's eyes, and I made a little 'oo . . . oo . . . oo' sound, and she stared with a really intense interest in what I was doing. I could sense Mrs Maynard relaxing a little. There was a montage of rather tatty photos on a pinboard on the wall, mainly of Hannah, and I looked towards them and got Vicki's eyes to follow mine. 'Who's that? Eh? Who's that? That your big sister?' I looked after them for the first time the next day.

Mrs Maynard had taken her full maternity leave, and a bit of holiday on top, and when she went back she sorted out a deal allowing her to work from ten in the morning to four in the afternoon, which meant she could get the kids up and sorted, and she'd also see them for a few hours before they went to bed. So most of my work was getting Hannah from school, and playing with them or taking them to friends. I had a couple of older children I used to see first thing and get off to school, from the posh side of the Highbury tracks, and I would sometimes have to babysit for them after school and into the evening too. Mrs Maynard often asked me to cook the dinner, and sometimes Hannah would help me with that, and we had a little joke going that if it was really tasty, she made it, and if it wasn't, I made it. So I was working long hours, but I think I had known all my life that looking after children was what I wanted to do. It is very demanding at times, and of course you do make mistakes, and you learn as you go, but I love it. I wish I had kept a record now of all the children I have looked after. I can remember most of them, but not in the kind of detail you need when you're trying to establish why some worked out OK and others didn't, and you're wondering whether you could have done anything differently to stop things going wrong. I certainly remember Hannah, and it's not all bad. She could be difficult, for sure, but she was smart, really pretty, conscious of it even as a small child. She once told me – she can't have been more than six or seven – 'You know, Chrissie, you could have a sweet face if you made a bit of an effort. Let's go and play with Mum's make-up.'

I decided to go down the children route after dropping out of university at the end of my first year. I was doing geography at Hull but it wasn't really for me. I don't know why I didn't like it. It wasn't like I was homesick, I had some good friends, and found the work reasonably interesting, but I found the whole student thing tedious. I'm quite serious about my faith but I'm not a prude, and I don't mind having a night out every now and then. I was really shocked, though, at how much drink and casual sex seemed to be the order of the day for so many of the students. I honestly couldn't believe Freshers' Week. There was a party I went to where one of the big beer companies was giving out free drinks, and the whole place was branded with their logos and their slogans and I remember saying I thought it was scandalous that alcohol companies could target eighteen-year-olds away from home for the first time in their lives like this, and everyone thought I was like some kind of alien from another age. They just laughed at me. It was like 'What else is university for but a chance to get away from home and do all the things your parents don't want you to?' One of them threw a condom at me, said Durex were handing them out free in the Students' Union. I felt quite alienated in behaving well. As well as being an engineer my father was a lay preacher, so alcohol barely featured in our lives at home. Also, I was never the rebellious sort; in fact leaving university without getting a degree is probably the most rebellious thing I have ever done. By the time I left home for Hull, I had been drunk once in my life, and I hated it. I didn't like the feeling of being out of control, nor how ill I felt the next day, and I hated the cold looks I got from my father. I know there are lots of kids who would go the other way when that kind of treatment was being meted out, but I didn't. I respected my parents and I didn't want to make them unhappy, or ashamed of me. So I just decided drink was not for me. I joined the Christian Union at Hull, but even though there was a fair amount of sobriety attached to that, the minute I left a meeting and went back to the halls of residence, I would be feeling I was back living in a tsunami of alcohol. A girl from Bournemouth called Alice was in the next room to mine and I could count on one hand the number of nights she went to bed sober. Heaven knows how she could afford it. I was always struggling financially. There was also a seemingly never-ending line of young men who would be drunk with her, and usually staying the night, and as well as listening to their loud music and their laughter, I'd have to listen to all the sex noises too, and then look Alice in the eye the next morning and pretend I had heard nothing. It was all a bit sordid. I'm not saying she was the reason I left, but she was one of them.

The main thing, though, was that I just couldn't imagine spending three years not really knowing why I was studying what I was studying. I was the youngest of five, and all my siblings had gone to college or university, and my father was really keen for me to see it out, but my mum was on my side, and during the summer break, we had a family sit-down and by the end of it we agreed I would call it a day and train as a childminder. Dad was disappointed, but also happy that it meant getting a diploma. As soon as I started on the training course, I knew that it was more my line than full-time academic studying. I got on a course through our local authority in Hertfordshire, and as well as learning things like basic first aid, there were sessions on business and management too, because in the end I was going to be setting up my own very small business, and I moved to London where there were so many people looking for childcare support.

I've had dozens of children now, hundreds even, if I count all the times I was looking after the kids of friends and siblings as well. It's true that they all have their own unique little character, but they do also meld into one, and as I look back, I cannot guarantee I have every detail right, nor that I don't sometimes mix them up in my own mind.

I've really thought about Hannah a lot, though, tried hard to think of anything that could have foretold what would happen to her. It was apparently the Catholic Order, the Jesuits, who said, 'Give me the child until he is seven, and I will give you the man,' and one of the reasons my mother didn't work was that she and my father both thought children should have constant parental support and influence in their early years, and that a lot of society's current ills are due to family break-down, and that a child with one working parent is likely to be happier and more centred than a child with two working parents. Who knows?

Well, Hannah was three going on four when I first looked after her, and I was her childminder on and off for five years, so that included when she was seven. If you'd asked me then what did I think she would be when she grew up, I wouldn't have known what to answer. Not a nurse or a teacher. I'm not saying she was uncaring. But she wasn't especially focused on other people and their needs. She was quiet a lot of the time too, quite brooding. I noticed it more when her parents were around. Unless you're living in, which I have never done, you tend only to get snatches of time seeing children with their parents. I have no way of knowing what Hannah was like as an only child, and what they were like with her, but there is no doubt that Vicki was her mother's special one. She was just so nice, not moody, but smiley and happy-go-lucky. You always felt a little bit happier when you spent some time with her. I'm not saying Hannah was all darkness because she wasn't. But she could be, in a way that Vicki never was. Mrs Maynard wasn't cold with Hannah, just warmer with Vicki, less strict when they were a bit older. Vicki was probably brighter too. I'm not academic, but I like reading, and one of the joys of my work is reading with children and watching them taste the joy that reading can bring. I read to Vicki long before she could actually understand letters let alone words and I like to think that was one of the reasons she took to books so avidly. I remember when she started at nursery school, Mrs Maynard wanted to take her in the morning but I picked her up, and the nursery teacher looked me out to say she had never had such a good first-day reader. Perhaps Hannah didn't have the same passion for books instilled in her when her parents alone were responsible for her upbringing. I grew up in a house full of books. The Maynards had maybe half a shelf full and a lot of them looked like unread Christmas presents. Sometimes I would take the girls to the library after school and Vicki's little eyes would light up as soon as I mentioned the idea. But Hannah tended to shrug, she would go along with it but without enthusiasm. I wondered whether she might have dyslexia, but they had her checked out and there seemed to be no problem.

You have to be very careful when you look after other people's children. Some days you are spending more waking hours with the child than their parents do, but you must never assume you are replacing a mother or father. You do get attached, though, and you do have favourites. You wouldn't be human if you didn't. So if you are asking me direct, did I prefer looking after Vicki to looking after Hannah, the answer is yes. And if you are asking me if I sometimes felt I would be a better parent to both of them than Mr and Mrs Maynard, the answer to that is yes too. I imagine that sounds a little arrogant. But why do we always assume parents will be good for their children?

I didn't actually meet Mr Maynard until a couple of weeks after I started. I had quite a powerful, even visceral reaction against him. I can't really explain it, but it was instant. He was quite a good-looking man, nice wavy hair, a strong jawline, and he had a warm smile but I sensed something deeply unauthentic about it. His Liverpool accent seemed to get stronger the longer he lived away from there, whereas his brother Malcolm, who visited occasionally, had softened his accent hugely. Perhaps my negative views of what I recall then are being reframed by hindsight, because now I know about the affairs, and I certainly know about the advances Mr Maynard made on me a good while later, but I am fairly sure

I felt immediately that he was not quite the good man he presented himself as, and perhaps he felt sincerely that he was.

There are all kinds of parent–child relationships, and they are all complicated, but as an observer, you tend to cut through the complexity and try to define them simply. Happy – there were a few of those, though not as many as you would like. Gushing. Strict. Proud. Wrapped around a little finger (usually a father). Disrespectful. Tolerant. Too close. Not close enough. Abusive. Defiant. Jealous. Tense. I've seen them all. So far as Mrs Maynard is concerned, I would say 'proud' was the closest a single word got to describing her relationship with Vicki. For Hannah, 'tense'. They never seemed to relax easily in each other's company. Vicki sensed that too, I think, and perhaps used it instinctively the way that clever siblings do. By the time they were both at school, it was really only the height difference that told you Hannah was the older sister. Vicki was more outgoing, more confident, more commanding as a presence. They had every reason to be proud of her. She was a lovely little girl, definitely one of my favourites. On the Christmas card list forever.

I don't find it quite so easy to define Mr Maynard's relationship with them. Confused maybe. Superficial. I sometimes got the feeling he loved the idea of children, and he loved to think, and have others think, that he was the head of a perfect loving family, but he didn't always appreciate the hard slog that went with it. He could be nice to Mrs Maynard, and sometimes the self-image appeared to match the mood and the circumstances. He could be tactile, considerate about what kind of day she had had or what pressures work or the children were putting her under. But when the key turned in the door, you never quite knew which Mr Maynard was going to walk through. I never saw him change a nappy, or make a meal for the children. There were times when I felt he took genuine happiness in arriving home to see them, and he would run to them as they ran to him, lift them, play with them, but then I always felt he was going through the motions, and often he would find a reason to do something else, make a call, watch something on TV, get himself a drink. He wasn't a drunk, but he certainly drank too much. It was almost like an instinct thing. Through the door, coat on the peg, hi to the wife and kids, then go to the fridge or the drinks shelf. It was usually beer, but sometimes it was whisky or vodka.

There was a lascivious side to him too. I dress for ease and my own comfort rather than to show off my figure – probably my best asset if a man were to think of me in those terms. Yet, when Mrs Maynard was not there, or elsewhere, perhaps upstairs getting ready to go out with him, I could feel his eyes running over my body and I would meet his look, and he would always hold my stare for just a moment too long before looking away. If one of the children were to drop something, and I would go to pick it up, he would go too and find a way of brushing against me, ever so creepily. The time he made a move on me, she was out and he came back first and it was so rank I can still get angry thinking about it. I thought about telling Mrs Maynard, but ultimately I had a simple choice to face – was it so serious that it merited me resigning there and then on the spot? I decided it didn't. It was unpleasant, it was mildly threatening in that he did place his hands on my shoulders and one fell down to my breast, and he moved as if to try to kiss me, but I pushed him away easily enough and didn't think he would ever dare try it again. I went to say goodbye to the girls in the sitting room. He followed me through, said, 'I'm sorry, I really don't know what came over me,' and I said, 'I think the less said the better, but I need to think about whether I can work for you now,' and he said, 'Oh please, don't do anything drastic, you've been wonderful, the girls adore you, and maybe that was why I went a bit far, because, well, you are a lovely young woman, and I guess I've had a couple of drinks and, anyway, look, I truly am sorry.'

'I'm not sure we should be talking about this here,' I said, making a point of kneeling down on the floor to help Hannah tidy away a jigsaw puzzle.

'OK.'

And that was the last either of us mentioned it.

I suspected he was a womaniser long before the terrible shouting match which I heard one Saturday morning as I arrived at the house. I didn't work at weekends as a rule, but Mrs Maynard called me first thing, said there was an emergency and could I maybe take the girls out for the morning? I had an immediate insight into the 'emergency', even as I was standing outside the door to the flat looking through my bag for the key. Voices were raised, including hers.

'This is not the way I want to live my life, Pat, and you need to decide what kind of life you want to live. With a family, or without a family, as simple as that. Because I am sick and tired of being humiliated. I am sick and tired of your lies. I am sick and tired of you telling me no, no, no, there is nothing going on, and then it turns out well yes there is, and it's all OK, OK, yes, OK, but I promise you it's nothing –'

'But it is, it's nothing . . . it's messing around . . . it's flirting . . . it's just what married men do . . . there is nothing more to it than that –'

'And do you think I believe you? Do you really think I

believe you? When I've heard it all before, and I know I'll hear it all again, unless you face up to what I'm saying, Pat.'

'I will, Kate, I will, I promise you I will.'

And then it went quiet for a few seconds and I wondered about going in, but it started up all over again, because she demanded to see his expenses claims for the past five weeks.

'What the fuck are you talking about?'

'I've made a note of where you've told me you've been when you haven't been home. One month. Five nights away. Birmingham, twice. Norwich. Cardiff. Shrewsbury. Conferences, you said. And I'm wondering why the Royal Mail has to have so many conferences for its assistant managers in the sorting offices. I want to see the hotel bills, Pat, and the petrol receipts, and I want to see your expenses sheets.'

'Who's trying to humiliate who now?'

'You say you're a changed man. All your philandering is behind you. Just want to be with me and the girls. OK, prove it. Prove to me that you were in Birmingham on the nights of 4 and 17 October, Norwich 8 October, Cardiff 27 October, Shrewsbury 2 November.'

'You are fucking crazy.' His voice was rising now and I was worried the situation could get violent. I'm not sure I would have known what to do. We had covered violent parents on the course, but sometimes reality feels very different to the theoretical examples of study, and I was turning to walk away.

'No, Pat, *you're* fucking crazy if you think I am going to put up with being shat on again and again. Do you think I'm deaf as well as dumb? I heard you talking last night, and it was not a Royal Mail colleague call to plan your next "conference". Not unless you tell all your colleagues you miss them and you love them and you can't wait to see their tits and kiss their fucking fannies . . .' and now her voice had reached screeching point, and I could hear a chair being dragged across the floor and it sounded like one of them had thrown it, and then I could hear crying, and at first I thought it was Kate, whimpering like a child, but the front door suddenly opened and Pat came charging past me, grunted 'get out the way', and I walked in and there was Hannah, holding Vicki's hand. It was Vicki who was crying, and she ran into her mother's arms, and Mrs Maynard let out the most awful scream, so loud, so shocking, that Vicki stopped crying, bit her bottom lip, and squeezed her mother so hard I thought she was going to strangle her. I turned to Hannah, but she had locked herself in the bathroom.

'You OK in there?' I asked.

'Yeah, fine, just brushing my teeth.'

'Good girl. See you in a minute.'

'Yeah, OK.'

# COLIN

**My name is Colin. I was Hannah's swimming coach.**

I'm retired now, sad to say. The local paper did an article on me, pictured by the side of the pool at Barnet Copthall, with a float in one hand and a whistle in the other. It looked cheesy to me, but the photographer was one of those pushy sorts who gets his own way, and the write-up and the headline – 'North London kids say thanks and farewell to swim coach Colin' – were nice enough. The reporter, a young girl called Alison I'd taught to swim fifteen years earlier, asked me what the highlight of my career was. I said I had hundreds – 'Every time a child I was teaching suddenly realised they could swim, without help from a human hand, a float or hanging onto the side. I never lost the thrill of seeing those first splashes.'

She asked how many children had been through my hands, so to speak. Hundreds and hundreds. Thousands, when I add in the school galas and the inter-school competitions I used to organise. I find retirement dull, perked up by the few hours of volunteering I still do for the swimming clubs. But the younger coaches are in charge now, and you have to be very careful not to fall into the trap of being bitter or resentful about that, or becoming an old bore complaining that things aren't being done as well as they used to be. Two of my former kids got into the London Olympics. I tried everything to get a ticket, but couldn't, so watched on TV instead. They both went out in the heats, but even so, they will be able to say for the rest of their lives that they represented their country in the greatest Olympics ever, in the world's best city – I was born and bred here and will die here too – and I can say I taught them their first strokes.

It's a nice feeling, to know there are a couple of generations of people out there who can appreciate the joy of swimming, not to mention the security it provides, because they came to the various teaching and training pools I have worked in over four going on five decades. What with the way people move around, and switch jobs the whole time – or don't have one, unfortunately, for a lot of people – there won't be many starting work now who do the same thing for forty years. I am very proud of my life. I have worked for clubs, councils, gyms, sporting associations, private individuals, triathlon teams, you name it. But the work I loved most of all was teaching beginners in the shallow pool at Caledonian Road, the Cally everyone calls it, watching fear and panic turn to confidence and fun in a few easy lessons. For some, the fear would never fully subside. For others, a minority, the water held no fear whatever, and they took to it naturally. My job then was to spot talent, and nurture it, like a flower.

Hannah was a bit of a late starter, seven or eight when she came to me via her primary school. She and her sister were naturals, graceful and confident, but Hannah was the one I sensed had a real, raw talent for the pool. Most kids start with aimless, energy-wasting splashing, graduate to a hopeless doggy-paddle, and then with proper teaching learn the basics of breaststroke. Hannah, however, had only been a few times when she spotted in the fast lanes in the 'grown-up' pool next to the teaching basin that there were some swimmers going faster than others, and they were all doing front crawl.

'That's not what you told us to do,' she said. 'They're not kicking like frogs. They're like dolphins and fish.'

I explained that once she and her friends had mastered breaststroke we should go on to that, but the next time she came, she was doing it anyway, rough-and-ready style to be sure, but recognisably front crawl. She had gone home and looked on a computer and learned all about it. It is such an exciting moment for a coach, discovering someone has the right build and shape, the right attitude, and a natural feel for what's required. She had all of that. Of course, with girls especially, you worry when puberty comes and you're waiting to see how their bodies change. You don't see many Olympic medals hanging down between a big cleavage and heaving bosoms, do you? Also, once kids become aware of the sexual side of life, that is a terrible time for a coach. I've lost so many good swimmers to the discovery that foreplay might be more fun than following the underwater white line for half a mile up and down the pool as a warm-up before we get on to the session proper. I don't know why pools always have 'No Heavy Petting' signs up. It's like an advert for it. 'Hey, try this, it's more exciting than what Colin's telling you to do.'

Her class teacher, Miss Fry, had told me Hannah was bright, usually attentive and with a sharp mind, but also that she could be a bit of a handful, prone to tantrums and sulks if she was challenged or pushed too far. I never saw that side of her. She would run in when the minibus pulled up outside, be first to change and first in the pool, asking what reps we were doing. You can only speak as you find, and I liked her. Maybe she was a loner, in that she didn't seem to have a special little friend, but I think that's because she loved the swimming. It's a total thrill for a coach when kids can't be bothered with too much larking around, because they're taking it seriously, properly seriously. The ones I couldn't stand were the bullies, the pushers and the shovers and the towel-flickers. That wasn't Hannah, and she had a presence about her so nobody ever tried any of that nonsense on her, and the one time a girl called Tanya tried it on Vicki, Hannah was straight in there, sorted her out and it never happened again. She always looked out for her little sister.

Outside of my work, I have always been a bit of a loner too. I'm married, to Muriel, but we have been left unblessed with children, and once we finally gave up trying, and the hurdles to adoption proved nightmarishly difficult and bureaucratic, the marriage meandered into a bearable nothingness. We ate together, slept together, went away to the south coast for weekends together from time to time, but we bore with us every moment the weight of knowing that our life together had not panned out as envisaged. It is a heavy burden and one that I escaped by doing a job I loved, with children who perhaps filled the gap left by my own infertility, which is a curse for any man, but I think especially someone like me, who loves kids and who has stayed fit and healthy all my life. Never smoked, never drank more than once a week, and then only a pint or so. I didn't need any of that. I just needed my work. It kept me afloat, I might say, even if it does sound even cornier than the *Barnet Today* headline. That explains why I looked so miserable in the silly photo with the float and the whistle, as the reality dawned that my purpose was being taken from me.

Hannah mastered the basics easily, and once we ironed out her freestyle technique, I realised that she was possible material for serious competitive swimming. Most of the top competitors come from the private schools with their own pools and buses and dedicated coaches, whereas at times I was covering dozens of local state schools, and often the kids could barely afford a decent pair of trunks or a costume, let alone the transport costs of training and competition. I had a secret stash of my own thick white towels for those embarrassed by the threadbare cloth their parents sent them out with. I loved it when my kids competed against the posh kids, and won. It didn't happen as often as I would have liked, but when it did, I would go home a very contented man. One of the happiest days of my life was when I persuaded the head of sport at Highgate School to let me put together a team to take on their best, two per event for all the main disciplines. We won it on the last leg of the last relay, Matthew Spence from Haverstock School bringing it home. I think my lads were aware of what it meant to me. They all dived in to celebrate, then some of them got out and threw me in too, fully clothed. That was up there, close to the top of all-time best experiences, especially seeing those rich kids and their fancy teachers slope off with their tails between their legs.

Hannah's main asset was her arms, long, slender, with good shoulders and flexible wrists and elbows, essential for maximising the force of each arm as it goes through the water. Most swimmers waste vast amounts of energy by thinking it is all about turning your arms as fast as you can. It is all in the technique, the rhythm, economic use of the shoulder, correct pitching of the elbow, good entry of the fingers into the water, use of the wrist so the hand is like a paddle and the body is the boat, the feet acting as the propeller. It can take some kids forever and they still don't grasp those simple basics. Hannah got them from her first day. She worked out that the fewer strokes it takes to get you from one end of the pool to the other, the more energy you'll have to do it again. For a 25-metre pool, most girls Hannah's age would require more than thirty strokes, many of them a lot more. She was in the mid-twenties within six months of her first lesson. I signed her up to my elite coaching squad – there were only two girls her age in it at the time – and that meant in addition to the weekly lesson with the school, she came out for two evening sessions, one at the Cally, one at Barnet. I entered her for a few races with higher age groups, warned her she wouldn't win, but said it was good experience for her, and it would help push her times up, seeing and sensing bigger, faster girls ahead of her.

Her approach to training was faultless, usually first in, last out, and she was capable of long, long training swims. If I'd said 'do a thousand lengths as a warm-up', she'd have done it. She was also a beautiful diver, and sometimes when she'd done a really good session, I'd let her mess about on the diving board and teach her a few of my special dives. I had her marked out as a long-distance swimmer for the future, but as a young child, her races were always one length or two, four max if there was a medley. When she was eleven, she won the freestyle, breaststroke and butterfly, and came second in the backstroke, in her school swimming gala. She was in a different league to the rest. She was so proud, standing there with her medals round her neck, doing that thing kids do where they're pretending to be all cool about it, but inside they're bursting. I asked if her mum and dad had been there to see it, and she said 'no, they're working'. She didn't seemed too fussed, but I always felt parents should try to be there for big moments like that.

As she started to win inter-school races, and then made county level, I decided I needed to go and see them. So one evening after training I drove her home and met her mum. She seemed a nice lady, thanked me for all my support, made me tea, said swimming seemed to be the one thing Hannah really enjoyed and excelled at, and I was the one teacher she didn't moan about. I don't know if it was meant as a put-down, but I could tell Hannah took it as one.

I explained that she was as good a natural talent as I had ever come across, I was aware children had to do English and maths and science and what have you, but I hoped she would see her way to supporting Hannah in her swimming. I was happy to coach her, but it might be she would have to start travelling distances to races and I might come looking for a bit of support for that, cost of petrol, or a lift.

'Is she really that good?'

'She's young, but if she develops as she has been doing, she has enormous potential and I would hate to see it go to waste.' She seemed genuinely shocked, like her assumption for Hannah would be of ordinariness, not something special. 'She is special,' I said.

Hannah was sitting silently as this discussion continued, and I noticed she was even quieter in the home than she was at the pool. But whereas when I talked to her, she always looked me in the eye, and listened with an eagerness and concentration I adored, when her mother spoke, she seemed detached, and struggled with eye contact. Her sister was around the place, and though she couldn't swim like Hannah, she had more confidence and seemed to get more give from her mother. You can't blame a child, especially a younger one, for working hard for that extra attention. I could see it came naturally. Mrs Maynard seemed stressed – she was friendly and polite, but I never felt I had her full attention, sensed there was something else going on in her head.

'Well, Colin seems to be really impressed, Hannah,' she said, standing up to indicate the meeting was over. 'Sounds like you're quite the little mermaid.'

'He's a good teacher,' she said.

'That's kind,' I said, 'but once you're in that water, it's not about the coaching, it's all about you.'

I suggested that she and her husband come to a race. 'Don't underestimate the positive impact of having support at an event,' I said. 'I mean, why do football teams win more games home than away?'

'We will,' she said. 'When's the next one?'

'She'll be in the South-East England champs in three weeks, at Crystal Palace. Won't be easy, but she's in with a shout.'

Bloody parents, honestly. I lost count of how many phone calls they made to check where, when, what. I sensed they were out of their comfort zone somehow. And when it came to it, her mum arrived five minutes before Hannah's 100-metre freestyle heat, and was waving and shouting to get her attention, and I wished I could have gone over and told her to shut up, because Hannah was all about focus and concentration, unusually for someone her age, and I could see she was distracted. Then her mother started making gesticulating gestures with her watch – I think to say her father was late.

Indeed, by the time he arrived, Hannah was already changed out of her swimming gear, having come fifth out of eight and failed to qualify for the semis. She swam three seconds worse than her personal best.

'Not to worry,' I said as she emerged from the changing room. 'We all have bad days.'

'But I wanted today to be good.'

'I know. So did I. But sport is about setback as well as success. Like life. We have to take the setback and turn it into success. Then we're stronger. You learn more from defeat than you do from winning.'

'Yeah, I guess,' she said. 'But they're going to think all that talk about being special, being a potential champion and stuff, was all . . . you know . . .'

'You are a champion, Hannah,' I said. 'Just not today.'

Her parents spotted us talking by the drinks machine, came bounding over, him saying, 'Sorry I missed you,' her saying, 'Didn't miss much, did he, love?' then, 'Sorry, didn't mean it to come out like that.'

It was the only time they saw her compete. Three months later, the local councils reviewed their budgets and I was put in charge of a much bigger area, and the powers that be decided I had to base myself full-time in Barnet. That meant a half-hour journey for Hannah. The public transport was OK, but it wasn't good for a girl as young and pretty as her to be making evening journeys on the bus and the Tube.

I made a call to both her parents, said she had phenomenal talent and they had to make an effort to get her to my sessions.

'You sure this isn't about you not her?' said Mr Maynard, and I reckon if he had said it in person I would have decked him. 'No,' I said, 'it is about your daughter being special and having a lot of potential and me not wanting to see it go to waste.' Mrs Maynard was at least more understanding but she was also brutally honest. 'We both work, Colin, and even with two salaries we're not rolling in it. Yes, I get a bit of help with the kids, but we also have another daughter to look after, and neither of us can really commit to regular schleps across town so Hannah can train all the time.'

'This is what makes me so angry,' I said. 'Rich kids have pools at their schools, coaches coming out of their ears, parents who drive them around or club together to hire or buy mini-buses, but Hannah – who has more natural talent than all the kids at Francis bloody Holland combined – has no chance, because we can't get her the support she needs.'

'I know,' she said, 'but when was life ever fair? I will try, Mr Shepherd, I really will.'

And for a month or so, she did. But soon, twice weekly became weekly, weekly turned to fortnightly, then it was monthly, and when her times dipped, she started to lose races she was capable of winning, became disheartened and eventually she stopped coming at all. It was sad. I wasn't fond of her in the way I was of the chatty cheeky ones, the characters. But there was something so special about her, something extreme almost, and that is a quality you need if you're going to get on in sport or in life, the ability to work that little bit harder, go that little bit extra, have people around you fearing you are more than capable of going over the top. She had that, did Hannah. That's why I'll always have her down at the top of my list of the ones who got away. I always felt, though, that whatever she did in life, she would do it better than the rest.

# ERIC

**My name is Eric. I was the judge in Hannah's parents' divorce case.**

The purest form of hatred I ever witness is in my courtroom when a once loving – one assumes – husband and wife are arguing over property, assets and children. Frankly the impact on the last of these appears barely to figure in their thinking, once the mists of loathing have descended. Mr and Mrs Maynard were not at the top scale of loathing, but from time to time she seemed perilously close to it. The divorce itself had been agreed on paper and only came to me after they failed to reach agreement both about financial settlement and Mr Maynard's contact with the children, issues which required separate hearings, the second of which was the most fraught. It is usually the other way round.

I have been a divorce court judge for over a decade now. It is not what I intended for myself when I was first called to the Bar. Employment law was my passion. However, I became involved in arbitration, and with that experience under my belt, the move from business–union or employer–employee dispute to husband–wife dispute had its own logic. Added to which, the divorce courts had an enormous backlog at the time, and there was a public appeal by the Lord Chancellor for QCs and judges to make the switch. I made the move as a barrister, and became a judge two years later. The arbitration experience comes in especially handy when we are resolving issues of cash. In this area, my guide is the Matrimonial Causes Act 1973, which, despite all the social turmoil caused by the rise in divorce and family breakdown, remains a fine piece of work, particularly Section 25. Here, a judge is having to establish the parties' income, their earning capacities – including how these might change as a result of divorce – property and any other assets that may have been deemed to be shared, the financial needs and obligations, expectations of standard of living, the contribution – financial and otherwise – each party has made to the marriage, any benefits that either party might lose as a result of the divorce. That is a list of the issues at their most simple. In practice, most cases tend to bring up their own complexities and it is never easy to be sure that the judgement is the right one. However, we are appointed and paid – albeit modestly compared with what one earns at the Bar – to make decisions. That is what we must do.

The Maynards' mortgage arrangement was complex for what I may call, hopefully without being too patronising or condescending, a very ordinary couple, in that they relied on three separate loans, one from a bank, two (of unequal size) from relatives on both sides of the marriage. The family loans were to help pay down a deposit and take care of the first instalments. They had been paid back only partially, and only on one side of the family, Mr Maynard's. Both parties were working, Mr Maynard earning an above-average salary, especially when bonuses and overtime were taken into account, whereas Mrs Maynard was on a salary slightly below the regional average. I decided in fairly short order, having read the papers the night before at home in Greenwich over a glass of Pinot Grigio, that Mrs Maynard was entitled to a small lump sum, ongoing maintenance to help with the costs of raising her children, and a part transfer of the property assets so that she should have a good share of the value of their main asset, their home. It was clear to me that this was likely to require a sale of the family home, and both Mr and Mrs Maynard were likely to have to move to smaller, possibly rented properties, until they were able to re-establish some kind of financial equilibrium concomitant with their new circumstances. This was of course regrettable, and likely to bring additional strain on the children already no doubt shaken by the events which led to the breakdown of their parents' marriage. But it was as satisfactory an outcome as I could deliver.

We required a separate hearing for the issue of contact, or what used to be called access, and at one point my clerk wondered if I had thought of calling the children, such was the anger – particularly from Mrs Maynard – that filled the courtroom. I did not give it more than a moment's thought. The divorce of their parents is hard enough for children without having to say what they think about their mother and father in front of both of them, and in front of a judge. Added to which I am aware they can be put under intolerable pressure by a parent to say bad things about the other parent in court. I have called a child only once in my career and I saw the emotional scars for a lifetime being carved into him before my very eyes. Calling them is always best avoided.

Mr Maynard accepted that the children would live with Mrs Maynard, who had been responsible for the bulk of their childcare. Mr Maynard was keen for regular contact. Mrs Maynard wished to restrict it to a minimum. When I asked her why, what I saw was raw anger, perhaps suppressed over many years, but now at bursting point.

'I don't trust him to look after them properly.'

'Did your husband ever use violence against you or the children?' I asked.

'No,' she said. (Mr Maynard would later tell me that he was the only victim of violence, when she struck him with a saucepan.)

'For most of the marriage, would you say he was a bad parent?'

'Not terrible, no. He was very loving at times, but in recent years he has been less so, much less so.'

'Less loving of the children, or less loving of you?'

'Both. He has been around less. Because he has been philandering more.'

'But if you have no fear of him physically mistreating the children, why, given it is accepted I think that children benefit from having two parents, even when they have split up, are you so vehemently opposed to him seeing them at all?'

'Like I say, I don't trust him to look after them properly, or give them proper attention. He goes from woman to woman, I know that now, and how am I to know the girls are not there with him, and he is just off with his latest floozy? He has shown he can't be trusted with me, he has hurt them as well as me in what he has done, so why would anyone trust him to carry out his responsibilities as a father to them any better than he carried out his responsibilities as a husband to me?' This was not convincing, and certainly not a reason to deny contact, though I declined from saying so at the time, instead suggesting to her lawyer, a rather impressive young man called Pinkerton, that he seek to discuss this position with her during the break. He knew what I was getting at.

Given the extent of his straying from the marital bed, I could well understand Mrs Maynard's anger, but anger is something to which a judge must not respond. The judge must seek to stay calm-headed at all times, and not be swayed by the often deep emotions surging through the court.

She had certainly been someone of considerable patience and forbearing in their marriage. Many spouses petition for divorce on the grounds of a single known act of adultery, whereas it was clear that Mr Maynard had been something of a wayward husband on the sexual front for most of their marriage. I learned all this from the horse's mouth, so to speak. Mr Maynard was not represented and so spoke quite eloquently, but at inordinate length, and with a lot more detail than I required to make a judgement.

He began by combining an apology for his adultery, which he made no effort to condone or explain, with an expression of unconditional love for his two daughters. He then went on to seek to refute Mrs Maynard's point that the possibility of future relationships with women meant he would not give his daughters sufficient attention when he saw them. His 'defence' appeared to be that he had managed to combine inappropriate relationships with being a good father when married, so he would be even better placed to do so when unmarried. I confess it was a new one on me, and I found myself rather warming to him as, to make his case, he ran through the level of extra-marital activity he was engaged in, while saying he managed to see his daughters at least first thing in the morning or last thing at night.

One assumes that he had admitted only to those acts of adultery of which Mrs Maynard was already aware, which included what might be described as a rash of such acts, when he falsely claimed to be away on business, but was in fact seeing two women with whom he was seemingly conducting extra-marital affairs simultaneously.

'I think this was the straw breaking the camel's back,' he said. 'She challenged me over where I'd been and I denied it, as you do. I think men always do that, so do women, but then she phoned my human resources department and said she had been with me on one of the trips, to Birmingham, and could she check the name of the hotel because we wanted to take the kids for a weekend, and the woman in HR fell for it, said I had not been to Birmingham, and Kate said, well, what about etc. etc., and this woman – not the brightest – said I had never made a hotel claim before. And it was true, I hadn't, and I was banged to rights, but let me say this, Your Honour, there was not one of those days, when I said I was in Birmingham, Norwich, Cardiff or Shrewsbury, that I did not make a point of speaking to the kids.'

He was quite convincing in his expression of devotion to his daughters, and I assumed all his affairs would surely lie on his conscience as he considered a life separate from the rest of his family. Though it does 'take two to tango', I regret that the male sex urge, often but not always accompanied by the presence of mood-changing substances, both liquid and solid, is the strongest single force driving through my court-room. Were I asked to choose a second such force, it would be greed, a sin shared by both sexes, with women perhaps slightly in the lead on that one, but that is by the by.

Equally by the by was Mr Maynard's decision to confess a compulsive attitude towards sexual conquest. He sought at one point, interestingly though irrelevantly, to say he had read about sex addiction and intended to seek counselling for this. He was going into far more detail than I needed to settle the issue, which is what often happens when respondents decline to have a lawyer. The issue of his adultery as grounds for divorce had already been settled before the case came to me. Marriage is a contract, fidelity is a key clause within the contract, and though I did not probe excessively, two children suggested that Mrs Maynard was not an unreasonable spouse with regard to the activity – 'with my body I thee honour' as it appears in the contract – that takes place between a man and a woman in the marital bed. Furthermore, I remain unpersuaded that it is possible to become addicted to the sexual act in the same way as one might become addicted to alcohol or drugs, with all their physiological and mind-changing attributes. I take a similar view of gambling, and harbour considerable doubt as to whether this too should be viewed as an addiction on a par with the two we know best, alcohol and narcotics. I did, though, see that in seeking to make this claim about his own conduct, Mr Maynard was, however clumsily and inelegantly, signalling clear acceptance of his own past wrongdoing, and a desire to change his behaviour, no doubt in part because he foolishly thought this might be a factor in persuading me to grant him the kind of contact he wished to have with his children.

The judge knows that he or she must always put the children first. Both parents will claim to have that same motivation.

Unfortunately, all too often, the children become pawns in the loathing game, and most of what their parents say before me is irrelevant to the decision I make.

That the children's interests are paramount when settling a divorce case is enshrined in the Children Act of 1989, one of the better pieces of legislation to emerge from Mrs Thatcher's late years. The key decisions for the judge are: where the children should live; and how much time, and in what circumstances, they should be expected to spend with the second parent. The decision as to where they should live was straightforward – with their mother. This was not because she was the wronged party, but because she was the one who looked after them. My final decision on contact was that they should be expected to see Mr Maynard every second weekend, including one overnight stay, that at least part of the annual family holiday should be with him, should he desire this, and that he was entitled to telephone the children up to three times per week. Mr Maynard seemed pleased, and Mrs Maynard did not seem overly disappointed. I was very clear that this was the best outcome in the difficult circumstances any divorce case presents to a judge. I was confident too that the children would prove sufficiently resilient to deal with any change to their situation. If I have learned one thing from presiding over this area of our national life, it is never to underestimate the resilience of children.

# JUNE

**My name is June. I was Hannah's senior-school form teacher.**

I was only Hannah's form teacher for one year, and I was ill with bronchitis for part of that, so she had supply teachers for some of the time. She was an interesting child, not easily pigeonholed.

I retired recently, am widowed and living on my own, and I often look back at the old class pictures, thirty-six of them in all, one for every year I taught. In my first year as a teacher, every child was white. By the time I retired the white children were in the minority. Quite a change.

I started in Southampton, but then met George whose work as an insurance adviser took us to London and I was fortunate enough to work in a succession of very good secondary schools. I was an English teacher, but it was the form-teacher side of things I enjoyed best, because that was as much about general development as helping with a specific subject.

A good number of my former pupils still live locally, so I see them all the time. They have their own children, some of them. I think children start far too young with that stuff these days. A couple of dozen or so still send me a card on my birthday or at Christmas, so I get news that way too. Sandra Spring, who was in my first class when I moved to London, has written to me twice a year for twenty-five years, and I get lots of titbits about her year that way. It's lovely to keep in touch, even if she seems to mention illness and divorce more than she does new jobs and new children these days. At a rough guess, I would reckon to know the names of about half the children in the photos without prompting, though if I sneak a look at the bottom of the photo, where the names are listed, they all quickly come back to me. There are very few, a handful, who spark no memory whatever. Teaching at its best is a wonderful vocation, the most noble profession of all. I can get quite emotional reading their letters and them telling me they're at college, or they've got married, or promoted. My favourites are the ones which start 'I've just qualified as a . . .' Whenever I hear that one of my children has become a nurse or an engineer or even a plumber – and especially if they have become a teacher, that is best of all – I think, I can't take all the credit but I can take some. I got a lovely letter last Christmas from Andrea George, who was a few years above Hannah. She said, 'It would be a bit much for you to remember all the children you taught, but everyone remembers Mrs Morrison, and thanks you for what you did.' I sat and read that over and over again. It makes a life worthwhile to get that kind of letter from a former pupil, like the time Terry McArdle sent me a copy of a job application form where he had listed 'my mum, my brother, Arsene Wenger and Mrs Morrison from my school' as the most important influences on his life. How wonderful is that!

The picture of Hannah certainly captures a part of her character. She was a pretty girl, and as I scanned the back row

– she was third from the left wearing a striped-red-and-white jumper, and had a purple band in her hair – she was the most striking. Quite tall for her age, certainly taller than the boy to her left, Adam, and Aliya to her right, with a high forehead and strong cheekbones. I could tell she was forcing a smile but her lips were closed and her eyes were emanating an irritation with her surroundings that I had come to know well. It was a cold and cloudy day by the look of it, which won't have helped, because we always did the photos outside, unless things got really torrential.

She wasn't the naughtiest child in my English class. That honour belonged to Samuel, a mixed-race fatherless boy from the Hornsey Road side of the Andover Estate who used to sit directly behind her. He was charming and lippy, and actually more academic than he let on, but utterly unconvinced of the benefits of learning, and someone of sufficient character and charisma to influence others in the direction of that attitude. Unfortunately, for a time Hannah was among those he influenced.

Boys were attracted to her, even at that age, twelve, thirteen, and she knew the effect she had on them. They wanted her approval in some way, and she enjoyed withholding it. She was nicer to boys than girls, though. She was quite intolerant of other girls if for whatever reason they got on her nerves, and she could lash out verbally and sometimes with venom, but she seemed to think it was OK for boys to do the same kind of things without them receiving the stare or the sharp put-down. I certainly noticed a change in the speed at which girls grew up across the three decades of my career. Today they are so much more aware, more socialised, more sexualised, open to more influences than we were, whether drink or drugs or advertising and music, more conscious of what happens elsewhere in the world, good and bad, lacking in the innocence that really defined the children in the early part of my career. Then there's all this Facebook and Twitter thing that has made life so difficult for teachers trying to keep their attention. I sometimes wish the mobile phone had never been invented.

Hannah was different from her classmates but not wildly so, whereas I suspect if any of them had been time-travelled back to my first class in Southampton, it would have been like watching children from different planets trying to mix.

Her attendance was not the best, and twice we had to get her mother in for a little talk. I tried to be cheery and smiley and not make them think it was too serious, though I feared that it was, and worrying too. A good teacher hates to see brightness in a child go to waste.

'It is not usual at this age to have this level of unauthorised absence, and I think it is very important that we nip it in the bud,' I said. Mrs Maynard agreed, as parents usually do, but she found it hard to get beyond straightforward anger, not always the best response. It is difficult for the teacher when the parent and the child just snap at each other, as though they were at home, rather than try to address constructively the reasons they are there.

'So perhaps you could tell your mum why you skip school from time to time?' . . . Pause, silence . . . 'You're one of the brighter pupils but perhaps you find some of the classes boring?' . . . Pause, silence, shuffle on seat, eyes to knees, slow chewing motion on bottom lip . . . Silence . . .

'What on earth are you thinking of?' said Mrs Maynard finally, leaving me wishing she hadn't. 'What chance do you think you are going to have in life if you don't do well at school?'

'I *am* doing well, though. Mrs Morrison told me I was doing really well, especially at English.'

'Yes, you are, Hannah,' I said, 'but you will fall behind quickly if you miss lessons.'

'I ain't missed that many.'

'Haven't, Hannah,' said Mrs Maynard, 'haven't, not ain't.'

'*You* say ain't.'

'I don't say ain't in school and you shouldn't either.'

'Oh, I forgot – do as I say, not as I do.'

'I don't know what's happened to her,' said Mrs Maynard, her eyes filled with pleading. 'I get this cheek all the time.'

'No, you don't. You usually tell me I don't talk enough.'

'Well, when you do, you can be very cheeky . . . and cruel.' Cruelty is a strong word, and as it left her lips, for a moment I thought she was going to cry. Tears from a parent tend to indicate issues other than the child's behaviour bubbling to the surface, but it is rarely appropriate for a teacher to ask about that, even when it may be the most relevant factor of all.

'The point is, Hannah,' I said, trying to steer things back to the matter in hand, 'that nobody enjoys every minute of every day in school, or if they do, they're a minority, but you cannot pick and choose when you come in and what lessons you take part in. Do you understand?'

'Yeah.'

'Yes, Hannah,' said her mother. 'Yes, not yeah. Will you please show your teacher a little proper respect?'

'It's all right, Mrs Maynard, Hannah is by no means one of the ruder children. But you do understand, don't you, Hannah,

66

that we cannot tolerate these absences? And next time it will be Mr Sharples who will have to see you.'

Mr Sharples was the head teacher, and quite a strict disciplinarian – he it was who insisted on all school photos being done in the playground. I confess Hannah did not seem terribly worried, however. She nodded curtly. She was definitely, and defiantly, hitting her anti-all-authority phase. The question was whether it was a phase, or a habit-forming characteristic. I hoped it was a phase because she had a sharp mind, could assimilate knowledge quickly, and I thought that if she really got into her studies, she would have been close to the top of the class in English, and not far off in everything else. When I saw her with her mother, though, it was hard not to imagine it was more habit-forming than passing.

'Are you listening to what your teacher is saying?' asked Mrs Maynard.

'Course I am. Nothing else to listen to, is there?'

I have children of my own, grown up now, and Hannah that day, aged thirteen, reminded me of mine in their later teens. In fact, two of mine did not really go through the bolshie teenager phase at all, but one did, the full works, and very tiresome it was too. When it came to that petulance and clever-clever answering back, Hannah was certainly advanced. She was not loquacious but she could be sharp-tongued. But there was also this other side to her, gentler, intelligent, the one who would tell others to stop making noise when she realised I might be losing control of the classroom. It happens. I'll be honest – there are some children that frankly I gave up on. Lost causes. No interest in work. No respect. Parents who made them worse, not better. Hannah was nowhere near that when I had her.

She had come to us from another school, ostensibly because her family had moved house, but when we explored a little we discovered there were one or two other issues that her previous head teacher had been rather concerned about. Concentration was one. Her choice of friends was another. The two sometimes came together to create discipline issues. She wasn't expelled, but the move to a new flat on the Highbury New Park social housing complex was seized as an opportunity to move school as well. She came to us mid-term, which is never ideal, as by then most of the children are settled, and know each other. It was much easier for Vicki, her little sister, because she came later, and started at the same age and same time as all the other first years. Also Vicki was much more naturally sociable, and made a nice little circle of friends more easily.

Things settled down for a while but then she started to go AWOL again, especially in the afternoons. I engineered a home visit. Mr Sharples encouraged us to visit the children at home if we could. It was always interesting to see inside their homes and families, as you get to know a lot more than you do from parents' evenings – assuming the parents show up – about family dynamics and home-life attitudes. You think you know what their home life will be like, because you know where they live, the way they dress and speak, you know which ones don't eat well and which are prone to ill health, you know which are confident with adults and which are scared. But I very rarely visited a child's home and came away having witnessed life as I expected it to be.

Hannah lived in a two-bedroomed flat about a ten-minute walk from the school, inside a functional and rather soulless block of mainly rented accommodation, for which I understand her mother had help from the local authority. The building was close to a small disused factory which used to make Christmas decorations and novelty cards but had been wiped out by Chinese companies which dominated the market now. They lived up one flight of cold grey stairs, though I noticed their next-door neighbour kept a lovely collection of potted plants on the balcony.

The flat was tidy and uncluttered. I didn't get to see the bedrooms, and it may be that Mrs Maynard had made a special effort tidying up because I was visiting, but the sitting room where we sat and talked was more like a low-budget hotel lounge than a home with growing children. It was the same in the kitchen. There was no mess, nothing lying on the table, nothing pinned on the fridge or the walls, one photograph of the kids in what looked like an adventure playground. The girl who helped out with childcare, a very intense-looking young woman wearing a loose grey sweater and dark jeans, took the younger daughter to the girls' bedroom so that the three of us could talk. I sat on an upright wooden chair directly facing Hannah and Mrs Maynard on a black sofa.

'So, Hannah, where are we?' I asked.

'In my mum's flat.' The way she said it, it was actually quite funny, and I smiled, but Mrs Maynard was immediately provoked.

'Hannah, behave . . .' she said.

'Well, we *are* in your flat.'

'That isn't what Mrs Morrison meant . . . And it's *our* flat, not just mine.'

Hannah shrugged.

'Perhaps I should be a little clearer in my question. When I said where are we, I meant with regard to the situation of you and your schoolwork.'

Silence. A shrug.

'Do you like school?'

'It's OK.'

'Where do you go when you're not in school?'

'Depends.'

'On . . . ?'

'Who I'm with, what the weather's like, how much money we've got –'

'Money?' It came out in a high-pitched squeal. 'What sort of money?' Mrs Maynard was keen to know.

'Pounds. Notes and coins.'

I sighed loudly as I sensed another provocation to which her mother would rise.

'I know what currency we have in this country but I would like to know where you get money from other than your dinner money and your pocket money.'

'Dad.'

'Dad?'

'Yeah, Dad.'

'How much?'

'Depends.'

'Depends on what?'

'On what sort of mood he's in, I suppose, and how good we've been.'

'Heaven help us.'

'Why shouldn't he give us a bit of pocket money too?'

'Well, if he does, I should know about it, and I should know what you're doing with it, and if you're using it to bunk off school and sit around in cafes then he shouldn't be giving it to you at all. I'm going to have to talk to him about this.'

'But you don't talk.'

'Yes we do. How can you say such a silly thing?' I could tell by the sudden half-smile that she wasn't telling the truth, and Hannah was. It is always a fine judgement for a teacher to know when to raise family issues but this one did seem relevant to her educational development.

'How often does Hannah see her father?'

'Supposed to be every second weekend but it doesn't work out like that really. He has a job which requires some weekend work. Also he has a new girlfriend and he's become less reliable since she moved in with him.'

'I see.'

'Can't blame her. She's probably thinking why should I have to spend my weekends looking after someone else's kids?'

'Yes, but he is their father.'

'I know, but I know what he's like and he'll be head over heels for a few weeks or months with this woman and he won't want to go against her. Till he finds the next one.'

'I see.'

'Sorry, this is probably more information than you want.'

'Well, my only concern here is Hannah, and if it is the case that these changed arrangements are causing her tension or anxiety then that may explain her reverting to these unauthorised absences and focusing less on her schoolwork than social activities outside.'

'I think she's found the Dad visits a bit of a pain, so I'm not sure she minds.'

'When was the last time you saw your father, Hannah?'

'Tell Mrs Morrison when it was, Hannah.'

'Three weeks ago.'

'Is that upsetting?'

'What?'

'That you haven't seen him more often?'

'No.'

'When are you due to see him next?'

'Don't know. He'll phone and say.'

'Does he phone often?'

'No. Texts.'

'I see.'

Silence fell over the room, broken only by the sound of Vicki and the babysitter laughing about something in the girls' bedroom.

'How much money does he give you?' asked Mrs Maynard.

'Fifty pounds last time.'

'*How* much?'

'No, sixty.'

'What?'

'Don't blame me, Mum. Why would I say no?'

'It's guilt. It's all guilt. It's guilt money. That's all it is.'

'You can't blame me for that.'

I had been teaching Hannah for seven months and realised that until now I hadn't given any thought to her father. As they sat there, Mrs Maynard overflowing with anger, Hannah containing hers behind a distant look that said 'this is happening to someone else, I am not engaging further', it struck me suddenly that he remained possibly the biggest force in their lives. Yet one never spoke to him and the other rarely saw him.

'Is it OK if I get a drink of water?' asked Hannah. Her mother stared away out of the window which looked out onto a cold damp sky.

'Yes, why don't you do that, Hannah?' I said. 'I'll see you at school in the morning.'

She rose quietly and walked to the kitchen. As Mrs Maynard

straightened her face towards me, her mascara was beginning to smudge. I passed her my handkerchief, said, 'I have to be going now,' and made my way to the doorway. As I went down the stairs to the street, I reflected that it had not gone as well as I had hoped it would, and wondered whether it might not be sensible to cut back on the home visits. They did nothing but depress me, and after a visit like this one, I worried they made things worse for the children I was trying to help.

# SAMMY

**My name is Sammy. I was Hannah's first 'proper' boyfriend, ha ha.**

I got my tongue in her mouth when she was twelve and a half, my fingers up her fanny when she was thirteen, finally fucked her when she was fourteen. Who said the age of romance and long courtships was over, hey? She wasn't my first, but she said I was hers, said she was really nervous, scared even, and I reckon she was telling the truth, even though I got a few shots down her when we went to a Blink 182 gig at the Garage near Highbury & Islington Tube. I knew it would get her in the mood because their stuff is funny and horny, which is the best mix. I even got my first tattoo because I liked the way they looked on their drummer when he was banging his arms around.

She was clueless when it came to sex. Men my grandad's age fantasise about shagging virgins. It's why those terrorists blow themselves up flying planes into buildings, because they think there's going to be hordes of vestal virgins waiting for them in heaven. Good luck to them. Kids the age I was when I shagged Hannah aren't so keen on first-timers, much prefer girls who know a thing or two. She was OK at kissing, in fact one of the best, and we did plenty of it, but when we got onto the Big One, the whole way-to-go-go, once I was in there, which was a struggle in itself, there was none of that rhythm you get with girls who've done it a few times. She kept saying she didn't know what she was meant to feel, and I was saying just go with the flow, but I'd be pushing in and wanting her to push towards me but she'd go the other way, or I'd be pulling out and wanting her to pull away so I could line up a monster slide, and instead she would come with me, thinking it was all about staying close. It was like I was poking in space, never quite getting the pressure where I wanted it. I decided just to pump away hard thinking about some of my nine out of tens – nobody is ten, and only Jessica Alba gets close – until I was done, then I rolled off without hanging around waiting to go limp inside her. I mumbled something about how the first time was always shit, and it would be better next time. Only there wasn't a next time, not with me anyway, though once we had broken her duck she found plenty of others to go with, and the word came back she was getting better, which I liked to think had something to do with me riding her in. With most guys, though, you can never get the truth from what they tell you of girls they've been with. If it was OK, they say it was the best ever. If it was OK bordering on not so OK, it becomes 'wouldn't screw her with yours'. It's like there's no in between, and of course there's a lot of lies, boys who've never been with anyone wanting you to think they've been laying their seed up and down the A1 when in truth they've been firing off into a sink, a toilet or a piece of Kleenex.

After we did it, we avoided each other around school, her more than me because I think she was a bit embarrassed about it all, not the fucking bit, I think she was OK about that, just the fact it was so amateur and low-grade, and she knew I wasn't impressed. Girls always like to impress me. It's why boys get jealous. I didn't get the feeling she told anyone else, and I only told a couple of pals who had both been trying to do her. If a girl tells her friends about a new fuck, it usually comes back to the guy who fucked her, but I had nobody, boy or girl, saying 'I heard you did it with Hannah'. Then a couple of Fridays later, Sam Cousins' folks were away for the weekend and he was one of the posher kids in our school, had a proper house on the other side of St Paul's Road, and he had a party, and there was a bit of music going on, and I was grinding with Abbi, who was like my most regular girl, almost like a proper girlfriend, which was getting a bit tricky to be fair, because most of her friends were in my notebook, and I look over her shoulder and there's Hannah making out with some spotty-arsed kid I've never seen before and as soon as she clocks me clocking her, she grabs this kid's bollocks and is giving him the big rub-down, all the time staring at me, like she's trying to make me think I was the one who fucked it up when we did it, and don't ever think she didn't know stuff. I wasn't going to let it get to me. I'd fucked her, and I went the whole way even if she never got past Base 2, and even if she wasn't a good fuck, not yet anyway, she was a good one to have on your list. Not in the top top league looks wise, she spent too much time with a sour face for that – though she was smiling big style as she played around with Spotty Boy's tackle – but she was a seven for the face, seven and a half for her tits, and eight going on nine for her arse. That is a good score in anyone's book. I had a list in the little red notebook I had at home, which I kept with other stuff in a box under my bed, and she went in high up my Looks Table, low down my Fuck Rating Table. Abbi was the other way round. Face in need of the lights going off. Fuck to die for. I know it's not all about the looks, and not all about the sex, but it's the one that leads to the other, and we're all pretending if we say it's not so. There was more to her than the looks, though, and so much more to her than the sex, which I guess is why we kind of stayed friendly once we got over that embarrassment. She will always have me in the list of key men in her life, because I was the first, and I will always have her because she was the only bad fuck I ever thought of as someone I still wanted in my life. She could make me laugh too, like she had this thing she did where she said, 'What did you do in a previous life . . . ?' like once, ages after we did it, I met her coming out of a corner shop and she said straight out, 'Hey, Sammy, you must have done something so good in a previous life to have been the first to get to go the whole way with me,' and she used it the other way too, like when she'd say, 'My God, Sammy, what evil did you do in a previous life to get a nose like that on your face?' and she did the same with passers-by and random famous people, like 'What did Jess Ennis do in her past lives to be given a body like that in this one?' It was like a little trademark thing.

So there I was thinking Spotty Boy must have done something good in a past life to have Hannah coming all over him now that I walked in on the scene. He couldn't believe his luck. They're just moping around, him looking eager to please, but his moves were woeful, her looking bored till she sees me with Abbi, and she is straight in, lips to neck, hands to waistband, and he looks like he has been prodded with an electric shock, then she stares at him and does that melting thing with her eyes and he is all lit up, thinking he is about to get his first ever lay. No idea if it was, or if he did, but when I watched her back to the corner the first thing she did was grab someone else's Corona from a table, and another for Spotty Boy, and she was putting it away sharpish, so I reckoned she was oiling up for a treat for SB. Abbi and I did it back at her place, on Balls Pond Road. It's a great name for a place to shag, but we had to keep the volume down because her mum was asleep next door, and I hated that, having to hold back on the groaning and the grunting, and the dirty talk which I love — when I watched porn movies on my computer, it was as much to learn about the talk as the action — but that night screwing Abbi, I put together a nice little composite, mixing Hannah's face with Jessica Alba's body and Abbi's style. Unfortunately I thought about Spotty Boy too, felt a bit sick at the idea of his cratered arse riding up and down on Hannah, and I felt sure he would be loving it more than she was, and in so far as she was loving it at all, it was as an act of revenge on me, because our time had been so duff.

It's like when kids are rejected by their parents and they want to do well to prove them wrong, or thickos are told by their teachers they will never make it who go on to become astronauts or brain surgeons or win a TV talent show, so I think girls who are told their first fuck was shit can go haywire trying to prove they can do it. By the time she was sixteen, seventeen, she had a reputation as an easy lay. It was probably unfair, because I doubt if she was even that far into double figures, but the ones she picked tended to be the ones who talked and boasted, and by the time Alfie fucked her — he was the only one I was sure told me the truth — he had her up as an 8.5, not just for face, tits, arse, but overall fuckery too.

He actually went out with her for a few weeks, but he heard she had given some salesman a blow job for cash and he wasn't having that. I didn't believe it to be honest. It was one of those things a guy says when he can't have a girl to himself. 'Problem is, you get a few drinks inside her,' he said, 'and she is close to being anyone's.' I didn't mind if it was true. I saw it as me performing a useful service for the men of London . . . She would be shagging away and thinking, 'I will show that bastard Samuel J. Mitchell I know how to do this.' I loved thinking that girls thought of me when they were shagging other guys. And I know she did. I knew it the second she grabbed that guy's bollocks, looked over at me, and gave me the stare, the one that said nobody is ever going to hurt me, and if you try, I'm going to hurt you back. She was spiky. I liked that.

I first saw Hannah when my class was halfway through a lesson with Old Ma Morrison, something about a poem on different creatures that lived in water, boring as shit, like anyone cares, and the door opens and Sharples comes in with this seven-out-of-ten girl. He says, 'Mrs Morrison, this is the Hannah I told you about earlier, who is joining us from another school and she will be in your form. Boys and girls, she is your new classmate. I hope you all make her feel very welcome.' Old Ma said, 'Hello, Hannah, why don't you take that place next to Ruhal there, we are just talking about poetry inspired by rivers and seas.' Poor kid. I thought I would not want to be brought into a classroom like that, with everyone turning round and staring because this poetry stuff is so much more boring than a pretty new girl arriving. Ruhal's desk was in front of mine, so I got a good look at the new girl as she came by. 'Could be an eight on a good day,' I whispered to Alfie. She went to her desk, sat down, and only looked at

Ruhal when she said, 'Hi, I'm Ruhal.' She was a cute-looking little thing, but she could have done with smiling more. At lunch break, Mrs Morrison had a word with three of her favourites and asked them to look after Hannah. But she wasn't their type, I could tell that, and they weren't hers. Alfie and I sat on the wall by the football goals and even though we couldn't hear them, we could see that Old Ma's creeps were doing all the talking and Hannah was saying as little as she could get away with.

'Come on, Alfie, let's have some fun.' We skipped down from the wall and sauntered over to where the OMM squad was asking if she wanted them to show her where the library and the computer rooms were. Hannah said she was fine, she liked the fresh air. I thought that was quite funny, as we could hear cars and lorries charging past and belching out stuff that made the air in the playground anything but fresh.

'So, Miss Hannah,' I said, 'I hope Old Ma Morrison's little helpers are making you feel welcome.' The other girls stepped back a little, and Alfie and I moved into the space.

'Yes they are,' she said. 'Thank you so much for your concern.' It was a nice put-down.

'I'm Sammy, this is Alfie, and we're more fun than these guys.'

'Why do you have to be so rude about Mrs Morrison?' asked Emily, who was numero uno OMM creepo.

'She ain't no more special than you or me, babe. Teachers ain't so special.'

'Yeah,' said Alfie, 'gotta eat, sleep, shower and shit same as the rest of us.'

'No need to lower the tone,' I said. 'I sense that Miss Hannah here has a touch of class about her, so we don't need to hear none of that shit talk now, Alfie.' I saw the slightest flicker of a smile, in her eyes if not her lips.

It didn't take long to get her onto my team. I was not, contrary to what Morrison or Sharples would tell my mum, 'deliberately destructive of a learning environment'. If others wanted to know all that shit about poems and life on the seabed, let them. They could go live on the fucking seabed if they wanted to, but I figured so long as I could read and write OK, know that 8 x 6 is 48, and you're best to wear a condom if you don't want to get a nasty illness or a snotty kid, I was getting the education I needed. I was never going to go to college, I knew that for sure, so why did I want to learn all this stuff that would make no difference to getting a job as a waiter or a labourer, or any of the other things I could do to make sure I had the money to live the life I wanted? Work to live, not live to work – I taught myself that lesson long before I met Hannah.

If she'd looked at me with the same disgust Emily and her two friends did, I would have got the message, done a touch of piss-taking and mild bullying every few weeks to remind her she had made her choice, but nothing nasty, certainly nothing to stop her learning every goddam Shakespeare play if she wanted, or any other bullshit Mrs M wanted to force-feed her lovely little kiddiewinks. But she didn't. She smiled with her eyes and even at twelve I knew enough about girls to know she smiled because I said she had a touch of class, and that was my in. A couple of years or more went by before I fucked her, but that smile was the start of it.

When she arrived, apparently because she got kicked out of her first school, so Alfie said, she was not a big talker, but she was a good listener, pretending not to be engrossed, but taking it all in and if she needed to throw it back at you later, she would. I once asked her if she loved me, just a little bit, and she gave me this amazing lovey-dovey look in the eye and then said, 'Sammy, no matter how much I ever love you, it's not going to be as much as you love yourself,' which was cute. True too. I am a gabbermouth, love the sound of my own voice, love making people laugh or think that I'm clever because of the way I see things and the way I can make any situation seem weird or crazy, and even if I never won an English prize, I am good with words and anyway it's easy to make things seem weird and crazy, because most things *are* weird and crazy.

I got the blame when she got hauled in with her mum for bunking off, but truth be told it was Hannah's idea. She wanted to go to the Odeon to see *The Dark Knight*, and asked me to go along. I had skipped lessons before and the school had asked to see my mum, but she told me to say she was too busy. She worked in a hairdresser's in Stroud Green and I was lucky because she totally shared my view of school. They sent her a couple of letters, but in the end I was bollocked on my own, and they sent my mum another letter, but she threw it in the bin and told me not to worry. It was tougher for Hannah because Mrs Maynard clearly wanted her to do well at school, and she felt ashamed at having to go in and get talked at by a teacher who doesn't know shit. Hannah was upset the first time, because her mum gave her such a hard time, but then it passed, and we started bunking off again, and it's like anything, from riding a bike to shoplifting to fucking to lying to your mum about money gone missing from her purse – if you've got through it once, the second time is easier.

'Got it in the ear from my mum big time again,' she said.

'All weepy-waily and why are you doing this to me, and why can't you be like the other children, and what she means is why can't I be like my little sister, want to help, always telling her the good things she wants to hear, not like me . . .'

'She made you, she raised you, raised you both,' I said.

'Too right. She wanted to have me, I didn't ask to be born . . . I said that, I said to her, you and my dad wanted to have me, I didn't ask to be born.'

'So what she say to that?'

'Says nobody ASKS to be born, but life is a gift and we are so much luckier than children born in Africa or children born with deformities and disabilities, and why can't I count my blessings?'

'Fuck! Heavy.'

'I know, that's what she does. Guilt trips. I hadn't even been in that much trouble this time. One lesson, that time we went to Camden Market, and I got a scarf and some tops. We didn't even get caught, so it's not like I was hauled in for stealing, it's just another missed lesson, and Mrs Morrison wants me to see Sharples, fair enough, but for my mum, it's like the world is ending, and she says she's not sure she can put up with this for much longer, and maybe I should live with my gran in Essex for a bit, and I say what about I live with Dad, and I don't mean it, because I reckon it would be even worse there now, especially with this new woman he's tied up with, but I wanted to see what she would say, and of course she goes crazy, because any mention of him and she is like wild, and she says, "Maybe if he'd stayed around I wouldn't have to deal with this all on my own," and I said, "Deal with what? I missed one lesson," and she says, "You know what I'm talking about, your attitude to school, your attitude to me, your attitude to everything is all wrong, and it doesn't need to be like this. You have a home, food on the table, a bed to sleep in, all the support I can give, and it seems to mean nothing." I said, "Mum, you're so going over the top, please just calm down," and she hates that, hates being told to calm down, because she thinks she is so calm, and she's not, she's always winding herself in knots, and it flips her, she goes crazy, says, "Don't talk to me like that, don't tell me how to behave with my own children. If I'm not calm – which I am – it's because of what you're bringing into this house with your attitudes and your temper and I want it to stop."'

Only I'm laughing now, because I loved that bit where she said 'if I'm not calm – which I am . . .' and I get a fit of the giggles, because it is so what mums say, like my mum when she says, 'Take that smile off your face,' like it's a fucking plaster, and I pretend to rip it off but it won't come off, and I have this picture of Hannah sitting there knowing she's been bad, but staying so calm, and it's her mum who's meant to be grown up, and giving calm advice and sorting things out, but she's flipping her lid. And as I started to crease up, I worried that Hannah would get angry with me, because girls take this stuff with their mums seriously, but she gets why I'm laughing and she stops halfway through a sentence, throws down a serviette she's been clutching the whole time, says, 'Fuck it . . . Fuck her nagging and her moaning and telling me I let her down, fuck it all,' and she starts laughing too and before long the woman behind the counter of the kebab shop is looking at us like she might have to throw us out.

I loved it when she laughed. I wished she'd done it more. When people see or hear something funny, their instinct is to laugh. When Hannah saw something funny, her instinct was to try really hard not to laugh. It was like an aversion to joining in with the crowd, because she knew she was special. I think that's why she didn't like football, even though she grew up near enough to the Emirates to hear the crowd, but she hated it, couldn't understand why her little sister spent every spare penny saving up to get tickets. I could get her laughing when it was just the two of us, and she loved my impersonations, but get her in a crowd and she was unbreakable. It changed when we started drinking more regularly. Then she could unwind and join in a bit more. But even then there was an edge to her and you had to be careful. She had a temper on her, one of the worst. I never did a temper league table but if I had she would have been in a Champions League place. There was one night when we had managed to get served in a bar near King's Cross, and we'd got two beers down us before the barman realised we were way underage and asked to see our ID. I had a fake National Insurance card, Hannah had nothing and she tried every trick in the book – flirting, flattery, a hint of sexual favours – but he wasn't moving.

'Cunt,' she said, throwing her glass against the wall behind the bar. I don't think I had ever heard her swear before that, certainly not 'cunt'. Girls hate that word, usually – I'm always being told off for it. The customers next to us moved away, one or two who were sitting down suddenly stood up, and the barman ran down to the little hatch at the end of the bar, so I grabbed her, picked up her coat from the floor, and forced her out of the bar before things got out of hand. We managed to get twenty, thirty yards away before the barman got to the street, and he was blocked by a group of lads arriving as he flung open the door, so we were out of sight and out of danger easily enough. We certainly had a laugh that time. We walked for a bit, hung around the canal, strolled up Caledonian Road, then went into a corner shop near the prison, tried and failed to get served, so I got Hannah to chat up a guy who was heading into the shop, give him money and get him to buy our booze for us, six cans of lager and a half-bottle of vodka. It was like the old hitchhiker trick my mum told me about. Pretty girl hitches, car stops, girl gets in, then calls over boyfriend from behind a tree. By the time Hannah had pocketed her change and taken hold of the thin yellow plastic bag with the booze in it, I was right beside her and the guy was looking like a promise had just gone walkies. We found a perfect-height wall at the corner of the next street, and sat there, talking and drinking, even though it was November and cold, with the odd spit of rain too. I said she needed to watch that temper, there was no need to lose it with that guy in the bar, and she looked like she knew I was talking sense. The cans lasted no time, the vodka not much longer, and Hannah wanted more. She always seemed to have cash on her.

This time she asked a woman, late thirties, a lawyer I would say, bad choice, and the woman was having none of it. So she walked into the shop, did her shopping, came out and Hannah went straight up to her, without giving me the slightest hint that she would, and she puts her face right up close, and she is snarling at her, says, 'Who the fuck do you think you are, lady? What makes you so fucking special that you don't want to help me out when that Pakistani toerag won't believe I'm legal?' I was like so shocked, because I didn't see it coming, and I didn't really see Hannah as one of those girls who go way OTT when stuff don't go their way. I've seen fights in our playground involving girls that are way more entertaining than the professional stuff on telly, but I would never, ever have put Hannah up as a possible contender. But she was going at this woman like crazy, and doing her 'previous life' thing, saying, 'You must have been Hitler or Stalin in a past life to get given your sin-ugly looks,' which was crazy because the woman was hot for her age, dressed really smartly and had a nice handbag she was carrying with her two bags of groceries and a couple of bottles of wine, and I can see she's thinking 'Am I going to get mugged here?' and she walks as fast as she can towards her car, big black Volvo estate, which is parked on the other side of the road, but Hannah follows her and as the woman reaches the car Hannah kicks her in the back of the leg, calls her a stuck-up cow, and I run over and I'm saying 'Hannah, fuck's sake, calm down', but the more I say 'calm down' the more she looks like she is going to do real damage to this woman. I just wanted the woman to get in her car and go, but now she is facing up to Hannah, calling her a disgrace, saying she is the reason people think Britain is going to the dogs and she will be reporting her to the police and Hannah goes 'yeah, yeah, yeah, go fuck yourself and go fuck the police too'. But this woman looked to me exactly the sort of person who *would* report her to the police, so for the second time in one evening I grabbed Hannah and I frogmarched her as far and as fast as I could, and when we finally collapsed on a wall opposite Pentonville prison, we were not laughing. Hannah was throwing up, saying she had never drunk vodka before. I was asking her 'what the fuck was that about?'

'Stuck-up bitch should have got me a drink. Deserved everything she got.'

'Come on, Hannah, you can't just tear into strangers like

that. It'll be on CCTV, guaranteed. We're outside a fucking jail for fuck's sake.'

'She won't do anything. Bitch,' and she threw up again, this time more violently. What was weird, with both incidents, was that there was no build-up to the moments of violence. She was pissed off the barman and the corner-shop guy wouldn't serve us, and she was pissed off the Volvo woman in the black overcoat wouldn't do what the young guy had done and buy her some booze. But the glass-throwing and the kicking came out of nowhere, I just didn't see them coming. I had known her for a few years by now, and she was quirky and a bit volatile, but until that night I never had her down as violent. It was a shock, I don't deny it. We stopped seeing so much of each other after that. I can take care of myself if I have to, but I don't like violence. How can I when I have a pair of underpants with the slogan 'Make Love Not War', front and back? I saw her around, we talked sometimes, it was great if she didn't have a drink in her, and I always felt a little tingle in my boxers whenever I ran into her. But something changed that night, for both of us.

# SOPHIE

**My name is Sophie. I was Hannah's best friend at school.**

We were very different, and from different backgrounds even though we lived near each other and went to the same school, but there was a time, a few months after we started being friendly, when I was so fond of her, and so much keener to be with her than with anyone else, that I worried I might be a lesbian. I longed for her approval, and for her touch. I loved her company even when she was having one of her big grumps, and I loved her to bits those times when she was chatty and fun and making me laugh or think about the world differently. I've got a boyfriend now, Martyn, and even if we got married, I don't think I could ever tell him about the time I thought I loved her, like real love, and it was the first time I ever felt it, and boy was I confused at the time, because I just could not imagine how I would ever have explained it to my parents. At first, my dad in particular found my friendship with Hannah hard to bear anyway, because he knew she was from a single-parent family, which was bad-vibe territory, and they knew she had a little bit of a reputation at school, and it wasn't for coming top of the class in anything.

I know it's not meant to matter, and people are straight or gay in the same way they might be blonde, brunette or ginger. But I found the whole idea terrifying. For the time it was happening, every time we sat down for dinner at home, I would try to imagine how my parents would react if I came in with Hannah and told them I would like her to stay the night and there was no need for her to use the spare room because we were an item, and she would sleep with me. Even today, after all that has happened, and all the time my family has spent with her, and the ups and downs we have endured, I can still feel a little chill of fear recalling that phase in my life. Once or twice, I tried to tease them out a little, told them for example our French teacher was a lesbian, hoped to get a 'so what?' reaction, but my mum looked nonplussed, and my dad said, 'Shouldn't she be thinking about teaching French, not having sex with women?'

'Dad, that is such a silly thing to say. If I'd said Mr Ramage was straight, you wouldn't even have thought about him thinking about sex. What you said is straightforwardly homophobic.'

'Oh, all this homophobia stuff is nonsense,' he said. 'Nobody minds any more if someone's homosexual, but do they have to stuff it down our throats the whole time?'

'How can you be such a hypocrite, Dad? You stand up in court doing all those cases, liberal this, radical that, and you're just an old homophobe.'

'I am not, but I don't particularly want to know about the sexual habits of your teachers when we're having dinner.'

'Come on now, you two,' said Mum. 'Don't argue. Who wants more vegetables?' Mum always thought food could settle an argument.

Hannah came to our house a few times, and having been

to hers, I was really uncomfortable about just how different our homes were. She lived in a flat in a badly designed block, with a tiny cluttered hallway, a kitchen with a table that could seat no more than four, a sitting room with wooden floors and no carpet, just a flowery rug between a black sofa and two non-matching comfy chairs, a TV, a stereo, a little table on each side of the fireplace. They had two bedrooms and a bathroom up a couple of steps. Her mum had the bigger bedroom. She had split up from her husband but had a boyfriend who spent two or three nights a week there. I only saw him a couple of times, and Hannah made sure we went straight to her room, which she shared with Vicki, so I never met him properly, and only spoke to Mrs Maynard once or twice.

Our house is one of the really big ones in Highbury New Park, near Highbury Grove. When my parents bought it, the estate agent said it had the biggest garage in the area. My bathroom was bigger than Hannah's bedroom, and I didn't have to share it. And I remember once when my parents were out I showed Hannah their bedroom and bathroom and when I took her into Mum's walk-in wardrobe, she said, 'Wow, you could fit our whole flat in here.' She wasn't resentful, and if anyone was embarrassed, it was me, not least by my dad, who was perfectly nice to her face, but when she wasn't there, all his questions revealed snobbish attitudes. Why did her parents split up? Does she live in a council house? Isn't that the place where that drug dealer was stabbed to death? ('It was five years ago, Dad.') If she came with us on holiday, would we have to pay for everything? Does she have a boyfriend? – which was his way of asking if she played the field.

I could never bring myself to tell her what I was feeling.

The second or third time she was in my bedroom, we did some Cold War revision, because we had a mock history exam coming up, and I think she saw me as her 'help with school-work' friend, not because I was much cleverer, but I was determined to do well enough to go to university and I had my parents, a barrister and a doctor, pushing me hard, and if I said I was doing two hours, that's what I would do, and I think she tagged along because she worried if she didn't she would do no work at all. We worked, talked, then I painted my nails, and asked if she wanted me to paint hers. She sat on the end of the bed and I was kneeling on the floor, and I loved holding her long, thin fingers, and stroking on the pink varnish. As I finished, and I stretched out my fingers towards hers, and she hers towards me, our fingertips touched, and I was so close to pushing my hand into hers. If only I had been braver, I would have done it, eased her downwards onto the bed, put my head above hers, stared long and deep into her eyes, and kissed her. But I wasn't brave. I was terrified that she would find the whole thing horrifying, and turn on me like I had seen her turn on some of the other girls who had annoyed her. She was a man's woman, and there were plenty of young men who would testify to that, and she always told me when she had been with someone, and it turned me onto her even more, because it underlined just how attractive she was that boys saw her that way too. I was such a coward never to find out if she thought about me the way I thought about her. I think I was worried that in trying to have everything, I would end up with nothing. Unrequited love is the worst love of all, particularly when the object of the love did not know it existed beyond the shared friendship with which she seemed to feel comfortable.

There was one day when we were in drama, putting together a play, in which I was a waitress and Hannah was having dinner with her 'husband', and there was a scene where I take over some drinks just as they're having a big argument and the husband pushes the table towards her, and one time he pushed too hard and I dropped my tray onto the table and one of the glasses of water spilled onto Hannah's skirt. We had to pretend it was part of the play of course, and I had an overwhelming desire to touch her, which I followed, and I patted her down, her waist and her thighs, took a napkin and wiped her dry. The play was part improvised and I even had the thought that I might just kiss her there and then, say her husband is a bastard, all men are bastards, she should come with me. I'm not lesbian, by the way, Martyn is proof of that, but I really thought I was, and when it was really bad, I used to kneel by my bed and pray to God that Hannah would be thinking about me, and as she slept she would dream of me, and wake up to realise that all she wanted was to be with me. 'Please God, make her bisexual,' I said, 'and when she comes with me, make her want to give up boys and be with me only.' I don't know if God heard, or if He did anything to her, but we never got it together in that way, and as I am now with a boyfriend and probably heading towards the same kind of life as my parents, I suppose it is a good thing nothing came of it.

I have never had sex with another woman, and there has not been any other woman, real or on TV or in the films, who made me feel like that, so it must have just been a phase I went through. But I really did feel something, and it felt like what I had been expecting to feel for a boy, and I just hadn't. I had never been with a boy, not properly, when I first started being friends with Hannah. The furthest was the time Simon from tennis came back to our house after the club singles finals, when my dad was umpiring, and we ended up in my bedroom, and I let him go as far as unhooking my bra and putting his hand inside my knickers, and I had a feel inside his pants too, and got scared by the noise he made when I touched it – like a cow bellowing – and it was so hard I felt its wildness and what with both my mum and my dad down-stairs with their friends, I worried about one of them coming in to find out where I was when lunch was ready. So I suddenly stood up, and said, 'We have to stop now because someone could come in,' and he looked so pained that I felt really bad, but then he made a lunge for me and so I pushed him away and felt better about calling a halt to the whole thing.

I am the youngest in our family, and the first not to be wholly privately educated. I did go to prep school, and then to a private senior school, but I really wanted to do drama and English at university, and everyone who knew about it said that for drama A level, the Islington school where I met Hannah was the best. It was a struggle to persuade my dad that I would not end up being raped and stabbed every day, but my mum is a terrific ally when I want something, and she won him round, saved him thousands of pounds of school fees in the process, and I got there in time for the sixth form, with some very good GCSE results under my belt. Hannah was doing the same A levels as me, English, drama and history. She nearly didn't make it to sixth form because she did badly in her GCSEs, but she got three good grades amid the fails and her history teacher, Mr Carpenter, persuaded them they should give her a go. He said that when she was interested in something, and she applied herself, she was as clever as anyone. She had a terrific memory for things that grabbed her. Nobody could learn lines as fast as she did. I was the opposite – I found it difficult to take in too much at any one time, and when it came to exams, I really had to work hard to have any chance of success. But I did work hard, which is how I got seven As and two Bs at GCSEs, and if I can do that, frankly anyone can. Hannah never seemed too worried about how she did. Before I got to know her, she used to hang around with Sammy Mitchell. He was half Asian, half Afro-Caribbean, and he really took pride in his indifference to learning. It was a bit of an act, though, because he always did better than his predicted grades. His mum's boyfriend worked in a factory that printed slogans on clothes, mainly T-shirts, and he used to come in with things like 'Skool Ain't Kool' in huge letters on a white shirt. He had another one that said 'OK to be f*ck', and everyone knew he was challenging the school to make him take it off, and when he got told by Mrs Morrison he had to wear something else because it was obscene, he said, 'It ain't fuck, Miss, if that's what you're thinking, it's fick . . . OK to be fick. It's my philosophy.' Most of the boys, and one or two of the girls, laughed.

'Well, I don't know about everyone else, Samuel, but I find it offensive and I would like you to take it off.'

'Hey, Miss, that sounds to me like borderline inappropriate – teachers shouldn't be asking young men to take their clothes off, but if that's what you want, Miss . . .' and he started to peel his shirt off, like he was a male stripper, humming that stripper song they use in the films, and Mrs Morrison was straight into panic mode. 'Samuel, stop that this instant, or I will ask you to leave the classroom.'

'Now she's asking me out,' he said, and the class started to laugh. He was a waster, but he was funny, and she didn't know how to handle him. She was losing the classroom, and Sammy started to do a rap about freedom of speech, and then said if he was made to change his shirt, it was an infringement of his human rights, and it was his considered opinion that formal education was overrated and it was far more important to learn the ways of the street, and he felt our teachers were OK at ramming facts into our brains but they knew nothing about the real world, and now he was almost into political speech mode, and he could certainly move people, and he was speaking in a way that built up to a crescendo that was demanding applause . . . 'They know nothing about the world where I will have to live my life. No qualification is ever going to feed me, and no teacher is going to tell me what I can and can't say,' and sure enough, about a third of the class applauded, and Mrs Morrison looked like she was drowning.

'Sammy, I think that's enough.' It was Hannah. Sammy sat down. Hannah asked Alfie to let Sammy borrow his jacket. Mrs Morrison went back to Chaucer. Hannah had a very quiet but real force about her. I know it sounds weird to talk about 'when I was falling in love with her', but I promise that is how it felt, and that was one of the key moments. Hardly anyone stood up to Sammy, but she did, and he just kind of melted whereas if it had been anyone else, he might easily have gone the other way. It was the same when we were doing another drama improvisation and there was a girl called Bella Hampson who was the classic type to be bullied, glasses, spots, skinny, bad hair in long pigtails, and she was playing this girl on a market stall and two of the other girls, Cynthia and Paula, were customers and all Mr Edwards had said was they had to go from asking for something on the stall to a discussion about a pressing social issue, and Bella was nervous as hell, and these girls were both mixed race and they had come up with a plan to accuse Bella of racism, only it went from being part of the play to something really nasty, where they were saying she was racist because she was so ugly and jealous because black girls were prettier, and I could see Mr Edwards thinking about stepping in but he didn't, and then Hannah did. She said, 'Excuse me, sir, but this is not on. They're not acting this out, they're picking on someone,' and at last he got off his chair and took them aside and talked to them. Hannah went and talked to Bella, and I thought 'wow, she is strong'. That was another moment, a big one, and I felt myself slipping, and I thought I wish I was Bella right now, the undivided centre of Hannah's attention. The very first moment I felt it was in my very first drama lesson, and I thought I would gravitate towards the posher girls, but we were listening to a tape of different regional accents, cockney, Welsh, Scottish, West Country, Geordie, Irish, and Mr Edwards played the tape and then went round us one by one asking us to do that particular accent. The posh girls – there were four of us that would probably go down as from well-off families I guess – were hopeless. We just couldn't escape our own accent and voice patterns. Most of the others were OK, if a bit embarrassing at times, and funny at others. But Hannah was superb. She could take them all off. I also noticed a softness to her voice that was quite rare in a teenager. Anyway, as if going from private to state school wasn't a big enough change in my life, the sudden bolt-like realisation that I actually felt like I was falling in love with a girl was the biggest change of all.

I was slow to realise she was drinking a lot. I was not a drinker but at that age most girls drank, and most got drunk from time to time, and quite a lot of us, though not me, took drugs, so you would have to be exceptionally drunk exceptionally often to draw special attention to yourself. Hannah could definitely drink more than the rest of us without getting drunk. Also, I saw her more during the week than at weekends. I had tennis Saturday and Sunday, church Sunday morning, Sunday lunch a three-line whip, homework, a bit of Saturday-night telly, and I had lots of other friends too. Hannah and I were a circle of our own, and our wider circles of friends didn't really cross, which was something else that I felt gave us a special bond. I think because she saw me as her 'school' friend, and her other friends as her social circle, I perhaps wasn't as exposed to the drinking side as the others were.

But then one Saturday night I was in bed, and I got a text which woke me up, and it was Hannah. *'I'm outside. Can I come in?'* I texted back, *'Wait there, down in a minute.'* Given what followed, I feel mortified that I added two kisses and a smiley face. It was 2.35 a.m. I put on a dressing gown, and for a few wonderful seconds, as I tiptoed along the landing and down the stairs, I thought God had answered my prayers and she was coming to say that she had something important to tell me, she loved me, and she wanted to be with me, and I was going to take her in my arms and hug her and we would tiptoe back upstairs and everything was going to be wonderful. My heart was beating so hard I thought I was going to faint, so I stopped at the foot of the stairs, breathed deeply, told myself to be calm and slow down. I had to plug in a code to deactivate the alarm, then I opened the door as slowly and quietly as I could. I saw the blur of her beautiful brown hair through the thick glass above the letter box. I pulled the door towards me, but it was a different Hannah that was standing there. She tried to say 'hello', but it came out as 'hiyo'. She asked if she could come in, roughly translated as 'k fi c'min?' I said yes, but made a shushing motion with my finger to my lips, took her by the arm and led her slowly through to the kitchen. As I switched on the lights, she winced, as though the dark felt a more comfortable place to be. We had a couple of old brown leather chairs in there, and I put her down in one of them, and asked if she wanted a glass of water. She shook her head.

'Got anything else?' I could hear the words, but the voice was different, lacking in her usual crispness and clarity, all the words rolling into each other . . . 'Gotnifenelse?'

I said, 'I can get you a cup of tea or some juice or something?'

'Not what I meant,' and she chuckled to herself, then sighed, and threw her head back against the top of the chair.

'Just one,' she said. 'Go on, I know where your dad keeps it all.'

'One what?'

'Glass of something.'

'What?'

'Anything . . . Come on, don't be hard on me now, just one drink.'

'But Hannah, you're totally drunk, you can hardly walk, you can hardly speak, you can't possibly want more.' Her chuckle turned into a cackle, then a full-throated laugh and I said, 'Shush, you'll wake everyone up.'

'OK,' she whispered, 'gemme one glass and no more noise, promise.'

'Why don't you come upstairs and you can get some sleep?'

'One drink . . . just one.'

We had a drinks cabinet in the sitting room. I poured a trickle of vodka into a thick tumbler, the one Dad sometimes used for an after-dinner brandy, went back to the kitchen and took a can of Coke from the fridge.

'Vodka and Coke OK?' She nodded. But before I could pour it, she sprang from her chair and came to inspect the glass.

'Aw, fuck off, Soph, that's not a drink, that's half a spit, come on, don't take the piss.'

'I'm worried about you, Hannah, I've never seen you like this. You need to sleep it off.'

She laughed again. 'Sleep it off, maleep it off, nadeep if off, praveep if off . . . OK, cup of tea, nice cup of tea, nice, nice, nice cup of tea.'

I went to fill the kettle, but the relief that she was moving towards my advice was short-lived. I looked around as she was slipping through to the sitting room and she came back holding the vodka bottle, laughing, triumphant.

'Hannah, please . . . Please don't do that. Let me pour you one drink, and then you must get some sleep.'

But she had opened the bottle and it was up to her lips, she took three large gulps, looked at me, smiled, lifted her finger to her lips, said 'Shush, don't wake Mummy and Daddy' in a quiet whisper, then laughed loudly. I walked towards her, saying 'Please, Hannah, don't wake them up, they'll go crazy if they know you're here', and I made to grab the bottle from her, but she clutched it with both hands, held it tightly into her chest, and I was reduced to standing there, saying 'Please, Hannah, please give me the bottle?'

'Shhh.'

'Hannah, please.'

'Don't want to.'

'Please. This isn't funny now, Hannah.'

'Not funny, no, no, no,' and she shook her head, said it

again, then laughed. 'Not funny, so laugh . . . No, no, no,' and she quickly took another swig.

'Hannah, how much have you had to drink?'

'Not enough.'

'Please tell me. Please.'

'Too much. But want more.'

'Why? You're making yourself ill.'

'Love being drunk. Love that feeling.'

'What? Being like this, upsetting your friends, making them scared.' I had to gulp hard to stop myself from crying.

'Love that feeling, love it, love it, love . . . glass to your lips, and the drink goes in . . . warms the mouth, then goes over the throat, and you feel it, going down through your chest, warmer and warmer, hits your gut and it's like a bomb going off inside . . . whoosh, kapow . . . only there's no damage, Soph, no blood, no pain, just a lovely warm bomb . . . and it takes the world away.' She put the bottle to her lips again and she took a swig, swallowed hard, pointed to her throat as the drink passed over, traced her index finger over her neck, down her cleavage, down her stomach, then said, 'Whoosh, kapow . . . The bomb explodes, but no pain, world gone away.'

'Please, Hannah, tell me how much you've been drinking.'

'You don't want to know, Soph, you really don't.' I sensed her mood changing a little as the effect of a sudden blitz of neat vodka kicked in. Hoping she was becoming more mellow, I went to sit on the arm of her chair, stroked her hair, said, 'I do, Hannah, I really want to know.'

'Can I have one more drink before I tell you?' and she had that lovely playful smile back, and I said, 'Only if I can put the bottle away afterwards.'

'OK . . . Promise.' She put the bottle to her lips, and it didn't leave them until it was empty.

'All gone, all gone,' she said. I looked at the clock. She had emptied a half-full bottle of vodka in seven minutes.

'Come on, Hannah, we had a deal. One drink, you said, and you would tell me how much you've had.'

'Tell you in the morning. Time for bed.'

'No, please, please, Hannah, tell me, please.'

'One drink,' and then she laughed again, and I was exasperated, said, 'Come on, Hannah, we had a deal, you promised,' but she was not the same person who had been in my house before, who revised with me, sat in the Hollywood cafe with me giving marks out of ten to the boys walking by, walked with me when I needed to clear my head, took me out of myself and made me feel a little less posh middle class, daughter of a barrister who could only bear sending his kid to a state school because he took on lots of left-wing causes, and made big bucks doing it, thank you very much, so it was probably quite good for his image. This was not a person I could rationalise with, when one of the things I loved about her was that she was so rational, so cold and calm and could see things for other people so clearly, because whatever her exam results said, she was as bright as they come. But looking at her now, her eyes half closed, odd noises coming from her neck as she choked back whatever liquids were pushing up from below, it was like watching a dream dying in a sea of drink.

'Do you promise to talk to me about it in the morning?' I asked her, and she nodded. She was close to sleep.

'Come on then, let's get to bed.' I helped her up, and slowly we climbed the stairs, my heart pounding this time because every creaking floorboard sounded like a tree falling in the darkness, and I was sure my parents would wake up, and go crazy if they saw me taking a drunken Hannah to my bedroom, but somehow we made it.

I had dreamt so many times of Hannah being in my bed, but now all thoughts of kissing and touching and feeling were gone. I took off her trainers, opened and pulled down her jeans, and suddenly those beautiful legs held no charm, no excitement for me. She was wearing a pair of white cotton knickers with red dots on them. I had fantasised about sliding her knickers down her legs, but not now, not like this. It was the same face, the same perfect body, but the desire had left me. Lust and jealousy had switched to sympathy, and hurt. Both diminished her, but didn't make me love her less. I hauled her up the bed, tried to rouse her out of her thick jumper, but after getting one arm free, I gave up. I managed to get her under the duvet, climbed in beside her, put one hand on her shoulder, then said a little prayer that she would not let alcohol take over her life.

I fell asleep, but dreamt my father had taken me to a park, and was reading a book on a bench while I played on a roundabout, but as the roundabout came back round to where he was sitting, he had gone, and an owl was sitting there instead. The next time it went round, the owl had gone, and then the bench, and I wanted to get off the roundabout but it was going faster and faster and faster, so that when I woke I was breathing heavily and suddenly conscious not only of a body next to me, but also of a dank wet feeling across the side of my leg. I lifted the duvet, looked down, patted the mattress where her bottom was, and the gruesome reality dawned on me, that she had wet herself. I'd been worried enough about how to explain that I went to bed when Dad was falling asleep in front of *Match of the Day*, and by the morning we had a house guest, who would doubtless be hung-over, bleary, unenergetic, all the things my dad dislikes in his clichéd view of young people. I'd decided that I was going to say she had gone home late, had a blazing row with her mum and her boyfriend, and she stormed out, then realised it was cold and she had nowhere to stay so she came to ours, texted me, I let her in and we went to bed. So long as Hannah didn't stay around too long for an inquisition – and she would have to be gone before we left for St Augustine's – that should have been fine, not perfect, another reason for them to think she came from a bad family, but I was sure they would think I'd had no choice but to help a friend in need. But a soiled mattress, that was a whole different league of botheration, it really was.

Hannah was unwakeable. A little trail of saliva was flowing from the corner of her mouth, her hand hung limp over the side of the bed. It was almost light now, and as I pulled back the duvet, a huge blonde stain went out from both sides of her. 'Oh my God,' I said to myself. 'They will go absolutely fucking mental.' I shook Hannah's shoulder, and she groaned gently. 'Hannah, Hannah, wake up, please, you've got to help me, you've wet the bed.' It was hopeless.

I sat in the chair by my desk, trying to work out what to do. I was so tired, and not thinking straight. I thought about carrying her out, then starting a little fire, just enough to burn the bed, and I'd say sorry, but I had been reading by candlelight because it was a mystery novel, the one Dad gave me last week. 'Oh, pull yourself together, pull yourself together,' I said. Time to think clearly. And – how crazy is this, but it shows she could still have a hold on me – I asked myself what

Hannah would say if she were me, and it was someone else lying there comatose.

That got me thinking more clearly, like a fog suddenly lifted. I reckoned my dad's reaction would be worse than Mum's, so my strategy had to be to take Mum into my confidence, tell her everything, no lies, no secrets, get her to agree to let me help get Hannah out of the house before Dad found out, and she would wash all the bedding after we got back from St Augustine's, our church, which was just down the road. Easy. Well, not easy, but the best option. Once I had decided on that, I felt more settled, but it would be another couple of hours before she was up. I slept fitfully on the beanbag by my TV, and was woken by the sound of life in my parents' bathroom. Annoyingly, it was my dad, as I could hear the sound of him peeing, then coughing as he brushed his teeth and shaved. Normally, Mum gets up first but for some reason he was ahead of her. Then I remembered, it was Mother's Day. He would be doing his annual 'Make Mum tea and toast in bed' thing. I heard him go down the stairs, then I slipped in to see her. I wished her Happy Mother's Day, then added 'but something dreadful has happened'.

'What? What is it, darling?'

'It's Hannah.'

'What?' she squealed loudly. I think she thought I was going to say she was dead.

'Look, please don't be cross, and promise you won't tell Dad, but she's next door in my room, she came round in the middle of the night, she'd had a row at home and she went out drinking and she was completely pissed, couldn't speak, nothing, so I put her to bed, and oh, Mum, please don't be angry, but she's wet the bed.'

'Oh my God, no,' she said, and I thought I was in for it. 'Well, don't you worry, it's not the end of the world, we'll just have to wash everything when she gets up.'

'But what about Dad? He'll go crazy.'

'Don't worry, Sophie, he's not as bad as you sometimes think he is, you know. You can leave him to me.'

# AMANDA

**My name is Amanda. I am a haematologist, and the mother of Sophie, Hannah's best friend at school.**

Even good families like ours are full of little white lies. I didn't mind Julian knowing Hannah had stayed the night, and wasn't feeling well. I most certainly didn't want him knowing about her being drunk to the point of alcoholic poisoning, and wetting the bed. He got on with most of Sophie's friends, but he was someone who felt much more comfortable mixing with his own kind, the Bar, tennis, golf, and so he preferred it when our children brought back friends from a similar background which, most of the time, they did. He was a very good lawyer, but when he took on these controversial cases involving terrorists or whistle-blowers, it was because of his fascination with the legalities, not because he liked the people terribly much. He abhorred what the terrorists did, but if there were loopholes in the law that he could exploit to their benefit, so far as he was concerned that was his job, and he did it very well. That's why we had the biggest house in Highbury New Park, another one on the Suffolk coast, and a plot of land in northern Spain, where we were building our own place. I never mentioned retirement there, but that was the plan.

I'm not making a direct comparison between a terrorist cell and a teenage girl's circle of friends, but I do think that Julian sometimes saw in Sophie's friendship group some of the same dynamics that went on among the IRA and al-Qaeda 'sympathisers' he knew – he would never call them terrorists because part of his job was to convince a court they weren't, which meant building as many arguments as possible to persuade himself that though they may be terrorists or fanatics, that did not make them guilty of the specific charges, nor that there might have been a defect in the handling of the case that allowed him to get them off on a technicality, or at least win the right to fight another day, possibly in another court. Loyalty; shared values; the feeling that it was 'them' (America/ Britain/Israel/authority/parents–teachers' generation) v 'us' (terrorists/freedom fighters/teenage girls wanting to wear garish make-up and very short skirts); a tendency to exaggerate right and wrong, slights and praise; and falling out with each other – Sophie always seemed to be having a fallout with one or more of her friends, and whenever Julian had lost a case, it was inevitably because a falling-out between individuals within the group led to the police and prosecuting authorities being able to find the hole in their defences, and once A blamed B, and B blamed A, it was possible to get the whole team turning in on each other. Then they were sunk, and he risked another defeat to put down alongside the many wins.

Oh, this must sound terrible, but when you're standing staring at one of your daughter's best friends, who is kneeling down naked on the bathroom floor, head plunged inside a lavatory bowl, throwing up a vile yellow liquid, you cannot be held responsible for the thoughts and comparisons that come inside your mind.

'Are you OK, Hannah?' I asked, as the vomiting calmed, which to her must have seemed like a particularly stupid question for a qualified doctor to ask. She was anything but OK. She said she was fine though, teenagers always do, mumbled an apology, but the effort of speaking sparked another convulsion inside her, her back arched upwards, I could see her chest filling out, her throat pulsing, and then another flood of yellow came charging out. I tore off some toilet paper, handed it to her and she wiped her mouth.

'So sorry, Mrs Harper, really am.'

'Don't worry for now. Let's just get you sorted for today. Is there any more to come?'

'Not sure.'

'That means yes. You just wait there while I go and check Sophie and her dad are OK.'

'OK, thanks,' and I could see the back arching again, and another wave was on its way.

She was like the outsider insider of Sophie's friendship group. In one of Julian's terror groups, she would have been the hitman, who took instructions from the group and then worked alone. All Sophie's friends knew she and Hannah were close, but she never seemed to be around when the others were. I wondered if Sophie saw Hannah as her guilty pleasure, like my tennis partner friend Donna who once had an affair – well, a one-afternoon stand – with the online shopping delivery man, which was so bad it was just funny, and her excuse was 'we all need a bit of rough every now and then'. This is terrible, I know. First terrorists, now the sex life of my tennis partner, all sparked by my daughter's friend wetting a nearly new John Lewis double-bed mattress.

We all tend to flock towards our own kind, I suppose, which

is why Hannah sometimes seemed a little out of place and perhaps why Sophie separated her out from the rest of her circle of friendship. Like her older sister and two older brothers, all now working or at university, Sophie was privately educated through her early years and into her teens. But when she heard about its reputation for drama, she became fixated on the idea of moving to the school in Islington, which actually is one of the closest schools to where we live. She switched when she was sixteen. She kept on with some of her friends from Francis Holland, and she had one or two from her new school, but they tended to be from our area, with parents who were middle-class professionals, and Hannah was very different. I liked her though. Our house was always full of debate about whatever was in the news, and what I liked about Hannah was that she said what she thought, or she asked direct questions if she didn't understand the issue.

'Would you ever defend someone if you actually knew they were guilty, but they said they weren't?' she asked Julian one Sunday lunch a few weeks after the bed-wetting incident. Julian wasn't overly used to being challenged at home and he waffled helplessly. Sophie and I ended up chortling so loudly he had to stop, and I said, 'That's a yes, Hannah. Bullseye.'

I unleashed a veritable snowstorm of white lies once I joined Julian and Sophie downstairs.

'How is she?'

'Fine, I think it's just a tummy bug. I've given her something to settle it down, and told her to have a lie-in.'

'What was she doing here in the first place, Sophie?' asked Julian, not unreasonably. 'I thought you'd gone to bed?'

'She called me just after I went upstairs. She wanted to talk about an essay we have to do, and I said to come round and we could work on it in the morning.'

'I didn't hear her come in.'

'You were out like a light, darling,' I said. 'Anyway what I suggest is Dad and I go to St Augustine's, you stay here and look after her, and I'll see her again when we're back.'

'But I thought we were having lunch at the Pringles'? He's got that judge from Canada over for a seminar at UCL.'

'It's not a sit-down, just a drinks and buffet thing. You can go and maybe I'll join you later. I'm not terribly keen on the Pringles to be honest.'

Julian harrumphed, which was his way of signalling that he accepted everything I said, reluctantly, including letting Sophie off church, which seemed to pass him by.

I spent the whole of the service at St Augustine's trying to think through the best way to approach things when I got back. Though there was the immediate problem to deal with, my main worry was ensuring that Sophie didn't get drawn too closely into the lifestyle that Hannah seemed to be choosing for herself. Of our four children, she was the least naturally academic, and Oxbridge had already been ruled out, but if she worked hard enough she would definitely be able to get to a good redbrick, which would give us a final tally, one Oxford, one Cambridge, one Nottingham and one wherever Sophie got to, the four of them split evenly between science and arts. So the genes must have worked somewhere along the line.

I had been a GP for almost ten years before deciding to retrain as a haematologist and switching to hospital work. But even back then, in a very suburban area like Hampstead Garden Suburb, I would say that a good proportion of the people who came to my surgery, whatever physical symptoms they were reporting, were there for reasons to do with their mental health and well-being, and in particular addiction to alcohol and to a lesser extent drugs. It became almost routine for me to ask how much they drank, and some would take offence, but I was in no doubt that drink was the force that was sending many of my patients to me, and my job was to help them to see the link as clearly as I did. Once they did, it was possible to put together a plan for recovery. Until then, doctor and patient alike, we were wasting our breath. I was also sure that for all the pubs that were shutting down – three have closed within half a mile of us in the last six months – more people were drinking to excess than ever before, and for young people, it was much harder not to drink than to drink. It was why, for all that she wasn't as superbright as her siblings, I was very proud of Sophie's approach to these issues, and never worried that she would go the way of her uncle Keith, my brother, who was the classic alcoholic-in-denial.

Julian dropped me back at the house around half past twelve, before heading on to Totteridge. I was quite relieved to miss both the journey – that traipse through north London is hell seven days a week now – and the lunch with a houseful of legal types trying to impress a foreign judge. 'I'll say you have flu,' he said, blowing a kiss as he switched the music system to Radio 3 – we have it on 2 when I'm in the car – and headed off. The lawn had taken a sudden drenching from a mid-morning downpour, and looked lovely now as the sun lit up the drops of rain rolling down slivers of grass in need of a trim. Sophie had put all the bedding in the washing machine in the utility room out at the back, as planned, and I started the wash, before throwing together a few snacks and sandwiches, pouring a jug of orange juice, then joining them upstairs. Sophie was lying on the beanbag, still in her pyjamas, and had thrown an old rug over the mattress. Though she had sprayed the room with perfume, and two cinnamon candles were burning on her bookshelf, the smell of urine and vomit still hung in the air. Hannah was sitting in the comfy chair. She was wearing her own jeans – with underwear borrowed from Sophie, I hoped and presumed – and a shirt and jumper Sophie had also given to her. I was quite used to seeing other girls wearing Sophie's clothes. She had showered and washed her hair, and though she looked a little tired, had I not seen it for myself, I would not have said this was someone who two or three hours earlier was throwing up the waste from a night's excess. Just how excessive she had been would come as a real shock both to me and, as I would see from the way she kept putting her hands to her face as the story unfolded, to Sophie.

I thought about trying to entice them downstairs, but Sophie was so comfy sunk deep into the beanbag, and Hannah looked remarkably well considering, and smiled so nicely as I walked in, thanking me once more for being so understanding by way of welcome. She was mortified about the bed-wetting, kept insisting she'd pay for it to be cleaned properly – which was a nonsense, of course.

I laid the tray on Sophie's desk, poured a drink for both of them, gave them each a plate, and took the sandwiches round.

Her colour and her voice had returned, but clearly there was still a lot going on inside her stomach that worried her.

'You must eat,' I said. 'Just take one of the tuna and cucumber ones, they're very light.' She did, and she started to peck at it nervously, suddenly looking more childlike than

I had ever seen her. Being a parent, and a doctor, my instinct was to want to fix whatever it was that had reduced her to this mess. But first I had to know if she would want to open up to me, even a little.

I remembered Sophie saying that they'd been talking and that it was important to see that Hannah had a very different life to us, in that sometimes irritating, sometimes amusing way teenagers have of acting as if they are the first ones ever to have experienced anything, or thought of its significance. But it also struck me that Sophie was such an innocent and trying so hard to say and do the right thing for her friend. I think she had an instinct that I really wanted to help, and she knew too that meant Hannah had to let out some of the things she was feeling and thinking.

'Tell Mum what you were saying to me, Hannah, the thing about happiness. She'll understand.'

She was a bit mumbly at first, and she clearly didn't want me to feel sorry for her, didn't want to make excuses for her behaviour, certainly didn't want to pile all the blame on her parents, but 'the thing about happiness' was that she just wasn't very happy a lot of the time, and drinking made her feel better, at least for a while. It is a horrible thing to hear, not that she enjoyed a drink every now and then, but that it made her feel better, at a deeper level. Not even eighteen, and already using drink to escape from herself or her life. Isn't that an awful thing for a child to say? And of course Sophie was right, Hannah's life was very different to ours, though when she talked about her mum and dad, not having met them it was hard not to see them as people like us, but the truth is I knew nothing about them, couldn't possibly make a judgement about whether they were somehow to blame.

Their constant fighting and arguing clearly upset her, though she seemed curiously un-upset about her father's eventual departure, and said that now her parents seemed to hate each other so much she wondered how on earth they ever got together, and what she seemed to be describing for herself was an absence of emotion about all of it, a kind of blankness, an inability ever to remember being particularly happy or particularly sad. She described the day her mother sat her and her sister down and went through how things were going to work, what had happened in the divorce court, how often they would see their dad, and though she was becoming more open and articulate, she might have been describing a guide from an instruction manual, so devoid of emotion was she. Her sister cried, she said, but she didn't.

I wondered how Sophie would respond to a similar situation, and hoped that somewhere in there would be those mother–daughter childhood moments of joy, the climbing into bed in the middle of the night, the wide-eyed wonder when Santa really did deliver what she had asked for, the laughter in the playground when the swing went too high, the shared sadness when something bad happened to someone in the bedtime stories I used to make up to help her get to sleep. And here was Hannah saying she knew that technically Mum was Mum, and Dad was Dad, but it sounded to me as if sometimes she felt like an orphan in her own home, like she didn't have parents the same way other children did. She said she felt she went through the motions, had run towards her mother when she came to pick her up from school, because she saw the other children doing it, but part of her wished it was the childminder who had come, because the emotions were more straightforward that way. And I don't know, I just thought that was so sad, and strange.

I asked her if she could remember when she'd had her first drink. Twelve, she said. Her uncle Malcolm gave her a taste of wine. He sounded like my brother, who drinks way too much but thinks no one notices because he's 'the life and soul'. She said she was fourteen when she first got 'properly drunk', at a party, on one of those lethal punches with a bit of everything out of a parent's booze cabinet chucked in, no doubt. It was then she seemed to come alive as she recalled the steady moving through the gears to the sensation of feeling drunk, of feeling looser and suddenly more in tune with the room, and everyone in it, than she had before. Like she had gone in lonely, and drink had helped her feel less lonely, and so drink was her friend.

I guess everyone knows that feeling of inadequacy or isolation walking into a social gathering, standing there suddenly amid friends and strangers and thinking, really, I don't know why I'm here – if I'm honest, escaping just such an occasion at the Pringles' with a bunch of lawyers and their excessively polite partners, all trying to impress a Canadian judge, was one of the reasons I'd been so willing to clean up after Hannah.

As she talked of drink, there was something frightening about how animated she became, and the concept of alcohol as a friend was particularly striking because it was the same kind of excitement I saw in Sophie when she first started getting friendly with Hannah. She compared drinking to that moment after you've had a cold – when you've been feeling bunged up for ages and suddenly your airways start to clear. I pointed out, though, that when you get better through using medicine for a cold, part of the joy of recovery is that you

116

don't need the medicine any more, but if you feel better through taking drink, you end up feeling worse once you have to stop, as we saw last night. She nodded, and she admitted it was how the spiral took hold, 'drink to feel better, feel better, feel worse, drink again'. I let those words rest in the air, so all of us could absorb both the silence and the significance of what she had said. But she said she didn't believe she had a problem, because she could stop when she wanted to, and often did, and she saw plenty of people worse affected than her.

In a fairly short period of time, she had gone from mumbling shame and shyness to a clear understanding of her own situation, even if she could not yet begin to define it as a problem. It felt as though she was opening up, though, Sophie following our conversation like a spectator watching a tennis ball go back and forth over the net. I have always believed talking is the best route to identifying and solving problems, so I wanted to keep going, especially as she seemed a little less tired now. I said, 'We're all unique, Hannah, but we're not alone.' It was something a therapist said to me, years ago now, and it had always stayed with me. It seemed the right thing to say and I really felt like Hannah responded. Her hair fell over her face as she nodded slowly.

'If there is anything we can do to help, Hannah, we want to do it,' I said. 'I am a doctor, and Sophie is a friend, and that's not a bad start, is it, having friends who care?' She nodded again, and rubbed her hands against each other.

'Would you like some more orange juice?'

'Yes please.' Sophie got up to pour it, and I went to the loo, just to give her a little break. As I washed my hands, and looked in the mirror, I remembered Matt, a young man who had been a patient of mine, who'd had a drink problem in his early twenties, but who could never admit it, and whose lies and denials became ever more inventive as he sought to convince me his health problems were down to anything but drink. He ended up dead at twenty-seven.

'Hannah,' I said when we started up again, 'whenever I see a patient, if they have headaches or stomach pains or the runs or they feel depressed, I always ask them a few questions about their drinking. And unless they're totally abstemious, I always assume they're not telling me the truth, and I add on a few drinks in my own mind when they say how much they drink. If I asked you a few questions, will you tell me the truth?'

'Yes.'

I felt she was becoming more reflective, perhaps even getting something from sharing what she was saying, but with the short break behind us, I thought a few sharp factual questions would open her up even more.

'How many days have you had a drink in the past week?'

'Since Monday?'

'Let's do Saturday to Saturday.'

'OK. Saturday yes, Sunday yes, Monday yes, Tuesday no, Wednesday no, Thursday yes, Friday yes, Saturday yes.'

'So not the two nights you were with me?' Sophie chipped in.

'Mmm.'

'On how many of those nights did you drink more than two glasses of wine or the equivalent?'

'All of them.'

'On how many of those nights did you go to bed in a state that you would describe as drunk?'

'Three, maybe four.'

'On which of those nights did you have the most to drink?'

'Last night, by a distance,' and she smiled.

'Glad to hear it. In your opinion, has your drinking ever had a negative effect on your work, your health or the key relationships in your life?'

She let out a tired sigh, and at first I worried I had pushed her too far, but she breathed in deeply, then out, and said that since hanging around with Sophie, she worked harder than before, but yes, there had been times when because she had been drinking she had not done her homework, and sometimes she missed school because of a bad hangover. 'So yes, yes to work.'

'Health?'

'Mmm, not sure. Never been to a doctor, but that's because the chemists are pretty good at working out what you need.'

'How often do you vomit as you did this morning?'

'Erm, last seven days, twice I think. Last Sunday, and today.' Then she remembered that on Friday, too, she had thrown up after her mother left for work, but she insisted that could have been food poisoning, because of all the solids in the mix. 'Sorry, that sounds disgusting,' she said.

'Hannah,' said Sophie, 'why did you never say anything? I mean, I know you drink more than I do, but I had no idea it was like this.'

'Maybe not something I want to shout from the rooftops. And anyway, perhaps you were my escape from it.'

'So who do you drink with?' I asked.

'Boys. Sometimes on my own. Parties.'

'On your own in pubs, clubs, or at home?'

'Hardly ever at home, though I have a few stashes in places nobody looks. Lagging and stuff like that. If I'm out and I'm really hammered I wait till Mum's in bed before I go home, and usually I'm pretty good at looking OK in the morning, or sneaking out before anyone sees me.'

'But she must know there's a problem if you're out late, or you're being sick or whatever?'

'She does, yeah, but there's only been once or twice when she's actually seen me worse for wear. Last night was one of them.'

'So we have a "yes" for work, a "yes" for health, though not so you've had to see a doctor, and what about key relationships in your life?'

She nodded again, breathed deeply, and then clenched her eyes, either thinking hard, or willing something away, it was impossible to tell. 'Depends what you mean by "key relationships"?'

'Well, usually we would mean parents, siblings, other family, boyfriends, friends, colleagues.'

'OK, mmm, complicated. Parents? Are things worse with my mum because of it? That's a yes. She's not a drinker, never has been, and it's one of the things she holds against my dad that his family was always big into booze. In fact I should have put my dad in the list of people I drink with. Last few times my sister and I have seen him, we've ended up in a restaurant and he hasn't minded me drinking and so we would share a bottle of wine or something like that. It makes the time pass more quickly. To be honest, these access visits have always been a pain, and even Vicki, who can get on with anyone, even she's wanted them to end as soon as we arrive, especially when he has a new woman in tow, which is often. So with him, I would say yes, my drinking has affected the relationship, but on balance for the better.'

'Your mum's boyfriend?'

'Not a key relationship. Not a relationship at all.'

'Boyfriend? Sophie said you've had boyfriends.'

'Complicated. I spend more time with Soph than any of the boys I hang out with. But I drink with the boys, and quite often one thing leads to another, and so I don't know if every time you sleep with a boy that becomes a key relationship, but I can definitely say I have never had sex with a boy without drinking first. Not sure what you would make of that in your clinic.'

I think she realised that a little note of petulance had crept into that last remark, and she apologised. 'Sorry, didn't mean to sound offensive. And sorry, there is no need for me to be talking about sex. I wouldn't want my mum hearing what my friends get up to, so there's no reason I should expect you to, what with Sophie sitting there.'

'It's really not a problem, Hannah. The thing is, I'm a doctor, and although I'm not an expert, I do have some experience in dealing with people who drink to excess.'

She nodded, and said, 'I've already told you more than I've told anyone else alive.'

'Thank you. Can I ask you this about these boys? Are there any of them that you would have sex with if you were totally sober?'

She looked to the floor, and I sensed she was running them through her mind. The fact that it took so long led me to believe there was more than the handful I imagined.

'One maybe, two max.'

'So you have sex because you're drunk?' She took a long time to answer and when she did, she part accepted, part rebutted my question. She was back to the point about getting drunk to feel better, and when she felt better she was more open to doing things she wouldn't do sober, and that included messing around with boys, from kissing at a party to going the whole way. She said sometimes she enjoyed it, but other times she would be halfway through and struck by the realisation she was there not because she liked the boy, or what they were doing, but because she was drunk, had lost control, and knew she would hate herself afterwards, and hate the reputation it would help to get her, so not only was the drink making her feel worse, but so were the things it made her do.

Sophie was looking more and more uncomfortable, so I moved things on towards a close.

'There are just two more things I want to ask you, Hannah, and then I think we should go downstairs and have a proper bite to eat. Have you wet the bed through drinking before? And how much did you have to drink yesterday?'

Again, a big sigh and heavy breathing, and I could sense from the length of the sigh and the depth of the breath that either she was about to shut down the conversation, or she was finally prepared to tell me the truth. It was as though I could hear and see the argument going on inside her head as she decided which it was to be. She stared for a while at the ceiling, then brought her eyes slowly to me.

'OK, first one first. Wetting the bed? This is humiliating for me but yes, a few times, a couple of times at home, and I have to do all my own washing and cleaning as punishment, and things have got worse between me and Vicki, because she's seen me drunk more than Mum and I can see it's not easy for her, and maybe that's another reason I find boys to sleep with, because it means I don't have to upset her more than I need to, because I can stay out. I did it once at a boyfriend's too, which is the last time he had me back, you won't be surprised to know.'

'And last night?' Three words to the question, but enough to unleash a torrent in the answer. If she had been a bit closed up talking about why she drank, she had no such hesitation revealing how much. It wasn't that she was proud, indeed I sensed her shame at various points of her account, which was probably why, once she got going, she directed more of her story to Sophie than to me, and quite a lot to the wall behind us.

'Well, it started earlier than usual. I had this essay to do, for history, and honestly, I was going to go to the library. I find it easier to work there than at home, especially when Mum and her bloke are around, and Vicki always has friends round, so I left about twelve thirty. I had a bit of a hangover but I was feeling nearly human and I set off, honestly, with the intention of going there, I really did. But I met Harry Collins – Sophie knows him, don't you, Soph? He's in our school, and he's someone I've been with before, and he's on his way to meet some friends, and I say, "I've got an essay to do, and I'm going to the library," and he says, "Come on, it's the weekend, just come and join us for a couple, we're meeting up at the Hercules, before heading into town, and you can go to the library then," and I knew I shouldn't, but I knew I would, and I knew as soon as I had the first one that I would not stop at two, and that's why I love working with Soph, because when she sets her mind to it, that's it, and there is no way she would have been sidetracked from the library to the pub, but yesterday she was out with her other friends from her last school, and when I was walking to the library, I was saying to myself, "I can't wait to tell Soph I've been working all afternoon," but Harry sidetracked me so easily, it was pathetic, but that's what happens. I can have good intentions but as soon as the excuse for a drink comes into the picture, I'm off. It didn't help that they were going to the Hercules. It's that one bang opposite the Odeon, on the corner of Hercules Road and Holloway Road, where I used to go to with Sammy after we bunked off to go and see a movie. I liked the gold signage across the top of the pub and they had comfy old leather sofas against the wall and we used to sit there with orange juices which Sammy topped up with vodka he bought from the offy.

'So I was in there, and I had a small lager to convince myself I wasn't really drinking – Harry and his pals were already on pints and chasers – and I drank the first one slowly, the second one not so slowly, and then Harry's cousin, a guy called Declan who was over from Ireland for the weekend, and they were going into town because Ireland were playing France at rugby and there was a sports bar they were going to watch it in at the bottom of Haymarket, this boy Declan is buying a round and he says, "No way am I buying a half, she'll have a pint like the rest of us, and she'll not just have a pint of lager, but she'll have a pint of Guinness too, my national drink," and everyone cheered, and I can feel the self-control cracking, literally like a chain inside me and it's cracking. After the first half of Heineken, I was still thinking I could make the library by one, and spend three or four hours there, but Declan blows the whole chain sky high, because he is taking control. Harry is laughing, his friends are laughing, and I am reluctant to join in, but the second half-pint has made a little hit, it's wiped out the last bit of the hangover, and then Declan is coming towards me, and he has a pint of lager in one hand, pint of

Guinness in the other, and he's trying to speak in a posh English accent and he says, "My Lady, your refreshment has arrived, and I do beseech you to knock the first of these back in a oner," and Harry and his mates crowd round, and we're all laughing, and suddenly the jukebox feels like it's gone from volume-level five to ten, a bar that felt half empty suddenly feels a lot more than half full, and I pick up the lager, and I take a small swallow, a larger one, then another, then another, then I open my throat wide, just pour it down, I feel it tickling the insides of my neck then filling my chest and my stomach, and I slam down the glass, let out an almighty belch, and then hear the cheers all around me, and Harry is slapping me on the back, and Declan is standing in front of me, applauding and he goes, "And now the Guinness," and I go, "Not without a double Scotch chaser and we all have to do it," and up goes another wild cheer, and he goes to the bar and orders six double Scotches and five more pints of Guinness, and brings them back, and now I take control, and I say, "Ready, steady go," and you have to do the Scotch first, pour the remnants into the Guinness, and I can see Declan is just ahead of me, but he is the only one, and he slams his glass down and I am a couple of seconds behind, then Harry, and the rest are spluttering and gargling and failing to get them down, so even though I didn't win, it was as good as, so far as they were concerned. Anyway, cut a long story short, we stayed in there till three, I laid off the spirits but had a few beers, a couple of red wines, and when it came time for them to go to the sports bar, Declan told me he didn't much care for rugby, and how's about he and I went somewhere else, and we did, first to a Spanish restaurant, El Molino, for a bit of paella to mop up the booze, and a bottle of wine. Declan said he wanted "just the house red", and the waitress said, "We don't do a house red but I'll get you the cheapest," which for some reason sent us both into uncontrollable fits of the giggles. We ate and drank quickly, paid and left, to the clear relief of the waitress, despite Declan's twenty-pound tip.

'As we walked out, it was sunny, and I got that headache you get when you're drunk during the daytime, like a pre-hangover hangover, and Declan says, "Maybe we should go have a lie-down." I knew we were going to have sex, but first I pulled him into the Herbert Chapman for a quick drink, just a half of lager and a Scotch. It had been my dad's local when we lived opposite the Coronet when I was a baby, and I knew I was on the edge of a 24-carat, full-on bender, and I guess I thought my dad's pub should be in there. Don't ask me why.

'So we walked on down the Holloway Road, past the library at the Met University I had been planning to visit, past the Famous Cock on Highbury Corner, and Declan shouts out, 'Oh look, I didn't know you Brits named a pub after me already,' and I creased up again. I was at that stage where everything either of us said was funny. We were almost at the Angel before we found a hotel, a Hilton, just beside the Business Design Centre. There were six Union flags fluttering outside and Declan made a crack about Irish freedom and we stumbled up the steps and through the revolving doors. I have no idea what Declan does for a living but he seemed to have plenty of money, and we were giggling away because it was so obvious what we were there for, what with no luggage apart from the bottle of champagne he bought at the Majestic opposite Highbury Magistrates', and him paying cash and asking if they do daytime rates, and the woman on the desk said no, she was so po-faced, but a customer is a customer, so he paid in advance, we went upstairs in the lift, finally worked out how to use the key, opened the champagne, had sex, just drunk stuff, over in no time, and then we finished the champagne, and Declan was raiding the minibar and by now we are both completely out of it, and he says, "Let's play a game," and the game is that you take out everything from the minibar, and you lay it on the bed, all spaced out, then you blindfold each other, and take it in turns to throw a coin towards the bed, then remove the blindfolds, and whoever's turn it is, they get to choose who has to eat or drink the thing nearest to where the coin has landed. So don't ask me what I drank while we played this stupid game. More champagne, I remember that, then some pretzels, a miniature of gin, a Mars bar, a small bottle of red, vodka, Chardonnay, and then he turned on the TV to watch the end of the rugby, and I had a little sleep. I felt rough when I woke up, and Declan made me a Bloody Mary, which he said was the best mid-bender settler known to man. We had sex again, then Declan called his cousin, and we met them later at a party in Shoreditch, and I was slowing down, a few wines, but it's amazing how you can get a second and third wind if you just persevere, so I don't know, some time before midnight, I peeled off from that crowd and I fell in with Paul Mellor, who Soph knows as well, and we went clubbing and so I was back on the spirits. Don't ask me how many I had, I was totally gone by then. I don't even remember where it was, or getting back home, but I did, and I was trying so hard not to make a noise, but one thing I know is that when you're really far gone, the harder you try to be quiet, the more noise you make, and when I had done the hard bit – getting the door open – I totally forgot about the little step in the hallway, and I tripped and landed bang on the floor. Next thing Dan, Mum's bloke, is standing there with just a towel round him, then Vicki appears at our bedroom door in a vest and pants, then Mum completes the team, wrapping her dressing gown around her and marching towards me, and I can hear her saying, "Oh, not again, please, not again." And then Dan says, "You've got to do something about her," which really makes her flip. "Like what?" and she looks back and is shouting at him. "What am I supposed to do?" So he disappears back into the bedroom and slams the door, and my mum is like leaning against the wall next to where I've fallen, and she says, "You can't go on like this, Hannah. Ruin your own life with drink if you must, but you're not ruining mine too. I've had enough shit in my life." And I say something like "very sympathetic I must say", and that only wound her up more, and so I can see Vicki getting worried and she comes down the hallway, and she says, "Come on, Han, let's get you to bed," and I try to stand up but I fall back and we've got a little coat stand just inside the door and I send it flying, and now my mum is screaming at me, she says, "You're not living here one day longer if you come home like this again," and I just stand up, and I say, "OK, if that's how you want it," and I walk back out the door. I honestly thought my mum would try to call me back, so I left the door open, but nobody came as I swayed towards the stairwell. I could hear Vicki saying, "Mum, get her back, anything could happen to her out there in that state." But if Mum said anything, I didn't hear it, and by the time I reached the stairwell, I heard the door to the flat closing.'

'And then you came here?'

She seemed startled to hear another voice, as if she had

been delivering a long monologue to herself. As she glanced towards me, I realised she hadn't been looking at me since the point in the monologue where she allowed herself to be distracted from the path to the library to the pub, and she had only looked at Sophie when she mentioned her name.

'Not straight away. I had a few quid left so I bought a bottle of cider and some cheese biscuits at the all-night supermarket, then I tried to call Declan but he wasn't answering his phone, so I sat outside, drank my cider, then suddenly I realised how cold it was. And I thought of Soph.'

The room fell silent, and was filled with the heaviness of her account, the sheer volume of alcohol, the twisted relationships that flowed in and out of her life, the sadness that she seemed to feel, and which she caused in others too. Right now, Sophie was one of them. She was masking her eyes with her hands, and I knew she was crying.

'I wish I'd known,' she said. 'I wish I'd known where you were, and come for you.'

'Don't feel bad,' Hannah replied. 'You're a better friend to me than I am to you. And I'm sorry I made you give me more drink when I got here.'

'It's OK.'

'We're always here if you need us, Hannah,' I said.

'Thanks. And sorry. I'm really sorry. It won't happen again, promise.'

I felt drained, and desperate to get out and mow the lawn or tidy the flower beds, even go to join Julian at the Pringles'.

She stayed upstairs with Sophie for most of the afternoon, and when she came down to say goodbye, I said I would give her a lift home. She said she wanted to walk, but I insisted. Sophie came along for the ride. Hannah directed me and I dropped her right outside the entrance to the flats. I was often struck by how remarkably peaceable London people were, considering that homes and lifestyles like ours lived cheek by jowl with places like this. It looked as welcoming as Holloway or Pentonville jail, both within another short drive from where we were.

I watched her walk in, but instinct made me drive to the junction, turn round and park.

'What are you doing, Mum?'

'Let's see if she goes in.'

'Oh, don't be ridiculous, of course she will. She said she was going to sit down and apologise to her mum, and promise to turn over a new leaf.' At which point the heavy green grille door opened, and Hannah emerged. She walked away from us, and once she reached the corner, and turned left, I started up the car, and followed her at a crawl. She was striding purposefully, walked for half a mile or so, and into the Alwyne Castle on St Paul's Road, her blue anorak lost, even before she got through the door, in the dozens of young people smoking and drinking at the big wooden tables outside.

'Oh no,' said Sophie. 'I don't believe it.'

'I'm afraid I do, darling. She's not the first, won't be the last.'

'But surely we can help her.'

'We can try, but if she doesn't want our help, there's not a lot we can do.'

The laughter coming from the drinkers spilling onto the pavement sat so oddly with the mood of despair that had fallen across Sophie's face, and made the short drive home one of the longest, and saddest, of my life.

# DAN

**My name is Dan. I was Hannah's mum's first boyfriend after her divorce.**

I tried, I really tried. It's not easy for a bloke to be with someone he thinks he loves, and as well as managing her, he has kids from an old marriage to worry about. If I had known in advance how hard it was going to be, and the extent of my failure, and the disastrous impact Hannah had on our relationship and all of our lives, I would never have asked Kate out in the first place. But you hope, don't you, that love will conquer all?

I was a rep for a shampoo company based in Hendon, though recently we'd branched out into soaps and perfumes. We'd just posted record profits, and I got a bonus almost as big as my basic, so I was feeling good about life. We sell direct to hairdressers, men's, women's and unisex, and most of my bonus came from a contract I won with one of the big chains. Then the boss asked me to take over sales to hotels and spas, and when I met Kate, she was working at a new luxury spa in Highgate. She was an assistant manager, which meant a whole range of things from manning the desk when they were short-staffed, to hiring and firing, making sure all the equipment was up to speed, and generally being on hand to sort out any problems, and deal with the many and varied demands of a particularly demanding clientele – affluent London. If you went in there, you'd have thought Kate was the boss, as the manager, Alan Brecker, sat in his office most of the time.

We had a new all-in-one shampoo and shower gel that we were hitting the gyms with, and I'd arranged to meet Brecker to talk him through it. But when I arrived, it was Kate who met me, and she said Brecker was in a meeting, so she would take care of it. I did the spiel about the cost and the quality, and how it had been tried out in a five-star Austrian spa and the feedback had been fantastic. Kate had worked in a hair-products place herself for a few years, but moved into leisure when it went bust in the first recession. So she asked more questions than I expected, and she was bright, no doubt about that. The tricky part came when I had to show her how the wall fittings worked, and the only way to do that really was to go into the showers, which if Brecker had been with me would have been easy, but with a man and a woman, not so straightforward. She asked two of her staff to check out how many people were in the ladies' and the men's changing rooms. Word came back – two men, five women. So we sent the male member of staff into the men's changing room to tell the two men the female assistant manager would be coming in with a salesman. One was taking a shower, the other was wrapped in a towel drying his hair as we walked in. Classical music was playing into the main changing area. The place smelled of sweat, chlorine and cheap soap.

The showers were in cubicles, classic aquamarine mosaic style, with a huge shower head, and wall sprays from the sides.

I took out the giant bottle of our new gel, and the holding gear, and showed her the optimum place to put it — head height for an average man, just below the shower, to the right, as most men are right-handed. I said some of the upmarket places go for two per shower, one either side, just to satisfy the left-handed market. She liked that idea. It helped that the gel system they were using, which had been around since long before I came into this game, was a small-container, low-quality product and badly positioned, on the wall to the right, waist-high. Also, to get the stuff out you had to squeeze the container on both sides with one hand, so the gel could come out into the other. I held the plastic bottle at the height we recommended placing it. A hand mark was printed at the base, and I asked Kate to slide her hand against the base of the bottle. She had barely touched it when a spurt of gel came into her hand. 'You see, nothing to push, nothing to squeeze, you just slide your hand in and out it comes.' She looked impressed. 'Now, when it came out, how did it feel? Cheap and nasty, or something you might actually want to use?' Women were far more resistant than men to using soaps and shampoos provided for them in gyms and hotels, but regular customers could be tempted if there was real quality.

'Yes, felt OK,' she said. 'Lots of substance to it, nice smell, nice colour.'

'Now give me your other hand.' I took her hand and placed it below their existing gel, I squeezed on the bottle, and a watery blue liquid gurgled out. 'Feel the difference?' She nodded. 'And that's without even putting any of it on your hair. It really is a whole new quality experience. Now hold out your hands,' and with that I turned on the shower, switched it to hand-held, and rinsed her off.

We left it so that she would speak to Brecker and call me back when they had decided. I was confident. No pun intended, but we gelled. It was quite odd to be standing, albeit fully clothed, in a shower with a woman I had only just met, but clothes or not, there was a charge about it, and I don't deny that from that first meeting, I was keen on her. I have never married, only once got close, and at the time I was going out with a girl from Chigwell called Della, but it was fizzling out, and I decided that if and when Kate called back, sale or no sale, I would ask her out.

She called when I was at a meeting, and left a message to phone her back. There was no indication whether it was good news or bad news, which probably meant bad news, I thought. My experience is that when you've made a sale, the buyer can't wait to tell you, because there is so much bad news around people love it when they can share good news, but Kate's message was very flat. 'Hello, Kate Maynard here, Highgate Hill Spa, you were here yesterday. Could you call me back please? – the number should have come up on your mobile. Thanks. Look forward to hearing from you.' I called as soon as I picked up the message, and it was the best news I could have had – 'Two bottles per cubicle, men's and women's, and what about ten per cent off in exchange for some advertising space in the spa magazine and the changing rooms?' Deal.

'One more thing,' I said when we had gone through the invoicing and payments process. 'I don't know if this is appropriate at all, and you could be married for all I know, though I noticed you didn't wear a ring when I was washing your hands for you, and I was thinking, that if you thought it was a good idea, we could maybe go out to seal the deal?' I knew she would say yes. That's not arrogance speaking, but when you've been in sales as long as I have, you get a sixth sense about how the person at the other end of the line is reacting to the words. People make a big deal about body language. I'm also into vibe language, and if you listen closely enough, you can hear the reaction, even when it's silent.

So two days later, I am pulling up in my company Nissan and parking opposite the Rising Sun, a gastropub that friends at work had been raving about. It's in Mill Hill. We both thought it was best to meet up a fair distance from her and my work. I got there early, and waited in the car. She was a few minutes late, and as I watched her park, and get out of her car, I had plenty of time to study her more closely. She was average height, good shape, her hair tied up in a way which showed off a face dominated by large brown eyes and strong cheekbones. She looked nervous, or maybe that was me reflecting my own feelings onto her. She was wearing a dark blue skirt, and a tight-fitting white blouse that emphasised good breasts and a trim waist. She threw her keys into her handbag and as she walked, heels clicking loudly, I nodded to myself at legs and hips that reminded me why I had felt as I did in the shower at Highgate Hill. I jumped out of the car so that we met at the door, and we walked in together.

The first few minutes of a first date are always agony, but we endured them, ordered food, and were quickly into basic life details. Where born, what schools, what parents did, jobs, family. I was halfway through my starter, a really sleepy avocado and mozzarella salad, when I first heard Hannah's name.

'I was married for over ten years, Pat, Liverpudlian, all charm but a bit of a shirker, and he couldn't leave the ladies alone. I put up with it for long enough, but it got so I was miserable the whole time. There's something very humiliating about having your husband unable to keep his trousers on when he leaves the house. Even when he's not doing it, you think he is. And every time you see him, you end up thinking "what a bastard", and I realised it was eating my soul away, I had to save myself and getting rid of him was the only option. Anyway, two kids, Hannah's just turned sixteen, Vicki thirteen, difficult ages for girls, and it's not easy, but we get by.'

'Any boyfriends since Pat?'

'Dates more than boyfriends . . . Nothing special.' I took that as a challenge.

The next time, we went to the Dominion theatre in town to see the Ben Elton musical about Queen. We were both big Freddie Mercury fans, though I'm not very PC on gays more generally. The time after that we met on a Saturday afternoon and walked around Alexandra Park, sat on a bench, held hands and kissed. And the following Friday, we decided not to bother with the restaurant booking, went to my place in Wood Green, and made love.

'My God, it's been so long,' she said.

'It felt like it,' I said. 'Thank you. That was as good as it gets.'

She left long after it was dark, saying the girls would be expecting her. But for the next few weeks we were seeing each other any time we could, and it became a running gag that we would arrange to go out somewhere, meet up, then decide to skip the date and go straight back to my place. And when we weren't together we were phoning and texting and emailing every spare second we had.

She didn't talk about the kids much, except to say she'd 'better be going', and a couple of times the young one phoned and asked where she was. I could tell she hated lying to her, usual excuses, working late, 'just buying a few bits and bobs on the way home, won't be long'. She showed me a photograph of them, and they were both pretty girls, but I sensed her time with me was very much *her* time, a chance not to think and talk about family. We were like young kids who had just discovered that the best feelings in the world come when you're falling for someone else and all you want to do is touch them, laugh with them, fool around, talk, fuck.

'I thought all this was just passing me by,' she said one afternoon when she had a day off and I threw a sickie. 'Thought my life was going to be work, kids, struggle to make ends meet, all work no play, and you've given me a whole new lease of life, and I love it.'

She just loved having sex, and I loved her for it. But I could tell it was putting a strain on things at home and the Hannah–Vicki mentions began to increase as the weeks passed. She always had a softer tone talking about the younger one, but Kate said Vicki suspected something was going on, and she was starting to complain more about getting her own tea, or being alone during the evening. And she worried Hannah was taking advantage of her absences to go out more herself, so she was falling behind with schoolwork again, which was a pity because actually she had been doing better recently, and she had found a bottle of vodka under her bed, and when she challenged her, Hannah just told her to get lost, she was old enough to make her own decisions, and it was none of her business if she took a few slugs of vodka to set her up for a night out.

'It's called "front-loading",' I said. 'The price of booze is so high in pubs and clubs kids tank up on supermarket booze first. I wouldn't worry about it. They all do it.'

'I just worry what she gets up to when she's been drinking. I mean, she just doesn't tell me anything. She's never brought a boy home, and yet according to Vicki Hannah is never away from the boys. Why wouldn't she want me to meet them?'

'Why would she? She might think you wouldn't approve.'

'When we had a row about the vodka, she ended up storming out, and I was in a complete rage, and I was looking through her drawers and her boxes for more booze, and I found a packet of three in there, opened, and only one condom inside.'

'Count yourself lucky she's using them,' I said. 'At least there's no chance of an unwanted pregnancy.'

'But Dan, she's my daughter, she's only sixteen, and the fact is I know nothing about what she does when she walks out the door. Nothing. I feel such a failure that I don't have a proper relationship with her any more.'

'It's a phase. She's doing the grungy teenager. You mark my words, she'll come good.'

'Maybe, but you know what, it's always been like this.'

'Like what?'

'Like I never seem to get it right with her, and she never seems to get it right with me. Vicki and I fit like a glove, but with Hannah it's always been hard.'

'You're not jealous of her, are you?'

'Jealous? Why on earth would I be jealous?'

'Dunno. She's young, boys seem to find her attractive, she seems to prefer them to being at home with you. And you feel like you're losing her.'

I shouldn't have said it. She looked hurt.

'I'm not sure I ever had her,' she said, 'not the way I thought I would when she was born.'

I didn't know Hannah at that stage, but as my relationship

with Kate deepened, I sensed she was angling for me to suggest moving in with her, but she worried that if she asked at the wrong moment, or pushed me too far, I would baulk. I wasn't sure, and she knew me well enough to realise that. I didn't want to lose my freedom but I didn't want to lose the fantastic excitement we had conjured up together, so I came up with what I thought was quite a clever compromise plan. First, I would meet the girls. If that wasn't a disaster, I would stay over for a night and see how they reacted. Then move in half the time, maybe up to a maximum of four nights per week. I didn't want total commitment, and I certainly didn't want Kate to think I was becoming a stepfather. Even if they were perfect kids – and from what Kate had told me, Vicki sounded OK but Hannah was scary as hell, and trouble to boot – I wasn't ready for looking after someone else's kids and frankly I didn't think I ever would be. In fact I knew it. It wasn't for me. And, to be absolutely frank, I had the heebie-jeebies about sharing a bathroom with three women, don't ask me why. I was even dreaming about it, going in there and finding my razors had vanished, and when I turned on the taps face cream rather than water came out, and Kate and her daughters were standing there naked, apart from towels round their heads, shouting at me to get out of the way. But the compromise plan sounded a runner, I put it to Kate and we went for it.

If I was nervous the first time I dated Kate, the first visit to the flat had me feeling mildly sick as I walked up the stairs, and realised I was ten yards away from what could be life-changing relationships with two teenage girls I knew only from a photo and a few snatches of chat with their mum. Kate, I could tell from the avalanche of texts, was as nervous as I was, even more. 'Just be yourself' was her most oft-repeated advice, but with all the different emotions swimming around me, I wasn't one hundred per cent sure what that meant. I had fallen for Kate, but I didn't particularly see why that meant I had to buy the whole family and all of her past and the problems it threw up for her, but if I didn't move towards entering her home life, the chances were the rest of it would crash and burn like my other vaguely serious relationships had, and for now, that was unthinkable. As I told my brother Stu when we went to Walthamstow dog track for his birthday, 'My dick has never been happier since the day I first realised it could stand to attention at the thought of the blonde one in Abba singing "Winner Takes It All".'

Kate answered the door, did a 'yikes' kind of face, half smile, half furrowed brow, and I followed her through to the living room, which was smaller than I expected, but clean and smart, more like an office than a home in some ways, which added to the uncomfortable feeling that I was being interviewed, as had the presence of a large woman along the landing, smoking a cigarette as she tended a window box, nodding and smiling at me as I waited to go in.

Vicki stood up and walked towards me to shake my hand. 'This is Vicki,' said Kate, and I said, 'Yes, I recognise you from the photos. You look even better in the flesh,' and I thought, oh no, mistake number one – patronising and actually possibly a bit pervy. It was the word 'flesh' I should have avoided. If I had said 'in real life', or 'in person', it would have been fine, but 'flesh' . . . best avoided, bad start. It was true though, she was far prettier than her photo, and if my reference to her flesh offended her she didn't show it, she smiled warmly and said 'hi'. She had a lovely mouth and fabulous white teeth like her mum, and she seemed to have none of the angst, not to mention the spots, that I associate with girls of that age. I felt she had made an effort, hair beautifully clean and brushed, nice trousers and plimsolls, a plain purple blouse unbuttoned a little bit too low to prevent inappropriate eye-lowering moments towards her, erm, flesh. I caught Hannah out of the side of my eye as Vicki was welcoming me, she was looking at her phone, only lifting her gaze to me when Kate said, '. . . and this is Hannah,' and I said, 'Ah yes, I've heard a lot about you,' possibly mistake number two, because it gave her an easy opening for a dig at her mum, which I was soon to learn was a staple of her conversation.

'All of it bad, I assume.'

'No, not at all. Far from it. Anyway, good to meet you.' She took the hand I offered, shook it unenthusiastically, then went back to her phone.

'So, Dan, why don't you sit there?' said Kate, steering me to an armchair close to the TV, 'and Vicki, you sit with Hannah, and I'll put the kettle on.'

I'd rehearsed what I intended to say, in front of the mirror, several times – how 'I met your mum through work, and we have become good friends, been out a bit and we really get along well, but I realise you are the two most important people in her life, so if she and I are going to take things to the next level, it's important I get to know you two a little, and I really hope we get along' – but Vicki chipped in before I could get a word out.

'So you're a sales rep, yeah?'

Looking at them side by side, I could see they were sisters, but only because I knew they were. Vicki had long light brown hair, almost blonde in parts, with big curls, and she had full lips on which she had dabbed a touch of gloss. She was sitting up ramrod straight whereas Hannah was leaning back, her feet perched on a little table. She had shorter hair, much darker, and her skin was slightly darker too, though not her hands, for some reason.

'How long you been doing that for?' asked Vicki, and I wondered if Hannah had been rehearsing too because before I could answer, she asked, 'Isn't that what Dad did, sales rep?'

'No,' said Vicki. 'He works for the Post Office.'

'Not as a sales rep? All those conferences and stuff?'

'Yeah, I am,' I said, 'for a shampoo company, not very glamorous, I'm afraid.'

'So that's how you met Mum, yeah, she told us.'

'Mmm, I tell my friends we met in a shower, and it was downhill from there. So what about you two, O levels and A levels, I suppose?'

'They're called GCSEs these days,' said Hannah.

'Yep, seems to be exams for one of us every year,' said Vicki.

'And how's it going?'

'Oh, OK, I don't think either of us is going to be Einstein, but we do OK, don't we, Han?'

'Yeah, we do OK.'

'That's good.'

'You married?' It was Hannah's first direct question, complete with laser-eye contact, rather than side-of-the-mouth barb.

'No, never met Miss Right, I'm afraid.'

'How old are you?'

'Thirty-nine.'

'Ooh, toy boy!'

'Your mum's a young forty-five.'

'So are you doing it?'

'Han – you can't say that,' squealed her sister.

'Why not? It's why they're here, isn't it? See how much we kick up, and if we don't, we have me and you in one room, Mum and Dan the Man in the other. That right, Dan?'

She had a glint in her eye that was half mischievous, half wicked, and not in the modern use of the word.

'Well, all I can say, Hannah, is that I like your mother a lot, and we have grown very close in recent months, and I would like to think I could come here from time to time, just as at the moment she comes to my place.'

'You live on your own?'

'Yes.'

'Bit weird, your age, never married, living alone, isn't it?'

'Come on, Han, give him a break.'

'It's fine, Vicki, you're both entitled to ask what you like. I have had girlfriends, and some have been serious, but none of them have meant as much to me as your mum. So . . .'

Kate appeared on cue, carrying a tray with two cups of tea and a couple of cans of Coke, and a plate of Jaffa Cakes and ginger biscuits. 'How we doing?' she asked as she passed me my tea, whispering that she had already sugared and stirred it, and offered me a biscuit, which I turned down.

Hannah and Vicki pinged open their drinks, and Hannah took a Jaffa Cake from the plate, and ate it chocolate-side first.

'I was just saying to the girls, you and I have grown close and we would like to see each other without always having to go out, and so sometimes that could mean here?'

'Yes . . . So what do we think of that?' In that single moment, I saw the two girls' characters so clearly. Vicki smiled, nodded and said simply, 'Sounds good.' Hannah stared at her mother, shook her head almost imperceptibly, and smirked with a tiny, inaudible flare of the nostrils.

'Hannah?' asked Kate.

'You're grown-ups. Free to make your own choices.'

Later, I suggested the four of us went out for a drink, and I drove them the mile or so to the Lord Stanley, where we took a table close to where a couple of old guys were playing cards, and I asked them what they wanted to drink. 'Orange juice,' said Vicki. 'White-wine spritzer,' said Kate. 'I'll have a large Jack Daniel's with ice,' said Hannah. I looked to her mum, who let out a pained sigh, and said, 'Do you have to, Hannah?'

'It's a celebration, Mum. You've found a man after all these years, let's drink and be merry.'

'Well, if I thought that was a genuine desire to share my happiness, I would go along with it, but wouldn't I be right in thinking it's an excuse to do two of your favourite pastimes – drinking underage, and annoying me?'

I was left standing there, not knowing what to order.

'How about I get a single to be going on with?' I said, and as neither of them responded, that is what I did. I watched them in the reflection of the wall mirror behind the bar. Vicki looked nervous, Kate livid, Hannah like she was trying to gain control of the situation. They sat in silence, other than an occasional plea from Vicki for them to get on with each other.

I took the drinks over, and by now the tension between the two of them had thickened, and poor Vicki was left trying to keep things light.

'Here's to you two,' she said, and we all raised our glasses.

No prizes for guessing who knocked her drink back in a single gulp, and then slammed her glass onto the table.

'My round,' she said, standing abruptly.

'Hannah, sit down,' said Kate. 'You cannot possibly need another drink already.'

'Don't need it. Want it. And if you'd let him get me a double, would already have had it. Same again for you, Dan?'

'I'm fine, Hannah.'

As she walked to the bar, and ordered a double, which she paid for after ostentatiously waving a twenty-pound note, then waited for the change, Kate tried to apologise to me.

'It's fine, really, don't worry. This is not easy for any of us, but you've got two fine daughters and I'm sure we'll get on OK eventually.'

'Hope you're right, but if this is a phase she's going through, I wish to heavens it would end.'

'Mum, I'll talk to her, she'll be fine,' said Vicki. 'This isn't the real Hannah. It's an act.'

'Thanks, love. Hope so.'

Hannah chatted to a couple of men at the bar while she finished her next two drinks, then came over to say she had arranged to meet friends in Canonbury, and she was leaving.

'Lovely to meet you, Dan,' she said. 'I'll be seeing you.'

'Yes, I hope so. Nice to meet you.'

'See you later, Han,' said Vicki. Kate couldn't even bring herself to look at her, as Hannah went back to the bar, and left with one of the two men she had been talking to.

I'd slept over at Kate's three times before I even really saw Hannah again. She came in a couple of times with a friend from school, a really posh pretty type called Sophie, another time on her own, and went straight to her room. She was polite enough if we bumped into each other in the hallway, or in the kitchen, but whereas Vicki seemed to be making an effort to make me feel at home, Hannah clearly had an avoidance strategy. She was spending as little time with me and her mother as was humanly possible given we lived under the same, not very large roof.

Still I tried. I tried to calm Kate down whenever Hannah had been drinking, or when she let off one of her verbal howitzers. I tried to talk to Hannah about what she was up to at school, even bought her a couple of books from the Oxfam bookshop in Upper Street when she said they were doing a Christopher Marlowe play in drama, and that made her mellow a little. 'And don't worry,' I said, 'I got them because I want to encourage you to work hard because it'll make your mum happy. I will never try to replace your dad.'

'Wouldn't be hard,' she said.

As I understood it, Pat was supposed to see the girls once a fortnight, but for the first couple of months I was half there, I think they saw him once, and Hannah made a point of telling her mum it was the second shortest period of time they had had together, but the second highest cash donation. 'Hundred quid,' she said. 'Said I had to get you something nice for your birthday with it, so what do you want?'

'Nothing if it's from his guilt money.'

'Oh, you're too predictable, Mum.'

'You should stop rising to her bait,' I said, but even when I tried to keep it jokey, Kate didn't like me getting too involved in her relationship with Hannah.

Despite the tensions, Kate preferred to be in her own home than at my place when we were spending the night together, and what with the two girls being at important stages at school, I got that. But the thing that had really made the last few months special – sex – started to take a dive. At my place in Wood Green, I didn't even know who lived on the other side of the bedroom wall. I saw them going in and out once in a blue moon, him in his bad suit, her in her veil, but I never had a proper conversation with them, and I'm not even sure they could speak English. So when Kate and I were at it, we weren't going to be inhibited by the worry that Mr and Mrs What's-his-name from Somalia could hear. Kate is a screamer and a yelper, I am a major groaner, and we screamed and yelped and groaned to our vital organs' glorious content, but at her place, it was impossible not to let the fact that two teenage girls were sleeping next door crowd in on the sense of abandon that had made our first encounters so wonderful. I found myself biting the pillow, and whenever a groan escaped, Kate would grab a chunk of my buttock and say 'Shhh,' while whenever she got close to a scream or a yelp, she would chew on her bottom lip, or sometimes grab my hand and bite on it. Once, she drew blood, so the only screaming going on was from me at the pain inflicted by her teeth on my hand. Sex went from five star to three star, and some nights one. Added to which there were a few nights when Hannah would come home and create a scene with her mum, who was getting more and more worried about how much she seemed to be drinking, and less and less confident that she had the slightest clue what to do about it.

When it came to the thought that Hannah might have a drink problem (which had crossed my mind almost from that first day we met, and certainly the next morning, when she looked near jaundiced until she slapped on a load of make-up), that was one area where I was determined to resist being pushed into the father role. There were limits to what I was going to do to hold things with me and Kate together.

Kate meanwhile had been promoted, and was now looking after operations for the whole chain, and she started to travel, not much, but maybe once or twice every fortnight, and I realised that bit by bit I was being sucked in, not just to be the stepfather, but also a babysitter, which really was not how I had planned things out.

She called me on the mobile one Friday morning as I was driving to a hotel spa near Watford. 'I've got to go to Oxford tonight,' she said. 'No idea what Hannah is up to, but Vicki's got coursework to do for Monday. Do you reckon you could be in, just to make sure she's OK, perhaps get her a takeaway or something?'

I liked Vicki, she was mature beyond her years and had always been nice to me and she was no trouble to look after, or to be with. Even so, I was pissed off. I felt like a big lead weight was dropping inside me, but I was still trying hard, you see. Kate was excited about her new role, and I still loved her enough, I guess, not to let her know how hacked off I was. Then again, maybe she is as good at reading unspoken messages down the phone line as I am.

'Well, OK,' I said, 'though I had been planning on seeing Stu tonight. His missus is on nights.'

'You can do that, Dan, my love. Just don't be too late, and give Vicki a bit of support.'

'Yeah, OK, well, maybe I'll see him straight after work, and get back around nine-ish.'

'How does half eight sound?'

Half eight it was.

I had a few beers with Stu, then called Vicki to ask what she wanted me to bring her home, stopped at Domino's to get a couple of pizzas, which we ate while she took a break from working, her drinking a can of Coke while I started work on a bottle of Sauvignon.

'Where's Hannah?' I asked.

'Dunno. Out drinking I imagine. It is Friday.'

'She drinks a lot for her age, doesn't she?' I said.

'Yeah. I try to talk to her, but she doesn't want to know. Always knows best. Says she drinks because she wants to, not because she has to.'

'You two are so different, aren't you?'

'Well, yes and no. I can see lots of me in her, and lots of her in me. But I guess I tend to see the sunny side of life, she sees the rainy side. But we're close, closer than you might think. The big difference is that Mum doesn't get on my nerves every time she breathes or speaks, and the other one is that I don't like drinking.'

'Because?'

'Because I did it once and I felt out of control, and I hated that feeling.'

'How come you manage to get on so well with your mum and Hannah doesn't?'

'Dunno. It's always been a bit like that. I don't understand it. I wish she could have the same attitude to Mum as she has to me. She's always looked after me. It was Hannah who taught me to tie my laces, helped teach me to swim, used to read to me, sing me to sleep, all the stuff you want a big sister to do, she did it. Mum's a good mum, Hannah's a great big sister, but I'd love them both even more if they could get on.'

Her coursework was for geography, something I couldn't really help her with, so she went to her room to work on it, while I cleared up, had another glass of wine, did a bit of admin left over from the office, then put on one of my old CDs, and did something I hadn't done for ages, namely roll myself a joint. I used to smoke a lot of cannabis, but since Kate came along, sex with her had been better than any drug, but being there in her home, on my own, a bit tipsy, listening to Sade – she used to live near me, when she went out with the BBC London DJ Robert Elms – it felt the right thing to do. I had a little stash which I retrieved from one of the side pockets on my suitcase, saw that Vicki's light was off, went back to the sitting room, sat on the sofa, pulled the table towards me, and went through the familiar ritual.

I was halfway down the spliff when I heard the key turn in the lock. Fuck. I had never told Kate about my occasional use, and was not sure how she would react. She knew I smoked cigarettes, no more than three a day, after meals, but cannabis was not the same. But there was no way I could hide what I was doing, with lights down, smoke in the air, Rizlas, tobacco and a lump of weed on the table, 'Your Love Is King' playing on the music centre, so as the door opened, I decided to play it cool, no big deal, chilling out on my own, nice to see you back.

Only it wasn't Kate. It was Hannah.

'My, my, my,' she said. 'Dan the drugster, who would have thought it?' She was drunk, though not on the scale of the weekend Kate kicked her out, when she was virtually incapable of standing.

'Do you want some?' I asked, and held the joint towards her.

'No thanks, Dan. Drink's my drug.'

'There's an open bottle of wine in the fridge.'

'Now you're speaking my language.' And she sashayed to the kitchen, singing her own lyrics to Sade's most sensual song, 'Drink is my drug' rather than '*Your love is king*'.

She came back with a large glass in one hand, the bottle in the other, and sat down beside me.

'Cheers,' she said, and I held my joint up to her glass.

'Cheers . . . Where you been?'

'Pub. With a friend. We had a fight. Fuck him.'

'Boyfriend, or friend?'

'If you mean, have I ever fucked him? Yes. Is he a boyfriend? No. He's not even a friend after tonight.'

'What happened?'

'Aw, who cares? Don't worry about it.'

I took another long draw on my joint, inhaled deeply, then blew out little gusts of smoke, aware she was watching me closely.

She laughed. 'You got any idea how big a dickhead you look doing that?' Now it was my turn to laugh, then I took another puff, inhaled even more deeply, created even more smoke, this time ending with a perfect smoke ring, through which she poked her finger, laughing, then finished her drink and poured another one.

'You sure you wouldn't prefer some of this?' I asked, holding out the joint once more. 'Got plenty more.'

'I told you,' she said, raising her glass, 'drink's my drug.'

When the next song came on, 'Smooth Operator', she said, 'Oh, I love this,' and she put her head on my shoulder so that I felt her hair fall across my face. She was moving her body slowly in time with the music and I glanced down to see the gentle rising and falling of her breasts. She had taken her bra off, presumably when getting her wine. I sensed real danger.

She stood, and she started to sway a little, at first I thought through drunkenness but then I realised she was dancing to the music, and she was adapting the lyrics again, not 'Smooth operator', but 'Drink is my drug, yeah, drink is my drug, yeah, drink is my drug, yeah . .' and as she sang, she came a few millimetres closer towards me with each 'yeah', at the end of each 'Smooth operator', so that as the song ended, her feet were touching mine, and her waist was so close I could have kissed it had I leaned forward an inch or two.

Instead, I pulled back, tried to signal a distancing from her, but either I wasn't clear enough, or she was too drunk to notice. She sat down beside me, and started to roll a joint. She'd clearly done it before, but after she licked it into shape, instead of smoking it herself, she put it between my lips, lifted the lighter from the table and lit me up.

'There you go, Danny boy, you suck on your drug, and I'll sip on mine,' and as she went through that single sentence, she spoke more and more quietly so that 'sip on mine' was no more than a whisper, her mouth now close to my ear, and as she said 'mine', she kissed my neck, then put her tongue into my ear, and slid her hand onto my thigh.

'Fuck's sake, Han, what are you doing?'

'It's Hannah, Dan. Only Sis calls me Han, nobody else. But you have other rights.' Her hand was now making long, slow movements up and down my thigh, and I was urging my dick not to respond, but that was a battle I had already lost, and I knew the only way I could stop this was to stand up, there and then, instantly, turn off the music, turn on the lights and say, 'No, Hannah, this is so wrong, no.' But I didn't stand up, I didn't move away, I just muttered the words 'No, Hannah, come on, this is wrong, so wrong', but with every second I stayed there, the harder it was going to be to move away, and she knew that too, and had her hand there and that same slow stroke was now working its way over my crotch. With her other hand she took hold of the joint, put it to my lips again and said, 'Come on, Dan, you suck on that, and I'll suck on you. You know you want me to.'

And I did want her to, though I also knew it was wrong, but even as I was about to say 'no, this is wrong', she flicked open the button on my trousers, the zip was down, her hand fished out my cock and her lips clasped it tight.

'No, Hannah, no.'

She sucked for a few seconds, then came up to look into my eyes, said, 'Yes, Dan, yes,' and kissed me.

'But your mum could walk through the door any time,' I said.

'I called her just before I got back in,' she said. 'She was still in Oxford. Promise.'

'Hannah, we're drunk, this is wrong, she's your mum, I'm her man, I might even marry her, you'll be my stepdaughter, this is just so wrong on every level.'

'Apart from the only one that counts right now, which is you want me and I want you, and I want to feel this inside me,' and with that she took my dick in her hand, put her tongue deep into my mouth, and I knew I was beyond saving.

'Do you want me to get a condom?' I said.

'Don't worry. I'm on the pill.'

She ripped off my clothes, and I hers, she straddled me and for those few wild minutes, 'Hang on to Your Love' as the backing soundtrack, Hannah whispering 'Drinking is my drug' every time Sade sang the title, I was lost in a physical joy that made me blind to the crazy risks I was taking. It ended, all too soon, and as I struggled to regain my breath, I just mumbled 'too good, too fucking good', over and over again.

And it was. As she lay there afterwards, her head on my shoulder, my cock still inside her but drained of all force by her riding on top of me, I stroked her back and said, 'Hannah, make me a promise. You'll never tell anyone what we just did. And you will never try to seduce me again.'

'I'll think about it,' she said, and she bit my ear. We lay there for a few more moments, and I was just thinking about stirring and clearing away the debris of drink and drugs, and tidying the sofa, picking up my clothes, when I heard the key enter the lock. I pushed Hannah from me, and Kate arrived to the sight of her daughter, naked, standing facing her, inches from her boyfriend, also naked, and she screamed 'What the fuck?' so loud that within seconds Vicki's bedroom door opened and she looked out to see her mother running towards her sister, throwing punches, saying 'you evil bitch, you evil, evil, evil little bitch', and Hannah was trying to grab her clothes from the floor, held them to her body like a shield, but she looked neither scared nor shocked. Then Kate turned her attention on me as I hurriedly tried to dress. 'How could you, how could you, how the fuck could you do this to me, my own fucking daughter, in my own home?' She picked up the music station, hauled it from its socket and threw it at me, landing on the wall behind the sofa where I had just been screwing her daughter. Vicki was standing pale-faced and crying, and not knowing who to help, who to hate. Finally she ran over to Hannah, put her arms around her and said, 'Come on, Han, let's go to our room.'

But just as Kate had reached a tipping point with Pat, so now she had reached it with Hannah. 'Yes,' she said. 'You go to your room, and you pack a bag, and you leave this house and if I never see you again, I don't give a flying fuck,' the last words said with such volume and venom that Vicki pushed Hannah behind her, like she was protecting a child in danger.

'Mum, Mum, listen, you can't do that. She's not evil, she's ill, and you shouldn't be punishing her, no matter what she's done, you should help her, we should all help her, because there's a good person in there, and we can find her.'

'I know she needs help, but I can't give it, because when it comes from me, she won't take it, and I can't keep taking the pain and the hate, and she can destroy her own life, she can drink herself to death if that's her choice, but she's not destroying me.'

And with that she collapsed to the floor, sobbing, her head sunk into her lap, and I was desperate to say something, anything, to ease her pain. But what could I say? Nothing. I had helped to cause the pain. I moved towards her but as soon as she felt the touch of my hand on her shoulder, she stood up, bolt upright now, the tears suddenly stopped, and she screamed at me, 'Don't you dare touch me, ever again, you're just as bad as her, you deserve each other, do you hear me? You're evil, you're evil, you're evil.' All the possible mitigation I could think of ran through my mind. I was high on drink and drugs. I had been led on. I had been used and manipulated by Hannah, who wanted to hurt her mum and punish me for loving her. Of course she hadn't phoned her. She never phoned her. I bet she wasn't on the pill either. But so what? There was nothing I could say. Kate was right. What I did was wrong, the worst thing I had ever done in my life. I just wanted out, and away.

Kate had recovered some of her composure, stood with a dignity that merely added to my shame, and spoke only to her younger daughter.

'Vicki, you're right she needs help. But she has to want it, and I can't give it. I have tried, but she has rejected me at every turn. I can't care for her any more.'

'Mum, you have to. She's your daughter, my sister. You have to.'

'I can't. I'm sorry. I know this hurts you too, Vicki, but I'm leaving here now, I'll spend the night at Grandma's, I'll be back at lunchtime tomorrow, and of the three people here, I only want to see one of them. The other two must leave. I'm sorry, but I insist.' With that, she moved to Vicki, touched her hand gently, stroked her face, then turned and walked out of the door.

Vicki collapsed on the floor, and wailed like a wounded animal. Hannah walked slowly to her room to pack her bag. I did the same, and left before she did. I never saw any of them again.

I asked to see my boss on Monday, and he agreed I could apply for the vacancy for regional sales director, North West. I moved three weeks later. I was based in Manchester but it meant regular visits to Liverpool, and every now and then I would see a man with a touch of the Hannah about him and wonder if it was Pat. Kate was the best sexual partner I ever had. But those memories were dwarfed by the memory of her calling Hannah evil, calling me evil, and at the time having right on her side. Even more powerful was the memory of the little smile playing on Hannah's lips, which minutes before had been sucking my dick, as she did so.

# JULIE

**My name is Julie. I am Hannah's aunt by marriage.**

Malcolm had made himself a plate of cold meats and salad
and taken it through to the TV room where he was about to
watch a football match, citing in his favour that as he had
tidied the leaves that morning, he was entitled to. He always
had different entitlement reasons, from 'profits are up this
quarter' to 'I painted the bedroom' to 'I managed to walk
down the stairs without falling over'. It was one of those little
running gags which, like sex and rows about washing-up, made
husband-and-wife relationships special and different. So far as
I could tell, he was undiscriminating about what the football
was; Manchester United, Real Madrid, Stevenage or Spartak
something or other, he would watch anything. Still, better that
than fall into any of his old ways which, touch wood, were
finally behind us.

Alan, our elder boy, was home from college for the weekend
with his girlfriend Fran, and I was sorting out his washing,
ready for him to head back to Southampton on Monday
morning. With his finals coming up, he was anxious, and I
was spoiling him even more than usual. Chris, who was in
his first year, had taken to university life better, and with

Newcastle being further away, he had not been home once apart from the holidays. Alan was doing a bit of work in his room, and Fran was sitting in the kitchen talking to me while I folded shirts, pants and sports gear. She was a lovely girl, but not academic – he had met her in the shoe shop where she was a bog-standard salesgirl – and she was telling me how hard Alan seemed to work, and how he was getting more and more het up, and it was a familiar story, like father like son, not in Malcolm's case through college work, but whenever he had a big decision, an important deadline or a new plan to hatch, he would work himself into a stew, and I was forever worrying he would relapse. So I counted my blessings that today all he seemed to want to do was veg out in front of the football, but worried about Alan being all work no play, with Fran having to talk to me more than him, and worried about Chris not seeming to need us at all. My own mother was forever telling me not to worry, that fretting only made things worse, but it was like telling waterfalls to stop sending rain into the rivers and seas. I was a neurotic middle-class mother who had made a nice life for herself and her family, and I was sure it would collapse around my ears any time soon.

Malcolm was totally dry now, and hadn't touched drugs for more than twenty years, three years before we met when he was a delivery man for a breadmaker in Cheshire, and I was training as a nutritionist at college. I had never taken drugs, never smoked cigarettes even. When we first started going out, and he told me about his addiction, how he started with cannabis, then graduated to cocaine, and in no time was on heroin and LSD, I was close to deciding to have nothing to do with him. I thought that if he had lost control of himself once, what was to prevent it from happening again? But he was such a charming man, and clever. He still had quite a lot of the Liverpool accent he grew up with, and the wit and street wisdom to go with it, and he had real drive too, had started his own plant-hire business with a loan and a rented one-roomed office, and by the time we were married had twelve people on the payroll, and a five-year plan to double then quadruple turnover, and I can honestly say this: he has exceeded every target every year. 'Underclaim, overdeliver' was his motto, and he lived up to it, in business at least and, most of the time, in our family life too. We have a lovely five-bedroomed house in Ponders End, with planning permission for a pool under way, and we owe it all to his hard work and recovery.

When he was in rehab up in Liverpool, it was in one of the first places that treated drugs and drink as a double addiction, but though he kicked drugs almost without a fight, he found drink harder. One of the reasons we moved to London was to help him get away from all his old haunts. Also, his brother and my two sisters had all moved south, so it wasn't as if we wouldn't know anyone.

When we were courting, he was a regular but not heavy drinker, but he was capable of unleashing himself on a real bender now and then, and it was hard to live with, not because he treated me badly – he didn't and in some ways he was more loving when he'd had a few – but because the anxiety I had about him going back on drugs would increase, and I suppose I became a nag, though it was for all the best reasons. His drugs era was before my time. He had essentially faced the choice between a possible jail sentence for a series of thefts to pay for cocaine and heroin, or an enforced stay in a rehab centre. It worked, and by the time I met him he was not only clean, but volunteering once a month at the place that sorted him out, Ashford House, where they encouraged their success stories to go back and talk to the current addicts. Malcolm has always had the gift of the gab, and he got on well with most of the patients, or 'residents' as the staff liked to call them, though the manager, Audley Parr, didn't like Malcolm to mention that he still drank from time to time. He wanted the message from the former residents to be 'Look at me, I was where you were once, but thanks to this place, I am fine, happy, healthy, my life back together again, and you can do the same.'

Malcolm worried about his drink lapses as much as I did, and when he was trying to stop, he would recall the lecture he got from Audley when he first told him he was 'off the drugs totally, off the drink mainly'. 'Addiction is like pregnancy. You either are or you aren't. With pregnancy, you can choose – abortion or birth. With addiction, the choice is just as stark – take the substance of addiction, or don't. There is no middle way.' I was with Audley on that one. But Malcolm was sure he could keep it under control until, one day, about the time Alan was going to senior school, he phoned me and said, 'Julie, I'm at Ashford House. I hope you don't mind, but I'm booking myself in again, for a month.'

Mind? I cried, with joy, with relief that just as he had faced up to his drugs problem, now he was doing the same with drink, and I just knew he meant it this time, that he would show the same determination he had brought to bear in making his business work, and in making his marriage work. He asked me to go to the office the next morning, get his chief executive to call in all the directors and staff for a meeting, and tell them where he was, and why. He had always been open about his challenges, and he wanted to set an example about openness at work too. I felt very emotional telling them the story, but held it together, and there was a warm round of applause when I finished.

He was not even drinking heavily at the time, but he knew that if anything bad happened, he was capable of falling off the cliff. When he told his brother he had checked himself in 'to sort out the drink same as I did the drugs', Pat was amazed. Having seen him almost kill himself with hard drugs, Pat felt the Malcolm who still enjoyed a couple of beers, wine with dinner, champagne on special occasions, was home and dry in the battle with addiction. But as an addict, Malcolm knew differently. As he spoke from Ashford House, and told me I could only visit at weekends, and there were family therapy sessions if I fancied them, he said he had been waking up thinking of drink, telling himself he would have a dry day, getting as far as dinner, and then cracking. To him, one or two glasses of wine was as significant a signal of addiction as a bottle of meths. He planned most days not to drink, and every day that the plan failed, he knew the addiction was digging in. 'I've also been drinking on my own,' he said. 'Again, nothing extreme or extravagant, and I doubt you even noticed, but it has to stop.'

'It will, darling. You've done it before and you can do it again. I'll support you whatever happens. Oh, and by the way, I had noticed.'

With the drugs, it helped that they were illegal. He often told the boys he was lucky not to have gone to jail, and once he came out of Ashford the first time, he said any temptation to go back was tempered not just by what he learned there, and how much better he felt, but by the worry that, if he did succumb, he would be straight back into his old habits, and end up in jail.

'The thing with drugs is that because of your upbringing, and because of the law, you know it's wrong. That doesn't make a blind bit of difference when you're mid-addiction, but when you're stopping it helps. With drink, it's almost as though the right thing to do is drink, the wrong thing to do is not drink. You try being in a business like mine, and not drink. Meet for lunch, drink on the agenda. Meet in a pub, drink. Meet in an office, fancy a Scotch or a brandy? Dinner, drink. And then you imagine just driving around, trying to give up drink, wishing the world was dry. Every other poster, alcohol. Ads on the radio, alcohol. Switch to the sport – sponsored by alcohol. Either end of every parade of shops, and staring out at you are shelves upon shelves of booze, two for one, reduced prices, reduced even more in the super-markets. Stop to get petrol, and you can say don't drink and drive all you like, but what chance does the alkie have when you can buy booze at the fucking garage? It's crazy. Imagine trying to give up drugs and having to face down an avalanche of marketing and advertising and sponsorship! These drinks boys don't do it for their good health. They do it because they know how to tempt us, and there are only so many times you can say no before you succumb. And I've been doing it too often of late, and I'm staying here until I feel about booze the way I feel about drugs.'

'Malcolm, I want you to know I love you very much, and I am very proud of what you're doing.'

'Will you tell the boys?'

'Of course I will.'

Once he was both clean and dry, he often said to the boys that giving up drugs was his 'proudest achievement – second only to drink' and I used to worry that glamorised it, but neither Alan nor Chris seemed to have gone down the same road, at least not to excess so far as I could surmise. Not that parents ever know the full story about what their children get up to; which is why I was asking Fran how Alan handled the pressure, and whether she ever worried he would follow in his dad's footsteps. 'No way,' she said. 'He's jihadic about the drug dealers at college, and if I've seen him drunk twice, that's as much as I can remember. He just wants to qualify as an engineer, and get himself a job, I don't think you've got any worries there, Julie.' I was less sure about Chris. I had read so much about addiction when Malcolm was in treatment, and when I went for help myself, because of the effect his drinking bouts were having on me, and the words 'genetic' and 'hereditary' kept popping up in my readings and conversations.

Fran asked if she could make herself a cup of tea, and she was putting on the kettle when the front doorbell went.

'Get that, will you, love?' Malcolm shouted through. 'QPR have got a corner.'

'You expecting anyone?' I shouted back.

'No.'

'Fran, do me a favour, would you, and just see who it is?' I put all Alan's clothes into a giant striped plastic bag, took it upstairs and left it outside his room so as not to disturb him. As I got back to the top of the stairs, I could hear Fran nervously engaging with a young woman on the doorstep. It sounded like it might be a God botherer. I got halfway down the stairs before I realised it was Hannah. She had two big canvas bags with her, one either side, and looked like she hadn't slept. I tried to recall the last time I saw her, and I think it was the Christmas before last.

'Hannah, what is it, what's happened?' and I helped her in as Fran picked up the bags and placed them in the hall by Malcolm's golf clubs, which I had been asking him to put in the cellar since he played on Thursday. Malcolm emerged from the lounge, picking up on the unexpected arrival, and he too saw immediately that she was in a bad way, and followed us through to the kitchen.

'What's happened, love?' he asked, as she sat down.

'I'm so sorry, I really am, I didn't know where to go. I tried to call Dad, but he's not answering, so I just . . . I just hoped you might let me stay here for a day or two till I sort things out.'

'Of course you can, Hannah,' he said, 'but where's your mum and your sister?'

'She kicked me out,' she said, and as she did so, I could see her body swelling with a wave of emotion, fear and anger mixed in her eyes, her bottom teeth biting into her top lip, she was trying to hold it all in but suddenly she started to cry in huge chest-heaving sobs. All three of us went to her.

'Hannah, what's happened? Tell us what's happened,' I said.

'I can't,' she said. 'I can't. It's too awful.'

Malcolm took her hand, forced her to look at him, and said, 'You're not in trouble with the law, are you?'

'No, nothing like that.'

'So you've had a row and she's kicked you out. But she'll have you back. Sure of it.'

'She won't, I promise you, and anyway, I'm not sure it's good for any of us I'm there.'

'Do you want me to talk to her?'

'No, please don't, not yet.'

'Where's your dad?'

'No idea, thought you might know.'

'No, I've not seen him for a while, but we'll find him, don't you worry about that.'

Fran gave her the tea she was going to make for herself and as Hannah took it, and said thank you, the sobbing subsided, and she started to tell us.

'Mum and I haven't got on that well for ages, and I know I must be a nightmare to live with, and she thinks I drink too much, but I honestly never thought she would throw me out.'

'But it must be more than drink, Hannah. She can't throw you out just because you drink too much.'

'She has. She said she can't take the hurt and the pain I cause her any more.'

'Surely she wouldn't do something as drastic as that without talking to your dad. Doesn't he get a say in this?'

'We hardly ever see him, to be fair. He and Mum don't speak, and when Vicki and I see him, we're all going through the motions. He's not a dad like you are to Alan and Chris.'

As she said that, it dawned on me how our own little family was fairly tight – though I was a tiny bit hurt Chris seemed to be wandering away – but so far as the broader family was concerned, we were not close at all. When they were very small, the boys would see Hannah and Vicki a few times a year, but once they were in senior school, if they saw each other once or twice a year, that was a lot. Malcolm saw Pat every few months, but that had slowed since Malcolm went completely dry, and avoided pubs, and neither of them got on terribly well with their mum, so hardly ever went back North. But I felt bad, both for Kate and for Hannah, that things had reached this point, and we hadn't even known there was a problem at all. She wasn't yet eighteen, for heaven's sake, not old enough to drink, yet seemingly so in its grip that she had been kicked out of house and home.

Fran was wonderful with her, had a lovely easy manner, which must come from all that small talk with customers in the shoe shop, sat alongside her and got her talking, and once Alan joined us, pleased to see his cousin but probably irritated it was eating into study time, it reminded me of the Al-Anon meetings I went to, when I had been finding Malcolm's lapses harder and harder to deal with.

The mood followed the rhythm of a bereavement. Shock when she arrived bearing unexpected bad news. Tears as reality hit home. Explanation and analysis as Fran and Malcolm coaxed out as much detail from her as they could. Then reminiscing, and finally a little humour.

'I'll never forget the day you were born,' I said. 'You'd have thought your dad was the one who had to put up with all the pain. But he was so proud of you, and so happy, I thought it would be the making of him.'

''Fraid not. He has his own addiction issues, and they're not the same ones Uncle Malcolm and I have.'

Malcolm put his hand on her shoulder. 'Do you think you're addicted, Hannah?'

'I don't know. I know I drink too much. But I don't know about addiction. I don't know. Don't think so. Think I could stop, if I had to, like you did.'

'Took me a long time, though, and I did a lot of damage

on the way. One thing I know though, Hannah, it didn't make a jot of difference other people telling me I had a problem. I only faced it down when I admitted to myself I had a problem. That's the step you have to take, and I'm not sure you're there.'

She clasped her hands together, and put her thumbs between her teeth, and bit on them.

'If I said to you, last night was the last time you could ever have a drink, what do you feel?' Malcolm asked.

'Scared.'

'What kind of scared?'

'Panic.'

'Because?'

'Don't know, just do, feels scary, not normal.'

'So you drink to feel normal?'

'I drink because how I feel when I'm not drinking doesn't feel normal, doesn't feel right.'

'And when you drink?'

'I forget.'

'And when you stop?'

'I hate myself.'

'And you have a drink to feel better again?'

She nodded.

Malcolm pulled her towards him and hugged her. 'I've been where you are, Hannah. You're not on your own. There are people in this street, this town, every town in this country, every country in the world, who are sitting where you are now. But no matter how much I have done it, and others have done it, each and every one of them has to make a decision for themselves, and that includes you. You understand that, don't you?'

'Yes.' She was crying again.

'So do you think you have a problem? And do you want to do something about it.'

The tears flowed. But she said nothing.

Vicki came round on Sunday evening with Hannah's things for school, and her friend Sophie came to help her with an essay, and the three of them sat with Fran and went over the whole story again. However, we didn't get the complete picture until several weeks later when Hannah came into my bedroom, where I was making the bed after Malcolm had left for work. Hannah had improved in the first few days with us, and with both the boys away I enjoyed having another young person around the house. We finally got hold of Pat a week later. He had got a new job working on a caravan site near Cambridge, and there had been no mobile reception. He managed to combine the sound of concern for Hannah, hatred of Kate, and gratitude to me and Malcolm, with compelling reasons as to why he couldn't do much to help. Malcolm and I agreed to a maximum stay of four months, which would take us to the summer, and then she had to find somewhere else to live. But by the end of the first month, we were already seeing why Kate had flipped out. She had her own key, but I found it impossible to sleep until she was in, and I would hear her stumbling around downstairs when she came in late, go down to try to talk to her, but get little sense. Then in the mornings she would be full of remorse and Malcolm would have another go at persuading her she had to get help. Then it would happen again, and again, and again, until Malcolm was beginning to lose patience. When I told him she had vomited all over the car bonnet, and slept on the doorstep having failed to get her key in the lock, he decided four months meant three.

But before we even got there, she came in, stood by my bedroom door, and said simply, 'Auntie Julie, I'm pregnant.'

# KISHORI

**My name is Kishori. I am the nurse who carried out Hannah's abortion.**

I absolutely love my job, and I won't have anyone tell me I am not doing a good thing. Good for my girls, and good for the country, and I am so proud to be British that my motto in life is 'If it's good for Britain it's good for the world.'

Hannah came in on a Monday morning, number 4 on the NHS list. We're a private sexual health, family-planning, sterilisation and reproduction clinic in Kilburn, but if you're passing by, what stands out on the signage is the word 'vasectomy', because of all the things we do, that's the least stigmatised. Sexual health? I think we all know what that means when you come to a place like this. Clap, clap, clap. Sterilisation? Sounds like something Hitler liked. Abortion? Well, there are almost a couple of hundred thousand of them in the country every year, but the stigma is still there, and even if Britain doesn't have all those nut jobs in America who go round slashing tyres on cars driven by people like me, and sending turds and bullets through the post with lovely messages like 'How'd you like it if we killed YOUR child, murderer?' it is still a political potato capable of periodic hotting up. We discovered that when we had a demonstration here, shortly after I started – I didn't take it personally – mainly Irish sorts and fanatical pro-lifers (like, I'm anti-life, am I?), after a Freedom of Information release revealed we were the second biggest clinic in the country for Irish girls coming over. One of our doctors got hit by a placard and we had to cancel a couple of abortions because we were busy fixing his broken nose and jaw, so I suppose the protesters could count that as a good hour's work. We got called in for an all-staff meeting, and a retired major called Barrington, who was so wet he made me feel about as secure as a blind man walking through a field of landmines, came in to talk to us about car bombs and how we mustn't watch TV with our backs to the window, and we all felt momentarily scared, and then carried on as per. You can't live your life looking under your car with an upturned mirror every time you drive down to the shops, for heaven's sake, and I reckoned if Inaction Man Barrington had survived all these threats, someone as smart as me would be OK.

We're private sector but we do get a lot of NHS patients. They go to their GP like Hannah did after doing a do-it-yourself test, or come through Brook, get told all the options, and we've marketed ourselves well, everyone who might want us knows we're here, despite the vasectomy blind, so most girls locally will pick us, and there are lots like Hannah who like to do it a few miles from their own backyard. So we bill the NHS monthly, and it really is a cash cow. Certainly, all the fancy-suit boss-class brigade look happy enough when they fly in from Switzerland.

I was born in Ealing, west London, second-generation Indian, but it annoys me when people ask me what part of India I'm from. The answer is I'm not from India and I've lived here all my bloody life. I'm as British as the Queen. In fact, as I have only been abroad once – to north-west India for my grandfather's funeral – and the Queen gads about the world all the time, as a proportion of life spent in this country, I am more British than Her Maj, someone I love and respect dearly. I will cry when she dies, I know that already.

If someone in a shop asks how long I've lived here, I'll have a right old pop. When girls at the clinic do, like Hannah did, I make allowances. It doesn't matter how hard a girl is, how street-smart, how uncaring even, an abortion is an abortion and it is a big bad thing to go through, and my job as the nurse is also to be a counsellor, make them feel at ease, help them live with the decision they've made, so I go easy on them when they talk to me like I'm foreign.

'I was born and bred here,' I said. 'Went to school in Acton, straight As, could have gone to Oxbridge but always wanted to be a nurse, trained at UCH, did two years there in A & E, three years on the wards at Hammersmith, then had a friend who worked at this place, and was earning way more than I was, so here I am. My mum still thinks I'm on the wards, wouldn't approve of this, and I can't be bothered to explain.'

We were doing the chit-chat thing that most girls do when they have been admitted, the GP's referral and the two doctors' signatures have been checked out as legit, and you're about to do the medical tests and take them through exactly what will happen.

'Seems busy in here,' she said.

'Oh my godfather, some days it's like Delhi bloody railway station. If any of the staff go down sick, we can be pushed, I tell you, but don't worry, I am your dedicated nurse for the time being, and we'll give you all the care and attention you need, and you'll be out of here right as rain before you can say "Where did I put those bloody condoms?"'

'You don't seem very Indian,' she said, which was pushing her luck, another lazy, close to being bigoted, 'can't be British if you're not white' comment, but I put it down to nerves.

'Wot? Cos oi tork loik this, all ow's your father, apples and pears?'

'Well, I suppose, maybe. The Indian girls at my school are also quite, er, reserved. Very hard-working, but reserved.'

'Well, first, miss, I ain't Indian. I am as British as you are, and more British than the Queen. Second, I am hard-working. And third, there ain't no point being reserved in this job, because you and I are going to be getting very personal very soon when the suction starts.'

'I didn't mean to give offence.'

'None taken, my love. Now come on, we'd better start on this.'

She didn't want to talk too much about how she came to be there, said she was pretty sure she knew who the father was – you'd be amazed how many don't – but no, he wasn't aware and she didn't want him to be. We did the usual tests. Both her pulse and blood pressure were a bit high and I told her to keep an eye on that. I asked her how her diet was. 'Pretty good,' she said.

'Smoke?'

'Only when I'm out.'

'Drink? Drugs?'

'Never taken drugs. Do drink, but so does everyone my age, just about.'

'Drinking when this happened?'

''Fraid so, yes. First time it's happened, though.'

'Well, try and make sure it's the last. We have some women through here so often, they might as well have their name on the bed. You'd think they'd have worked out how it happens by now, eh, love?' Hannah laughed at that, chuckled anyway. She had a lovely face when she relaxed a little, and there is nothing more relaxing than laughter. That's the secret to my nursing technique. Relax them with small talk, amuse them with stories and banter, but always level with them about what's going on, and make sure they know that I know what I'm doing.

There are three basic ways to do an abortion, but it's amazing how long the image of gin and knitting needles has endured. Hannah didn't even know it was possible to do it with medication, two doses a few hours apart, mifegyne and misoprostol, with the pregnancy dropping out not long after the second dose. We only do that for up to nine weeks, though, and the scan showed she was closer to twelve, so Hannah had to go for suction, and I had a doctor in with me for that. I think if ever I had one, I'd get in early so I could go for the pills, but I never say that. If they leave it too late, say fifteen weeks, it gets more complicated, and you have to stretch the cervix. I only told her that so she'd be relieved when I said we wouldn't need to do it.

It's not without pain, but really no worse than intense period pains, which pass quickly enough, so I try to steer them towards doing it without major anaesthetic, which can screw your head up for ages. All of it is very much their decision, as we don't allow anyone else in with them. I don't care who they are – parents, siblings, friends – they only get in the way, so no thanks, you can drop off and we will give you a collection time, but we don't need you hanging around all day, and no, there isn't a visitors' car park. I'm not being harsh, just practical. They don't help, so I don't want them around.

Hannah agreed to do it with only mild sedation. The ones who go for heavier anaesthetics tend to be using it to take their minds off whatever situation it was that landed them here, and the life they'll be heading back to. Hannah was what I would call stoic. She listened, followed every instruction without ever needing me to say the same thing twice, and though she looked upset, I didn't sense it was because she fancied a shot at motherhood and the chance was being taken away from her. She just had very sad eyes when she was in repose.

'Will I need some time in bed afterwards?' she asked.

'No, you'll be right as rain tomorrow. If you don't feel so good, maybe rest up, but you look fit as a horse to me, so I'm betting you'll be back at work in no time. What do you do?'

'I'm still at school.'

'Do they not teach you girls about contraception in sex education?'

'Yes, but sometimes things happen you can't control.'

'Well, I guess if that wasn't so, I'd still be doing dressings and injections at Hammersmith.'

'Do you like this job?'

'Well, nobody can say we don't make a difference, can they? Your life would be very very different if you weren't here with me today, and I like to think I'm changing your life for the better.'

'Hope so,' she said.

'We're helping the country too. When any of our rich private patients complain about having to share with "poor people" I always say the few hundred quid used up by the NHS is money well spent for all that'll be saved on welfare and child benefit and what have you. So I don't have to defend my work to anyone, even if I can't bring myself to tell my mother.'

'Mums, eh?'

'Aw, she's lovely, but the world she was raised in is so different to mine, a place called Pali in Rajasthan, and it's best just to be honest about that, and a little bit dishonest about the things I know we won't agree on. Now, how are you feeling?'

'Is it all done?' she asked.

'It sure is. Not nearly as bad as you thought, was it?'

'No. Thank you.'

I busied around her clearing everything up, making her tidy, assuring her there were strict procedures to follow with regard to disposal of the foetus, and I didn't need to go through all that unless she was particularly keen to know. She wasn't. So I zipped into my usual little post-procedure talking-to. 'Don't be surprised if you have a bit of a dip in your mood, it's almost inevitable. What you've done is not easy. If you feel particularly down, we have post-abortion counselling services. No sex for a fortnight, because there could be an infection, and if you do it before that, you could fall pregnant again. So just don't do it, and if you do, use a bloody condom. You'll bleed a bit, don't worry, and don't use tampons unless it's your period. If you're still bleeding after a month, come and see me, and don't be upset if you get stomach cramps, clots and a horrible-smelling discharge. I'll give you a fact sheet with all this, but always best to hear it.'

'Thank you.'

'You might get irregular periods for a while. Of course, a missed period could mean a repeat pregnancy – though not if you use those condoms, OK, get the picture, get with the programme – but it is also possible to get a positive pregnancy test when you're not pregnant because the hormones from the one you've just lost are still kicking around. Does that make sense?'

'It does. Thank you.'

'My pleasure. And here, young Hannah, listen to me,' I said, as I passed her a box of standard-issue condoms, 'take these and keep a few in your handbag if you're ever going out on the razzle-dazzle in a testosterone zone, aka the whole bloody world, from Kilburn to Karachi.'

'Thanks, I will. Promise.'

'Anything else you're worried about?'

'Does it go on my medical records?'

'Ah, I'm afraid so. If you had come direct, or gone through family planning, we could have got round it. But you were referred by your GP and we have to write and tell him the procedure is done. Still, you'll know next time,' and I laughed, and she beat me to it –

'There won't be a next time if I use the condoms,' she said, also laughing, this time more freely.

'Thanks for making this so painless,' she said. 'What's your name?'

'I told you that when I met you. Kishori.'

'Kishori? That's a new one on me. It's lovely.'

'Yes, I am pure British but my name is pure Indian. It means "young girl", but I get to keep it when I'm old.'

'I can't imagine you being old.'

'Oh, I'll be old one day. We all get old, Hannah. There are not many certainties in life, but that's one of them.'

# JULIAN

**My name is Julian. I am a QC and the father of Sophie, Hannah's best friend at school.**

I was not best pleased to hear Hannah was back at the house. I was preparing for a very big case defending a Department of Work and Pensions official, Eliot Connell, who had leaked a policy paper exposing the true intent of the government with regard to benefit cuts. It was hugely complicated, with a mass of technical information and legal points I wanted to tease out from the contents of the research papers to my fingertips and then to the innermost recesses of my brain. I am a detail person. I am a preparation person, which is why I have a framed quotation from Benjamin Franklin on my study wall, a copy of which I gave all my children as they came of age . . . 'By failing to prepare, you are preparing to fail.' It was a philosophy which led to me becoming head boy at Highgate, getting to Oxford, a first-class law degree, pupillage with Adrian Murtagh, who went on to be the finest silk of his generation, silk myself at the age of forty, a string of high-profile wins to my name, head of chambers, a judgeship only a matter of time. The kind of preparation I had in mind for this latest case was not compatible with having a teenage psychodrama playing out in the house, and one which risked having a deleterious effect on my own teenage daughter's already downgraded aspirations for a good degree.

However, Amanda and Sophie are the sort of people who, if they see a rabbit limping by the roadside, will stop the car, retrieve the injured bunny and drive it to the nearest animal sanctuary. My attitude would be that the rabbit wouldn't be limping in the first place if it wasn't stupid enough to hang around a dual carriageway in one of the most populated urban centres on this great planet of ours, and the lack of brain power thus revealed explains why it is rightly so low down the species power pecking order.

I knew something was up the moment I walked through the door. Isn't that remarkable, how you can park the car, close the garage door, walk through a garden untouched since the last time you saw it in the morning, go up the steps to the front door, open it, and, before you have set sight on a single soul, or heard a word your lovely wife has said, you know, you just know, that something has changed since you kissed her goodbye and headed into chambers? I could smell it the second I took my key from my pocket.

'Julian, is that you, darling?' That was another sign. I wonder if she realised she had different verbal tics according to which part of the house she was in. Normally, if she was in the kitchen, it was 'Hiya, I'm in here'. If she was in the lounge, it was 'In the lounge, darling', and if she was upstairs it was a loud 'Yoo-hoo, down in a tick'. 'Julian, is that you, darling?' meant trouble, so my sensors were up and active from the off.

'We're in the kitchen.'

'We're . . .' This was getting worse.

The 'we' turned out to be Amanda and Sophie, who smiled

but it was a smile shorn of its usual warmth and confidence. She looked unusually earnest and preoccupied. When Amanda asked me to sit down, and poured me my usual gin and tonic at least half an hour before my normal time – I like to change into slacks and a less stuffy shirt for dinner first – I was prepared for ghastly news, though I confess Hannah did not cross my mind. Amanda's father had been in for blood tests at the Cromwell, and I thought perhaps the results had come back bad; or one of our grown-up kids had had an accident, or was about to produce a sprog – but that would have been an Amanda in the hallway as soon as I arrived, beaming from ear to ear, Veuve Clicquot at the ready, with one of her 'you won't believe the good news?' shrieks. So what else could it be? Had our broker called and said that last investment went belly up, or was Sophie planning to tell me some mumbling oik of a teenage boyfriend was about to move in? None of the above, I learned soon enough.

'I really want you to try and help on this, Julian, and be understanding, but you remember Sophie's friend Hannah –'

'Hard to forget when you're throwing a smelly mattress on the skip –'

'OK, but listen, she's really not well and Sophie's worried about her, and also I think with all my medical contacts and what have you, we think we can help her, and so I would just like you to accept her for a little while.'

'What do you mean, accept?'

'Well, she's upstairs resting, but I've said she can stay here just while she sorts herself out and gets better.'

I knew I was going to go along with it, because when Amanda is in this calm, straightforward, bunny-rabbit-rescue mode, she has such a warmth and sincerity to her that, for all my grumbling, I find her irresistible. But it didn't mean I wasn't going to ask the difficult questions.

'What sort of ill?'

'Well, I would say she has quite a serious alcohol addiction problem.'

'Oh, great, so perhaps we should bulk-order a few mattresses.'

'Dad, can you just listen?'

'I'm listening, Sophie. But forgive me if I sometimes think alcohol addiction is little more than a medical term for lack of discipline and self-control, plus poor parenting.'

'She is basically a lovely girl, darling, but she needs a bit of help.'

'Why doesn't she just stop drinking?'

'It's not always so easy. How would you be if there was no G and T when you get home from work, and none of your favourite Vouvray on the table night after night?'

'Oh, for heaven's sake, how can you possibly equate my drinking with hers? That is absurd. When have I ever come home vomiting or rolling around the floor or peeing myself?'

'It's only a question of scale. You need your little rituals, she needs hers. The point is she has nowhere else to go.'

'What about her parents, for crying out loud? She didn't come from under the stork.'

'Her father is working away, and anyway seems to be a bit of a wastrel, and her mother has kicked her out.'

'Kicked her out? Well, that's quite a signal of what we might have to deal with, when I have a case that is going to be front-page stuff, "Lawyer of the Year" material if it goes well.'

'Darling, you have your study. You will be fed and watered and cherished as usual. We will keep the rest of the house as quiet as possible. I just want her to stay here for a while, go to school with Sophie, come back from school with Sophie, eat with us, they can do their homework together and meanwhile I am going to find her someone to see about her drinking.'

'She's not even drinking age, Amanda. Sometimes I wonder why we have all these bloody laws when nobody pays a blind bit of notice to them, and here we are, the family of JH QC, widely tipped to be a High Court judge within the year, conspiring to reward her for years of teenage excess and law-breaking.'

Sophie had sat silent in the main, but she could tell I was relenting. She knew me far too well. It was probably the pomposity that signalled it, and Amanda having done the softening up, Sophie moved in.

'Dad, we know you have a big case on, because we've read about it in the papers, and everyone said how worried the government is that hotshot Harper has taken up the case of the leaker. But we also know that underneath all that wig-and-gown front, you're a loving, lovely man, and when Hannah is around we're just asking we see a bit more of that, and a bit less of JH QC at Highgate Golf Club telling his buddies what's wrong with the world. Is that OK?'

It's hard to push back on that kind of flattery. 'I can see I'm outnumbered. But I'm the head of the household, and I can make conditions. One, you must agree limits to what she can drink before coming in, and in my view that should be no more than three units. Two, under no circumstances is she bringing home boys. If there's one thing I cannot cope with it's drunken youths. Charles Moreton let his son have a party recently and by the morning Charlie had lost a watch from his bedside table, a pinkie ring from the mantelpiece and a watercolour sketch from the bathroom wall. I would trust Sophie on the kind of youth she might bring in, but you must agree, someone who drinks as much as Hannah does could bring in any old riff-raff, and I am not having it. Three, I must be entitled to make a judgement as to whether this is affecting your schoolwork, Sophie, and thus your chances of getting to university, in my view already imperilled by your decision to go to this damned state school, and if I make the judgement that it is, she must leave, and there is no right of appeal. Fourth, there must be a time limit to this arrangement, and I think Christmas would be a reasonable deadline for her to establish her own long-term arrangements.'

'Perhaps New Year,' said Amanda. 'I think throwing her out at Christmas might be a bit harsh.'

'OK, well, let's see if we get that far.'

Sophie stood up, and threw her arms around me, kissed my head and said she loved me. But just as abruptly she pulled away, and put her hands to her mouth. As she looked to the door, I turned to follow her gaze, and there was Hannah, standing in a pair of flowery pyjama bottoms and a sleeveless red T-shirt I recognised as Sophie's.

'Oh my God,' I said. I just couldn't hold in the words. Her hair was matted down on her head, her skin was a browny-yellow colour, her face thinner than I remembered it and she had dark bags under eyes now drained of life and energy. Worse, I noticed twin scars on her right arm, from which trickles of blood were flowing. Sophie went towards her, picking up a kitchen roll on the way, and as she helped Hannah clean herself up, I could tell that it wasn't the first time she had done it. I noticed a line of old scars on her upper arm, neat, evenly spaced, like slivers of bodies wrapped and lined up in a morgue.

Amanda poured her a glass of water as Sophie led her to the table, barefoot, shuffling.

'Hello, Hannah,' I said. 'This isn't so good, is it?'

'No, Mr Harper. I'm really sorry, I really am.'

'Well, not to worry, let's just see if we can't help you get better.'

'Thank you.'

We ate together later, Hannah now thankfully wearing a long-sleeved yellow cashmere sweater I had bought for Sophie at Edinburgh airport a few weeks before when I was up for a conference on the potential implications of independence on the various legal systems of the UK. It is a much more complicated field than might commonly be imagined and my main point was that the politicians seemed not to have thought it through. I was feeling quite pleased with myself, even had the legal correspondent of the *Scotsman* telling me he was planning to write his column on my speech, so I was in generous mood when I had an hour to kill at the airport, bought Amanda a lovely piece of Celtic jewellery, and Sophie a sweater that I made the mistake of taking to the till before checking the price. Oh, what the hell, I'd had a good day and she had been doing really well at school, so she deserved it. I was a little surprised to see Hannah wearing it, but both Amanda and Sophie were showering her with love right now.

She barely ate, despite Amanda's constant exhortations. I counted two spoonfuls of leek and potato soup going in, the bread on her side plate untouched, and perhaps three small bits of the lamb shank, and half a potato. She kept apologising to Amanda for not eating, said her stomach felt tight and shrunken and knotted, and she was worried she would be sick again.

'I'd be surprised if there's anything left by now,' said Sophie.

It turned out she had done another middle-of-the-night arrival, this time with luggage. She'd been staying at a relative's house but had gone back there very drunk, been sick, had a row, and either left or been asked to leave, she seemed unsure. Apparently her uncle was also an alcoholic, and trying hard to stay off it, so he had a booze ban in the house, and she broke it by going home with two bottles of cider for what she called 'a little nightcap'.

I couldn't imagine how someone so slim could consume the quantities she did. I remember when I was a young junior barrister being led by a prominent silk in the case of a man who murdered his wife because she switched channels on TV, and the only defence was that he was incapable of knowing what he was doing because of the amount of alcohol he had taken on board. Twelve pints of beer, a bottle of Scotch, a bottle of cider – it was Amanda telling me of Hannah's cider carry-out that reminded me – and, in a detail which allowed the brief to suggest madness as well as inebriation, a half-pint cocktail of milk, Pernod, his own aftershave and his wife's perfume. 'I don't recommend you try this at home, members of the jury,' the judge said, a moment which stuck with me because of the exaggerated obsequious laughter it produced from all around the courtroom, something I looked forward to when I became a judge myself. Frankly, I never thought the defence stood a chance, and so it proved, and the man was sent away for a minimum of twelve years, but until now it was the high watermark of my drinking stories. Given her tender age, Hannah was already pushing him close.

I reflected on what Amanda had said with regard to my own consumption. 'I challenge you,' she had said, 'to take a month of your life, do all the same things you always do, same work patterns, same social and leisure stuff, and just take drink out of the equation – could you do it?' I admitted that no, I probably couldn't, because I didn't want to. It was true that I had a large G and T and two or three glasses of wine every night of my life. So I tried to imagine how I would feel if for whatever reason – let's say we were invaded by the Saudis – the Queen and Parliament were replaced by Islamic law strictly imposed so that Britain became a dry country and I was to be deprived of those little treats in my life. How would I feel? Not very happy, to be blunt. So I was dependent on those drinks for the oiling of a reasonably contented life. 'It doesn't make me a bloody alcoholic,' I'd said. Amanda had said it was a question of scale, and perhaps she was right. But I wouldn't be capable, physically or psychologically, of putting away the quantities Hannah could. I drink to bring about mild positive changes in mood and help me unwind at the end of the day, and I never lose control. What little I knew about dangerous drinking – mainly gleaned from my early days as a criminal barrister, when drink and drugs seemed to crop up in virtually every case of GBH, ABH, mugging, domestic violence, child abuse, death on the roads, you name it – led me to believe Hannah drank to destroy her life, rather than improve it. The self-harm, which Sophie told me was a recent phenomenon, after she had had men trouble of some sort, confirmed me in that view. I vowed to be as sympathetic as possible, and told Amanda I was all for trying to help her stop. But my main concern was what it was that Sophie saw in her that made them so close, and the possible influence she might have, not least on her schoolwork. I was frankly worried enough, as I told her many times, about her leaving a private school full of girls of good breeding, to go to the local comp.

Day one back at school seemed to be fine, though Hannah had been called in to explain a series of unauthorised absences. That was the first I heard of the abortion. 'God alive, Amanda, an abortion?! What are we dealing with here? This is getting well out of my comfort zone. Who was the father?'

'Some questions are best not asked.'

'Christ, we're not talking incest, are we?'

'Oh, for heaven's sake, Julian, stop imagining the worst. No, we are not. All we need to know is she had an abortion, it appears to have made her even more depressed, and that's probably what unleashed the two-day binge that brought her here.'

'It's quite hard not to imagine the worst. We've gone from a pissed bed to blood on the carpet because of self-harm, via abortion and expulsion by two members of her family, in pretty sharp order. I am a lawyer, Amanda, not a bloody social worker, and I dread to think what comes next.'

What came next was another good day at school, Hannah beginning to look better, and she and Sophie working hard on history after dinner. And what came after that was a visit from one of Amanda's colleagues, a stern but clearly highly professional and rather handsome woman, Clare Lister, who worked at Lambeth Hospital, the psychiatric place in Clapham, and who Amanda knew through a 'Women in Leadership' conference organised by the NHS to encourage more women to go for senior positions in management.

She arranged for her to come round on Wednesday evening, after supper. Amanda was really pleased with herself, sure that Dr Lister was the right kind of person for Hannah – 'I think she'll respond better to a woman,' she said; I resisted pointing out that her relationship with her mother suggested otherwise – and happy that she was described in one medical magazine report which popped up in her Google search as 'an innovative addiction specialist, whose work on gambling and alcohol has been widely adopted by health authorities around the world'.

Dr Lister arrived on time, 8.45 p.m., to a house already brimming with stress because Hannah wasn't there. She had told Sophie she was going to meet her sister for a cup of tea, but would be home to eat. Sophie called her at 7.30, to be told she was just saying goodbye to Vicki. By 7.45, she was 'nearly there, just met an old friend'. By eight, Sophie's calls were going unanswered, and so were texts. By 8.45, Sophie was in tears, Amanda was fretting about wasting Dr Lister's time, and I was trying hard to resist 'told you so' mode.

'Don't worry,' said Dr Lister, 'I'm used to this. The power of the addict to deny addiction is very strong. Seeing a psychiatrist or a counsellor is a way of admitting something you don't believe to be true, and so you may seek to resist.'

'How can she not know she's addicted?' I asked.

'Oh, it really isn't hard to find ways of convincing yourself. They wake up sober, usually. Then they go the morning without a drink, and they tell themselves real alcoholics have to drink in the morning. Or perhaps they were sick yesterday but today they're not. They tell themselves real alcoholics are sick every day of the week, sometimes at both ends of the day, and in the middle too. And they can stagger out of a pub, and bump into a tramp living rough on the street, and they say to themselves, "Thank God I'm not an alcoholic like him."'

'Well, I'm sorry to have wasted your time,' said Amanda. 'I really don't know what to do.'

'It might not be a waste of time. Some of my most successful consultations have started with a host of missed appointments.'

'You really are understanding beyond reasonable expectation,' I said, and she smiled. She was very warm and pleasing on the eye when she smiled.

Sophie suddenly leapt up excitedly. 'She's texted, she's texted. Says ten minutes away.'

'Oh, great,' said Amanda, but Dr Lister's countenance remained unchanged. She had clearly been present at such a delayed arrival before, many times.

She finally left at ten to ten, having had a bite to eat and a Bloody Mary, and told us a little about her research into alcohol and drug addiction. She said her day job was no longer in addiction counselling but if we managed to persuade Hannah to see her, we could call and she would try to fit her in at the hospital any time.

'You have my mobile number. Just ring me whenever.'

Amanda showed her to the door, came back in enthusing 'what a lovely woman' but found her positivity quickly punctured as I was arguing with Sophie that I really didn't want Hannah to come in if she was drunk.

'But Dad, we can't expect her to sleep on the streets.'

'She must have drinking buddies who have a roof.'

'Julian,' said Amanda — I hated it when she used my name at the start of a sentence, as it was usually a staging post to an argument — 'we don't even know she has been drinking. There might be something happening with her sister, or her mother or something.'

I paused, and made a mental note to myself to remain calm and dispassionate for the next few minutes so that we could navigate the argument zone without escalation to rancour.

'Darling, you have been wonderful to Hannah, and so has Sophie. But the fact is you have gone to considerable effort, and put a colleague to considerable trouble, and Hannah has thrown it back in your face, and wasted the time of a professional psychiatrist to boot.'

'A psychiatrist who said it was not wasted time, not necessarily.'

'Well, it seemed pretty wasted to me. Now, all I'm saying is we had rules of engagement for her stay, and if one of them — re drink quantities, three units — is broken, she cannot come in. That was the deal. We have to see it through.'

'But Dad, what if she agrees to see Dr Lister?'

'She already did, and didn't show.'

Amanda could see we had reached an impasse, and suggested it might be better if I went to do some work on the Connell case in the study. I did, but I found it impossible to focus, kept thinking of things I could have said to Dr Lister, arguments I wanted to mount to Sophie to suggest she unpick herself from this friendship. Amanda came in an hour or so later to say she was going to bed.

'No sign?'

'No.'

'Oh shit.'

'Sophie's texted ten times, but she's not replying. Be gentle with her, she's worried witless.'

'I know, but we can't have this eating into our everyday life, Amanda.'

I got to bed at one, fell asleep easily enough as I always do, but woke abruptly, and the bedside clock flashed 4.32am at me. She wasn't even my own daughter, yet I couldn't sleep.

'You awake?' It was Amanda. She couldn't sleep either.

'Yes. And bloody angry to be so. I can't bear the effect she's having on our lives.'

'I know, but let's just see where she's got to, and give it one more go with Dr Lister.' She snuggled up, and with sleep coming to neither of us, we made love. It was many years since we had done that at half past four in the morning!

Amanda texted me the following afternoon when I was in a planning meeting with the team and the client. '*Call asap.*'

'*Is it urgent?*' I texted by way of reply.

'*Quite. Dr L can see H 6pm. I'm on lates tonight. If S brings H to chambers post school, could you take to Lambeth hosp?*'

I closed my eyes, and hoped the anger over the intrusion would pass quickly. Technically the answer was yes, I could. But did I feel inclined to? No, I didn't. I decided not to reply, and to reflect. Yet again my concentration on the case in hand was disturbed by Hannah, and I was angry about it.

Then Sophie started to text. '*Did Mum get you? Can we take Hannah to doctor at 6?*' Followed a few seconds later by '*Pretty please, love you, you're the best dad in the world xxxxxxx*' and then one of those awful smiley faces. I tossed the phone onto my desk, suddenly realising Eliot Connell had been speaking to me, and I had not been listening. This was becoming intolerable.

I called the meeting to an early close, dispatched the juniors to complete various tasks we had decided needed doing, and I agreed to speak to Connell, who was an irritating self-righteous sort, as the fascinating cases often are, over the weekend. I called Amanda who could tell from my silence when she answered that I was not in the best of humour.

'Is that you, darling?'

'I assume my name came up when I called, so who else would it be?'

'Oh, OK, er, well, what do you think?'

'You know what I think in general, but what I think specifically right now is probably best unsaid.'

'Look, this isn't easy for anyone. I can ask Sophie to take her on her own, but I thought it would be better if an adult went.'

'Well, perhaps you could get me telephone numbers for the man and woman who brought this child into the world, and I will call them and suggest they take responsibility for the product of their sperm and egg, which they created when doubtless pissed at the time.'

Amanda paused, realising I would know I had gone over the top, which I would regret, not merely because it was gratuitous and vulgar, but because if the conversation was a tennis rally at deuce, I had just ceded the advantage to her.

'She came back this morning, after you left,' she said. 'She'd been waiting in the shed for an hour for you to go because Sophie texted her you were cross. So she does respect you, darling, and she says she wants to try.'

'These people always say they'll try. So where had she been all night? Not in the shed surely?'

'I don't know, but she said she was scared to meet Dr Lister, because she didn't want to feel any worse than she already did.'

'Doctors are there to make you feel better.'

'Not if you don't like the message they're trying to give you.'

'So what's the plan now?'

'Sophie came for her at lunchtime, they have lessons together, and she will not let her out of her sight, and she will get to you by five fifteen at chambers. How does that sound?'

'Utterly ghastly.'

'But you'll do it.'

'Yes, I'll do it, and if I lose the Connell case, and go back to the end of the queue for the next High Court appointment, I'll know who to blame.'

'Please, darling, let's just try to get through this calmly and rationally and without falling out. She is Sophie's friend, Sophie is our daughter. We have to help. It won't go on forever.'

'I hope you're right.'

She said thanks, I said I hoped I was still awake when she got back, and ended the call, reflecting on what a very special mother she was, which is probably what makes Sophie such a very special child.

# CLARE

**My name is Clare. I am a psychiatrist who had several consultations with Hannah.**

I hope this doesn't sound harsh, but given the day I'd had at my beautifully named PICU, Hannah came as something close to light relief. When Amanda Harper called to tell me Hannah had surfaced, was sober, and had agreed to come to see me later that day, I had just spent an hour drifting between Adam, who was speaking in tongues, Ciaran, who required constant supervision because of his ever more determined and imaginative suicide efforts, and Gabriel, who amid other more dangerous paranoid delusions believed he had been recruited as the first black member of the Rolling Stones. I was the duty senior psychiatrist for the Psychiatric Intensive Care Unit at Lambeth, part of the equally beautifully named SLAM (South London and Maudsley) NHS Foundation.

I suspect when most people hear 'intensive care', they imagine drivers close to death after road traffic accidents, heart attack victims surrounded by doctors, nurses and machines working overtime to save them. Well, for a PICU, try to imagine the human mind in the kind of mess a human body needs to be before qualifying for the cost, expertise, machinery, medication, volume of care and security systems of intensive round-the-clock treatment. Adam, the postgraduate student speaking in tongues, had another doctor and three nurses dedicated to him for the time it took us to calm him down, a task not helped by his refusal to sit or stand still, nor by the sound of 'duh duh da duh, Brown Sugar' being belted out by Gabriel, in between his screams to 'hit dem fuckin' drums harder, Charlie, else you ain't gettin' no skunk tonight', a plea which caused further complications in that our latest arrival, a remand prisoner in the throes of a full-on psychotic breakdown, was a gentle-seeming armed robber named Charlie Blackwell, whose road to crime had been ordered by Jesus following a secret meeting with the Devil, the Pope, and the global head of the Freemasons, who needless to say ran MI5 in his day job. Unsurprisingly, Charlie found himself drawn to Angus, a white, working-class former soldier from Wick, who came to us via a hostel near Euston Station whose staff became concerned at his seemingly sincere insistence that he and his fellow residents were the London Central wing of al-Qaeda. Welcome to my world, a secure men-only unit comprising eight beds, with an extra one we try to keep spare for when the police have to bring in someone who may be severely sick but also has to be kept under police guard because of crimes they may have committed. Murderers and rapists have been among our police-accompanied residents. The last time we used the police room was when a patient in another part of the hospital tried to burn the whole place down, and ended up causing an evacuation. Evacuations at a psychiatric hospital in a busy area of south London are not fun.

None of this is intended to minimise the seriousness of Hannah's situation, or the concern of her family and friends.

But as heavy days go, I had had the full lead-lined battleship, to the point that when Steven Loughlin took over from me at teatime he said, 'You look tired, Clare. Get some rest tonight, promise me.'

'I'll try. Got to see a friend of a friend now for a bit though.'

'Oh no, poor you. Bane of our life, eh?'

'I know, tell anyone you're a shrink, and they'll soon find a friend or a rellie who needs to see you.'

'Well, don't give them too long. You look knackered and these people need you more.'

I didn't even know Amanda Harper that well. I had met her at an NHS away-day conference in Cheam, where she and I ended up as team mates in role-playing exercises which were enjoyable enough, but taught me nothing ascertainable with regard to the senior management positions we were being encouraged to apply for. Meeting her, and listening to a wheelchair-bound woman who had sailed solo from one end of Britain to the other, were the high spots of an event that was otherwise just a brief escape from the day-to-day pressures of my new job, which I had taken after twelve years working exclusively with addicts of alcohol, drugs, gambling and sex. It was my interest in the mental health consequences of cannabis – potentially severe, I might add – that brought me to SLAM, where the drug is a cause of a lot of our patients' problems, but alcohol has always remained something of a passion for me – not the consumption but the study of it.

Even so, it was marginal as to whether I would put myself out for her, rather than just get her lodged into the normal referral process, when she first called me. I also did my best to hide my intense irritation when Hannah failed to show, after I had driven over to Highbury on a Wednesday night when Arsenal were playing at home and the traffic had been dreadful. But I knew that if I was in need, or I was trying to help someone in need, Amanda was the kind of person who would help.

'Oh, Clare, thanks so much for taking the call. Hannah has emerged, and she is up for seeing you asap if the offer still stands. I think I know her reasonably well by now, and I am fairly confident she will show, and in any event we are going to man-mark her all the way from school to you if, as I say, the offer stands, if it's convenient.'

She knew how to work a phone line.

'Yes, definitely best to get her when she says she wants to do this, and a good idea for someone to bring her. I've got a busy day but I can be free at six.'

'That's so kind of you. I know it's a pain when people land out-of-office hours friends and family on you, but I really think you're the right person to help Hannah.'

'Well, let's see.'

The consultation got off to an unusual start. Mr Harper and Sophie, who looked so healthy and lustrous compared with her friend, brought her in, and I went to meet them in the main reception area of the PICU building. The reception looks like a fairly standard NHS establishment. It's when you start making your way through the three separate coded double doors that you realise this isn't a conventional hospital ward. I spared Hannah and Co. the ordeal, and instead booked a standard meeting room just off the entrance, yards from where Mr Harper parked his maroon Jaguar, with a cold grey table, two hard-backed plastic-covered mauve chairs and a jug of water with a stack of paper cups. I suggested Mr Harper and Sophie waited in one of the nearby cafes in Landor Road, but

Hannah immediately said she would like them to stay. I saw Mr Harper flash a look to his daughter that said he did not want to stay, and his daughter flash a look back that said they should do whatever it took to get Hannah talking. I had to think for a moment about how appropriate her suggestion was. I knew from Amanda that Hannah was estranged from her mother, but she remained a minor, just as Sophie did, and though it might be that she was in pursuit of a father figure in her life, Julian Harper didn't strike me as a man volunteering for the role.

'Why would you like them to be here?' I asked. I was really just giving myself a little time to think.

'I just would. I feel more comfortable if they're here. Also, they've had to put up with me, and I think they're entitled to hear.'

'I see.'

'Also, I think I'll tell the truth more if Soph is here.'

'I certainly want you to tell the truth, so I like that as a reason. I have a horrible feeling I shouldn't be going along with this, but as it's what you want, and this is very much an informal preliminary session, I will, at least for an opening chat perhaps. Are you happy with that, Mr Harper?'

'Please call me Julian.'

'Julian, I beg your pardon. Are you happy with Hannah's suggestion?'

'If Sophie is, yes.'

'I am,' said his daughter, with a triumphant wink at Hannah.

'OK,' I said. 'Better find more horrible waiting-room chairs.'

If I hadn't been so tired, and ready for home, I would have talked to colleagues about the ethics of agreeing to Hannah's request that Mr Harper and his daughter stay to witness our exchanges, but the truth is I was shattered, ready for home, and I knew I would get there more quickly if I went along with what she suggested.

Once we were settled, I reached into my holdall, and asked Hannah if she minded if I recorded the conversation. 'It's nothing to be alarmed about, but in addition to my work with patients, I do research and teaching, and if the patient is happy, I film and record the interviews. You'll be given a signed guarantee that this will only ever be used for research and teaching.'

'And you have a Queen's Counsel as witness,' chipped in Mr Harper.

Hannah nodded and I hurriedly set up the little camera on its tripod, and pointed it directly at her. Experience had taught me the camera makes people nervous for a few seconds, but they adapt to it quickly.

The first questions and answers are always among the most important. I sometimes feel like an actor or an athlete, knowing that those opening words in the play, or moments in the match, can be the difference between a good performance and a bad one, between victory and defeat. I'd had no time to prepare properly, so I was going to have to rely more than usual on instinct.

'So, are you ready?' She nodded. 'I'd like to ask you first why you think you're here.' She paused, and I waited five or six seconds before chivvying. It may not sound long. It is in those circumstances.

'I don't mean that in an existential sense – why are you here on the planet? I mean it very specifically. Why are you here, now, in this hospital, talking to me, a psychiatrist who has specialised in addiction?'

'Sophie's mum.'

'Yes, it's right that she's the one who contacted me, but why would anyone feel that necessary, that you should see me here, to talk about you?'

She paused again, but this time I let the air hang heavy, looked at her with a certain intensity, signalled I would not be the next to speak.

'Drink, I suppose.'

'Go on.'

'Drink, why I do it, what it does to me, what it does to my friends when I'm doing it.'

'How would you describe your relationship with alcohol?' It was one of my favourite questions.

She looked at her feet, and I could see she was searching for the right description.

'Relationship?'

'Yes, if you think of yourself and alcohol as being in a relationship, how would you describe it?'

'Like a bad marriage.'

'Bad because . . . ?'

'Well, maybe good and bad. Good because it makes me feel better. Bad because it makes me feel worse. Bad because it screws me up with my friends, my family, my schoolwork, my head, I suppose.'

'So that's more bads than goods.'

'Yeah, but the goods can be awesome. Sometimes.'

'When the relationship is good, what does that feel like?'

'It helps me feel that my life is not quite as shit – can I say that?'

'Yes.'

'– not as shit as it was before.'

'And does that good feeling come when you decide you're going to drink, when you first taste the drink, or when you begin to feel drunk?'

'It goes in stages. Let's say I wake up feeling bad. I don't want a drink. But I want to know I will have a drink later. I'll start to imagine it. I can wait a long time, you know, all day, and as the time gets nearer, my mood is picking up.'

'So you like the thought of the drink?'

'Yes, but only because I know it's going to happen. The thought on its own isn't enough. It's not like sex, where you can think nice thoughts about having sex and feel something positive, and even get excited, even though there's nobody else there. I can't think of drink, and feel the pleasure it gives me, in the same way.'

I could see Mr Harper turning nervously in his chair. Like most fathers, he probably found the subject of sex and teenage girls a difficult one to handle.

'For now, let's stay with alcohol. We know you like the prospect of drinking, provided you know the drink will materialise. When it does, how do you feel?'

'You mean the first taste?'

'Yes, but also what do you think and feel immediately before?'

'I like the rituals. Like, in a pub, standing at the bar and holding a note and having small talk with a barman. I like that. I like watching the drink being poured, because it builds the expectation. I love spirits in pubs best, when they take the glass and push it against the thing that shoots out the measure. I love that.'

'The optics? Any idea why you like that so much?'

'It means it's near, it's coming.'

'But why would the spirits measure be nicer for you than a beer being drawn or a glass of wine being poured from a bottle?'

'Oh, don't get me wrong, Miss, I like them too, but I suppose it's that spirits pack a bigger punch.'

'So you like the hit? A big hit?'

She nodded.

'Let's imagine you're drinking a beer, not a strong one, an ordinary beer. How does that feel when it's the first drink?'

'OK, but I'll usually only drink beer to get warmed up for spirits. Like you have different rituals for different places. Like in a corner shop or a supermarket, I like the idea that I'm shopping, so I might buy a packet of nuts, or even something I won't even eat like a box of cereal, and then I'll buy a four-pack or a six-pack or a bottle of something. It's like a little game I'm playing and I'm the only one who knows the rules.'

'I see, I think. Just back in the pub, for a moment, which are your favourite spirits?'

'Toss-up between vodka and Scotch. Scotch in a pub, I think, vodka if I'm just out and about.'

'Any reason for that?'

'There's so much cheap vodka on the market. So if you're just hanging around on the street getting drunk, it's the best. I prefer the hit from Scotch, and if I'm in a pub, I think I want people to know I'm drinking. Vodka could be anything.'

'So you care what impact you make on people when you're drinking?'

'No, I don't mean it like that. Well, hold on a minute. I like being able to drink boys under the table, I do. But that's not what I mean either. Maybe it's just that if I'm in a pub, as far as I am concerned, a pub is for drinking, and I want to belong there.'

'You want to belong?'

'Yes.'

'What does that mean?'

'It means what it says. If I'm in a pub, I want to feel like I belong, like, I don't know, at home.'

'Is that because you don't feel you belong anywhere else? In your home, your family, your school perhaps?'

She took time to think about that one, looked at Sophie, who I could see was following this with total concentration. She just smiled, and moved her shoulder and nodded as if to say 'keep going, you're doing well, this is good'.

'I don't want to do that "blaming the parents" thing,' Hannah replied.

'I agree the blame game is usually not a good one to play. But I'm asking something different – whether you feel you don't belong anywhere.'

Another long pause.

'It can't all be my parents' fault. If it was, why hasn't my little sister started to go down the same track?'

'How big is the age gap?'

'Three years.'

'Do you feel being the first child was a burden?'

'No.'

'Do you feel your sister was spoiled more than you? Older children often do feel that, that they pioneer things, get all the boundaries in place, and by the time their siblings come along, Mum and Dad are more used to having a child, and the second one gets away with more. Does that sound like your family?'

'No, not really. I'm aware my mum really likes her, but so do I. I love my little sister.'

'You're not jealous of her in any way?'

'Well, I am now, seeing how she has a home, a room of her own, and isn't causing all this grief I seem to cause, and everyone thinks she's great and I am just trouble. But I didn't grow up hating her, if that's what you mean.'

'Did you grow up hating your parents?'

'I don't think so. I mean, my dad left us, well, my mum kicked him out, and to be honest, I can't blame her for that. He wasn't a good husband and he isn't a good dad. I've kept in touch a bit but he's just a flake, really, and I know it's made life a lot harder for Mum, and . . .' Her voice trailed away.

'And?'

'And I've made it worse for her, I suppose. But . . . Oh, I don't know.'

'Are your parents heavy drinkers?'

'Dad, a bit, Mum no.'

'Other family members?'

'Dad's side yes, Mum's side no, Dad's dad alcoholic, never met him, Dad's brother alcoholic, but now dry. I've talked to him a bit about this. I know he thinks I have a real problem.'

Sophie leaned across the table and whispered, 'Tell her you were there,' so she did, told me the story of her recent stay at her uncle's.

'So two members of your family, mother and uncle, have asked you to leave, and one of those people, your uncle, is himself – or certainly was – a problem drinker?'

'Yes.'

'Let me ask you this, Hannah . . . if you had to stop drinking, how would you feel?'

She paused. 'Not good. Bad that I say that, I know, but I don't like the idea.'

'Because?'

'Because sometimes he's the only friend I have.'

'He?'

'Drink.'

'Interesting you see drink as he not she?'

'I wouldn't read too much into that. People usually say "he" when it could be either he or she.'

'Perhaps. So you see drink as a friend?'

'Well, you said relationship.'

'I did, and you said friend. A friend is a good thing, yes?'

'Yes.'

'But you said drink was good *and* bad. Are friends good and bad?'

'I don't know what you're getting at.'

'I'm not getting at anything. I am trying to establish why you drink to excess, and what I have learned so far is that you see drink as your friend. I think that's an interesting insight and I would like to explore it.'

'And I would like to know where all this is leading.'

I had had a good start, but was now moving into a more uncomfortable phase of the conversation. She was irritated. She felt suddenly threatened for some reason. It was important for me to try to find out why. There might be no reason. It could be tiredness, lack of concentration, boredom, an irritation with me and my mannerisms and way of speaking. There doesn't always have to be a reason, like there doesn't always have to be a reason that some people are addicts and others are not. But the reason why I often felt psychiatry, and dealing with mental health, was harder than dealing with physical medicine is that most of the time all we have to go on is what the sick person tells us. There is no X-ray for truth, no scan for emotion, no test that can tell us what the patient is thinking, what scars the past has inflicted, what hopes still lie in their hearts and souls. And when the patient doesn't want to speak, or lies, or refuses to engage meaningfully, there is absolutely nothing the doctor can do.

I knew I had to shift tack.

'When were you at your happiest?'

'Don't know.'

'Are you happy now?'

'No.'

'Why?'

'Because I wouldn't be here if I was.'

'You might be happy if you thought this would lead to you having a better, healthier, happier life?'

'Mmm.'

'Do you want to be happy?'

'I don't know what that means. Happy can mean anything you want it to.'

'Are you happy when you're drunk?'

'Not always. Sometimes, yes, I feel happy.'

'Do you think you would be happier than you are now if you didn't drink at all?'

'Got no way of knowing that, have I?'

'No, but that's why I was asking you what you thought. I'm trying to get you to envisage a life without drinking. On a scale of one to ten, how unpleasant a thought is that to you?'

She put her right hand around her left wrist, then laced both hands into a knot.

'Is one pleasant or unpleasant?'

'One is pleasant.'

'And ten is unpleasant?'

'Yes.'

'That's a ten then.'

'I see. And how scary do you find it?'

'Eight. Nine.'

'And right now, today, sitting here with me and your friend and your friend's father, how likely do you think it is you could stop, again on a scale of one to ten?'

'One.'

'So you're scared at the idea of not drinking, and you find it almost impossible to imagine a life without alcohol?' She didn't reply. She was looking at her feet, and rubbing non-existent specks of dirt from her jeans.

'I'm just telling you the truth. That's what you said you wanted.'

'Indeed, and I am grateful. Let me ask you this: have you heard of the phrase "drink problem"?'

'Course I have.'

'What does that phrase mean to you?'

'Means someone has a problem with drink.'

'What could that problem be?'

'Drinking too much. Damaging your health through drink. Losing all your money on drink. Doing crazy stuff because of drink. Dying through drink. I guess.'

'I really want you to think about this question, Hannah, really think about it, and try to be honest with yourself, and honest with me.'

'OK.'

'Do you believe you have a drink problem?'

She looked over to Sophie, who stared back passively.

'I don't know,' she said. 'I know my drinking is causing problems, but I don't know if that's the same thing. I think there are plenty people drink worse than I do, and I think if I really had to stop, I would.'

'What state would you have to be in for you to know that you "really had to stop"?'

'My whole life collapsing. Down-and-out. Living on the street drinking day and night.'

'I see. But the down-and-out didn't start out as a down-and-out, did he? The man or woman living on the street drinking day and night didn't start there, did they? They started as children, and didn't know what drinking was. Then they started drinking and they were experimental drinkers, then social drinkers, then habitual drinkers, them problem drinkers, then drinkers who lost the support of family and friends, then drinkers who couldn't cope with living in hostels, then they found they had nowhere else to go but the street. And at every stage of the journey, Hannah, they thought they could stop if they had to, thought they could control their addiction. But they couldn't. Because somewhere along that journey, the addiction took control of them. And you have to face up to the possibility that you are already well down that road, and you need to think about getting off it.'

I stopped. I never liked lecturing patients. I prefer to ask short questions, and get them to think about the answers more than they think about anything I might say. It was a sign of my tiredness and frustration that I went into stern finger-wag mode, even though I have years of experience and hundreds of examples of it not working. It was so obvious to me that she had a serious problem, but she was struggling to accept it because she was scared by the vision of a life without alcohol. She said many of the right things, things I wanted to hear. But she didn't say she had a problem. She couldn't bring herself to admit she was addicted. And I knew that until she could, there wasn't much anyone could do to help her.

'Would you like to see me again?' I asked.

'Could do.'

'And would you do one or two exercises before you see me again?'

'What, gym and stuff?'

'No. Would you try to make a note of every time you drink, when you drink, where you drink, how it makes you feel?'

'I can try.'

'I'd be really grateful if you would. I would really like to try to help you. But you need to help me a bit too.'

'OK. I think I understand. Thank you.'

She looked at Sophie and smiled. Unfortunately, I knew it was a smile that said 'This is over. She can't think of anything more to say. She's knackered. Can we go home?' I wanted to go home too, but I also wanted one last go at opening her up.

I asked if anyone needed water, and Mr Harper asked 'Any chance of a tea?' and Hannah eyed me nervously.

'Yes,' I said. 'We don't have a visitors' canteen, I'm afraid, so you'll need to go to a cafe. We're nearly finished here, but you certainly have time for that.'

'Anyone else?' he asked.

'No thanks,' said Sophie. Hannah shook her head and put her hands on the table, then folded her arms, angrily, and sighed.

'I'd like a coffee,' I said. 'Plain black.'

'Thank heavens for that. I was dreading having to ask for a skinny latte with soy milk. Amanda's tipple.'

As he left, I took a sip of water and prepared for the final round.

'Hannah, Sophie's mum told me you had been self-harming.'

She drew her arms closer in and, though her sleeves were already down to her wrists, pulled them even further so they covered half of her hands.

'Can I see?'

'Why?'

'Because it's important I know what form the harm has been taking, and how serious it has been.'

She looked down at her clothed arms, chewed on her bottom lip and let out another loud sigh.

'Go on, Han,' said Sophie. 'You've been honest about drinking. Be honest about this.'

Slowly she peeled back first her right sleeve, then her left, which she pulled right back to her shoulder. I had seen a lot worse, many times, but just as she was well along the alcoholic route, so the volume and recent nature of the marks and bruises suggested she was in the habit-forming stage of self-harm.

'When did you first do something like this?'

'On my arms? After the abortion. Week ago, maybe two. Partly it was the bleeding. Just kept bleeding down there. Also the pains were worse than they said they would be.'

'Nothing else? Nothing else you were feeling that might have brought it on?'

'Well, I didn't enjoy having to have an abortion if that's what you mean.'

We explored her feelings around that for some time, talked through her sex history, and the link with alcohol consumption – it was close – then Mr Harper came back in at the worst possible moment, just as she was telling me the circumstances of how she fell pregnant. She stopped in mid-sentence, at the point where she was rolling a joint for her mother's boyfriend. Mr Harper placed my coffee on the table in front of me, then resumed his place beside Sophie. As he sat down I noticed a smattering of raindrops against the window. It was dark outside, and I felt even more tired suddenly, saw the day stretching into the night, and bed still a long way off, and I would need to be back at the PICU by seven in the morning.

'We're talking about sex now, Julian. Hannah, would you find it easier if Mr Harper left the room?' He stood, seemed eager to leave.

'No,' she said. 'It's fine.'

'Julian?'

'What do you advise?'

'Let's see how we go.'

I took a mouthful of lukewarm coffee and waited to see if she would resume where we had left off. She didn't.

'So, Hannah, you were just telling us about Dan, your mum's boyfriend, how you quite liked him as a person, but hated him staying over. Why was that?'

'We've only got a small flat. Me and Vicki share a bedroom smaller than this room. My mum's room is not much bigger. There's one bathroom, one living room, a little kitchen.'

'So you felt your space was being crowded?'

'Just annoying having someone else to think about, worry about, have to talk to and try to be nice. I had enough going on. Also, I'm not a heavy sleeper, and I'd have to listen to them, you know, doing it . . .'

'Sex?'

'Yeah.'

'And how did that make you feel?'

'Bit sick to be honest.'

'Would you have felt different if it had been your father?'

'No, to be fair, I don't think it was about Dan. It's just not nice listening to anyone doing it, but especially not your mum.'

'But if your mum and dad had never "done it", you wouldn't be here.'

'True, but I didn't have to listen while they made me, did I?'

'Did Vicki hear all this too?'

'Yeah, sure. Her bed's up against the wall that joins on to Mum's, and Mum has a headboard, and sometimes it would bang against the wall and we could hear Mum trying to shush him, but, anyway, you know what men are like when they get going.'

'Mmmm, well. So you have no personal animus against Dan, but you didn't like having this other man in the flat and you found your mother's sexual activity difficult to deal with? Is that fair?'

'I think I could deal with it. But I didn't want to listen to it.'

'OK. Now just before Mr Harper came in, you were telling us about the night you fell pregnant. Dan was definitely the father, is that right?'

Before she could get her answer out, Mr Harper spluttered out a mouthful of tea and muttered what sounded like 'Jesus!'

'Dad!' said Sophie. 'I thought you knew.' He shook his

head. Hannah looked at him, apologetically, then turned back to me.

'Pretty sure. I mean, I had been quite active around then, but I usually insisted on boys using a condom, and the times I didn't was well before that time.'

'Could there have been other times when you were so drunk you forgot you'd had sex?'

'Don't think so.'

Sophie leaned towards her and whispered again. 'Tell her about the book.'

'Oh yeah,' she said. 'The other thing is, I have a little book, and I write in all the names of boys I've, you know, slept with. I've done it ever since my first one, Sammy, because he had a little book, and I think everyone is in there. Apart from Dan. I've not put him in.'

'Because?'

She shrugged, then added, 'Not been anyone since.'

'How much had you had to drink the night you had sex with Dan?'

'Not bender quantities. I'd been out four hours maybe, hour or two front-loading outside the offy, then pub with a few friends, but I got bored to be honest.'

'So how much, roughly?'

'Er, bit of vodka, couple of beers, few Scotches, glass of wine maybe. Can't remember. Fair bit, but not as much as other times.'

'Did you set out to seduce him?'

'Well, I didn't even know he was going to be there, let alone that he was going to be drinking and smoking weed.'

'But once you noticed that, and that your mother was out, did you set out to seduce him?'

'Well, I did seduce him, so I suppose I must have done.'

'And would you have tried to seduce any man that night, who was reasonably good-looking, if I can put it like that?'

'No, because there had been a couple of guys in the pub who had been trying to get off with me, both better-looking than Dan, and I wasn't interested. I was honestly intending to go to sleep when I got in.'

'So you got in, had a drink, smoked some cannabis, then seduced him?'

'I didn't smoke cannabis. Never have, well, once, hated it.'

'And as you seduced him, what were you thinking, and feeling?'

'I was in drunken shag mode, I guess, like we talked about when Mr Harper was getting your coffee.'

'But this was a much older man, more than twice your age, old enough to be your father, and he's your mother's boyfriend. And you were doing it in your own home, with your sister down the hall, and you knew your mother could have walked through the door at any time, as indeed she did, shortly after Dan climaxed inside you. This was not an ordinary drunken shag, was it?'

'No,' she said, as I looked away from her to see Mr Harper's mouth fall open.

'And what I'm interested in knowing is whether you felt any kind of revenge in what you were doing. Revenge against your mother for not being there, then or at other times in the past when you might have needed her. Against Dan, for taking up space in the flat and for taking your mum's focus away from you and Vicki. And your dad perhaps, for not being there, for not knowing what you had become, and probably not caring either. Did any of those emotions come into play?'

'I don't know. To be honest, it just started out as a bit of fun. He was quite warm and mellow and friendly when I came in. I thought I would try and be a bit nicer than usual. Then one thing led to another, like it does.'

'You don't feel there was more to it? That in having sex with Dan you would get between him and your mum, hurt them both, and maybe drive them apart, which is what happened.'

'But like I say, I didn't know he was going to be there. I didn't know he was a pothead. I didn't know he would be such a flake, just fall for a bit of flirting and then let his prick take over. Sorry.'

'Or at a deeper, even subconscious level, do you think it is possible you wanted to do all that, hurt them, cause mayhem, but also show that you could create something – a child, a foetus – so that you could also then display the power you have to destroy, this time via a termination?'

'I don't go big on all this subconscious stuff. I can assure you the word "foetus" did not cross my mind.'

'So this was just a situation that developed, rather than an event that you planned, either consciously or subconsciously?'

'Well, look who got hurt most of all. Me. OK, Mum lost her boyfriend, and she had to see her daughter and her boyfriend naked together after they had just done it, and I am not saying that was nice for her, course it wasn't. And he loses his girlfriend and his regular sex partner, and is humiliated I guess, and gets kicked out like my dad was. But I'm the one with nowhere to live, and no earnings of my own, and I'm the one who gets pregnant, and has to have a fucking abortion because he couldn't resist the idea of shagging the mum and shagging the daughter. So if I set out to hurt them, I did a fucking good job of hurting myself, didn't I, Doctor?'

She emphasised the word 'doctor' aggressively and with a nastiness I noted for the first time.

'But these were all choices you made, Hannah. You chose to drink to excess. You chose to get Dan to smoke more. You chose to have sex. You chose to risk hurting your mum. You chose to –'

'But I didn't choose to be fucking born, did I? What fucking say did I have in that?'

For a moment, I thought she was going to hit me, or rush from the room. Instead she started crying, gently at first, then loud chest-ripping sobs. Sophie moved to get up from her chair, but I shook my head, held up my hand and motioned her to stay seated. I let Hannah cry for fifteen, twenty seconds, then it stopped, then started again, this time for almost a minute. Sophie was crying too, and Mr Harper put his arm around her. Sophie looked at me, her eyes pleading with me to let her comfort Hannah, but I gently shook my head again. I wanted Hannah to cry out all her tears, because as the tears left her, so did some of the pain, and when she had stopped crying, her eyes and her throat and her chest would be sore, she would have a raging headache, but she might start to find out why she acted as she did, and she might tell me, and I might be able to help.

'I'm sorry to put you through all this,' I said. 'We'll soon be done. You said a moment ago you did "a fucking good job of hurting myself". Do you think when you're drinking, and when you're being promiscuous, and when you're putting yourself in difficult situations, you are deliberately hurting yourself?'

'Dunno.'

'Like when you scratch your arms and punch yourself?'

'Dunno.'

'Is it possible, do you think, that they are all part of the same thing?'

'I suppose so.'

'When you cut yourself, you *know* you're harming yourself. When you drink, you think you're making yourself feel better, but you're not. Does that make sense?'

She nodded.

'So, to get you well, we have to stop all the self-harm, don't we, and understand it is all part of the same problem?'

She nodded again.

'The thing is though, Hannah, that we – me, Sophie, your mum, your sister, Mr and Mrs Harper, your school – we can't do it. Only you can. And that means being honest about why you do it, and it might take time before we find all that out.'

'I know.'

'Are you prepared to work at it, to put in the time we need to get you better?'

'I mean I know why I do it.'

'You know?'

'Yes.'

'Tell me why, then.'

'Because the pain of the knife is not as bad as the pain inside. So I cut to let the pain out.'

'And that feels better, does it?'

'For a bit. Like a drink makes me feel better. For a bit. And then I feel worse, and the pain inside comes back. Worse than ever.'

I paused, but the silence was heavy, and this time Sophie

could hold back no longer. She rushed over to Hannah, her shoulder bag flying from her lap, hugged her, and both of them sobbed into each other's arms. Mr Harper, who knew a thing or two about questioning reluctant witnesses, nodded to me and I saw in his eyes the recognition of one professional to another of a job well done. Where it went next, I had no way of knowing. That would be down to the choices Hannah made. But as I looked at my watch, and saw it was seven fifteen, I had a sudden yearning to be on the couch at home, falling asleep in front of a black-and-white movie with a takeaway curry, a glass of red, and the cat sleeping at my feet. It felt like a long time since I told Gabriel that no, Ronnie Wood hadn't phoned, but maybe he would in the morning.

# VICKI

**My name is Vicki. I am Hannah's little sister.**

Until the horrible thing with Dan, when Mum went –
unsurprisingly – completely, totally spare, I could have counted
on my fingers the number of nights in my life when I had not
shared a room with Hannah. There are only two ways to go in
those circumstances, when your beds are almost touching because
your first bedroom was tiny, and your second one, when we had
to move out because of the divorce, is even smaller. Either you
get very close, or you long for the day when you hope you never
have to share a room with anyone, and you never have to see
your sister again. We got close.

She can be the most infuriating creature on earth. She has
a chip on her shoulder big enough for both of us. She can
swing from cuddlesome to sulk and back again in a matter of
moments. She can invade my space and steal my stuff and play
her naff music when I'm trying to read or talk to a friend.
She can come home pissed and fall all over me when I'm fast
asleep. She can – and she does – hijack my Facebook page
and put on all sorts of rubbish about boys I'm supposed to
fancy, and she'll even say I love One Direction and Spurs when
she knows I love The Wanted and Arsenal. I might flare up,

but I will always come down on her side again pretty soon. And since the thing with Dan – again unsurprisingly – it has felt like taking sides in a war. Mum pretends to be over it, but I can tell it eats at her all the time. Why wouldn't it? I may only be fifteen, and I only caught the aftermath, when Han and Dan were covering themselves up, and Mum was screaming they were evil, and that was bad enough. But, oh my God, to be a mum – my mum – and come back all cheery because you've been told by your boss they were all really impressed at the conference in Oxford, finally to be getting over your husband being serially unfaithful, and to have found a nice new boyfriend who treats you with respect, and treats your kids nicely, even though the older one is surly as a dinner lady serving the boy who always throws his bread roll when he thinks nobody's watching, to be on the train home, looking forward to seeing him . . . and then she walks through the door, and they're locked together, on the sofa . . . every time I think of it, even now, I feel so sick, and I feel such sympathy for Mum. But I can't help loving Hannah. I'll never stop loving Hannah.

She once said, I think I was about ten or eleven, certainly after we had moved from Holloway Road to Highbury New Park, 'Do you realise we have been asleep together for more than thirty-five thousand hours?'

I'm a whizz at maths and said straight away, 'That's 2,100,000 minutes.'

'How many seconds?'

I had to scribble that one down to work it out, but got in soon enough. '126 million. Wow! That is soooo long.'

'And you're too bleedin' clever.'

She didn't mean it. She was good at some things – swimming,

acting, history, words, being my big sister – I was good at others, and maths and science were right up there.

Mum couldn't believe I could 'still defend her' after the thing with Dan. But I didn't defend her. What she did was wrong, so wrong it tested even my faith in her. But when all is said and done, she is my big sister, she has always looked out for me, and I hope I would always look out for her, no matter what. Her drinking makes it hard, but I've always believed in her, and I always will.

My problem – if problem it is – is that I can always see everyone's point of view. Mr Ramage says that's what makes me a good mathematician. I can look at an object or a situation and see it from every angle, and work out how it changes if you look at it from a different angle. So I totally got why Mum was livid. But the minute she asked Hannah to leave, I got how scary a prospect that was for someone who was seventeen, knew deep down in her heart she had a problem with booze, knew deep down too that what she had done was so wrong it would haunt her forever, and it showed her life was careering out of control, but suddenly she had nowhere to live, no money except for what Dad coughed up when he bothered to see us and thought a few notes would make us feel warm towards him – actually it had the opposite effect – exams coming up, her school getting fed up with her, one or two good friends but actually most of them either guys who wanted to sleep with her, or girls who liked drinking with her because no matter how drunk they got, and no matter how stupid that made them, they could always say, 'Well, Hannah drank more than I did.' Then chuck in an unwanted pregnancy and an abortion on top, and 'I'm sorry, Mum, but there has to be sympathy for Hannah too, even if she is the cause of her own problems.'

We are so different, Han and me, but we're so the same. I look at her, and I know there is nobody else in the world who could be my sister. But I think Mum's a good mum, whereas Hannah has never seemed able to see it. I love school, always have, loved it from the moment Mum dropped me off for the first day, used to look forward to telling Chrissie what I had done when she picked me up, and then telling Mum when she came home. It didn't bother me that she sometimes seemed not to listen because she was cooking dinner or doing paper-work from the office. But as far back as I can remember, there was this thing between Han and Mum that was just so irritable, like an itch that never went away no matter how much cream or lotion you put on it. We probably had more in common in the way we felt about Dad. He could be good fun, but he wasn't a great dad. But again, while it got Hannah down, I remember thinking, once I'd got over the shock of him being kicked out by Mum – my God, I hope I have better luck with men than she's had – 'Well, he wasn't much of a dad, and not much of a husband, so maybe home life will be better with just me, Mum who I love to bits, Han who I love to bits, and we can see Dad from time to time and try to get along.'

I can't say I found it easy to see things from Dan's point of view when he did what he did with Hannah. It's one thing for a young girl to be drunk and stupid, quite another for a grown man. Then again, Hannah is a very attractive girl. I've seen her when she's in man-charming mode, and if this was a jungle, it's like lion v sheep, only one winner.

We're different when it comes to drink, for sure, and sex as well. I've only ever really kissed two boys, that's it, Nathan and Paul, one after school once, one at a party. I do not go to bed full of angst because I am still a virgin. I do not feel in any way inferior or inadequate. I have a long life ahead of me. I will meet someone I will want to go the whole way with. It might be next year, might be the year after, might be when I'm twenty, twenty-five, who knows? I am not losing sleep about it. But Hannah had to be ahead of the pack on that one, and she got a reputation as being a bit of a slag. Emma Knighton once said 'your sister's a fucking slag', when we were changing after PE. It is the only time in my life I have slapped anyone. But she had a point, to be fair, so when she slapped me back, I left it at that.

As for drink, I am at a total loss to work it all out. I hate the stuff. At the party when I was making out with Paul, which was a few days before Hannah's thing with Dan, I thought, yeah, well, I don't want people to think I'm a square, there was a big black dustbin full of ice and bottles of beer, and I took a Budweiser because I'd seen a really cool advert on TV, with this ripped guy taking his shirt off, and I guarantee it lasted me all night. I took a swig, and didn't like the taste much. I took two or three more, and I didn't like the effect, and for the rest of the night I just hung on to this near-empty bottle so people didn't keep asking me if I needed a drink. I felt totally out of place by half ten, eleven o'clock time because everyone else seemed to be out of their trees. Friends I know and like who you can usually have a good conversation with were talking absolute rubbish, and laughing at things that just weren't funny. The next morning, I was up at eight and Hannah was lying in a heap, smelling of drink, groaning because she felt ill, and there was a half-bottle of vodka on her bed. And I sort of stood there, I stared at her, and I thought, Why her? And why me? Why does she love it, and I hate it? We have the same mum, the same dad, the same grandparents, we have slept in the same two rooms in the same two flats all of my life. We go to the same school. We watch the same telly, listen to the same music, give or take her obsession with Snoop Dogg. Yet there she is, drunk again, about to wake up horribly hung-over, again. And here's me, can't stand the sight or the smell or the taste or the effect of the stuff. Why? How can we be the same and yet be so different? It's the one point of view I cannot fathom, no matter which angle I'm coming from. Why does she drink so much, when it's making her so ill, doing so much damage to her life? I don't get it.

I went over to her that morning, sat on her bed, and I said, 'Han, you OK? Wake up, listen to me, you OK?'

She grunted, she rolled away from me, but I can be as determined as she can and I kept shaking her until finally she opened her eyes. Those beautiful brown eyes were bloodshot and dazed.

'Han, you can't keep doing this to yourself.'

'We'll talk later.'

'Please, talk now. Talk to me now. Come on, wake up.'

'Sis, it's fucking Sunday, we don't have school. Let me sleep.'

'No, I'm worried about you, because we've done this in citizenship at school, we've studied addiction, and I'm worried you're hooked on booze and binge drinking, and I know it can kill people, because it *has* killed people, lots of people, and I just can't bear the idea of that happening to you.'

'It won't. I promise. I like a drink. Saturday night out, everyone was there. But it's not a problem, trust me.'

'Can we talk about it later?'

'Yeah.'

'With Mum?'

'Nah, come on, it'll only worry her. I'll talk to you, promise.'

Only we didn't. She went out when I was round at my friend Sasha's. By the time she was back, I was asleep. And the next morning, we had school.

It was hard getting used to having a room to myself, after Mum kicked her out. I was trying to look after Mum, but I really missed Hannah, and I worried about her every night she wasn't there. Sometimes I'd fall asleep quickly. But some nights I would be lying there, hour upon hour, fantasising about where she was, what was happening to her. She was being raped on the canal at the back of King's Cross. Or she had been kicked out of a club and as she left she insulted a group of men coming in, and one of them pulled a knife and stabbed her. She got rushed to hospital and was in intensive care but she had no ID and they had no way of knowing who to contact, and the first we knew was when her face flashed up on the London evening news on the telly because the police put out a plea for witnesses. No matter how fanciful these random fantasies which kept crowding in upon me, ever more violent as I tried to push them away, and prayed to a God I didn't really believe in to help me sleep, the truth dawned that they were not fanciful at all.

That none of these things happened to her is the reason I love, I mean love, Sophie Harper. I was so happy when Sophie came and found me at break time and told me Hannah had moved in with them. And even happier when she said that they had been to a psychiatrist at one of the best psychiatric places in the country – Sophie even said 'one of the best in the world' – and Hannah had admitted she had a problem and when they were driving home with her dad from the hospital, she had said, 'I know what I have to do. I can see something now I couldn't see before. All my problems come from the choice I make to drink. And I know I have to choose to stop. And I want you to help me.'

I hugged Sophie so hard, and I said I could not thank her and her mum and dad enough.

'Are you sure they're OK with her staying with you? I know what happened the last time.'

'Dad's come round to it. And Mum is a woman on a mission. The thing is, Hannah has got something so special, that other special people like my mum, or Dr Lister, they can see it. Like I can see it, like you can see it.'

'I know,' I said. 'Shame Hannah can't see it herself.'

I arranged to go round and see her that evening. I agonised about whether to tell Mum. I don't like lying to anyone, but especially not her. It's one of those decisions you have to take yourself, so I didn't tell anybody, not even Sasha, my best friend by some distance, and instead went for a walk after school, around the little park behind St Mary Magdalene Church, where we used to go with Chrissie when we were little. A young Polish or Czech woman was emptying the bins, and I wondered how many of my friends would even think about joining the council refuse department as a job. She stopped for a smoke on the bench opposite the one I was sitting on. She smiled. I smiled back. 'I love this place,' she said. 'So peaceful. Best part of my job is the bins in the parks.'

It's funny how you can get guidance from random events. Just behind her, a mother was playing with her toddler, who was so wrapped up against the cold I couldn't work out at first if it was a boy or a girl. The mother was throwing a yellow tennis ball, and the child was throwing it back, usually a long way from its intended target. As the ball bounced from a tree, a Labrador, black and sleek, came bounding up, took the ball in its mouth, and ran off in the direction of its owner, marching purposefully ahead, oblivious to this little child's drama unfolding. The toddler looked first impressed, and pulled down her hood. I could see now it was a little girl. The look of intrigue at the dog's exploit then turned to bemusement, followed by sadness and finally, as the dog disappeared from view, she pointed in its direction, and began to cry. The mother walked towards her, big smile never leaving her face, and as she reached into her coat pocket, she pulled out a second identical ball.

'Magic!' she said. 'The doggy took the ball, but magic made it come back to me.'

It was a lie. But like the lie I was about to tell my mum – that there were auditions for the school play – it was a lie told for the best of reasons . . . to buy time, and to avoid hurt to someone she loved.

The Harpers' house was like a new world to me, even though it was only a few minutes' walk from our flat. Big garden, with its own gate and pathway. A big garage set off to the side, separate from the house itself. Four storeys and windows with criss-cross grilles, a tall steep roof, a light that went on as I approached the lowest of the seven stone steps leading to an oak front door. It reminded me of the family home in my favourite film, *Home Alone*, where Macaulay Culkin is left to run riot. I rang the bell nervously and, when nobody came, rang it again a few seconds later.

'Coming, coming,' shouted a voice whose impatient sound made me more nervous still. The door opened to reveal a nice-looking woman wearing a red jumper and plain grey skirt.

'Hello,' I said. 'I'm Hannah's sister. Did Sophie say?'

'Yes, yes, come in, come in. Vicki, isn't it?'

'Yes.'

'Do come in.'

'I got you these, to say thank you.' And I held out a small bunch of tulips I had bought from the flower seller at Highbury Corner.

'You really shouldn't, but that is so kind.' She was just like Sophie, full of niceness and warmth, but I felt a little silly about my three-pound bunch of flowers on seeing in the hallway two upturned pillars with vases on top of them, filled with enormous and varied bouquets.

'The girls are just doing some history, I think. You go in here while I get them down and we'll have a bite to eat.'

She showed me into the sitting room, where what looked like a real fire was burning, and where there were so many sofas and chairs I didn't know where to put myself, and so many paintings I didn't where to look. The sofas in particular looked too expensive to sit on, all puffed up and furry. I went to the piano in the far corner, sat on the stool, and waited. Moments later, Sophie ran in, followed by Hannah who rushed over and hugged me so hard I fell against the piano and made an almighty and discordant racket. Sophie and her mum laughed.

'Let's leave these two together while you and I sort something to eat, Sophie,' said Mrs Harper, and off they went.

'They are so nice it's ridiculous,' I said.

'I know. I don't know what I would have done without them.'

'And this house, my God, Han, it's like something off the telly, not a real house.'

'Her dad's loaded. Said in the paper he gets as much as a million for a case.'

'A case of what?'

'He's a lawyer.' And she laughed and pulled my hair gently.

'Sophie said you saw a doctor?'

'Yeah, a shrink. She was OK.'

'And she said you were stopping drinking.'

'Well, yeah, going to try. So far so good. One day. One day at a time, they say.'

'Well, you must, Han, you really must. I was so happy when Sophie told me. I've never been so happy. You can make people sad, Hannah, and you have. But now you can make us happy. How good will that feel?'

'Yeah, good.' She sighed though, heavily, and I could feel a sense of burden.

'It won't be easy, sis. You've all got to help me.'

'We will. Everyone will. I mean, what better place to live in than this? What better friend than Sophie?'

'I know. I'm lucky, and I've got to try to stay lucky.'

'Well, I'm always there for you. You know that. Any time you think you're going to go back on this, you call me. Promise?'

'Yeah,' she said, and she sighed again.

Sophie's dad arrived. He was not at all what I expected. I imagined a male version of Mrs Harper, smiley and bouncy and small. He was big, over six feet tall, with two chins and a fat belly beneath a waistcoat which was a couple of sizes too small for him. He was also, despite apparently being a great lawyer, not a very good diplomat, as his first words, after hellos all round, were: 'Now then, Mrs H, enough of your falling down on the domestic duties – I could murder a very large G and T.'

'Dad!' exclaimed Sophie and only after a withering look from his wife did Mr Harper realise it was not the best thing to say in front of someone struggling to complete their second full day without alcohol.

'Oops, sorry, Hannah. Tell you what, make it a water with ice and I'll pop up and change.'

One of their sons telephoned during dinner, and as they all had a brief word with him – he was a TV journalist apparently – I looked at Hannah, and I could tell we were thinking exactly the same thing . . . 'Why can't we have a family like this?'

Sober as a judge – his words not mine – Mr Harper dropped me home. It wasn't that far but he insisted I couldn't possibly walk back in the dark. He wasn't as easy to talk to as his wife – she had instantly become one of my favourite people of all time, in the whole of humankind – but as I stepped from the car outside our block, I said, 'Mr Harper, one day my mum will thank you for being the most wonderful family in the world. She can't bring herself to do it right now, but I know she will. Anyway, I can. You have saved my sister and I will always love you for that.' The big man looked like he was going to shed a tear, so I turned and ran to the entrance to the flats, which felt like a real comedown after my first taste of a luxury home.

I chatted to Mum for a bit, stuck by my lie, and ran through the various parts I'd 'tried for'. She looked tired, and sad, watching TV without taking a word of it in. It was a film about a priest who struggled with all the thoughts he had about women that he wasn't supposed to have. He was always praying, and that must have been why, before climbing into bed, I knelt on the floor, hands on the duvet, closed my eyes and prayed as well. 'Dear God,' I said, 'I know you don't exist because if you did, my mum and dad would still be together, and we would have a lovely house like Sophie's, and Robin van Persie wouldn't have gone to Manchester United. But on the off chance that you do exist, my sister is called Hannah and she is the best, the loveliest, the most beautiful sister in the world. Trouble is, my mum always says your enemy the Devil works his evil ways through alcohol, which is why she doesn't believe in you, and the Devil is working on Hannah right now. If you really do exist, and you're up there watching us all the time, you'll know that Hannah drinks an awful lot for someone of her age, and it's making her ill, and making us ill, and it's driven her from me into someone else's home – it's a nice place, don't get me wrong, God . . . well, you've seen it, you know what it's like – but I would still rather have her back here. I'm not sure my mum will ever speak to her again, but I want her to, and I want you and the Harpers to help me make that happen. In RE at primary school, Miss Charlton used to say you were our guide, so I am praying to you so that you might think about guiding Hannah, every day, day after day, because she says she has to do it a day at a time. I hope you do exist, and I hope you're listening and I hope you can do this little favour for me . . . well, big favour, really. Anyway, good to talk to you. Sleep well. Night-night.'

I got into bed, stared at Hannah's pillow, and smiled at least knowing she was in a comfy double bed in her own room with an en suite bathroom, and a bedside lamp with a switch actually in the wall, not on the wire to the lamp like mine.

# JONATHAN

**My name is Jonathan. I am a TV journalist, and the brother of Sophie, Hannah's best friend at school.**

Hannah cost me my job, inadvertently, but I didn't mind. Because, equally inadvertently, she helped me to learn a wonderful lesson in the difference between right and wrong, which is important to a lawyer like my father, but just as important to a journalist like me.

This is not a good time to be a journalist. The phone-hacking scandal, alongside the skulduggery and arrogance of journalists, editors and owners exposed at the Leveson Inquiry into the 'ethics [*sic*] culture and practices of the press', have given ample ammunition to those who wish to place us beneath politicians, second-hand car salesmen, drug dealers and paedophiles as the lowest of all the lowlifes. I still see journalism as a noble calling, yet I am aware most see us as people who parasite off the sufferings of others, who believe the impact of what we write and say is far more important than its veracity, who really would sell their granny if it got them a front-page byline or a two-way piece to camera with Huw Edwards on the BBC news. We have all been tarred with the same pungent, shit-covered brush. It really isn't fair.

When I was growing up, and first developing opinions of my own, my father often yelled at me, 'Don't just scream "it's not fair", do something to make it less fair.' As a lawyer, though, his mind and his life have always run on reasonably straight lines of logic. I never fancied law, or medicine, my mother's world, because though I like logic, I prefer emotion, and journalism to me is about emotion and feeling, which inspires us to use the power of language and belief in justice to expose the bad and highlight the good in the world. Despite having a lawyer and a doctor for parents, I am an idealist. If I really want to wind up Dad, I say, 'I am in the justice business, the same as you are, only you care about winning the case, I care about the truth.' The best stories, for an investigative reporter like me, come not from everyday events – the general news guys and the policy specialists take care of those – they come when I feel something deeply, when I react viscerally to something I hear or read, and I say to myself, 'I cannot be the only one who would feel like this. I will go out and discover more.'

I was working for the current affairs show *Focus*, which is ITV's attempt to persuade the public, politicians and regulators that the TV world has not all gone to the bottom of a downmarket, soap-sudded, Cowellised barrel. It is a one-hour programme, usually made up of three items and a studio discussion with an audience, with ad breaks in between, but which occasionally devotes the whole hour to a single issue. I had a wonderful boss, deputy editor Andy Cape, a Geordie, who was giving me a lot of time, and freedom, to come up with the ideas and the research for the one-hour shows. Investigative reporting is dying, but people like Andy will ensure it doesn't fully expire without a considerable fight. I came to the programme from the *Sunday Telegraph*, where my father helped me get on the first rung after my local paper training in Blackpool via his friend, the legal affairs correspondent, and after a few shifts with him, I was put under the news desk, had a string of good exclusives, which led to a call from Andy, asking if I fancied telly. I did. I always had. When it comes to the power to move, nothing can beat the moving picture and the spoken word working in unison.

So, aged twenty-six, I found myself visiting an online print store to get new business cards, 'Jonathan Harper, reporter at large, *Focus*, Britain's leading current affairs show'. I could have happily left it at *Focus*, and gone straight to the phone, email and Twitter contacts, but the management insisted on that last bit. It was part of the 'programme branding'. Yuk.

The idea for a film on young women and booze came when I was in my flat in Kew, stirring a risotto as I waited for my girlfriend Angela, who works for an architecture company in Hammersmith, to come home from work. It was a Thursday, and as *Focus* goes out on Wednesday night, most of us take Thursday as a day off. I'd poured myself a glass of white wine from the fridge, showered the risotto with it too, and I was thinking that it had been several weeks since I had successfully pitched for a full-hour show. I'd not been slow in putting forward ideas, and some had led to good shorter packages and decent discussions. But the specials were what I lived for, and as I turned down the gas to leave things to simmer, I decided to spend the next morning writing a note to myself about the possibilities. I often write memos to myself, as a way of thinking things through.

However, sometimes the best ideas come straight at you, without forethought or warning, and one such came at me from the radio that was chirruping away as I cooked and wished Angela would hurry up. I was drifting in and out of listening, something Radio 5 Live is particularly good for. Suddenly my attention was caught by a stentorian-sounding man, described as Professor something, I didn't catch his name at first, who said that when he started out as a liver specialist, cirrhosis was almost exclusively a male disease. Now, he said, his cases were evenly divided between men and women.

'It's not sexist, but a fact,' he said, 'to say that women cannot drink as much as men can. But they try to, increasingly so, and I see the results in my clinic every single day. I am not prone to sensationalism or exaggeration, but frankly what I'm seeing is an epidemic of alcohol abuse among women, young women in particular, with all the implications that has for health-care costs, childcare, marriage, social cohesion, frankly the happiness of the nation. We are sleepwalking to a disaster and it's time we woke up to that.'

I walked over to the radio, and listened more closely as the interviewer said, 'But surely Britain has always been a drinking country. One thinks of the gin laws, of the –'

'Possibly,' interrupted the liver expert – nice to hear the interviewee doing the interrupting for once – 'but what is new is the disproportionate impact on women. I have looked into drinking patterns and the medical impact all over the world, and I believe there are now more young female problem drinkers in Britain, per head of population, than anywhere in the world, including Russia and northern Europe. The medium- and long-term consequences of that are nothing short of catastrophic. The problem is the alcohol lobby is way too powerful, and politicians and regulators lack the courage to take it on. But they must, before it's too late.'

'Professor Michael Childs, Southampton General Hospital, thank you. Now . . . Katy Perry, how's things on the roads? . . .'

I scribbled the professor's name on the top of Barack Obama's head on the front page of *The Economist* which lay on the kitchen table, got through to Professor Childs' secretary the next morning, explained the purpose of my call, and she came back to say he could see me late on Friday afternoon. In a couple of neat, crisp sound bites, he had given me the basis for a special. Meeting him at the end of the week, passionate, quirky, well informed and with a mass of unpublished research material, convinced me it could be a good one, and the memo I wrote over the weekend convinced Andy Cape, who in turn convinced Deborah McHugh, the series editor and head of commissioning.

'The thesis is strong,' she said when we met to discuss it. 'Your man Childs is clearly a good talker, he has some great facts and figures, not least on all the money the companies spend on lobbying and marketing, and he has fascinating trends on the health stuff, but listen, Jonathan, it will only work with real faces on screen, young women, telling their stories of the road into oblivion through drink, and I'm not interested in distorted voices or back-of-head shots, all that identity-protection bullshit. I want real people, real fucking stories, and I don't just want people who have come back from it, I want people who are still suffering from it now.' I felt fired up, because though Deborah could be grating when she tried too hard to be the tough exec woman in a tough man's world, she was decisive, and what she had set out for the special was what Andy and I wanted too.

Childs reckoned he would be able to lead me to plenty of recovering alcoholics, but he would need to think carefully about whether he would encourage any of his own current patients to talk on camera. In any event, he wouldn't pressurise anyone to do anything they didn't want to. 'We're talking about fragile and often damaged people, and we cannot do anything to make it worse for them. But I am determined to get the government and the country to see sense on this.'

I was clear that I would give whatever guarantees I could, but I knew these face-to-face, no-hiding-place interviews would make or break the programme, and they might not be easy to get. I spent the first couple of weeks directing the research team, working up filming possibilities in different hospitals, drop-in centres, women's groups, and of course inside the alcohol industry, who were remarkably cooperative considering I was honest and straightforward about the thesis – Britain was sitting on a time bomb, an epidemic of alcohol abuse among young women, fuelled by a tsunami of booze marketing.

I was confident that as we dug into the issues we would find people to talk on camera. What I didn't bank on was that one of the best possible talkers on the subject was at the time living with my parents. Mum had mentioned they had a friend of Sophie's staying with them for a few days, who had fallen out with her parents, but I only got the full story when Angela and I went round for Sunday lunch. I hadn't even said what I was working on. When I met Hannah, though, I 'declared an interest', explained about the programme, and went through some of the facts I had dug up. She had gone ten days without a drink, apparently, the longest period since she started drinking. She struck me as bright, very pretty, but I could tell she was still struggling to hold off the urges to drink. She was confident when she spoke – except when the subject of alcohol came up, which, given how I was diving into it with my usual bit-between-the-teeth obsessiveness, was often. I should probably have been more sensitive but at the time I didn't realise how far gone she was. She didn't look so bad. In fact, if she hadn't been my little sister's friend, and I hadn't been with Angela, I could definitely have fancied her, even fallen for her.

After the girls had gone off, Dad filled me in on the meeting with Dr Lister, which sounded quite an event. When he said she filmed and taped all her interviews because she was a world-class authority and researcher on addiction, I said simply, 'Wow.'

'The only thing is I specifically recall her saying to Hannah these interviews would never be shown other than for research and education. There is no way she would ever go back on that.'

'No, but she might have leads for other people. There might be women who actively want to talk about this. According to one of our potential interviewees, sometimes people trying to give up need to say something publicly to give themselves the pressure they need to see it through.'

'I understand that. But go easy on Hannah. I don't want her thinking we're doing this so our son can land himself a BAFTA award.'

'Course not. I will talk to this Lister woman. But Hannah is off-limits.'

Mum called Dr Lister the following morning, explained the rather unusual set of circumstances and asked if she would see me for a background chat. It turned out she had watched *Focus* the week before, when I had fronted a shortish piece on how the media campaign against vaccines had led to a rise in measles. It helped that she knew and liked the programme, and associated me from the off not just with my parents, good and responsible people, but with what she viewed as a good and responsible piece of journalism about health.

We met in her almost anally uncluttered office, which I had to access through three separate security doors, escorted by a man with a shaved head and a huge fob of keys on his belt. It felt more like entering a small and rather smart new prison than a hospital.

'Don't tell your lodger this is my day job,' she said when finally we met. 'It might frighten her. This is the Psychiatric Intensive Care Unit. There are some very sad cases in here, and I wouldn't want her to think this is her league, let alone her destiny.'

'How's she doing?'

'OK. She has a slight habit of saying what she thinks I want to hear, but she's at least conscious of the issues.'

'Still, twelve days isn't bad.'

'Twelve days?'

'Dad said she hasn't had a drink for twelve days.'

'And he believed her? That's what I mean about telling people what they want to hear. I took blood tests last time. She's still drinking.'

'Oh.'

'She's in what we in the shrinking industry call DENIAL mode – Don't Even No I Am Lying.'

'Oh. Should I tell Mum and Dad?'

'No. I shouldn't really be telling you, but it's difficult when there's no adult member of the family for me to talk to, and I'm still being engaged informally. I don't know if she knows, but I'm seeing her as a private patient, and your dad is paying the bill.'

'Bless him,' I said. 'Parades as a legal hard man. He's as soft as his belly.'

I showed her the research notes I had done so far. It didn't take long for professional rivalry to surface.

'Childs is a good clinician, but he does love the sound of his own voice.'

'It's quite a voice.'

'Certainly is, and at least he's using it to get the issue up in lights. He's right on the substance too.'

'ITV likes to have as many women on as possible, and as this film is about women alcoholics, it would be great to have women doctors and experts, so I hope you might take part too.'

'I'd be happy to, though this is my world right now, seriously disturbed people, not just addiction.'

'I'd love to read any of your papers. I'm at that stage where I'm getting all the vomit on the page, as we say, totally immersing myself, then working out a way forward. Your work could be absolutely central.'

It was she, in the word 'tapes', who raised the hundreds of hours of films she had, and though she emphasised they could only be used for teaching and educational purposes, she felt, if some of the interviewees were willing, she might consider that a programme like this was educational.

I asked about the quality of the film and the sound.

'Well, Hannah's was the last I did. As she was happy for your family to be there, you can take a look while I just have a wander round the unit.' She had a new patient in who was refusing all food and medication. He had come to them from the police the night before, who had found him on the London Eye, trying to smash his way through the glass when he'd got to the top.

'Are you sure?'

'About what?'

'That I should see the interview with Hannah?'

'No, you're probably right. I should get her permission. In fact, I should probably get her parents' permission, but I'm not sure how to do that.'

I went for a walk, and a coffee, and by the time I came back, she had spoken to my mum, my sister and to Hannah. She was a little uneasy, I could tell, but she was also desperate to help me, I could tell that too.

She showed me the tiny camera she used, which had a flick-out viewfinder, and I had to watch through that. The camera focused tightly on Hannah, who looked so different to the pretty girl I'd met a couple of days earlier. She was paler, almost yellow, gaunt, her eyes ringed with tiredness and filled with sadness. But when she engaged, she was spellbinding. Dr Lister would make a good TV interviewer, I thought. Short, sharp questions, to the point, good use of the pause, stern but sympathetic. However, nothing prepared me for the emotion at the end, as Sophie moved in to hug Hannah as she equated her drinking with her self-harm. I'm a bit of a weeper myself, joined them in crying, alone, as I looked at a five-inch-by-three-inch screen, and felt a tide of love and hurt come towards me. I felt so proud of Sophie, and of Dad, and so sorry for Hannah, who looked to me like someone who just needed a switch to go on inside her head, the switch marked 'feel good, live good', and she would be fine. I'd seen a shrink for the research yesterday and he said something wonderfully simple:

242

'If you think bad thoughts, you feel bad; if you feel bad, you act bad; if you act bad, you think bad; and so it goes on.' That sounded like Hannah.

Dr Lister timed her return to perfection, as I rooted through my pockets for any remnants of tissues with which to wipe my eyes and blow my nose. She opened a cupboard, and handed me a toilet roll. If good journalism really is driven by emotion, this was going to be the best film I ever made.

'I shouldn't really have let you see that,' she said. 'And I shouldn't let you see any of the other tapes. But I will. And hang the consequences. Because I am totally with Childs on this. We are facing an epidemic and we are doing nothing as a country to face up to it. If alcohol didn't exist, and a company invented it, and took it along to all the governments in the world, there is not one of them, not one, that would allow it to be manufactured and sold. Trouble is, we've gone too far. It has a total grip on every level of society, from the rich with their Pimm's and their aperitifs and digestifs, and the middle classes with their wines and their nights out, to the kids on the estates with their cheap cider, and nobody in power wants to admit it. I've seen dozens of Hannahs, maybe not as young as her, but she's just ahead of her time. And you know, I have seen so much damage to so many people that I think I have got to do something more than just treat them.'

'I don't want to get you into any trouble though,' I said. 'If you have the slightest doubt about showing me your tapes, you mustn't.'

'I did have doubts, but I've thought about it. I want you to see them so you can see the damage being done. You'll have to sign a non-disclosure agreement, but it will help you under-stand the issues. Then if you log the ones you think would

243

help the programme, I can decide whether to approach them on your behalf, and discuss possible participation. We have to wake this country up, and maybe your film is the way to do it.'

When I arrived on Monday with Simeon Morris, a trainee, as support, I felt utterly daunted by the scale of what lay in front of me. She put us in a meeting room near the entrance to the building, where she had set up two separate video machines. She had listed all her old patients in an A4 folder, by number, location, age, sex, occupation, brief history, and length of interview. It went on for dozens of pages. The shortest interview was fifteen seconds, a man who stormed out because she asked him whether he had ever felt sexual attraction towards other men. The longest was four hours eleven minutes, an Australian knee surgeon. Her system at least allowed me to separate out the women. At a rough count, flicking through her folder, I reckoned we had about 140 interviews to dip into.

The sound quality came and went, but there was something really special about the films. The camera was always at the same angle, and the face filled the shot. Nothing but the talking head. Even watching their faces as they listened to a question could reveal something of their character or their pain. Dr Lister came in after a few hours, and I said, 'If these women were all game, you could become a TV star in an instant. This stuff is fantastic. It would make a series on its own.'

I sent a note to Andy, explaining what we had, pointing out that we still had to face the prospect that none of them would talk. But what would make for a great hour's show, I said, would be for me to watch back these interviews with some of the women concerned, both those who still drank and those who were dry, and talk to them about their lives that took them to see Dr Lister, and their lives now.

'I love it,' said Andy. 'With Childs, Lister, your other shrinks, the refuge women and the industry voices, we only need four or five max. So let's aim for ten and see how we go.'

By the end of the week, between us Simeon and I had watched and made notes on almost seventy hours of tape. I asked Dr Lister if we could come in over the weekend and, ever helpful, she said yes. I brought in Andy and two more researchers so we could blitz the lot. By the end of Sunday, I had a wish list of twelve names to give to Dr Lister. Hannah, for obvious reasons, wasn't on it.

I called Mum and asked if I could bring the guys back for a drink and a bite to eat, as two of them lived not far from Highbury, and Angela was in Madrid, where her firm was bidding for the design of a new theatre. We were at that stage of the film where I knew it was going to work, the research was building up beautifully, we had some half-decent stuff in the can, plenty more planned, and what ought to be a truly fascinating series of interviews with women about the admissions they made in the Lister films, and the different stories they told as to why they descended into the drink. We were at the tipping point you need to feel before you can really start to motor on the creativity and the emotion that separates the great TV from the average.

Dr Lister, despite having what my limited access to the PICU suggested was surely one of the most tiring and stressful jobs in London, worked as hard as we did to try to make it all work. I wondered if she might be finding it a nice distraction from looking after the poor souls I saw on the two occasions I went with her through all the security doors and into her office. One was lying on the floor, face down, with a male nurse crouched down on either side. As we arrived at Dr Lister's office, I heard a kerfuffle behind me and the man had started to bang his head against the floor as hard as he could. 'That's been going on for four days,' she said. She took our list, crossed out three names immediately, for reasons I didn't press for, and then began contacting the remaining nine, one by one. Within three days, she had seen or spoken to all but two of them – one was not responding to calls, the other had emigrated to Canada with a new husband – and of the seven, she decided two were not suitable to be put out in public, two more were unwilling under any circumstances, which left us with three. I got Simeon to go through our reserve list, and we produced ten more names for Dr Lister. A similar process left us with two to add to the initial three names. Over the next few days I met each of them with Dr Lister, gave them what assurances I could, sought to make clear that I saw this as classic public service broadcasting – members of the public providing a service to others by revealing their own stories. Two of our five were dry. Two drank moderately. One remained a heavy drinker, and yet was the keenest to appear. Expenses and the offer of a modest 'disturbance fee' might have had a role to play in her enthusiasm. She was a university dropout who had recently been sacked from her job in a sales office, and was living in a hostel.

I had been so immersed in the making of the programme that I had stopped asking Dr Lister about Hannah, though she did tell me we were working in the room where she interviewed her. It was my mum who told me she was worried Hannah was back drinking again, worries exacerbated when she asked my dad how I was getting on with my programme, and 'do they pay the people they interview?' I suggested he said he didn't know – which at the time was true – but the following morning, I received a text. '*Jonathan, this is Hannah, your sister's friend. I would like to help with your film. Call me on this number after school.*'

I phoned Dad. He was about to leave for court and said, 'Let me think about it.' I called Mum, who was at her clinic, where the mobile reception was always dire, and after three aborted calls, I gave up. I called Sophie, who I still tended to see as my baby sister, eight years younger than I was, but she was old enough to vote now, she was sensible and mature for her age and I owed it to her to take her opinion too.

'I gave her your number. She'd be great, Jont, she really would.'

'I know that, but would it be the right thing for her to do?'

'But she's barely touched a drop for weeks now.'

'Are you sure?'

'Pretty sure. She's not been here every night but when she has been she hasn't been drunk, put it that way.'

'But she's only just turned eighteen, Sophie. Could she cope with being on the telly, having people write about her in the papers, maybe dig into her family life and all that stuff about her mum and the boyfriend?'

'But you don't need to talk about that.'

'I don't need to talk about anything. But she'll be the best interview in a programme of interviews about a big subject. For a while, the press will be interested. They might dig around. Can she cope?'

'The thing is, Jont, I think she wants to do it as a way of putting real pressure on herself to stay off it. She is good when she puts herself under pressure. I've seen it in our A-level revision. When she focuses, she's brilliant. She was down for three Ds six months ago, now they're talking maybe Bs, and even the outside chance of an A in drama. She could get to university, Jont, imagine that as the end to your film.'

I recalled the editor's strictures that she wanted women 'still suffering', and I wondered if we did do Hannah, who would be seven years younger than our youngest Lister patient signed up so far, we would be making future suffering more not less likely. I was horribly torn. Had she not come across my radar via the family, I would have pushed hard to get her on. But she did come through the family, who now virtually saw her as being a part of the family herself, and though I wanted to make a great film, I didn't want to damage her as she seemed to be making a half-decent fist of recovery.

When finally I spoke to Dad, he was borderline sceptical. Mum, clearly got at by Sophie, trotted out all the reasons for doing it, said, 'This will be like a public declaration she is on the mend. She isn't the sort to go back on that.'

'You sure she doesn't see it as the chance of a few bob, Andy Warhol's fifteen minutes of fame?'

'I don't think so.'

'Or sending a message to her mum?'

'That would be no bad thing.'

I called her head teacher, Mr Sharples, who said he wouldn't encourage it in the run-up to exams, but he had noted an improvement in her recently. Ultimately, he said, it was a matter for her and her parents, but he knew that was a fraught situation and not exactly a helpful observation.

The casting vote had to be with Dr Lister. She came up

with a great idea when I phoned her at her PICU. 'Watch the interview back with her, then do your own interview, then we all watch it, you decide which bits you're likely to use, we review again, you, me, Hannah, your parents, your sister, the head, and we don't decide till we absolutely have to.'

'Brilliant,' I said. 'Brilliant.'

We did the interview at my parents' house, but we made it dark and moody, with a plain black backdrop. It could have been anywhere. We had agreed to pay her £120 disturbance fee and rather than go through the bureaucracy I paid her in cash which I would claim back as expenses. It was a bargain given that renting a house like Mum and Dad's would normally cost thousands for all the palaver TV creates. I did two of our other Lister interviews there during the afternoon, but Hannah was the one I was most excited about.

We had pushed all the furniture in the sitting room against the walls, and set up a viewing area, where Hannah and I would sit, a camera to our left, a camera to our right, and watch her chat with Dr Lister. The format we had agreed would work best was that I would run the tape, but occasionally pause it, and ask her questions, at which point the third camera would focus on her, tightly, to echo the tape we were discussing, but from a slightly different angle so viewers could tell the difference between the hospital interview and mine.

A TV studio can be a scary place for people not used to it, even when it is set up in the place where you live, so I made sure Sophie and Mum brought her in, fussed around her as she sat down to get TV make-up applied, generally made her feel this was an exciting adventure, one with the capacity to help her. Before we started, I said she could stop at any time, and I reminded her she could pull out of being used at any point, right up to TX, transmission date, which was looking like being two weeks away.

There were some good moments. I stopped the tape at the point where she was telling Dr Lister about her 'relationship' with alcohol. 'Can you imagine never drinking again?' I asked her. Her face filled with a fear I had not seen since watching the interview. She looked down at her hands, cupped together in the lap of one of Sophie's patterned skirts. She breathed in, deeply, then formed her mouth into a little 'O' and let out a long, slow sigh, which ended with her closing her eyes.

'Is that hard to imagine?' I said.

She looked at me for four or five seconds – a lifetime on TV – licked her top lip as though suddenly it had lost all its moisture, and said, 'Hard, yes, it's hard.'

'How many days is it since you had a drink?'

Another long pause, and I saw her trying to bring Sophie and Mum, sitting by the piano which had been shoved to the far side of the fireplace, into her line of vision.

'One,' she said. I heard Sophie gasp.

'I've been managing a few days at a time, but it's not easy. I had a couple yesterday.'

'Last night?'

Pause. Tilt of head to the right. Scratch nose. Lick lip. Sigh.

'No, at school, between history and drama.'

'At school? What time was that?'

'Two thirty?'

'Do you take drink to school?'

'Look, I'm really trying, I am. I've seen Dr Lister five times, I've only missed three, I do most of her exercises even though I've got my exams in a few weeks, and I think I am doing better. I know I am. But even when I'm not drinking

250

I like to know drink is around the place. So I have bottles hidden here and there.'

'Like what kind of thing?'

She now looked over to my mum and Sophie, mouthed the words 'I'm sorry. I'm trying', and Sophie said softly, 'It's OK, just tell the truth.'

She looked back to me, and said, 'Right now, Eristoff vodka, cistern, toilet by the science block. Blossom Hill white and red wine at the bottom of the equipment box in the gym. Scotch in the lawnmower bucket in the caretaker's shed.'

I was stunned, and must have looked it.

'Towel on top. He doesn't use the lawnmower, because we don't have any lawn.'

There was a great telly moment when we got on to viewing the discussion about self-harm. I stopped the tape as Dr Lister made the comparison between self-harm and excessive alcohol consumption. I wanted to get something close to her cutting herself 'because the pain of the knife is not as bad as the pain inside' in my own interview.

'Had you thought of that before she asked you about it?'

'About what?'

'What you went on to say, when you said you knew why you did it. Do you remember what you said?'

'Kind of. I said I drank to feel better, but ended up feeling worse. I cut myself to feel better, but the same.'

'So why do you cut yourself?'

'To let out the pain I feel inside.'

'You have drunk less since seeing Dr Lister, though you haven't stopped completely. Have you stopped cutting yourself?'

Another nervous look towards the piano. Another deep

breath. Another 'O'. Another sigh. Then she unbuttoned the bottom of her sleeve, and rolled it up, to reveal a new scar, scrawled across several of the old ones.

'Can we have a break?' she said.

'Sure.'

I sent the rushes to Andy later, and when we reviewed the edit the next evening, Dr Lister was a little more sceptical that the broadcast would be good for her recovery. Hannah remained keen to press ahead. I said we would keep it under advisement and meanwhile we would get on with the rest of the film. We were really pressed now to make it for the week after next. I had not even sketched out my script and pieces to camera.

Thanks to sleep deprivation and a great team, we got everything done in time. The one outstanding decision, with two days to go, was whether to use Hannah or not. We had arranged a final meeting at my parents' house with her, her sister Vicki, my family and Dr Lister where – this was probably sacking material if ITV found out – I was intending to show them two versions, one with her, one without. They were both strong, but the one with her was the difference between good and great TV. No matter how many times I watched those two sections in the edit, and the bit where she talked about her love–hate relationship with her mum, and her non-relationship with her dad, I felt the same power and emotion I felt when doing the interview. Andy reckoned it was award-winning stuff, and the device of watching back the old tapes, both hers and the other women in the final edit, was brilliant, though I say so myself.

However, the meeting to view it never went ahead. I was

working at the Farm, a film and TV edit centre overlooking Soho Square, when I got a text from Andy back at base. *'I know you're busy, but call. Urgent.'*

'We're not running it,' he said when I phoned.

'What?'

'We're not running it.'

'Why not?'

'Don't fucking ask me. Deborah just told me, said she'd explain, then went to a meeting.'

'But it's in the listings. They've done trailers. I just heard one on the radio in the cab.'

'I know. Fucking nightmare.'

'What the fuck can it be, Andy?'

'I really don't know. It's the best thing we've done this series, by a fucking mile.'

I could hardly breathe I was so angry. All that work, all the commitment and emotional input from doctors and patients, all the negotiations we'd done. Above all, the fact we were bringing to public attention something that had to be out there, because the more I had gone into it, the surer I became that Dr Childs and Dr Lister were right. The title for the programme, 'Women Drowning in a Booze Tsunami', may have been a bit tabloidy, but it was true. And for reasons that were unfathomable, the truth was being cancelled.

I tried to call Deborah but was told she was in a meeting. I told the team to carry on, left the edit suite, jumped into a cab and headed to ITV. I found the meeting she was in, and walked in.

'Jonathan, not now, please,' she said. She was with the chief executive, the head of marketing, the head of advertising and the chief press officer.

'Sorry, but yes now. Why is the film on young women and alcohol being pulled?'

'Jonathan, I will explain to you. But let me finish my meeting, and I'll see you in ten minutes.'

The marketing man, Vic Andrews, was sitting next to her. He had a folder on his lap. One of the most important journalistic techniques I learned from my old editor on the *Blackpool Gazette*, Sam Foreman, was the art of reading upside down.

Memo from VA to DMc, cc HK, LR, OT
Re: Sponsorship and ad revenue risk from *Focus* film on women and alcohol.
Urgent. Can we meet asap?

I walked towards Deborah, and I could feel all eyes in the room on me, and minds worrying I was about to do something very silly. Olly Tendler, the head of press, stood up in anticipation. 'Jonathan, no.'

But as I arrived close to Deborah, I reached over to Vic Andrews, grabbed the folder from his lap, and ran out of the office, chased by at least two of them. I was three floors up, raced down the stairs to get to the lobby where word had gone out to stop me. I leapt over the exit barrier, pushed aside a security guy who was hopelessly overweight, got out into the street, and hailed a cab.

'Where to?'

'Anywhere. Just drive. I'll decide in a minute.'

As we headed towards the river, I read Andrews' paper which showed that ITV had been coming under pressure from some of the big alcohol companies, and the supermarkets, in the light of what they feared was a 'hatchet job' on the industry.

There were memos and letters which included veiled threats about shifting ad spend to other channels, or other media. But 'of far greater risk', wrote Andrews, 'is the multimillion-pound programme sponsorship deal being put together with Australian wines. As you know, we are in advanced negotiations with Aussie wines generically, and a number of specific Australian wines which will act as sponsors for soaps, talk shows, and the post-9pm talent shows. We are looking to build an ongoing partnership for several years, such as the one Stella have built for Film on Four, and Foster's for Channel 4 comedy shows. But in the deal we're negotiating – wine not beer!! – the female demographic is central and we should at least have a proper discussion before going ahead with the *Focus* special.' There was then a puke-making selection of quotes from brand managers extolling the success of past tie-ups, the best of which – worst of which – was from Baileys. '*Sex and the City* is an effective sponsorship vehicle for Baileys in that it will help add flirtation, sensuality and mischief, as well as a touch of bare-faced cheek, to the brand. Our aim is for consumers to reappraise the brand and consider it outside the traditional Christmas period. We want consumers to feel good about being a fan of the programme and the Baileys brand. To this end, the idents that we are creating will bring the best of both *Sex and the City* and Baileys together.'

The marketing, advertising and sponsorship issue was just a tiny part of the film. We did mention that alcohol companies spent more than £85 million on TV advertising in the UK in 2011, and the latest edit included a short section on how the industry got round advertising and marketing restrictions designed to limit any suggestions of a link between alcohol and social and sexual success. We had unearthed an internal memo from one of the vodka manufacturers that sponsored programmes with a disproportionately young, female audience, and spoke explicitly in terms of 'using our celebrity ambassadors in the bumper breaks so they become associated with the product as well as the show'. We had interviewed the author of the memo. He had defended it, denied our 'insinuations', insisted his firm stayed within the Portman Group rules, rammed home the industry line that most people drink responsibly, they encourage responsible drinking, they have no desire to see young people drink to excess and – this line survived all edits – 'Listen, let's not be silly about this, we would hardly want our customers to become ill. They're not much use to us dead, are they?' And there he was in this note, one of eight industry executives, clearly organised, warning of 'serious consequences for our relationship with the station if this blatant misrepresentation of our industry is allowed, for purely sensationalist reasons, to go ahead'. Another claimed – falsely – that 'we understand on the basis of a single interview, you intend to allege a link between alcohol promotion and self-harm among young women, when we have reputable and respected research showing there is no such link'.

And then a paragraph on four MPs, three Tory, one Labour, who had written in to ask that we ensure the economic benefits of the industry are properly examined in the programme, and that we focus also on the alarming loss of pubs across the country, 'something which somewhat negates the idea of a booze tsunami'.

My anger was now turning to rage, and I had to apologise to the driver as I punched the seat beside me.

'Sorry, listen, just drop me here. I need some fresh air.'

I called Carole, the sound mixer, who was still in the edit suite. I told her to make copies of everything we had and meet me at the Chancery Court Hotel in Holborn when she had them.

I walked there, ordered a coffee and a glass of water, and read the whole grisly folder. To me, it was worse than anything that emerged at the Leveson Inquiry. I was staring at a Venn diagram on the growing importance of alcohol to programme sponsorship, with a long footnote on the importance of product placement in the film and TV industries – 'the latest James Bond film was a total triumph for Heineken and is already seeing benefits among younger and female demographics' – when my mobile rang. It was Deborah.

'You spineless bitch,' I said.

'Jonathan, I am with the company lawyer and Olly. I need to warn you that the document you have is company property and you have stolen it.'

'Have I? Well, perhaps it will find its way to a newspaper and they will show more guts than you and they will claim a strong public interest in exposing it to the world, alongside the issues in our film.'

'Jonathan, you are too close to this. The best thing you can do is take a day or two off, and come back refreshed. You've been working too hard. We may be able to salvage something, but not this week, and meanwhile we have Wednesday's programme to fill, and not much time to fill it. So let's meet Thursday or Friday and go over this calmly and sensibly.'

'No fucking way.'

'Jonty, it's Olly here. Look, can we meet up? Regardless of the background – I know nothing about that – it is in nobody's interests for this to become a big bad story on anything other than our terms, so let's sit down and work it out.'

'Olly, I don't know about you but I work in telly because it can shine a light on things that we should all be worried about. I'm worried about young women killing themselves and the big people, the politicians, the business guys, now it seems also the media, doing nothing to help them. I am not working for a company that can see the right thing to do staring it in the face but for its own reasons of cash and cowardice does the wrong thing.'

'Oh, spare us the fucking lectures, Harper.' It was Deborah again. 'You want your pretty young face on the telly, same as all the boys. You picked a nice easy subject which gave you access to lots of sad women with sad stories and you saw the chance to pump a few fucking tears. You even milked your own sister's best friend which is on the edge of the ethics border I would say, but let that go for now. She clearly means a lot to you.'

'What are you trying to suggest?'

'I am trying to suggest you are too close, and I am saying this is not Watergate here, Jonathan. It is not thalidomide. It is not even MPs' expenses or phone hacking. It is a programme about drunks. I am not saying we're canning it. I am saying it is under review. But as a company with obligations to share-holders, and regulators on our backs, the issue of where our money comes from is not without some relevance. Who do you think pays your fucking wages to sit around making three or four worthy films a year? The adverts do.'

'So you admit it? The programme was made, it was announced, it was trailed, and it is being pulled because you need the cash the booze companies give you and the cash won't come if we tell the truth about what their products do to our fucking viewers.'

'No, I am saying yours is not the only view that counts, and I am listening to the views of others. Meantime the film is on hold.'

'Deborah, go fuck yourself. And if your silent company lawyer wants his document back, I suggest he gets himself a good silk. Don't call my dad though. He'll be working for me, because unlike you lot, he knows the difference between right and wrong.' With that, I ended the call. I had never felt better in my life.

# FRANK

**My name is Frank. I was on duty when Hannah reported her mugging.**

My brother Alfie, who works for Special Branch and is at the moment looking after the Israeli ambassador, takes the piss, says night shift on the main desk at Snow Hill is the same as time off. True, Snow Hill might not be as busy most nights as nicks in the West End or out east or up north in Camden or down south in Streatham, let alone round-the-clock protection work like his. It also has to be one of the cutest stations in the country, with its two *Dixon of Dock Green*-style blue police lights either side of the entrance, and a nicely designed four-storey frontage that makes it look more like a fashionable old town house than a working cop shop close to the national capital of fraud and corruption, not to mention the most important criminal court in the land.

Alfie's mockery hit a new height when I made the mistake of inviting him in for a cup of tea and a look round, and the first thing he noticed was the blue plaque on the wall outside, commemorating the 'Site of the Saracens Head Inn, demolished 1868'.

'Fuck me, there's me thinking you were a copper and you're

working in an old pub. Still, only three years till you retire on full sick pay with a bad back from lifting all those barrels into the bar.' Ho ho. Snow Hill is no holiday camp, but Alfie has his joke and I can't take it away from him. 'Oh look, you've even got your own little hallway before we go through these lovely double doors and there's your desk. Where's your bed then?'

The City boys do tend to work hard in EC land, then play hard somewhere else, and tourists round these parts are more St Paul's and Bank of England than the younger ones hanging around Piccadilly. But it can be a fucking war zone at times, and because we're staffed for quiet times, it's not great when things kick off.

Pete Danton was on a break, I already had two in the cells, and another being processed, when in comes what I can only describe as a big dose of female attitude. I was on the phone, and she leaned over, close to my face, said, 'Scuse me, I just been mugged.' I nodded and held up my hand for her to wait a few moments while I dealt with a call from someone who had forgotten where he'd parked his car. As the young woman picked up on the relative triviality of the case I was dealing with – 'Tell him go look for the fuckin' thing himself' – I reminded myself that I had an offer of a job in private security in Gunnersbury, which had to be better than this.

'Now,' I said, when finally I got the lost-car man off the phone, and I decided to try to be firm but reasonably friendly despite the language and the attitude, 'how can I help?'

'I've been fucking mugged. Three guys, riding round on bikes, surround me, push me around, I hit one of them, but the other two are into my pockets and off with my purse. Cash, Oyster card, hole-in-the-wall card, everything. Then they see I've got a plastic bag tucked inside my coat and the bastards make off with that too.'

'OK, let me get some details.'

'OK, but fuck's sake, can't you get your people out looking? There can't be many gangs going round bike-mugging at half three in the morning.'

'You'd be amazed. Now listen to me, I know you are upset –'

'Course I'm upset. How'd you feel if some guys whacked you around and made off with near on a hundred quid and some jewellery?'

'I'd probably ask myself why I had so much cash on me.'

'Because I got a hundred and twenty quid for a telly thing I did, and I don't have a home, so I keep my money with me.'

'You're a TV personality, are you?'

'No, I'm not. I'm a young woman and I've been mugged and robbed and you're supposed to fucking help me.'

'I'll find it easier to do that if you calm down, stop swearing, and move a few inches back so I don't have to smell a night's drinking and smoking.'

'I don't smoke.'

I stood silently and waited for her to calm down. She raved on for two or three more incoherent sentences, and duly did.

'Now listen, I can only help with this if you tell me calmly who you are, where you were, what happened. OK? So let's start with your name.'

'Hannah Maynard.'

'Age?'

'Eighteen.'

'Address? You said you didn't have a home, but if someone wanted to send you a letter, where would they post it to?'

'My mum's, but she kicked me out a while back.'

I resisted the temptation to say 'that doesn't entirely surprise me', and instead asked for her mother's address.

'Flat 22, Killingbeck House, Highbury New Park.'

'I grew up near there,' I said, hoping small talk might further lighten the mood.

'I wish I hadn't.'

'Do you have a mobile?'

'Yes, but they took that too.'

'Give me the number anyway, in case they use or try to sell it.'

She did so, once she had dug around the recesses of her mind to remember it, then went back to attitude mode. 'Do you have any street patrols? Do they do anything? The time this is taking, these scumbags and their fucking bikes could be cycling round the Olympic Park by now.'

'Where did the incident happen?'

'Outside Sainsbury's, Holborn Circus.'

'Three youths?'

'I told you that, yes?'

'Colour?'

'What? Their bikes or the hoodies that made sure I couldn't see their faces?'

'Their skin.'

'One definitely white, one mixed race, didn't see the other one at all. He was at me from behind.'

'Clothes?'

'For God's sake, I don't know. Hoodies. White guy's was grey, mixed race black, I think. Jeans, trainers, I guess. The uniform, you know?'

'Notice the make?'

'Nike trainers, the mixed-race guy. White guy, Lonsdale top.'

'You see, these details may be useful. Notice anything special about the bikes?'

'Two wheels each, no stabilisers. I'm not a bike expert, I'm a mugging victim.'

'Miss Maynard, you're getting very close to being drunk and disorderly. Even closer to causing a nuisance in a public place. And you're abusing a police officer carrying out his duties.'

'What duties have you carried out? Faffed around and taken down information so slowly on this form they'll have spent the money by now. Look, I've been mugged. No phone, no money, I need you to help me.'

'Not if this abusive behaviour continues. If it does, I will arrest you.'

'What the fuck? A young girl gets mugged within an inch of her life, and the ones who get the help are the muggers, probably getting a police escort out of the patch so you don't have to do a fucking thing, while the young girl is locked up. Brilliant. Fucking brilliant. Well, fuck you, mister, and fuck your fat lazy arse.' And with that she went through the door into the foyer, stopping to pick up a chair, which she threw towards me before running out of the building. She's right that I'm overweight, but I jumped over the desk, chased after her and, helped by a PC parking his patrol car in the 'Police Only' bays outside, caught her by the time she reached the Viaduct Tavern, next to the Bank of America on Giltspur Street. She had a little go at escaping as we walked by the Royal Fusiliers Garden of Remembrance, so we whacked on the handcuffs by the water fountain, and marched her back in.

'Now, young lady,' I said, once we were safely back inside the station, 'I'm going to tell our patrols about your mugging. But I'm also going to ask you to go into the cells, and I'm going to get a WPC to come and take a statement with regard to the mugging, and also the criminal damage offence with which we might charge you, alongside all the others I mentioned earlier.'

I radioed out the mugging alert, and she didn't correct me so I must have got the details right, then asked, 'Any WPCs near Snow Hill?'

'Yes, Frank. Judith here. How are you?'

'I've got a young lady here I'd like you to see. Where are you?'

'Warwick Passage, just by the Old Bailey.'

'Yes, Judith, I know where Warwick Passage is.' It was a covered, narrow, tunnel-like passageway running down the side of the Old Bailey, and a favoured spot for courting couples and police officers enjoying a smoke out of the cold.

'I can be back in a couple of minutes,' she said.

'See you then. Over and out.'

I turned to the girl, said I was taking her to the cells to cool off, I would keep her informed of any developments with regard to the mugging, but as for her own situation, WPC Peters was a nice woman, and she would be reasonable, 'but if you're unreasonable in return, don't be surprised if you stay the night here, and face a charge in the morning. See this as your last-chance saloon. OK?'

'I've got an exam in the morning.'

'It must have escaped your notice that it has been morning for some time. You should have thought of that before you got drunk and started hurling chairs at me.'

And with that, I took what limited possessions she had, asked for her shoelaces and the scarf she was wearing, and led her to the cells, where I put her between a Russian labourer sleeping off a heavy night on the floor, and a Nigerian minicab driver who had punched an officer and fled when pulled over for touting, and was now headbutting the stone wall in a slow, regular rhythm.

# JUDITH

**My name is Judith. I was on duty when PC Frank Lockyer arrested Hannah.**

I was relieved to get the call. I was on nights all week, had just gone out, and despite it supposedly being the start of summer it was perishing cold. I was due to be out for a couple of hours, back in for a break, then take over front-desk work from PC Lockyer. The streets were quiet, apart from the council cleaners out early, a few black cabs roaming around, vans heading to the flower and fish markets. I've been trying to stop smoking since my birthday, but Wally Bould was incorrigible, forever getting me to have one when he did, which was as often as he could. It was frowned upon for on-duty officers to smoke in public, so we snuck in by the public entrance to the Old Bailey and lit up. Wally used the call from the station to head back with me, and have a cup of tea with us as Frank explained the case of the young lady in the cells. We had a good laugh at her crack about the bikes having no stabilisers, but he had clearly just about had enough of her.

'I'm prepared to put a lot of it down to being drunk and being in shock because of the mugging. But I've said she's in the last-chance saloon and I think we have to stick to that,' he said.

I finished my tea, helped Wally with a couple of crossword clues, then went through to the cells to see her. I took a look through the spy-hole and saw she had stripped to her underwear. She was sitting on the hard wooden bench, and seemed to be reading the graffiti on the walls. Frank had put her in the cell that still had the shit stains on the ceiling. That was a heavier night than this, for sure. I tapped three times on the door, which prompted silence from Hannah, a couple of drunken, abusive shouts from the cells next to her.

'OK if I come in?' I said as I opened the door and walked in.

'I doubt I have a choice, do I?'

'Is it too hot in here?'

'No, just fancied taking my clothes off. I'll put them on now.'

'It's fine.'

'No, I will.'

It was only when she stood up that I noticed the patchwork of scars on her arms and shoulders. There was also a big one across her abdomen, and another at the top of her thigh, right at the trim of her knickers.

'Any of those happen tonight?' I asked.

She shook her head. 'They only pushed and shoved really. I can fight, but three v one, no chance.'

'So all your own work, eh?'

'What?'

'The scars?'

'Yeah.'

'My daughter does that.'

'You're kidding me?'

'No.'

'How old?'

'Fourteen.'

'Shit. Four years ahead of me. Funny, seeing you walk in, I'd never think of cops having families.'

'Yep, and they're not all happy either.'

'Mmm.'

Dressed, and with the beginnings of a sobriety of sorts returning – a bare cell with a bright shadeless bulb in the ceiling has that effect on a lot of people – she suddenly looked so much younger. Despite the self-harm, she had a lovely slim body, which reminded me of myself before my kids, too much fast food and too many fags intervened. She had long, slender legs which, but for the gruesome marking on the thigh, would not have looked out of place in a fashion magazine. But as she sat there now, sitting upright, hands on her lap, bare heels tapping against each other, she had gone from young drunken woman to scared, vulnerable child in an instant. It's rare for someone to appear stronger naked than clothed, but Hannah did.

'So what are we going to do with you?' I asked.

She shrugged and tapped her feet together more firmly. 'Dunno. Any news of my muggers?'

'No.'

'What about your man at the front desk? Still angry?'

'Yeah, but he's seen worse.'

'I guess so.' On cue, a voice came from several cells away. 'You might have a fucking uniform but you are the fly on the shit of global humanity.'

I smiled. 'New resident,' I said. She smiled back.

'Do you want to hear my plan?'

She nodded.

'We get in a car, we take you home, we see if your mum lets you in. If she does, fine. If not, we come back here and we think again.'

'No point. She won't let me in.'

'What makes you so sure?'

'I don't tell this to many people. But I got drunk one night and screwed her boyfriend.'

'Ouch.'

'Yeah, well . . .'

'Yeah, well, as things stand you have two options. Stay here, because I'm not letting you back out on the streets when you've had so much to drink and you've not got a penny to your name. Or see if your mum has forgiven you. Then hope Frank forgets all about a silly chair and a bit of bad language.'

'What time is it?'

'Almost half three.'

'She'll go mental.'

'Let's try it.'

I retrieved her scarf and laces, borrowed a yellow plastic jacket from the storeroom to keep her a bit warmer, collected Wally from the back office, and we set off in a patrol car to Highbury New Park.

I sat in the back with her, and could feel her nervousness mounting as we drove through the night and past Smithfield Market, already humming, then signs to the Angel, Islington, Holloway and Highbury, A1 and the North came into view. She complained of the heat and removed the jacket as Wally turned down the fan. We were about five minutes away when I leaned over to her, took her hand, and then ran my other hand up her lower arm, slowly, so I could feel the little ridges on her skin even below her jumper. She looked at me, her eyes blazing with sadness.

'I hope your girl works out OK for you,' she said.

'Me too,' I said. 'Thanks.'

She directed us from Highbury Corner, off at the second exit, next left, first right, and into one of those odd roads with beautiful huge houses on one side, and tired-looking council blocks on the other. Her block was one of four looking onto a patch of green, with a single lime tree and 'No Ball Games' signs dotted around. It was a classic 1970s public housing project, four floors, walled balconies, green grilles with entry-code buttons and speakerphone, next to big industrial dustbins.

'Will she answer the entryphone?' I asked.

'If she hears it.'

'Is she a heavy sleeper?'

'No.'

'Wait up,' said Wally. 'Afro-Caribbean guy coming up behind us, looks like he's heading in there.' I looked round. So did Hannah. 'That's Albie Marchant from 27,' she said. 'He works in a club.'

'Wait there,' said Wally, jumping out and walking in behind Albie, leaving it a few moments before calling us in through the green door.

'Lead the way,' I said, as Wally wished us 'good luck' and returned to the car. She walked up one flight of stairs, then along a landing. Six paces on, we were outside number 22.

'You OK?' I asked.

She breathed in two deep breaths, breathed out, chuckled, and said, 'No.'

I rang the doorbell. It was loud and I kept my finger on it for five seconds. Hannah stood back from the door to see if any lights went on. They didn't. I rang again, and also rattled the letter box up and down a few times. Still nothing stirred. I took my mobile phone from my belt and asked Hannah for her mum's number. I had punched in '077' when a light went on behind the door and I saw a blur move towards us from behind the frosted glass.

'Who is it?' Hannah nodded and mouthed the word 'Mum'.

'I'm WPC Judith Peters from Snow Hill, City of London Police.'

'Snow Hill?'

'I'm going to let you see my ID through the letter box.' I pushed it through and saw the blur bend down to examine it.

'What's it about?'

'It's about Hannah.'

'She doesn't live here. She lives with a school friend in Highbury Grove.'

'I'm afraid she's been mugged.'

'Oh. Is she OK?'

'Well, yes, she is, Mrs Maynard. She's with me now.'

'Where?'

'Here. Outside. Now.'

I moved to take Hannah's arm so that she would be in sight as her mother opened the door. Only she didn't. She turned, switched off the light, and went back to her bedroom.

I rang the bell twice more, but to no avail. I called the mobile number Hannah had given me, heard it ring inside, but she didn't answer. Hannah shuffled back down the stairs and as we walked out together, Wally had the look of a bull who had been hit with a lead pellet. He is such a softie for a big man.

We drove back in near silence. I called Frank to say Mrs Maynard had refused entry, and I suggested he put an extra pillow and blanket in the cell so that Hannah could get a couple of hours' sleep. It was getting light as we arrived back at base, and Frank's shift had already overrun by an hour, but I asked him to stay another few minutes while I spoke to her and settled her in. I looked through the spyhole. She was in her underwear again, this time just her knickers. And she was digging the fingernails of her left hand into the flesh above her right nipple, digging so hard that her eyes and mouth scrunched up in agony. She gritted her teeth and dragged her fingers slowly across her breast, leaving a trail of tiny red droplets as she went. She ran her fingers through her hair to wipe them clean of blood.

I waited till she was lying down, and had covered herself with a blanket, before taking in a glass of water and two bananas.

'How you feeling, Hannah?'

'Hung-over. Bit sick.'

'Here, have a drink of this.'

'Thank you.'

'I'll be on the front desk for the next few hours. I'll pop in and see you every now and then.'

'OK, thanks. Do you know something?'

'What?'

'I've got to stop hurting all these people who try to help me.'

'Your mum?'

'I think she's given up on me.'

'She rejected you tonight. But in her heart she'll want you to get better.'

'It's all the other people, though. My little sister, Vicki, who is the best, my uncle Malcolm, who knows what this is like and tried to help me, my gran up in Liverpool who's been writing to me and I never reply, my friend Sophie and her brother and her mum and dad who have been amazing and all I did was take from them and give them nothing but trouble. The doctors, the psychiatrists, people like you. All I am is trouble, and all because of fucking drink.'

'Don't swear,' I said. 'I had a bet with PC Lockyer I'd have you off the F-words before he clocked off.'

'You're a proper little community in here, aren't you?'

'We can be, but the police are no different to anyone else. People with their own lives and their own problems and all the while trying to do a difficult and important job to earn in a year what some of the City types earn in a second. Oh well, as long as we have strength and health, Hannah. Now eat these bananas, drink your water and see if you can get some sleep.'

I looked in at five thirty, again at seven, and she was sleeping soundly.

At seven twenty, as I was catching up on paperwork, two people came through the front entrance. One was a woman nearing middle age, maybe my age, though she had kept herself in better shape. The other was a young girl, probably a daughter, with a lovely round face and smiling eyes.

'Can I help?'

'I'm looking for WPC Peters,' said the woman, and I could see in the shape of her hair that she was the blur from behind the frosted glass.

'Mrs Maynard?'

'Yes. How did you know?'

'I'm WPC Judith Peters. Do you want to see Hannah?'

'Do you know where she went?'

'She stayed here. She had nowhere else to go.'

I explained that Hannah was sleeping, and asked if she would rather I woke her up and arranged for them to meet in an office rather than a cell.

'It's fine,' she said. 'I'd like to see her now.'

'And this must be Vicki?'

'Yes,' said Mrs Maynard.

'How do you know my name?' asked a younger, blonder, healthier version of Hannah.

'She told me all about you. Said you were the best sister ever.'

'We'd both like to see her,' said Mrs Maynard. She seemed quite detached from all that was going on around us, whereas Vicki couldn't stop sneaking little looks as we went through the back offices, then down to the cells, where the smell and the noise and the atmosphere suddenly changed.

'Get your tits out, love,' someone shouted from behind a cell door on hearing female voices pass by.

I looked through the spyhole again. Hannah had turned but was still sleeping. I opened the door, walked in, and Mrs Maynard and Vicki followed me. Vicki burst into tears and in two steps fell upon her sister, holding her up and kissing her head and her cheeks. Mrs Maynard walked over slowly, stood over them for a moment or two, then crouched down, touched Hannah's hair, then her scarred shoulder, and said, 'Come on, let's get you home.'

Hannah roused herself, stood, still only dressed in her knickers, and pulled her mother towards her.

'I'm sorry, Mum, I am so so so so sorry. I'm sorry. Please,

you have to forgive me. I'm sorry for everything I've done and I'll do everything I can to get better.'

Vicki put her arms around them both, and now all three were crying. I walked over, tears streaming down my face, and joined them, a quartet of women who all loved, and all hurt, and knew at that moment that love was the better way.

I left them to talk while I arranged for a cab to take them home. Then came more good news, then bad. Can stories about girls like Hannah never have a happy ending?

The good news. The three youths on bikes were caught trying the same trick on a German woman in Liverpool Street. They had Hannah's purse, and the remainder of the £120 that she hadn't spent on booze. The bad news was that they also had her plastic bag, and it contained thousands of pounds' worth of jewellery. A standard search showed up that a jewellery theft had been reported by a Dr Amanda Harper, of Highbury New Park, and it coincided with the departure from the Harper home of a girl who had been staying with them. The girl, of course, was Hannah. I was beyond exhaustion now, and the family's tears flowed again, first in trickles, then torrents when I went through to tell Mrs Maynard. She looked poleaxed.

Vicki, so happy when she saw her mother hugging her sister a short time ago, suddenly looked drained of all hope. The optimism that had shone from her face when she walked into the station had been replaced by a dull, grey pain. 'Mum, I have to go to school,' she said.

Hannah found in that statement the energy to get up, dress, take Vicki by the hands.

'Sis, listen to me. This is my last chance, I know it. Get to school, tell Sharples I won't be in for the exam, and I won't be coming back to do the others. Tell him I'm sorry. Find Sophie – wait till she's done her exam – and tell her this . . . I am sorry. Yes, I stole the jewellery. I know it was wrong. But I had a reason. And if you and your mum and dad show me one last act of kindness, and let me explain, I know you'll believe me, and I know you'll understand . . . Will you do that for me, Sis?'

Vicki nodded, hugged Hannah, and I showed her out. The hurt and the scars of life which had ground down her mother suddenly seemed to fall on her. She had gone from being a young girl to a sad woman in one night.

I got back to the cell to find Hannah and her mother arguing, Hannah saying she could explain it all if they gave her the chance, Mrs Maynard saying there could be no explanation for taking the kindness of such a good family, and stealing in return, and if it was her 'I wouldn't show you the time of day'.

In a short spell, she had lifted the veil of forgiveness suffi-cient to hold her daughter once more, cried tears of joy and relief as she and her daughters came together, made plans for a return home, then been hit with the reality that Hannah could be facing a serious jail term, and the fear that her daughter was a lost cause after all.

# ANGELA

**My name is Angela. I live with Jonathan, who made a TV programme about Hannah.**

Jonathan was on a high for a while after quitting his job, loved the 'TV journalist of principle' profile in his old paper, the *Sunday Telegraph*, who splashed with 'ITV cave in to admen over booze "tsunami" film', and it got raised at Prime Minister's Questions in the House of Commons, after Jonathan put the whole film online, which caused a real storm for a few days, but David Cameron said it was not directly a matter for him, and the fuss died down, as invariably happens. That was quickly followed in Jonathan by a real burning rage that I worried was out of character, and also, having grown up with my mother's illness, I could see the beginnings of depression in him. I had a lot on at work at the time, and I wasn't able to be with him as much as I wanted to, in those first few days after the storm, but when I did, he switched quickly from anger to an aching, non-communicative silence. He was also drinking more than usual.

I asked my boss – I work on business development for a firm of architects in Hammersmith – if I could have a half-day off 'to deal with a family situation'. I thought that the gesture of arriving home early, a good chat, perhaps a spell in bed making love, then an outing to the theatre or the cinema, would take him out of himself, start to turn the negativity of what had happened – which I agreed was a scandal, and I wanted to be supportive – into something more positive. He was a good journalist, everyone accepted that, and he had a great future if he could get back on track.

As the taxi turned into our road, I had it all worked out in my head . . . he would be watching some terrible daytime TV, he would perk up as soon as he saw me, be really thrilled I was there, we would have a bite to eat and talk everything over, then the bed bit, which I was really excited about, as we had both been way too distracted of late, a short sleep, and off to the movies, followed by dinner.

It is never good to anticipate in such detail, because when the first detail is wrong, everything else tends to go wrong thereafter. He wasn't watching TV, but sitting on the stairs, talking on the phone, and though he signalled momentary surprise on seeing me walk through the door, it was quickly followed by a hand-waving shushing motion, and I stood there still and silent. I realised instantly he and his father were talking about Hannah.

'But Dad, listen, you were there with Clare Lister. You know this is someone who can't control herself when the addictive side kicks in. She needs a drink, she needs the money, it doesn't matter how she gets it. Surely you can see that . . .

'I know, Dad, but you're thinking it through as though you are you, logical lawyer, not her, addict. Of course *you* wouldn't steal from someone who helps you. Nor would I. Nor would Ange, nor would anyone else we know. But we are not Hannah. We are not eighteen, addicted and bombarbed by influences from friends and marketeers and media and the whole bloody world telling you it is great to drink . . .

'You have got to stop thinking it through as though everyone is reasonable, Dad . . .'

It is frustrating to follow only one side of a conversation, and I mouthed 'What's happening?' as Jonathan listened to what sounded like a diatribe from his father.

'Dad, Dad, Dad, listen, sorry to interrupt, Angela's just walked through the door. She knows nothing about this. I'm going to put you on loudspeaker. Tell her what's happened. Be cold, logical, fact-based. I want to hear what she thinks.'

He pressed the speaker button on the phone, laid it on his thigh and asked me to join him on the stairs.

'OK, Angela, here's the story. We had a break-in, or so we thought.'

'Yes, Jonathan told me.'

'All that went was a single box of Amanda's jewellery. Just been insured recently, fourteen and a half grand. It's gone. We report it to the police. OK? Fact-based enough so far, J?'

'Yes, doing fine, Dad.'

'Today, still in bed, we get a call. Police. They've found the jewellery. In the possession of three youths caught mugging a woman at Liverpool Street whilst riding on pushbikes. The jewels came from an earlier mugging. And the victim of that mugging was one Hannah Maynard.'

'Your Hannah?' I asked.

'Well, I don't know about "our", but certainly the one that we took into our home, so she could soil our beds, vomit on our geranium beds, ruin our daughter's preparations for A levels.'

'Dad, that was not so fact-based, not quite so calm, logical, top-lawyer-in-the-land stuff.'

He snorted. 'So here's where we are now. Hannah is in custody at Snow Hill nick. She has admitted the theft. She has a lawyer. The police are indicating she will be charged later today. She got a message via her sister to Sophie at school, asking – "begging" was the word Sophie used – to see us, so that she can "explain", and saying she is sure we will accept her explanation if only we give her the chance to provide it.'

'And?'

'And what?'

'And why wouldn't you?'

Julian seemed taken aback.

'But she stole from us, not just a few pounds for a drink, but thousands of pounds' worth of personal and highly senti-mental possessions.'

'I'm not defending it, but I heard Jonathan before and he's right, she doesn't know what she's doing when she's at that moment when she needs a drink. She will do anything.'

Jonathan put a thumb in the air, encouraged by the silence at the other end.

'What does Amanda think?'

'Very mixed up about it. Devastated Hannah stole. Relieved we'll get the jewels back. But sort of feeling there isn't much more we can do to help.'

'What if she's telling the truth, though? What if there *is* a reason why she did it, that you *would* believe? All she's asking for is a chance to be heard.'

'But how many chances can we give her? She's not even our child.'

'I know, but you've all grown to love her like she was family. I know Jonathan has. Or else why is he out of a job?'

Jonathan leaned his head on my shoulder, and we both stayed

silent for the few moments it took his father to compute what we had been saying.

Julian said he was going to talk to Amanda, and call back in five minutes. When he did, it did not go as we had expected.

'I'm afraid we're going to let justice take its course,' he said. 'Your mother is virtually in grief with this. Sophie has to get her studies back on track, or else she might as well wave goodbye to university, and I am way off the pace in this case I'm doing, which requires all of my attention.'

'But Dad, you saw my script, you know what she's like, you know she needs help, you know how much this whole issue means to me —'

'I do, Jonathan, and I am proud of you, proud of the film you made, and proud of the way you made sure the arguments got out there, and I know you will continue to do so. But your mother and I both feel we have done all we can do. I'm sorry, but that's final.'

Jonathan looked devastated. I put my arms around him. We went to bed later, but sex was not on the agenda. He was plunged into a despair that made me fear for him, but love him all the more.

# SHEILA

**My name is Sheila. I am the magistrate who heard Hannah's theft case.**

It was certainly a more interesting case than the usual drink-driving, petty crime and minor acts of violence – if any act of violence can be deemed minor – that come my way. It caught my eye even when I looked down the listings the night before it came before us, because the girl's date of birth – 12/02/95 – was the same as our twins, my fourth and fifth children respectively, the fifth of which, Veronique, was our first girl so that, *enfin*, we could put our reproductive ambitions behind us. All I ever wanted was a daughter, and now I had her. Eighteen years on, she remains *la prunelle de mes yeux*. You must forgive my lapses into *le franglais*, but my husband, Alain, is from Brittany in western France. We met shortly after I had graduated with a first-class honours law degree from Bristol University. Rather than go straight into work, I decided to do a Master's in Napoleonic law, and with the help of Professor Sellers, my tutor, I won a six-month placement to Nantes University law school, where Alain was a visiting lecturer. *Le reste, comme on dit, c'est l'histoire.*

Veronique is about to go off on a similar, even more exciting adventure, once she gets her A-level results, in French (unsurprisingly since all five of our children are bilingual, as we spoke both English and French when they were growing up in Potters Bar), Spanish, English and history. She has a conditional offer of three As from Trinity Hall, Cambridge, to do Spanish and Italian, which she also speaks fluently as a result of our many holidays at our second home in Tuscany – well, third, if you count the cottage in Brittany – having inspired her to do after-school classes since she was eleven. First, however, she is taking a year out to travel around South America, and turn her Spanish from good to excellent. Alain, who now lectures in European business law at the London Business School, as well as running his own hugely successful commercial law firm, has given her £25,000 to take care of all her expenses for the year, as a reward for her hard work and astonishing achievements. According to her headmistress at Cheltenham Ladies' College – I'm afraid Alain has become a sucker for all the great English traditions – she secured marks of over 90 per cent in all of her mock exams, which she said had never been achieved before across four arts subjects. So dedicated was she to the task of learning that when her and her twin brother Charles's eighteenth birthday was upon us, she said she would prefer to wait until she was twenty-one for a major party so that it did not get in the way of her schoolwork. Alain used to tease me when I trotted out son after son, as 'tout ce que je veux, c'est une petite fille', but the reality is that though obviously we have had the ups and downs that are part of any mother–child relationship, she has so far been pretty much la fille parfaite.

I never did go into law in the end, not unless you count my work as a magistrate, which I have done now for six years.

I became an interpreter after finishing my Master's, first living with Alain in Paris, then moving to Brussels where his firm was expanding and I got myself a position as a translator and adviser to the then British Commissioner for Energy, at which point we started a family, and later moved to England to set up home, which allowed Alain to establish a third base for his commercial law firm. They now have offices in fourteen different countries. He is that rare creature, a man able to combine academic excellence with extraordinary entrepreneurial skills, the latter making it possible for me to enjoy a very, very long sabbatical from work until the twins were off to senior school, Charles to Ampleforth like his brothers – *Alain est catholique, hélas* – and Veronique to Cheltenham. With all of them away for large parts of the year, I needed something new to fill my time, so I took up a part-time lecturing position at Hertfordshire University, became a patron of three different children's and young persons' charities, and also trained to become a magistrate, in addition to sitting on a number of boards in both paid and, in the case of my charity work, unpaid roles. I am very proud – and Alain is even prouder – that my various hats combined to secure me an OBE in the last New Year's Honours List, and next month is our date at the Palace to receive the medal from Prince Charles. Unfortunately, it seems the Queen is due to be on an overseas tour, *mais il ne faut pas s'en plaindre*.

Hannah Maynard was the sixth case on the lists for the Tuesday morning at Highbury Corner Magistrates' Court on the Holloway Road, a stroll down from Highbury Islington station. I sit there because it is neatly placed in north London, close to the A1 escape route to Herts, but also a good base for my other business, charitable and social activities around

London. It is not the nicest building, four storeys of greying, once white, stone slabs and glass, but the entrance is quite bright and airy, the facilities for lawyers and magistrates better than many courts if my fellow magistrates are to be believed and it has the added bonus for me that it is right opposite a Majestic warehouse where I pick up our favourite wines once a quarter. Alain and I are very regular in our drinking habits. The order barely changes quarter to quarter.

In the covering notes that my clerk Clive Cooper prepares for me and my fellow magistrates – on the day in question Michael Hayman and Jill Kennedy – he had written simply: 'Guilty plea, first offender, drunk at time, sizeable sum involved but considered OK for mags. Defendant represented so likely to be mitigating circs, but unlikely to drag.'

'Unlikely to drag' was one of Cooper's favourite phrases, and code for 'deal with it quickly so that we don't end the day with any further additions to our backlog, which has been growing since our budgets were cut by the Justice Department'. He tends to view me and my fellow magistrates much as a director might view actors – we are the front people whose names may appear regularly in the *Islington Gazette* or even the *Evening Standard* from time to time, but everything depends on him, and he is the boss. As the day wore on, and my colleagues and I took more and more of an interest in the Maynard case, I hope I did not allow my emotions to be swayed overly by the coincidence of her birthday, and the particular love I have for Veronique. We are all human beings though, not machines, so it is foolish to assume even the hardest-headed judge in the land does not from time to time allow their own views and experiences to come into play. At one point, Michael Hayman did ask me – doubtless prompted by the note slipped to him by Cooper — whether we were not 'taking too long on an up-and-down theft by a drunk', but as the chair of the bench, I was able to swat that aside fairly easily.

We had dealt swiftly with three driving offences, a mugging and an ABH when Hannah was called in. I tend not to look too closely at the accused when they arrive in the dock, other than to suggest they make themselves comfortable, point out that there is water there should they need it, then wait for them to be sworn in. But there was something which drew me to her instantly, and it was more than the date of birth I had noticed the previous evening, after Alain had poured me a glass of our favourite burgundy rosé. She was tall, slim, with lovely dark brown hair resting on her shoulders, smartly dressed in a light blue blouse, buttoned grey jacket and dark blue skirt. I am well used to young defendants who live their lives in the uniform of hoodie, jeans and expensive brands of trainers appearing before me in badly fitting smart clothes worn for the first and last time. But she looked like the smart clothes belonged on her back, and she held herself with a poise that was unusual for someone so young in the dock. As she listened intently, and then replied, to the words she was being asked to read, I heard a strong clear voice with a marked London accent, but also a gentleness and respect for what she was saying. Hers was not the kind of visage I was used to seeing from the bench. She was clearly white working class, but had quite brown skin, with a hint of make-up around the eyes, high cheekbones, a nose that the French would call mildly retroussé, full lips, again with a hint of lipstick or gloss, and good strong teeth.

Once the theft charge had been put, and the guilty plea

entered, the prosecuting lawyer, a nasally man named Kiddle, who read through every case as though it were the dullest and most insignificant event he had ever been asked to consider, ran swiftly through the details. 'Miss Maynard had been having difficulties at home and was staying with a friend, the child of a well-known lawyer and a doctor' (slight emphasis on lawyer, nod to the bench). 'The accused has had difficulties with alcohol addiction, and you will have reports in front of you from a psychiatrist, Dr Lister from Lambeth Hospital, on that. You will hear that a combination of homelessness and drink led her to steal, in the form of jewellery from the mother of her friend, value estimated at close to fifteen thousand pounds. This came to light because the accused herself was mugged in Holborn by youths after a long drinking session. She reported this to Snow Hill police, the said muggers were later apprehended and found to be in possession inter alia of her purse and the jewels taken from said mother of said friend. This all took place in the early hours of the morning when she was due to sit her history A-level exam. She has since been expelled from her school and is currently unemployed. The youths who allegedly mugged the defendant have been charged with this and other offences, and the case is scheduled for Tower Bridge Magistrates' next month. Miss Maynard is likely to be called as a witness for the prosection. Date not yet set.'

'Thank you, Mr Kiddle. Miss Maynard, I believe you are represented?'

'Excuse me, Miss?'

'I understand you have a lawyer to represent you?'

'Er, no, I did at the start, but no, not now.'

'Oh, I see. Now, we have heard the facts as set out by the

prosecution, and you have entered a guilty plea. Would you say Mr Kiddle's brief presentation of the facts of the case, as opposed to the background which I would like to come on to in a moment, was accurate?'

'Yes, except for one little thing.'

'Would you like to tell us what that is?'

'I did get a message to the head teacher, Mr Sharples, that I was not going to sit my exams, and not going back to school. So I would say I left rather than was expelled.'

'I see. And may I ask this: was the fact that you had an exam coming up relevant to what happened, in terms perhaps of extra pressure you were feeling?'

'No, Miss.'

'Thank you. Obviously this is a serious offence, and the value of the items you stole much higher than the sums this court often hears of. So it will be no surprise to you that my colleagues and I take a very dim view of what you did.'

She nodded and whispered, 'Yes, sorry,' so quietly it was as though she was saying it to herself.

'I think the public would expect me to deal quite firmly with what is not only an act of theft, but an act of betrayal on your part, having been taken into the home of another family. I'm sure you can see that.'

'Yes, Miss,' she said, this time more firmly.

'So I suspect you will realise that you could well be facing a custodial sentence. Before we decide on the punishment, however, it is only fair that you should be able to put your side of the story. So is there anything you would like to say to the court, anything you think we should be expected to take into account by way of mitigating circumstances?'

'Should I stand or sit, Miss?'

'Whichever you feel more comfortable with.'

She stood, her head straight and still, her chest moving slightly as she settled her breathing, her hands clasped together and placed on top of the dock.

'First I want to say sorry. What I did was bad, so wrong, because Mrs Harper and her family have been so good to me. They took me in because my mum kicked me out –'

'We have heard about alcohol, Miss Maynard, a subject that we hear a lot of in this court, as you will know if you were sitting through the earlier cases.'

'No, Miss, they told me to wait outside till I was called.'

'Yes, indeed, and was alcohol the reason your mother asked you to leave the family home?'

'Yes, well, yes in that I had been drinking a lot and had been sick in the house, and also we'd had really big rows, but the night she actually chucked me out, I was drunk and she was out and I did something really, really bad. I am sorry about that too.'

'Would you like to tell us what that was?'

She bit her lip and shook her head. Mr Kiddle came to the rescue.

'I think the bench will find a mention of the circumstances in the psychiatrist's report, Your Worship.'

'Ah, thank you, Mr Kiddle.'

'Page 8, paragraph 32, Your Worship.'

Mr Hayman and Mrs Henderson flicked through the report from Dr Lister – I confess none of us had read it in advance – and Mrs Henderson found the relevant sentence. '. . . after, in a state of considerable inebriation, seducing her mother's then boyfriend, and having intercourse with him . . .' Both she and Mr Hayman looked particularly stern and troubled.

'You clearly drink a good deal, Miss Maynard.'

'Well, yes, I do, Your Worship. It is bad, I know. I have been trying to stop, and actually I've been good these last few days, because I've been staying with my uncle Malcolm and auntie Julie, and staying in, and they don't allow drink in the house, so I've done four days without, which is, well, a bit of a record, because obviously I was nervous about coming here, and I wanted to do my best, so I was keen to go as long as I could.'

'Your uncle? Is this your mother's brother?'

'No, Your Worship, my father's brother.'

'And where is your father?'

'My parents are divorced, and I've not seen him for a while.'

'I see. Carry on.'

'Carry on?'

'With your statement.'

'So like I said, I am sorry, not just sorry in, like, saying the word, but sorry so it hurts my whole body and my whole head just to think of all the trouble I have caused to people who tried to help me. Sorry to you for taking up your time with all this. Just so sorry to everyone.'

'And is there anything you want to say about the theft itself, why you took the jewellery? Presumably there were other things to steal if you were just raising money for a few drinks?'

'Oh yes, the Harpers live in an amazing house, and they have everything you could dream of in there. But the jewellery was worth exactly what I needed.'

'I don't understand.'

'Well, this is a bit complicated, Miss, and to be honest it's the reason me and my lawyer fell out, because he didn't think it was a good idea to say all this. He said it was best to fess up, plead guilty and hope the court went easy on me because it was a first offence. But I think it is one of those mitigation things you were talking about.'

'I see. And what is it?'

She rubbed her hands nervously against each other, looked towards the public gallery, I assumed to a member of her family, resumed her earlier pose and began to talk, more quickly than she had been speaking up till now, never taking her eyes from mine.

'Sometimes, Miss, events happen that make you think you are meant to do things, even though you know they are wrong. You think they might come out right. The bad you do can lead to good. I know it's not logical, but we all do things that aren't logical. I know drinking is bad for me, so it is not logical to do it, but I do. Because drinking makes me feel good, some of the time.'

She pulled back her right sleeve and I noticed a number of scars and scabs instantly. 'Cutting my skin makes me feel better, some of the time,' she went on. 'But both drinking and cutting make me feel worse, most of the time, and make life worse for everyone else too, but the only thing that keeps me going is the feeling good might come from bad. Or else – and believe me I have thought about it, many many times, and tried it a few times, as my friend Sophie knows – why don't we just top ourselves when the bad feelings are so bad, and the pain inside is so hard to live with? I have been there, and Mum told me when we were in the cell together the night I got arrested that she has been there too, not just because of me, but because of my dad, because life has been so, well, "so shit" is what she said. Sorry, Your Worship.'

'That's all right, as you are quoting someone else,' I said. 'Just a couple of things on what you said. I understand you have been drinking steadily for four years or so, heavily for perhaps two, dangerously so for around one. Is that fair?'

'Yes, roughly, that's right.'

'And, forgive me if this is in the papers I have not yet had time to read fully, but when did you start harming yourself physically, as we can see you have?'

'After I had an abortion, Your Worship, after the incident Mr Kiddle pointed out to you.'

'Thank you. And tell me this, who is Sophie?'

'She's my friend, Miss. Sophie Harper. She is the one whose house I was in, whose mum had the jewellery.'

'I see. And I presume she is no longer your friend.'

'No, she is, she's here in the court, supporting me, Miss, the only one though, yes.'

'You have no family here?'

'No, my sister wanted to come but she has school, my uncle Malcolm is working, and my mum and dad, well, you know, and to be honest I didn't want my grandparents to know.'

'I see. You mentioned suicide, or thinking about it. Is that something you have done often?'

'Every day, Miss, for a long time.'

'You said you had tried to do so. In what way?'

'Pills once, but I just kept throwing them up as soon as I put them down me. Knives on my wrists a couple of times. Once went to Archway, to that bridge where people try and jump off, but I couldn't get to the top.'

'I see. So what good was going to come of stealing a large quantity of expensive jewellery, other than providing money for drink?'

'The thing is, I'd been seeing Dr Lister. Mr Harper, Sophie's dad, he was paying for me to see her, which was really kind,

293

and it did make me think about things differently, and I knew I had to do something to change my ways. But I couldn't. I was trying, honestly I was, and the Harpers, they kept telling me how well I was doing, because they thought I wasn't really drinking. But I was. I had stashes all over the place. In the garden. At school. You get good at covering it up. That makes you feel good too, little secrets nobody else knows. Till you feel bad. Then you feel really bad, because secrets remind you deep down how lonely you are, with nobody to tell the truth to, including yourself. So bad goes to worse. Then you want to do something to stop. But you can't. Because the urge for the taste and the hit is too strong. And the relief from the pain is too great when you get the hit. So the vicious circle goes round again and again and again, and you know where it's heading, but you can't stop it turning.'

'This is all very interesting, Miss Maynard, and may well be leading to some kind of mitigating circumstance, but I am still not clear as to why you stole Mrs Harper's jewellery box.'

'Sorry, Miss, Your Worship, this is what the lawyer said, that it was too complicated and nobody would believe it, but it's all true and I am trying to make it simple, as simple as I can, but it's not easy, because it is complicated.' I could sense Mr Cooper becoming irritable as he saw the rest of the day's cases stretching into the afternoon and beyond. I didn't blame him too much, but his main interest was that guilty pleas should take up no more than a few minutes, and he was never happier than when striking his black marker pen through a case we had concluded quickly. Not-guilty pleas he considered to be a menace, and this had the feel of a guilty plea that would take longer than many of the not-guilty cases we heard.

'Very well, carry on, but do try to come to the point,' I

said, trying to sound stern in the hope Mr Cooper would desist from gently flourishing the list for the day every time Hannah went into a long subordinate clause.

'So, a couple of Tuesdays before I did it, we were having dinner, and we were talking about a film Sophie's brother was making, about women and alcoholism, and I was asking if they paid for interviews, and I mean I knew nothing about his world, but I thought maybe there would be thousands of pounds in it, because you read how much these TV people earn, and it turns out I would get a bit if I did an interview, but not a lot. And anyway, later on, after the pudding it was, Mrs Harper was talking about her jewels, the ones on the table with the big mirror in her bathroom – Sophie has shown me in there once – and she said she had had them insured for £14,500.

'Well, the thing is, that day I had bunked off school, I went in with Soph, but I went back to their place –'

'Whose place?'

'The Harpers', Miss, and I went into Mr Harper's study, and I went on his computer, because I had heard him say he never switched it off and it doesn't have a password and so I went straight on and do you know why?'

'Tell us, Miss Maynard.'

'And Sophie believes me on this, because she went and looked on his search record, but unfortunately I'm not sure Mr Maynard did, and I don't blame him because he had had enough of me by then –'

'Sorry to interrupt, I can see this is indeed complicated, but please try to help the court by getting back to the issue of the theft.'

'OK, I'm nearly there, Your Worship. The thing is, I was

googling residential rehab centres, because I knew Dr Lister was right, I needed proper help, and the one I really liked, it was up in the countryside, near Lancaster, a former convent which did one-month initial rehab for addiction and had a specialist self-harm unit for young girls too. And I looked at loads of places, all over the country, one even in South Africa, one in Austria, but the only one I phoned was this place in the hills near Lancaster. And I got through and I said to the woman, "I'm calling for a friend and she is drinking a lot and she harms herself with knives and needles and pens and her nails, and what does she have to do to get in?" and this woman on the other end, she said, "Does your friend have private insurance, either herself or through an employer?" and I said, "No, she's still at school," and the woman said, "Well, we do get people referred through various agencies, probation, local authorities, and also the NHS; is she a registered addict?" and I said, "No, I don't think so," and she said, "We also take people through charities and I could send a list of the kind of charities we work with and you could see if your friend might have access to any of them," and we went round a few options but none of them applied to me, and then she said, "The only other way is – and I don't know what kind of background your friend comes from – but it would be simply to pay the standard fee for a month's residential stay, which covers accommodation, food, treatment, medication, and transport to and from anywhere within the UK." So I said, "How much is it then?" and she said, "Fourteen and a half thousand pounds." And I put the phone down and I thought, oh well, nice idea, no chance. Then that night, we're at dinner in the dining room, and the jewels come up in conversation, and Mrs Harper says she got them reinsured, like her husband had suggested, and they were valued at "fourteen and a half thousand pounds". And I think, oh my God, there is a message being sent to me here. But I knew it was wrong, I really did, and the only way I could bring myself to do it was to get tanked up. So how? Well, Jonathan had given me some cash for the interview I did for his film, a hundred and twenty pounds, so I went out, had a few, nothing extreme, but enough so they would have noticed, so I said I would be back late and I might stay with a boyfriend. They were used to that, because if I got really drunk I didn't go back there. What I was actually doing was drinking for Dutch courage, then I came back when I knew they were all in bed, and I wasn't so drunk I couldn't get up the stairs without being heard, crept into Mrs Harper's bedroom, through to the bathroom, made away with the box, got a plastic bag from the kitchen, took a couple of swigs from the fridge, looked around to say my goodbyes, and off I went.

'I was feeling flush with the Jonathan cash, so I got a cab, headed into town, and I'm saying to myself, "Tomorrow I am going to sell this jewellery, get on a train to Lancaster, get a cab to Fairburn Lodge Rehab Centre, hand over the cash, and get better. But tonight, because I have just done something so bad, I am going to drink myself to oblivion for the last time in my life, I am going to shred my arms and my thighs and my breasts and I am going to let the pain out, but then I am going to learn to be sober, and I am finally going to take charge of my life, and take responsibility for my choices.

'And who knows? Maybe it was all rubbish. Maybe, even though I thought it at the time, maybe I was just going to get drunk, get sober, get drunk again, but this time with even more money to spend. But all I am asking you to believe is that is why I stole from them. I'm sorry, I truly am. But

Dr Lister, in her main job, she was looking after people who thought they were getting messages from God or Muhammad or the Queen or an ancestor who died hundreds of years ago. I am not as crazy as them, but I did think I was getting a message. It said: "Go to rehab. It costs fourteen and a half grand. The jewels are there waiting for you. You'll get fourteen and a half grand for them." But because life is never easy, I got mugged, and they must have thought, "Boy, this is our lucky day, a placky bag full of gold and diamonds," and then it was me that got lucky because of all the police stations in all the world, I went to the one with a woman called WPC Peters in it, and she wanted to help me, because she has a girl like me, and she knows what it's like, and she thought, "I can't help my own girl right now, and I can't help myself, but I can help this girl, and I can help her mum," and that's what she tried to do.'

Mr Cooper was shuffling ever more impatiently but there was something mesmerising about her in full flow, and I let her go on.

'I love Sophie's family,' she said. 'They tried to help me, and I don't blame Mr and Mrs Harper one bit that they are angry with me, and think I betrayed their trust. I did. But the thing I learned from Dr Lister is that I have to learn to help myself. In stealing, yes, I was helping myself to their possessions. But it was because I was trying to help myself in the way Dr Lister meant it as well. And do you know what, having an exam that day, my first exam, history A level, that was the last piece in the jigsaw coming together to make me do it, make me get the money to go to Lancaster. Because Soph and I had been talking about university at breakfast, and she has been so great trying to help me get my grades up so I could go to university like she will. And we were talking about tuition fees and debt and how she would come out owing thousands and thousands of pounds, and I was thinking, "I can't do that. I've got no parents looking after me, I've got no means of my own. I don't even have a bank account. I'm going to have to work as soon as I'm out of school." Even if it meant going on the game, Miss, because that's what drink does to you.'

'Are you telling the court you became a prostitute?' I asked, prompting a snort from Mr Cooper.

'No, not properly, but we all know how it works, because the only stealing I've done before now, apart from a few quid from Mum's purse and Dad's wallet every now and then, has been from blokes I've been to bed with, near strangers who get what they want and I think I should have something in return. I could see that life coming too. Do it once, and it's easy to do it again, and you tell yourself, "Oh, it's not so bad, and it gets you a bit of money and that gets you drink," and on you go. And I didn't want it. I wanted something better.

'So I thought, I know . . . Sophie will go to university and she will get a great degree and then a great job and eventually pay all that money back to the government. As for me, I will go to rehab, and that will sort me out even better than uni will help out Soph, and when I'm better, I'll get good jobs and earn good money and one day I am going to go back to the Harpers and say, "Here is fourteen and a half grand, with interest. Thank you for saving my life." Thank you for letting me into a house which I loved so much that, after I had taken the jewellery box, I walked around downstairs because I wanted to take time to remember all you had done for me, remember the comfort, the food, the smells, the lovely welcoming warmth, and I went into Mr Harper's study and I sneaked another look at the rehab place on his computer, and I said to myself, "Tomorrow, Hannah, you'll be there, looking at those fields, sitting in those therapy groups, relaxing in that meditation centre, training in that gym, writing your thoughts in speech bubbles on those whiteboards, painting in that art room, sleeping in one of those beds in those clean simple rooms, with no wiring and a thick duvet not sheets in case you try to do anything daft, and you're going to get better, you're going to get happier and when you've done it, all on your own, you're going to come back and make all these other people happier too, and proud that you did it."'

She paused, looked again at the public gallery, and I could see that the girl she was looking at had her hands on her chin, and was crying. It was Sophie. And yes, she did remind me of another well-brought-up, pretty, confident, well-educated, much-loved eighteen-year-old, my own *fille parfaite*, Veronique.

'So when I say I am sorry, Miss, I really, really mean it. I will be sorry for the rest of my life. But I just ask you at least to believe that what I've told you is the truth, the whole truth and nothing but the truth.'

I felt exhausted.

'Is that all, Miss Maynard?'

'Yes, Miss, thank you, Your Worship.'

'OK, sit down, thank you.'

After conferring with Mr Hayman and Mrs Henderson, I announced, to Mr Cooper's considerable and instantly grunted irritation, that the court would break early for lunch so that we could have time to consider the case properly.

'Quite a performance,' said Mr Hayman as Cooper brought

in our sandwiches and tea to the robing room, grumbling loudly that there were now so many people waiting outside the courtroom as the case dragged on (my fault) and held up others that he 'wouldn't be surprised if we had a riot on our hands by the end of the day'.

'I don't think so, Mr Cooper,' I said. 'And I'm sure the police can cope if we do.'

'Not sure I can if this drags on much longer. I take it you've seen the new budgets?'

'We'll manage, Mr Cooper. I think it important we reach the right outcome here.'

'So long as we reach one,' he said.

'Quite a performance indeed,' said Mrs Henderson, belatedly replying to Mr Hayman. 'But one cannot escape the fact that it was a serious crime.'

'No, absolutely,' he said. 'Theft is theft.'

I feared I was going to be in a minority of one. Also, Mr Hayman was something of a hanger and flogger, who thought of me as the kind of affluent liberal who, when it came to what he called 'that "tough on crime, tough on the causes of crime" nonsense peddled by Blair', was too interested in the causes bit, not enough the crime. Mrs Henderson was more reasonable, and she was the one I needed to work on.

I suggested we read the psychiatric report in silence, but made one or two leading observations as I went, such as Dr Lister's point that Hannah was basically a good person, certainly not a sociopath, and would have no criminal tendencies at all, were it not for her addiction.

I could tell by the end of her reading it, and my summation of Hannah's statement, which I was minded to believe, that Mrs Henderson had moved.

'What a waste of a life,' she said. 'Only just eighteen and her whole life wrecked by drink already.'

'Been breaking the law every day to do it,' said Mr Hayman.

'That's not why she's here,' replied Mrs Henderson.

'She's here because she has bad parents and she does bad things because there has never been discipline in her life,' said Mr Hayman.

'But where was she to get it from if she had bad parents?' I asked.

'I sincerely hope you are not considering letting her off,' he said. 'How would you feel if you were Mr and Mrs Harper? Julian Harper is one of the country's top QCs, a man of enormous integrity and, as we have heard, generosity too. How would you expect him to feel if he is the victim of a serious theft and betrayal of trust, and we let her off scot-free? How would you feel if it was you that was the victim, and he was the judge deciding the crime should go unpunished?'

'Of course she has to be punished, but what Mrs Henderson and I are asking is whether, given her life has been so damaged by alcohol already, as Mrs Henderson said, there might be a better way of dealing with this?'

'She wouldn't get any drink in Holloway,' he said.

'Oh please, Mr Hayman,' said Mrs Henderson. 'Have you ever been there? You can get a lot more than drink, believe me. She'll go in a drink addict and come out hooked on drugs too, I wouldn't bet.'

Mr Cooper came in to remind us we had a long list of other cases to get through. 'Yes, yes, yes,' I said, 'but this is important. The decision we make now has the potential to shape this girl's future, and we shouldn't underestimate our responsibility in that regard. Also, I do not take lightly the point she made about suicide, and that is something I would consider to be a real possibility if the next step in her life was to Holloway.'

'Well, send her to an open prison then,' snorted Hayman, 'with all the art therapy and the yoga classes and the bungee jumping and all the rest of it. Just don't send a message to the public that we don't take theft seriously, because we must and we do.'

'Suicide?' asked Mrs Henderson sweetly.

'In my experience, if people are serious about suicide, they do it, they don't talk about it.'

His bluster was definitely pushing Mrs Henderson towards me.

'Surely we can check whether she was telling the truth about looking up rehab places?' she said. 'She mentioned computer searches.'

'Get that Sophie girl in,' said Hayman. 'She can tell us about all these failed suicides too.'

'Perhaps that is exactly what we should do,' I said. I asked Mr Cooper to find her, and to ask if she would be willing to be called as a witness. She was.

We finished our tea, went back into court, and Sophie Harper was sworn in. I explained that I was only interested in two points of confirmation – did she check the search record on her father's computer, and did it show Hannah had googled residential rehab centres? And had Hannah discussed suicide with her before? The answer was yes to both. I then asked why her father, a very intelligent man, and her mother, clearly a very compassionate woman, had chosen not to believe her story.

'It wasn't that they didn't believe it,' she said. 'Mum was

heartbroken to be honest. She had put so much into helping Hannah that she just felt she was at the end of the road with her. My mum is an optimist, glass half full kind of person, but I think she became depressed.'

I noticed Hannah hanging her head, and shaking it from side to side.

'And your father's attitude to Hannah at this time?'

'Well, he has been involved in this big case you might have read about.'

'The Connell case, yes.'

'That's right, and he just felt I think that he wasn't paying it the attention he needed to, so as far as the police investigation into the theft was concerned, his attitude was "let them do whatever they have to do, let justice take its course".'

'Your brother?'

'He was more with me on this one, totally believes Hannah and still wants to help, and also because Mum got the jewels back, he said the only loss was emotional, not financial. But he's had problems too, because he lost his job and is trying to find a new one – he has an interview with an American TV station, otherwise he would have come with me today. And like Hannah said, we all understand why Mum and Dad are so cross.'

'Thank you, Miss Harper. You've been very helpful.'

As Sophie left the witness stand, I turned to my left to whisper to Mrs Henderson, a conversation that went on for a minute or more.

I could sense now not just Cooper's irritation at my dawdling, but Hayman's angst that I had turned to Mrs Henderson first, which was not my usual practice. She had definitely shifted from her hardline position, though was also clear a tough message had to go out.

I then turned to Mr Hayman.

'Michael,' I said, allowing my pinkie finger to touch his wrist as he flicked through the papers once more, 'I think Jessica and I have come up with a good compromise.' The court was not particularly full, but as we conferred, most who were there were looking towards us, and I was gambling on the fact that Hayman wouldn't want to be seen to be having an argument he might lose. So he nodded portentously, asked a couple of questions, and concluded with 'good compromise, and I think you should give it both barrels in telling her the discipline and sort-yourself-out bit'.

'Quite.'

I looked towards Hannah, and motioned for her to stand.

'Miss Maynard,' I began, 'we have listened carefully to all the evidence, and have concluded that this was a serious offence, for which the court has a duty to punish you. We note your guilty plea, which has saved the court considerable time and expense, though frankly given the circumstances of your arrest, which we read about during the lunch break, I think anything other than a guilty plea would have been incredible, and foolish. In committing this theft, which you admitted was not your first, you abused the hospitality of a good, loving family, who took you into their home, gave you comfort and solace, and hope of a better future. Your response was to steal from them, adding further emotional pain to that which you had already inflicted upon them and upon your own family. The public has a right to know that laws passed in their name will be upheld, and that the sentences available to us will be used to show the seriousness with which we view crimes that blight our country. I am therefore sentencing you to six months in prison . . .'

Hannah's head fell and her hands shot up to the back of her neck, while I heard a shout of 'oh no' from the public gallery.

'. . . the sentence to be suspended for a period of two years,' I continued. 'This means that if you commit any further crime, or fall into further trouble, this custodial sentence can be restored or added to any punishment for those future crimes.

'In making the sentence suspended in this way, we were struck by the report from Dr Lister, who assessed you as being of basic good character, except for what she called your "relationship with alcohol", which she suggested "acted as a negative and transformative force in your life". It strikes us that if you are to have any kind of future, you must address this relationship in a way you have tried thus far unsuccessfully to do. Neither I nor my colleagues on the bench are persuaded that a spell in Holloway jail is likely to help you do that. I am, however, insisting as a part of this sentencing that you should have appointed to you a probation officer who will explore with you ways of finding the kind of residential care you were seeking at the time of the offence. I am also persuaded that, should this result in a burden on the public purse, that will be as nothing to the cost that would result, now and in the future, from you going to prison at this time in your life. I will ask to be kept informed of your progress, and will consider calling you back if you do not agree to residential care for a period of time to be agreed with the probation service. I believe this sentence carries the right balance between the need to punish you for the wrongs you have committed against others, but also provides you with the opportunity to face up to your own demons, and face them down. You may go.'

She nodded, sighed, said 'thank you' quietly, and left to join Sophie Harper at the entrance to the public gallery. Mr Cooper passed up the papers for our next case, a shoplifter, Harry George, one of our regulars, who last year sent me a rather nice Christmas card.

# PAULINE

**My name is Pauline. I am a cleaner at Fairburn Lodge, where Hannah was sent by the court for rehab.**

I love it up here. I was born and bred in Somerset, but when Jack came out of the army, he got offered a job as a driver with Eddie Stobart, and as he was once based at Catterick, and always liked the north, he went for it, and we moved up with the kids. I've done all sorts of jobs, dinner lady, lollipop lady, barmaid, call centre, but this is the best I've had, and the one I've done longest. I reckon I'll be here till I retire.

People – even the kids to be honest – ask if it isn't a bit scary having all these 'nutters' around – I hate that word, though I admit I used to say it myself, before I worked here. The answer is 'no, not really'. There have been a few moments, and yes, one or two can get violent from time to time, but never with me or any of the other cleaners, and the medical staff are fantastic, they really are.

I've been here five and a half-years now. It's a half-hour drive south from where we live, down the motorway, off by Lancaster University, then a nice little jiggle through the best scenery in the world not counting Somerset, A-road to B-road to country track, at the end of which is a high blue gate, entrance to Fairburn Lodge. I work Monday to Thursday, and one weekend in three, and I start at ten, when the residents are all up and about doing whatever it is they do, and I can get going on the bedrooms. There are twenty-eight in total, and though men and women mix in all other activities, they sleep in separate wings, and I always do the men's rooms first, then the women's. They are supposed to make their own beds, and most do, but I tend to make it all nice and tight and tidy. If anyone is particularly messy, or I spot anything lying around that they shouldn't have — we get a lot of drug addicts and they are very adept at getting stuff in through visitors and deliveries — the doctors and nurses expect me to tell them. I don't like snitching on the residents, but I see myself as part of the medical team, not just a cleaner. Jack once told me a fantastic story about President Kennedy visiting NASA Space Centre and he bumped into a cleaner like me, only this cleaner was a man, and Kennedy said, 'What do you do, my man?' and the cleaner said, 'Mr President, I am helping to put a man on the moon.' Well, I'm a cleaner like he was, and I am helping sick people to get better, drug addicts to get off drugs, alcoholics to stop drinking, problem gamblers to stop gambling, sex addicts to stop thinking sex with any passing stranger or prostitute is a route to happiness, girls who self-harm to address the causes of their pain, not think they can ease it by inflicting more pain. I'm not qualified medically at all, apart from my first-aid certificate, but Jack always says I have a 'first-class honours degree from the university of life', and I certainly like to think I make a difference to the souls who come here, beyond keeping the place neat and tidy.

You get to know them all, because they tend to stay for several weeks at least, and even when it's full – which is hardly ever – I would usually see most of the residents at some time most days.

Albert Rishton, the boss and the founder of this place, whose son died of a drugs overdose, likes to keep spare capacity at all times in case of emergency admissions. He went potty recently when he heard a Lancashire mental health crisis unit was being closed because it only ever operated at two-thirds capacity.

Hannah was here through one of our charity link-ups. I'm never quite sure how it works, but as I understand it, she was in trouble with the cops and she was going to go to jail unless she came here, and someone high up in the courts system, a magistrate or a judge I think it was, found a charity that paid for her to do a full five-weeker. She was here as a double-issue patient – alcohol and self-harm. This place specialises in treating multiple addictions, drink and drugs being the most common.

She was very quiet at first, as you'd expect. She was only eighteen, way younger than most of the people here. My oldest is twenty-one now, but I wouldn't like the idea of her arriving in a place like this, long way from home, nobody popping in to see you, lots of really quite disturbed people around, not allowed out, and if you legged it, you'd have a long walk before you met another soul.

They put her in the end room on the third floor, which has windows looking out in two directions, across some of the most beautiful moors you will ever see, even supposing you go to every country from here to the moon. I could look out of those windows all day long if I didn't have so much cleaning to do. The nurses do the first medical tests when residents are admitted, and Hannah was not in bad shape considering, but she had high blood pressure, a spot of liver damage unsurprisingly, stomach lining a bit of a mess, but nothing a few weeks without booze, and lots of good food couldn't cure. We have our own farm here and the chef gets most of his ingredients home-grown, beef, lamb, chicken, and one of the best vegetable gardens in Britain, according to the brochure. The harder stuff was the mental side of things. She must have been drinking a lot to get labelled an alcoholic before she was old enough to drink. And the first time I saw her in her room, she had a towel wrapped round her having just come out of the shower – it's all en suite for the women, whose rooms are nicer than the men's I think – I couldn't miss all the cuts and scars. The only good thing was they didn't look too new, but the nurses had to be on the alert for signs when she was spending time on her own. They can't drink in here, not unless visitors are daft enough to bring it in, and sometimes we search them, but they can self-harm, and often with the double-up drink/self-harm girls, the withdrawal from the drink makes them do more of the self-harm.

A week or so in, she was definitely more settled, and she knew all the names of everyone, and was getting into the routines a bit. They tend to let them rest a lot for the first few days, but once it picks up, it really does. Breakfast at seven thirty, full breakfast or continental, help yourself to tea, coffee or juice. Then group sessions, and we had three or four self-harmers in when she arrived, so that was the obvious place for her to start. Then maybe a talk from either one of the staff or an outsider – we have good links with Lancaster University, and they send people up from time to time. Then it might be an hour of art or music therapy, which Mr Rishton swears by. Lunch at one, back into it at two, when they mix the groups up, then maybe a one-on-one session, or a physical review, then there's the gym, or a walk round the grounds, and before you know it it's five o'clock and I'm heading home, and they're getting ready for the evening meal. It's the perfect job for me, in that I love the feeling of arrival here in the morning, and I love leaving to go home too.

You don't become friends with the residents, I wouldn't say, but you do become friendly while they're here. You learn their stories, you get to know their little habits, and of course the staff – I can't begin to tell you how dedicated they are – they talk about them all the time, and they trust me enough to give me a lot of detail about the new arrivals, because they know sometimes the patients will talk to someone like me more than they would to someone with a big fancy title. It can be intimidating talking to psychiatrists who are trying to get right into you, like a surgeon gets in with a knife when he's operating on a cancer, it really is no different, except the cancer surgeon can knock you out, and is always likely to have your undivided attention and total cooperation. It's not so easy for a shrink. So the clever psychiatrist knows he can glean a thing or two from a cleaner who makes it her business to get to know the residents as they settle in. In fact, it was Dr Meredith, who is a young woman doctor specialising in self-harm, she was the one who said to me they were finding it hard to get Hannah to open up, and they were sure she was harming again, so could I maybe work on her a bit.

I got her talking one day when I was doing the top landing, and she came by saying she was skipping art therapy because she had a bad headache. I let her get to her room, which I hadn't cleaned, left her for a while, then went in to see her. 'Mind if I clean around you, love?' I said, and she said, 'No, that's fine.'

'Can I fetch you some aspirin or something?'

'No, I'll be fine. Just feeling really down today.'

'Aw, yeah, we all have days like that, love.'

'Sort of dawning on me how hard this is going to be, and how bad it is that I'm here.'

'Bad? This place is paradise, love. Look at those hills out there. Never seen anywhere better in my life.'

'No, I mean bad because of the reasons I'm here, the drink and everything, and the fact I've sort of lost everybody really. I get a text or two from my friend Sophie, who's on holiday in Mauritius with her parents after finishing her exams . . .'

'Nice,' I said. 'All right for some, eh?'

'. . . my sister who keeps asking when she can come, and that's it really. I saw Miranda in the self-harm group today, she gets more letters in a day than I've had in total, which isn't hard because it's none.'

'Yes, but this place is about finding yourself, so the isolation is part of it, really. You've got to dig quite deep in here to get the best out of it, find out who you really are, so you can be true to yourself. Have you seen the message on the stairwell? "To thine own self be true, and it must follow, as the night the day, thou can'st not then be false to any man." *Hamlet*. Mr Rishton's friend Billy Shakespeare. You should think about that, Hannah.'

'I just can't stop thinking negative thoughts, you know, about myself, all the bad things I've done, how I've hurt everyone, screwed up at school, got a criminal record, lost my family, most of my friends, and I can't see how I get over all that. And you know, I'm not drinking now, because I can't, but there's a part of me thinking as soon as these five weeks are over, I fancy getting onto that university campus down the road, getting into the students' bar with their cheap booze and their happy hours – you see, I've googled it already – and getting blathered and then shacking up with a first year. I can't stop thinking about it, and that shows this isn't working, doesn't it? If I can't stop thinking about drinking and all the bad stuff it makes me do, what chance have I got of stopping? Yet I know if I get out and do all that, I'll do something crazy again, and I'll be back in court, and this time there won't be a nice woman like the one I had in London, it'll be a hard-man judge and I'll be off to jail. And if I can see that so clearly, why can't I see that I must, I must, I have to stop drinking?'

'But you're working it all out, love. You're not even halfway through. Don't beat yourself up so much.'

'I'll try.'

'You're not cutting yourself again, are you?'

'Only a bit.'

'Only a bit's still too much.'

'I know.'

I sat on the edge of her bed, and took her hand. 'Listen, Hannah, you're a lovely girl. You've got a lot going for you. You sort out your drinking and you know what, everything else is going to fall into place. I've seen plenty like you in here, not many as pretty as you, mind. And they all have doubts, and they all wonder if they can do it, and there's times when they all think this is a total waste of bloody time and money, and they might as well take a walk. And one or two do take that walk, and they never come back, and then some-times we hear of them . . . we had one a couple of years back, older than you, Jill Kerry, Scottish girl, lovely, lovely girl, but addicted to drugs and drink. She was doing so well, she was a fabulous painter, they discovered that of her, that painting of the buildings burning down, the big one on the stairwell, that's one of hers, and she seemed to be all set, and everything was going to be great. Then three weeks in, she did a runner in the middle of the night. It's not a prison, we can't stop people leaving, and she left. And two weeks later, the day she was due to finish here, we got a message from the police in Aberdeen that she'd been found dead in a bed and breakfast, surrounded by cider bottles, aspirins and a syringe. She couldn't see it through. So she killed herself, got herself drugged up to the eyeballs, but not so she couldn't work a rope and a chair. But I reckon if she had stayed those extra two weeks, she'd still be with us.'

Hannah nodded slowly, and squeezed my hand.

'She was one we lost,' I said. 'But there are plenty more we saved, and I want you to be one of them, because you deserve it, and so do we.' She smiled, but it was the sad smile of someone whose life had taken too many wrong turns to identify with the successes of Fairburn Lodge, and I could tell she was thinking about the failure, Jill Kerry.

'Have you got a family?' she asked.

'Yes. Husband Jack, four kids, girls twenty-one, nineteen, sixteen, boy fifteen.'

'That's Vicki's age. My little sister.'

'Do you love her?'

'Yes.'

'Well, you stay alive for her then. And you see through your time here for me, is that a deal?'

She nodded.

'What about your mum? Mums are the best, you know.'

'It's hard. I guess I must have loved her once, but I can't remember when. She's not a bad person. Vicki loves her to bits, even forgives her for kicking me out. And before I was charged, the policewoman got Mum to come and see me in the cells, and we hugged like we have never hugged before and I thought, "She's forgiven me for all the bad things I've done, and we can start a new life together." And then the news came about my stealing, she left me again, and we haven't exchanged a single word since.'

'Why don't you write to her? Then you might get a letter back.'

'I'm not very good with words.'

'Rubbish. The nurses say you're bloody brilliant with words when you can be bothered speaking.'

'What would I say?'

'Just tell her what you think.'

I emptied her bin, swept the linoleum floor, ran a cloth over her sink, and left her to it. I had no idea if she would write to her mum, but writing is something I often suggest to the patients when they're stuck, or struggling with their thoughts. 'Put it down on paper, see if you can make sense of it all,' I say, and I give them a song to listen to, just to remind them they aren't alone. I ought to be on a commission from R.E.M. the number of times I've recommended them, especially to the girls.

# WENDY

**My name is Wendy. I was Hannah's psychiatrist at Fairburn Lodge.**

In so far as I noticed Hannah in our first session, it was because she was so quiet. She was new to the group, and the only other new girl, Trixie, had given the nurses far more cause for concern, both in terms of her physical state, with liver capacity well down on what it should be for a 26-year-old, and because she had tried to kill herself several times, most recently when she attempted to jump out of the taxi bringing her from Lancaster station. Thankfully, she was accompanied by a social worker from her home in Sunderland – Trixie was a local authority case – who was able to haul her back in and had her reasonably calm by the time she arrived here. She had the full cocktail of Fairburn Lodge problems – mother an alcoholic, abused by her father and an uncle, addicted to drugs and alcohol, a self-harmer who had been involved in prostitution on and off since she was fifteen, in and out of prison, both routes also trodden by her mother, and a young son taken into care. She was also a talker, and from that first session, I could see she intimidated the other girls, but fascinated Hannah.

I am the youngest doctor here, and I have yet to master the art of the group session. When I was a student at Glasgow University, I used to marvel watching Professor McDonald, conducting group therapy sessions like a maestro leading an orchestra, bringing everyone in at different times so that by the end the patients all felt they had played their part, and they were enthused by what they had heard and what they had said, and the mood of learning and sharing they had created together. Perhaps that only comes with experience, but I felt my group sessions were like a clash of individual consultations never quite reaching the point, because just when it felt like it was getting close, I would feel I should bring in someone else.

That first time, a few days after Hannah's arrival, she and Trixie were the newcomers, Chloe had been with us two weeks, Sandra and Mo were in their third week and Hilary was in her fourth. It wasn't very satisfactory to have them all mixed up in that way but Mr Rishton liked to view self-harm as its own issue. We didn't get that many self-harmers and they were mainly women, so they tended to get lumped together. I would say that apart from Hilary, a student who had started cutting herself when revising for her finals, these girls were primarily drink and drugs cases, with self-harm a linked but secondary issue, and I felt both Hannah and Trixie would have been better off going straight to the mixed-sex 'alcohol/narcotics' group therapy sessions, but when you are the youngest doctor on the team you are the least likely to be listened to. Thankfully, though, Steve, the senior nurse sitting in on that first session, agreed, so at the staff meeting the following day, when we took stock of all the residents, it was decided to switch them both.

Trixie was just as domineering with the men in the drugs and drink group as she had been with the women self-harmers. Our male drinkers at the time were predominantly middle-class professionals, with us either because their employers did not want to lose their talents and write off the investment they had made in them, or because they had their own private medical insurance covering the costs. Trixie took particular delight in trying to shock Lionel, who was the chief operating officer of a Japanese electronics firm based in the West Midlands, and who was very well spoken, in a privately educated, upper-middle-class kind of way. When Trixie was describing – as she had in her first group – how she was driven to prostitution both to make ends meet, and also as a means of buying drink and drugs 'on demand', she couldn't resist embarrassing Lionel, seated to her immediate left in the group. 'You know how it is, Lionel, darling,' she said, putting her hand on his thigh, 'you need a bottle of vodka, you give a guy like you a handjob in the car outside the offy, and you get the bottle. Need a few beers or a wrap of heroin on top, and lucky Lionel gets a blow job too,' and then she made a loud, slurping noise, followed by an even louder, brown-toothed cackle as Lionel shifted uneasily. We have strict rules on bullying and I had to warn Trixie she was getting close to unacceptable behaviour.

'Come on, Lionel, you saying you've never done it with a tart like me?' she asked, and I said once more, 'Trixie, please, that's enough.'

'Oh, OK, just trying to liven things up a bit. Like a fucking morgue in here. No hard feelings, eh, Lionel?' Lionel nodded, and smiled weakly, with the look of a man who had never been bullied by a woman before.

'Can I go out for a fag, Doctor?' asked Trixie.

'I would rather you stayed for the whole session, Trixie,' I said.

'It's fucking crazy we can't smoke in here. Bunch of addicts giving up booze and drugs. Giving up smoking on top is too much.'

'You can go to the smoking area afterwards, but for now, please stay with us if you can.'

When she was being serious, rather than merely trying to fill the space with her personality and crowd out everyone else, making me feel I was too young to command these groups, Trixie made good contributions, and I could sense Hannah was an attentive listener, with a bright mind, if only I could get her to open up more. I made a point of leaving her till last when I asked everyone in the group, even though most would have met already, to say their name, where they were from, what work they did, and state briefly why they were there. Lionel, Telford, businessman, alcoholic. Trixie, Sunderland, unemployed, alcoholic, crack-cocaine addict, self-harmer. Neil, local, university lecturer, alcoholic. Robin, Manchester, actor, alcoholic, cocaine addict. Michelle, Edinburgh, investment banker, alcoholic, prescription drugs addict. Hannah, London, school-leaver, 'here because I ended up in court after drinking too much'.

Trixie's was without doubt the most dramatic and compelling story. Hannah had heard parts of it in the earlier group, but this time Trixie piled on detail that had the others hanging on her every word. It was the matter-of-fact way she said it all that created such a powerful impact on people unaware of life in Britain's underclass.

'. . . so I get home from school, and my mum'll be fucking

a punter and she'll shout, "Get your own tea, love, there's some packets in the freezer bit of the fridge" . . . My uncle feeling me up when he was pissed, I fuckin' hated that, but my own dad, Jesus fuckin' Christ, and when I say "I'll tell Mam", I'm thinking he'll say "don't you dare", because that's what blokes usually say when they abuse their own kids, but no, he says "she won't give a fuck". And he was right of course . . . I left home at fifteen, just couldn't see the point living with her any more, she was horrible to me, I was horrible to her, he had fucked off years ago thank God, and all I saw was her getting worse and worse, more and more horrible dodgy blokes in and around the place, and I thought I'd be better on my own. I was better-looking than I am now, so it wasn't hard getting the blokes to give you the money to get the stuff you needed.'

The others' stories sounded like tales of middle-class indulgence rather than the torture of the human condition, and when it came to me asking Hannah, 'What do you think of what you've heard so far?' which was my way of trying to tease her out to tell her own story, she asked back, 'In what way?'

'Well, I suppose what I am asking is which of these people do you feel your story relates to most?'

'Neil,' she answered, which surprised me.

'Why?'

'Because with the others, I can see why they ended up here. With me and Neil, I can't. Lionel lost his parents and his wife around the same time, his parents because they died, his wife because she left him. Michelle was working too hard, and like she said "trying to be like a man in a man's world", and drink and pills became a crutch. Robin was struggling.

But me and Neil, it's like it just happened and there's no reason. So Neil, I think.'

'Neil, how do you feel about that?'

'Not sure. Need to think about it. I felt more like Michelle to be honest.'

I returned to Hannah. 'And Hannah, how does that makes you feel, the feeling that you understand why Trixie is here, but not why you are?'

'Well, when I hear Trixie talking about her life, and all the bad stuff that's happened to her, I feel a total fraud to be honest.'

'A fraud?'

'Well, like what the hell am I here for? I don't have problems like she does. I had a tough life compared with, say, my friend Sophie, whose parents are loaded, but I never felt poor. Two parents, never harmed me, lovely sister, did OK at school, OK flat growing up, good at sport, shelf full of medals, enough friends, never short of food, just got into drinking too much and got into trouble.'

'You may not have had Trixie's childhood. But you drink to excess like she does. You self-harm like she does. So perhaps deep down whatever hurt it is you feel is even deeper, because you don't have those external circumstances to contend with.'

'I don't understand.'

'Well, as you say, Trixie has had a very tough life, and therefore we all understand, almost without question, why she has gone down this route of drug abuse and alcohol abuse and self-harm and prostitution. You have had a more comfortable life, by no means pampered but with none of the awful experiences Trixie has had, and yet still you do some of the same things, so perhaps your internal hurt is even greater. Do you see what I'm saying?'

Trixie intervened. 'What she's saying, love, is that it's fucking obvious why I'm a fucking loony, but what have you done to deserve it?' and she laughed. Others joined in nervously.

'Hannah?'

'What?'

'How does that make you feel?'

'Pretty desperate to be honest.'

'Why?'

'Because if I was Trixie, I'd be thinking "I know why I am like this", because I had a shit mum, a shit dad, a shit family, a shit house, no money, nobody looking after me, nobody caring if I did OK at school or not, got a job or not. So I'd be thinking "Here I am at Fairburn Lodge, if I can get myself clean, I can go out of here to a life that doesn't have those people and those situations, and I can start again." But me, I don't know what it is that makes me like I am, and makes me do what I do. I didn't have a great childhood, but it wasn't terrible, and yet here I am, in the same boat as Trixie, and I'm thinking she's got a better chance of getting out of here well than I have, because I can see what she needs to fix.'

'Maybe,' said Trixie, 'but I don't miss anything out of my life in Sunderland apart from the crack and the smack and the booze, and I miss them so much I can't wait to get back on the whole fucking lot of it.'

'Let's hope not,' I said. 'Let's hope there's time for you to see another way.'

It was Hannah's first real contribution to any of the discussions she had been involved in, and it worried me. In a more understated way than Trixie had expressed it, she was indicating difficulty in imagining that she would not go back to her old ways.

'What has to be fixed is your addiction to alcohol,' I said.

'But that's the what. How do I fix the why, when I don't know what it is?'

'What the fuck does that mean?' asked Trixie.

'What Hannah is saying is that if her problem is addiction, what are the things that make her an addict? That's what we need to try to help her find out.'

Now Neil spoke up. 'I don't feel that. I feel I do know why I'm an addict. I'm an extremist. I like excess. I don't like one or two drinks. I like obliteration. If I work, I like to work all the time. It's why I became an academic, because you can study forever. Every subject is inexhaustible. It's why I love to be in love, because I can go completely over the top in how I express that. So I'm pleased Hannah identified with my story, but I think it's because she only knows me a little.'

He said it nicely, but I sensed Hannah took it as a slap-down, and she retreated into herself again, and her face spoke of a sense of isolation. She stayed clammed up at the next one-on-one, so much so that I cut it short, and later I asked Pauline the cleaning lady to have another word if she could. I felt totally inadequate, relying on a cleaner, but sometimes needs must.

# TRIXIE

**My name is Trixie. I was a patient with Hannah at Fairburn Lodge.**

It was all fucking bravado, all the laughter and the banter with the other patients. I wish to fuck they didn't call us residents, like we have just popped into a country hotel for a weekend break, when we were all in Fairburn Lodge, even the posh ones like Lionel and Robin, because we were sick. In my case, not just sick in the head but sick to death of fucking living. That's what I mean about the bravado. If they wanted to think I was a bit of a character, great, but there was not a single second of any minute of any hour of any day that I was there that I did not feel sick and sad and wishing to fuck I was dead. They knew that. That's why I was in the room off the landing halfway up, so that 'one-on-one obs' was easier. They were quite subtle about it, but there was always someone passing every few minutes, including at night, and popping in and asking if I was OK. What a stupid fucking question. If I was OK, why would I be there? It was the one totally suicide-proof room in the building, according to Chloe, who had been in there before me. The shower didn't have a lead, just a fixed big head in the ceiling. There were no plugs, just wall switches.

The cupboards were made of plastic not wood. The windows, made of unbreakable glass, were bolted shut. I recognised some of the tricks from prison, though at least I had a bit of fucking light in here, and a comfortable mattress. No sheets mind, just a nice duvet with no cover. And I had to wear Velcro shoes, no laces. Pauline the cleaning lady told me I'd be up with the other girls in a few days. I wasn't so sure I wanted to be.

I liked Hannah though, she was nice enough. She didn't say much in the groups, but after the first one, she came and sat with me when we were having dinner – it was help yourself and sit anywhere you like – and at first I thought maybe she was just a rich southern girl who fancied a bit of poverty porn, but it turned out she grew up in a block of shitty flats the same as I had. She was asking a lot of 'did you really, was it really, oh my God?' type questions though, and the thing that really got her was this idea that I was actually living in the same place where my mum took her punters.

'When did you first see her taking drugs then?' she asked me.

'Fuck knows, love. Long as I can remember.'

'Why didn't anyone move you out, like your school or your council? I remember when I was falling back at my school in London, the teacher came round. If someone had come round to your house then, there's no way they'd have let you live there.'

'We had a social worker, but they had so much on, those poor fuckers. And Mum would always put on a bit of a show. I don't know, everyone gets good at lying when they're in a mess, don't they? Maybe the social worker lied to herself too, went out thinking things weren't as bad as she'd expected.'

Drink was very much her thing. She didn't smoke, she didn't

do drugs, and I think the second session with the booze boys troubled her. It was like she needed to have a reason for why she was like she was.

We'd become quite friendly by then. People do pair up and group up in places like this, and it's funny to see which ones get together. I was pretty sure Robin and Michelle were fucking by week two. Neil was gay, and gravitated towards the younger men. I remember my first time in Low Newton prison I paired up with Maria, the biggest butchest lesbian you've ever met, and everyone thought I must have been a dyke – which I'm not – but it just happened like that. She was there when I fancied talking to someone, and she listened. I reckon that was why Hannah and I hit it off OK. She came and sat with me, treated me with respect, rather than as a curiosity, and took my advice about her own situation. Even with her though, I hid how I was feeling most of the time. I can't stand people who just moan on about how terrible everything is and how death would be preferable to life, because even though that's how I felt, I couldn't see the point in dragging everyone else down with it. So we talked about the other patients, the doctors, the staff, what was on the telly, what it was like living in London compared to the north. We talked about men we'd fucked and films we'd seen and places we dreamed of going to, and I reckon between us, me, the doctors and nurses and Pauline the cleaner – Hannah was always talking to Pauline – we got her into a better place after a while. Me, though, I was in a worse place, because I felt as shit after three weeks clean as I did when I went in. I don't mean physically. Obviously I was physically better, and I was eating OK, and taking the medication most of the time, and walking a bit round the fields with Hannah – they stopped following me after two weeks so they must have seen some improvement in me I guess – and of course not having any booze or drugs makes you a lot better, medically at least. Hannah was fucking gorgeous once she had got all the crap out of her system. There was a young ned called Barry arrived in our third week and he so had the hots for her, and she wasn't interested and I had to step in and tell him to lay off or else he would have me to answer to.

'Oh, didn't realise you were fucking dykes,' he said, and I clocked him one, bang in the mouth, and he went off screaming to the nurses and everyone else thought it was funny, but I had to apologise in front of everyone and I said, 'Only if he apologises to Hannah for chasing her like she is some piece of skirt out for a shag with any fat Geordie cunt on a Friday night in Newcastle,' and he did, and Hannah said thanks later and we went for a walk.

'Funny how it works here, isn't it?' she said. 'I mean, you have the doctors and the nurses and the other staff and they do what they do, but then there's everything else going on too. Pauline, Paddy in the kitchens who is such a good laugh, the food, the scenery, I never realised how beautiful country-side was till I came here, and then the other patients, I owe a lot to them, Trix, especially you.'

'Aw, that's kind,' I said, only what she couldn't have known, because I hadn't told her, was that I was on a major dive at the time. I had a week left and I just couldn't see I'd made any progress at all. I'd been up the night before, wandering round seeing if I could find a few more meds lying around. The staff aren't always as careful as they should be with that stuff.

On the Sunday before our last full week, we went for a little mope around the farm buildings. It was a proper farm, with cows and barns and milking machines and pigsties and fuck knows what else, and one of the farm workers, Arthur, who brought the vegetables in for Paddy the chef every day, he was pretty hot and even though we weren't serious about chasing him down, we sometimes walked over there to pretend we were out on the pull and it just got us out of ourselves a bit. There was a massive corrugated-iron shed which was filled with hay bales and oil cans and farm machinery, and Arthur was up on the red sloping roof, painting it black, listening to some music on the radio. He had a ladder laid out on the roof, and was painting strips of a foot or so at a time, then shuffling the ladder along, and painting the next bit. Another bigger ladder stretched from the ground to the start of the roof.

'Come on,' I said, 'we can have a fucking good laugh here.'

'What?' she said and then, quickly realising what I was doing, said, 'No, Trixie, you can't do that. We'll get into trouble.'

'Oh, we'll put it back soon enough. Don't be so soft.'

So I slowly, as quietly as I could, pulled the big ladder away, and we managed to get it down before Arthur had even noticed.

'Hey, Arthur,' I shouted up to him, 'need any help?'

'You any good with heights?' he asked.

'Yeah.'

'Well, there's a ladder there.'

'No, there's not,' I said, and Hannah and I picked it up and marched off towards the Lodge.

I turned round and he had come to the bottom of his fixed ladder on the roof.

'Fuck's sake, come on, girls, that isn't funny.'

'Trixie, we can't wind him up,' said Hannah. 'Let's put it back.'

So we did, and she was right because it meant he could just about see the joke, but we didn't scare him too much. We put it back up and he came down for a smoke.

'You had me worried for a minute, I'll give you that,' he said.

He had only done half the roof – the shed must have been thirty feet high and twice as long – but said he was coming back to it later, because he had to get the cows in for milking. We walked with him for a while, until we got to the really muddy bits, then started to head back.

As we passed the shed again, I said to Hannah, 'Come on, let's climb up and see the view. It must be even better up there.'

'I'm not sure about that,' she said. 'I don't like heights.'

'It's not that high, come on.'

I climbed the first ladder easily enough, clambered onto the second one, and once I was on it, it was a doddle to get up to the top, and I was sitting, like a bird, perched on the join between the two sloping sides of the roof. The view wasn't that different because the farm buildings were at the bottom of the valley. But it was nice enough.

'Come on, Hannah, you'll love it up here,' I said, lighting another cigarette.

She looked nervous as hell when her little face appeared at the top of the first ladder. I was smiling and said, 'All you do is grab the bottom rung of the next one and climb onto it. It can't budge because it's locked on the top here.' I tapped the top of the ladder next to me.' She was starting to look a bit panicky but she made it and then slowly came towards me. She couldn't quite bring herself to make the final step to sit on the top of the roof with me, so she lay on the ladder instead, holding onto both sides, occasionally sitting up to look around.

I honestly hadn't gone up there with a view to jumping off, but as we chatted a bit, it became fucking obvious that's what I should do.

'You ever tried to top yourself?' I asked her.

'Yeah, a few times. I think about it a lot, but only tried a few times.'

'I think about it all the time, Hannah. Never stop thinking about it. It's why you were wrong, you know, in group, when you said you could see how to fix my life. It's not fixable. There's too much has happened that's bad, and it's in me, and it's never going to get out of me.'

'It can though. I've seen a change in you.'

'It's an act, Hannah. Even with you, it's an act.'

And with that, I lifted my hands from the roof, leaned backwards, and let my body weight do the rest. I slid and bounced down the roof in less than a second or two, and I could hear Hannah's scream and her crying of my name as I left the roof and hurtled to the ground, trying to twist my body like a diver, hoping to land on my head and put the whole sorry fucking mess of my whole sorry fucking life behind me.

I couldn't even do that right.

# HANNAH

**My name is Hannah. This is the letter I wrote to my mum the day after Trixie fell from the roof.**

Dear Mum,

Mrs Morrison used to say stories should have a beginning, a middle and an end. Same for letters, I guess. It's just that I don't know where to start.

Pauline has been nagging me for ages to write to you, to tell you what I really think, about you, me, why things have turned out the way they have. She is a cleaner here, but that doesn't say the half of it. She's like everybody's favourite auntie, some of the girls even call her Mum. She mothers us all.

It's especially hard to write now, because I'm in a bit of trouble. You're used to that, I know, and probably sick to death of hearing it, but this is bad, and really sad, because my friend Trixie tried to kill herself yesterday. If she dies, Mr Rishton says there will be an inquest, and the police will need to interview me, because I was with her on top of a roof when she threw herself off. He accepts it wasn't directly my fault, but we all knew she was a suicide risk, so it was silly of me to let her climb up there in the first place.

Maybe it's because I'm so tired, but it looks like I've started my letter with the end not the beginning, because it only happened yesterday. I haven't slept for a second since, and every moment, I've been thinking it should have been me, I should have been the one to fall off. I must admit I did wonder about following her. Partly to avoid facing the music and the question 'why didn't you stop her?' but mainly because I've thought about killing myself often before, so why didn't I have the guts to do it? Perhaps I'm a coward, and Trixie was brave.

I screamed and screamed and screamed, I thought I was going to slip off the ladder I was screaming so hard, then Arthur the farm worker came running from the cowshed, then Dr Meredith and Mr Rishton, who is like the overall boss here, then patients and nurses and everyone came running over from the Lodge and then an ambulance arrived and I watched all this mayhem from the roof but I had no idea if she was living or dead, all I could hear was shouting and screaming down below. Arthur spotted me first. He told Mr Rishton I was there and they helped me climb down into this nightmare of sobbing and sighing as the ambulance sped away, sirens blazing even though there was barely another car between here and the motorway. She's alive, Mum, but only just. She's in intensive care at the Royal Lancaster. Broken neck, broken back, never going to walk again probably, still might not pull through. And that's what she wants of course. She'll be lying in hospital wondering why on earth the doctors and nurses are bothering trying to save her.'

I thought she was getting better in here. But she wasn't, I can see that now. As the day approached when she had to leave, I reckon she couldn't face what she had to go back to. If I thought my life was a mess . . . Her dad and her uncle abused her, and let other junkies do the same. Her mum was a prostitute. She used to inject her with heroin, can you imagine that, a mother so out of it she did that to her own child? I've heard so many stories here that have made me realise that however bad Dad was, and however much you weren't the perfect mum (and I know I'm not the perfect daughter), you are good parents compared with a lot of others. Trixie could see nothing in the life ahead of her but more pain, more drugs, more crime, more prison. She liked this place, but it didn't sort her out, not fundamentally. So she tried to end it all again.

It was the scariest moment of my life, Mum, much worse than being mugged or having an abortion, even scarier than that night you found me with Dan. Seeing her legs go up in the air and realising she was committing suicide, I will never forget it as long as I live, and I'll never know what stopped me from joining her. It would have been so easy. Do you remember Colin my swimming teacher? When I did good reps he used to let me play on the diving board and he taught me how to do a rolling somersault dive. One of those off the top of the roof and I would be dead in no time. But I didn't. Was it because I was scared of dying, or was I thinking maybe she was alive and she would pull through, like those babies you read about who fall out of skyscrapers and survive, and I would be able to help put her back together again? We like to think we can help others, don't we? I wrote a list last night of all the people who've tried to help me, who maybe thought they could save me from myself, fix me. You, Vicki, Uncle Malcolm and Auntie Julie, Sophie and her whole family, especially her mum, Dr Lister at the hospital, the policewoman who tried to get me back home with you, the magistrate whose charity is paying for me to be at this place, Pauline, Mr Rishton, Dr Meredith, the nurses and counsellors here. I started to write little letters to them all, but this is the letter that matters. Pauline is right about that.

She was at me again this morning. She said I should just sit down and say what I really think. 'Tell your mum what you really want to say,' she said. I said you wouldn't be interested, because I have hurt you too much and you have given up on me, but she said mums never give up on their kids. She also gave me a CD, and said I should listen to it while I write. It's R.E.M., 'Everybody Hurts', a bit corny, but it is such a lovely song, and it is playing on my computer now. If ever I do what Trixie did, I would definitely want it played at my funeral.

If there is one thing I want to say to you, Mum, it is sorry. Sorry for drinking. Sorry for lying. Sorry for stealing. Sorry about Dan. Sorry for all the pain I've caused you. Thanks for what you've tried to do for me, and sorry for letting you down so much and so often. Sorry for being me.

If I tried hard enough, I could find plenty of things to say that put a bit of the blame on you, like I sometimes felt you weren't there for me, and I sometimes thought you loved Vicki more than you loved me – I think all kids feel that sometimes – and sometimes you were there but I felt you were there only in body, your mind was somewhere else, and sometimes I really wanted you to say things that you didn't say, or you said things that I wished you hadn't. I could give you lots of those. But my point is I am not blaming you for me being who and what I am. And right now, I am just sorry, really, truly sorry.

I've been here nearly four weeks now. Longest I've gone without a drink since I first touched the stuff! It's a nice place, lovely scenery in every direction, cows and sheep wandering around in the fields outside, weather a bit ropy. I've got my own room – for the first time in my life, eh? – a nice comfy bed, a sink in the corner, my own toilet and shower, a blue armchair, a lamp and a painting of a man lying on a beach done by a former patient. They're big on art therapy here, but I still can't paint! There's also a little framed slogan – they have these sayings all over the place, a different one in every room. Mine says 'One day at a time, and remember the battle is never over.'

The food is nice, three meals a day, no sweets, no crisps, no junk food at all, and no alcohol allowed in the building, not even wine for cooking. The head chef was in prison for stabbing someone apparently, but he ended up here as a patient and now he runs the kitchens. He's called Paddy, he tells dirty jokes all the time. He's from Liverpool like Dad, only he supports Liverpool not Everton. I see Arsenal lost again at the weekend – we have a telly and games room downstairs and I watched a bit of the second half – I hope Vicki isn't too upset. Maybe if I had fallen for Theo Walcott like she did, I wouldn't have gone down the booze route. Has she still got his picture on her side of the bedroom, or has that Podolski taken over? She'll be amazed I know his name! Give her a big hug. We were asked to write down three good reasons to be alive the other day, and I put her first, followed by fresh air and rap.

We have lots of sessions talking in groups, I've done the self-harm group and the drugs and alcohol group, and we do one-on-one sessions too. They say my physical health is OK, and I do feel better. It's the mental they worry about. So do I. Even before the thing with Trixie, I wasn't sleeping well. I would just lie in bed and think all night about why I've ended up here, all the bad things I've done, all the hurt I've caused so many people, asking myself again and again if it wouldn't be better for us all if I was dead. I'm fine during the day, when they keep us busy, but at night I just can't stop thinking about it, and now Trixie has done her thing, I know it can only get worse. Pauline was telling me about a Scottish girl called Jill, she left here early and two weeks later she hanged herself. I don't want to end like that, but I have thought about dying so much, and I lie here thinking about my funeral, and who would come, and would you sing hymns, and would Dad show up, and would the Harpers come or just Sophie, and would you have a eulogy and if so who would do it, and I usually end up thinking it would have to be Sophie or Vicki, but they would both cry so maybe someone from school, Mrs Morrison maybe, or Mr Harper because he does a lot of speaking in court, or their son Jonathan who looks really good on the telly, and who wrote me a smashing letter before I went to court. His eulogy is the only one I have actually started to write, the other night when I couldn't sleep. He talks about you and Vicki, how sad everyone is for you and how he hopes you find peace, then some of the stuff I did at school, and how I helped Sophie with her drama, and how I brought a different dimension to the Harpers' lives, what a great friend I was to his sister, how I tried my best to make something of my life, how bright I was, and at times full of life and hope, but drink obliterated everything, because it got into my bones, and then he does a big political thing about his telly programme and how he was blocked from telling the truth, tells some of the things I said to him and to Dr Lister, and says until we face up to the truth about the damage drink is doing to our young people, we are going to hell in a handcart. He says how tragic it is that I have been taken so young, and it can only make sense for those I have left behind if others can be helped to avoid the path I took. Then he says, 'We will miss you, Hannah,' and goes from the pulpit to the coffin and stands and bows. And it's weird, Mum, it's like when I'm having these thoughts, it's dark outside, it's dark in my room, my bed feels like a coffin, I am dead at my own funeral, but I can listen to what every-one's saying, watch the different emotions in different people, and it doesn't make me scared, or sad, but leaves me feeling maybe this is what was destined to happen. But then I think, and especially now, you have had plenty of chances to do it, Hannah, but you haven't, so maybe you want to live not die. And that choice goes round and round my head night after night, and it is torture. That's what I really think.

So here's what I really think about you, Mum.

I think you deserved better than you've got from life. You deserved a better husband than Dad. And you deserved a better first child than me.

I think you are bound to wonder if it is your fault that I am like I am, but I don't think you should, because I look at Vicki and you raised her too, and she is brilliant. So don't blame yourself. Don't imagine you did something terrible in a past life and I have been sent as punishment. I used to think that, you know – crazy, isn't it? – but now I realise life is not like that. It just is. I think some people get some illnesses and other people don't. If I had cancer, nobody would say it was because my mum didn't bring me up very well. If I broke my leg falling down the stairs here, nobody would blame you, would they?

We had a talk on it last week. A guy from a university who was a bit posh explained why alcoholism is a disease, and drinking is just a symptom of it, and how if the disease is in you, you can't control it, so you have to get the disease out of you, and he said that's why we are here. He said every time we pour a drink, or raise a glass, and put it to our lips and drink, we are making a choice. Every time we spend money on it, we are making a choice. We are choosing to feed the disease when we ought to be choosing to starve it. We are letting the symptoms control us, not the other way round. And he said there was always a reason for making that choice: we felt entitled to it because we had done something good; we felt relieved by it because we had done something bad and the drinking symptom made us feel a bit better; we felt happy and wanted to celebrate; we felt sad and wanted to commiserate – he called that one the 'poor me, pour me another drink syndrome'. He said we also drank because we were bored, or tired, or wired, or fearful and anxious, or we wanted to feel normal and it was normal to enjoy a drink, we wanted a little lift, we wanted a treat. He said we could always kid ourselves there was a good reason to drink, but for addicts 'there is never a good reason, there is only feeding the disease'.

Did you know that William Shakespeare invented the word 'addiction', Mum? Yes, we learned that too, in a lecture from Mr Rishton, who is big on art and music and literature as a way of helping recovery. Apparently Shakespeare was always making up new words and hundreds of them are now used by all of us all the time. To think I was doing A-level English and nobody ever told me that. Another of his words, from a play called *The Tempest*, was 'abstemious', which means not drinking alcohol, or not having sex. You wish!

He went through a few Shakespeare phrases that he said we might think of in relation to drinking. 'Fool's paradise.' 'Too much of a good thing.' 'It smells to heaven.' 'Give the devil his due' (I thought you would like that one seeing as how you always used to say the Devil did his work through drink). 'Get thee to a nunnery' (this place used to be a convent, as it happens). 'Good riddance' (I wish to God I could say that to alcohol).

When he called me in last night, he said I should think about 'bloodstained mortifying silliness' – all

Shakespeare words – every time I thought of poor Trixie and her fall from the roof.

He is one of those people who is so enthusiastic you can't help liking him – he reminds me of a male Mrs Harper funnily enough. He said Shakespeare had a phrase or a saying for every situation that any of us ever faced. He even did the first 'knock knock' joke apparently. Did you know that? What a legend.

Anyway, I was crying about Trixie, and saying I was scared about leaving Fairburn Lodge, and he said the Shakespeare phrase I really had to think about was from *Macbeth*. 'What's done is done.'

He gave me a hanky because I was crying so much, and he said, 'You can't live in the past, you have to learn from it.' And once I'd stopped crying, he told me how after his son died from drink and drugs, he knew a part of him had died too, and he and his wife would never be the same again, but they took a decision to honour their son's life and death by trying to help others, to get something good from the worst thing that could ever have happened to them. That's how this place started, and he said every time someone comes in sick and goes out healthy, he feels not only that his life is worthwhile, but so was his son's. He was called Craig, and there is a bust of him in the hallway downstairs, and Mr Rishton gives it a little pat every time he walks by it.

I am trying to get good from bad, Mum, but I am not going to pretend it is easy. 'What's done is done.' The life I've had. The upbringing you gave me. The choices we've made. They're all in the past. If I want to make something of my future, I need to make the right choices, not the wrong choices. 'To be or not to be', that's the most fundamental choice of all, and the one I have to make now. Only I can make it, I have learned that much, and I know what it is . . .

It's the funeral I've been fantasising about, and you and Vicki standing beside a gravestone that reads

HANNAH RUTH MAYNARD, 1995 to 2013, RIP

. . . or it's me going into the group therapy session tomorrow morning and saying something I have never said before, even after a month in this place.

'My name is Hannah, I am an alcoholic.'

XXX